AN ARCHER'S AWAKENING

OF CROWNS & QUILLS
BOOK 1

Casey Morales

Contents

Before You Begin . . .

To say thank you for joining me on this journey, I would like to give you a gift, a free copy of my first contemporary mm romance novella, My Accidental First Date.

Visit https://dl.bookfunnel.com/foxhchxb5r to tell me where to send it.

Fontaine
Abedil
Clude
Featherstone
Marlo
Spoke
Kingdom of Spires
Oliver
Jeston
Cradle
Lake Irina
Irina's
Seat
Cooper
Rubin
Huntcliff
Gull Town
Stark
Grove's
Pass
Brighton
Crelt
Kes
Vint
Mort
Barbadi

Riz
Pez
Baz
Alm
n
Kitchton
Bo
Lynn
Sil
Aria
Fersh
Fleet Town
Amnel
Cobb
Anfar
Saltstone
Melucia
Pantrel
Crees
Cret
Traders' Gate
Orn
Drea
Cvn
Huntcliff
Tuvlai
Uvo
Rea Utu
Vel

— ◦ —

PROLOGUE

A THOUSAND YEARS AGO

I rina surveyed the battle from her mountainside perch.

Banners of cobalt faced emerald and gold as tens of thousands clashed on the plains below. The clamor of swords and pikes sang with a melody of anger and pain beyond any heard in generations. The height of the lone peak spared Irina from the stench of death, but nothing could deafen the cries in the Reaper's wake.

The flesh of her arms pimpled as power coursed through her veins. Magical fire raged from her staff, scorching men and earth alike, leaving blood and madness where enemies stood only moments before.

She poured the last of her energy into the enemy line. Her magical endurance far outpaced anyone alive but still had its limits. She would need to eat, rest, and recover before casting again.

Time to watch the men battle it out.

Irina had spent the last year hunting every Mage she could find and repaying them for her stolen youth. Of the original ten, she'd already killed six. The remaining four scurried and hid like rats across the border in Melucia. She'd never dreamed of ruling, power, or war—not before they'd ripped her future from her grip.

Now it was *her* turn. The thought had consumed her. She didn't care how many innocents would die in the wake of her wrath. *Innocence* had died when her mother fell. She would destroy every last Mage and take everything they held dear.

As the enemy lines buckled, something in the sky shimmered. It was distant but growing closer. She shielded her eyes. A brilliant . . . something . . . flew toward her.

Irina stepped to the edge of the cliff and raised her spyglass. Far to the east, a massive cerulean flame streaked across the sky, leaving a trail of light in its wake that twinkled, then faded. Her breath caught as the form sharpened in her lens. Its outstretched wings dripped iridescent flames. She stumbled back as the beast lifted its head and uttered an otherworldly cry that stilled the battle below. Men on both sides cowered and stared in disbelief. Cries rang up all around her.

"That's impossible!"

"It cannot be!"

Irina turned toward the robed men nearby. "Get me the Orb! *Now*!"

They jolted, then scattered in all directions. A moment later, one man approached, clad in black and cradling a velvet bag. He pulled his hood back, revealing oily, slicked-back hair and onyx eyes. He kneeled and bowed his head, holding the sack aloft.

"Your Majesty."

She snatched it out of his hands and removed a perfect scarlet sphere. Elegant lines of ancient runes lay etched within, like tiny spiders caught in an amber web. They pulsed as though a heart thrummed inside.

"Listen to me," she said, snapping the man's gaze to hers. "The spell I'm about to cast will draw on my essence and the magic of the Orb. It will send you far from here and guide your path."

"It what?" The man's eyes widened as they darted from woman to Orb. "But . . . Your Majesty—"

"There's no time," she snapped, looking up at the fast-approaching Phoenix, a bright haze of blue fire hurtling toward her, then turning back to the man. "If it takes a thousand years, bring me back, Danai."

"Irina—" His hand reached toward her cheek, then snapped back. "*Your Majesty*, could you not face—"

"If you ever loved me, Danai, bring me back." She reached down, and he pressed his cheek into her palm.

"Irina—"

The flaming bird bellowed, and the screams of men and beast rose above the maelstrom below.

Irina snatched her hand back and stiffened her spine. "*The Phoenix* has risen. Even fully recovered, my power might not stand against hers. And I am *tired*, Danai." Her voice hardened. "Now, open yourself. My strength is spent, and yours will have to do."

Irina closed her eyes and chanted in the language of Mages. With every phrase, the pulsing of the Orb grew until its brilliance forced those around to look away. Bright scarlet light flooded them.

Danai peered past Irina as the Phoenix belched fire in massive streams, scorching thousands in a blink. Then the mighty bird snapped its head, looked directly at Irina, and launched itself toward the ledge.

Irina grasped Danai's wrist, slamming his palm onto the Orb, and spoke the final words of her incantation a heartbeat before the Phoenix reached the mountainside.

Irina's body flared, then dissolved into liquid smoke that poured itself into the Orb.

The sphere of crimson pulsed one final time.

Danai vanished.

The Phoenix dove headlong into the ledge, obliterating everything in her path. Flames billowed in every direction, filling the sky with waves of energy and heat. The world trembled, and the sound of earth rending and rising was heard across the continent. Mountains rose, replacing the battlefield plains, forming a range—a barrier—between aggressor and foe.

Far to the west, on the edge of a distant capital, an ebony stone rose from frozen earth.

A lone man pulled his hood off his head and gawked as brilliant symbols flared white then faded to gold, searing deep into the monolith. Line after line appeared, offering guidance, giving him purpose and direction, a path to restore what was lost. In that moment of chaos and fear, he raised the now-dulled Orb above his head and pledged his life to her cause.

To her Return.

PART I

Chapter One

Declan

Ten archers stood, their shoulders inches apart, longbows gripped in their right hands with one end resting on the ground. Seven men and three women stared intently across the field. Every quiver was full and slung across their backs. Spare arrows packed ancient barrels a few feet behind their line.

They stood at the base of the longest mountain range on the continent, but bare arms and shoulders still baked beneath Melucia's merciless summer sun. A gentle breeze drifting through the forest offered little respite, and sweat glistened on foreheads and arms. A few struggled to keep their eyes fixed forward but snapped to attention the moment they saw their leader's raised brow.

I peered down the line. These were my cadets, my charges. Over the last year, I poured myself into their training, and whatever happened next would determine their fates.

No one moved. They barely breathed.

"Archers to the line," I ordered, my voice as taut as the cadets' bowstrings.

As one, the unit took two steps forward.

"Ready your bows," I commanded, and each lifted a bow and drew an arrow.

"Nock."

Arrows found strings in swift, practiced motions.

"Draw."

Most drew easily, but a few struggled, their muscles straining.

"Loose!"

Nine *thwacks* were followed by the rustle of a tenth arrow landing somewhere in the foliage.

"Cease fire. Parade rest."

Before I could move, two additional cadets arrived, chatting loudly. One was familiar enough, another Second Year who'd risen to lead his own unit of Firsts, but the other man was new. Thousands wore the green of Melucia's Rangers. Most lived in the massive headquarters compound or in the nearby town. It was unusual to see a new face beyond raw recruits raising a bow for the first time.

The newcomer stood over six and a half feet, near my height, and carried himself with the surety of the son of a wealthy nobleman. His deep green tunic and leather leggings hugged an impressive frame.

The whole thing likely cost more than all the bows on the line combined, I thought.

The spectacles that circled the man's bright blue eyes made him look more like a scribe than any field Ranger I'd seen, but his fitness made me wonder, as fiery red hair fell across broad shoulders. His perfectly tailored tunic hugged his well-formed chest.

The pair laughed at some private joke, then surveyed my cadets. The redhead's mouth twisted like someone had squeezed a whole lemon down his throat. His gaze shifted toward me, and his scowl deepened. Then the man's expression smoothed, and an odd glint filled his eyes.

I shook myself free of the stranger's stare and stepped from the line, crossing the field to examine the targets. Ten tightly woven thatch shields stood in an orderly row. Each was painted with two white rings encircling a solid red center dot. The mountain's steep ascent, blanketed in a thick forest, began a dozen paces behind.

Bullseye. Bullseye. Inner ring. Inner ring. Bullseye. Inner ring . . .

Forest floor.

Every cadet in the unit had struck the inner ring at least five out of ten times that day. Most had hit at least two bullseyes. Every cadet except . . .

"Dempsy!" I bellowed, my voice no longer neutral. "Here. Now."

A scrawny boy of seventeen summers fumbled his longbow, struggling to rest it against a barrel, then thought better of it and grabbed the bow before taking off down the range.

"Leave your bow," I shouted. "Don't run with your weapon."

"Yes, sir." The boy flushed, ran back to the line, leaned his bow against the barrel, then resumed his jog across the field. He'd only made it a few yards when the clatter of the bow falling to the ground turned every head.

I had to resist the urge to cover my face with a palm.

Aaron Dempsy was a good kid, but he was the runt of the litter, more attuned to battling ledgers and sums than bandits or wildlife. Gangly arms hung off his slender frame, and a mop of dark, unwashed hair bounced with every stride.

There were only two reasons Aaron had made it through his first year as a cadet. First, he was brilliantly smart and would make a fine scribe for the Command staff. He scored far above any other classmate in any subject focused inside a classroom.

Second—and far more important to his seniors—he was Captain Whitman's nephew, which made him the nephew of the commander of *all* Rangers.

Now, the hapless boy faced the final tests, which would either advance him into his second year at the Academy or send him home.

Captain Whitman was a solid man and a fair leader. He demanded excellence and had no patience with failure. Despite Whitman's reputation for unflinching standards, the pressure to help his nephew pass the five First Year Tests was intense, and I felt it.

Still, Aaron had to earn his place or he would never be accepted by the rest of his cohort. It was a fine line to balance on.

"Sir." Dempsy skidded to a stop before me, losing his balance and tumbling forward.

I had to reach out and brace the boy, biting the inside of my cheek to keep from smiling. I painted on an annoyed gaze, then blew out a breath. "Cadet, was there a boar I didn't see?"

The boy's nose wrinkled. "A boar, sir?"

"Yes, or a deer? A bear, perhaps? Some kind of animal you thought was a threat?"

"Uh, no, sir. I didn't see anything in the woods."

I crossed my arms. "Then what were you aiming at? Your arrow isn't anywhere near the target. In fact, I can't even see where it landed."

"I, uh . . ." He glanced past me. "I don't know, sir."

The cadets on the line heard every word, and muffled laughter flowed across the field. Aaron's head dipped. His cheeks flushed with embarrassment.

"Eyes up here, cadet," I snapped, then lowered my voice and leaned in. "Listen, Aaron, you've got to hit the target or I can't pass you. You know what another fail would mean, don't you?"

Aaron nodded and muttered so only I could hear, "Please, don't send me home, Declan."

"That's *Cadet-Sergeant*, Dempsy," I grumbled loudly, then whispered. "I won't have a choice if you fail again. I want to help you, I really do, but you've got to give me something to work with. You don't have to hit the bullseye, just get inside a ring."

"I'll do better, I promise." Aaron's voice shook almost as much as his lower lip.

I glanced up to find the cadets on the line getting restless, so I straightened and raised my voice. "Dempsy, find your arrow and retrieve the others. You're staying on this line until the sun fries you to a crisp. Got it?"

One laugh rose above the others, turning a few heads of those on the line. I glanced over, annoyed by the interruption, and found the redhead puffed up, a broad grin on his lips, and his companion doubled over.

"Who is that?" I grumbled to myself.

"That's Ayden Byrne, Lord Byrne's son," Aaron answered, "They're—"

"I know who the Byrnes are," I snapped. Then I noticed something odd and murmured, "Where's his gold?"

"Sir?" Aaron's brow knitted.

"His collar. It's bare. I'd figure a prick like that would have his stripes made of the actual stuff."

"Oh, that. He can't wear gold. He's Mute." Aaron squinted, covering his eyes with one hand.

"Huh," I grunted.

"That's what everybody says, anyway. Must be terrible not having . . ."

Aaron's voice trailed off. He tried not to glance at my barren collar but couldn't help himself.

"Declan, I'm sorry. I didn't—"

"Forget it," I muttered, my eyes fixed on the redhead. I shook myself free, took a step toward the line, and barked across the field, "You two, either keep it down or step away. This unit is testing."

The laughing quieted, but the redhead lifted his chin and glared.

I squinted, as if searching for something. "Do you know why he's wearing Second Year bars? He wasn't here last year."

"I . . . I don't know." Aaron shrugged. "He could've trained in Saltstone."

"Saltstone?" I cocked my head. "The only Academies there are for Mages or the Guard. That doesn't make sense."

"Sometimes, they do different things for the major houses. Maybe—"

"A rich arsehole, right."

My gaze shifted from the redhead to Aaron, whose eyes quickly found his boots.

"He's not worth worrying over. You have yourself to think about today."

Aaron nodded without looking up.

I stared a moment longer, then barked loudly for all to hear, "Dempsy, arrows."

The boy snapped to attention. "Sir, yes, sir!"

When Aaron didn't move, I added, "Now!"

The cadets on the line chuckled as Aaron startled and darted into the forest behind the targets, got his feet tangled, and promptly tumbled onto his face. The redhead's friend pointed and laughed, but his companion's eyes remained fixed on me, his mouth set in a thin line.

I stepped forward and yelled toward the rest of my unit, wielding one finger in the air like a sword. "You idiots are finished!"

They stilled, eyes wide.

I glared at each cadet in turn, then allowed a grin to tease my lips. "You've all passed the Archery Test. One down, four to go. Have a drink or bed a bear or whatever it is you fools do to celebrate, but be clearheaded and ready for the Test of Swords at sunrise. Dismissed."

A relieved cheer rose as they clapped backs and clasped forearms before gathering their tunics and drifting away from the range. By the time Aaron emerged, his arms laden with arrows, a half hour had passed, and the sun was beginning to creep behind the mountains. None of the others remained, leaving Aaron and me alone on the field.

I pointed to one of the barrels filled with arrows and spoke as Aaron shuffled past. "You know your uncle can't—"

"I don't want his help, Declan."

I glanced around, making sure we were alone. I couldn't afford such familiarity from an underclassman in front of the others. I liked the kid. He was a reminder of how lost and alone I felt most of the time, but it wouldn't do either of us any favors to be seen going soft on him.

Aaron slumped against the barrel. "This part's so hard. If I could take a test on history . . . or strategy or tactics . . . anything but fighting and shooting." He hung his head. "I'm just not built for all this."

Everything about Aaron's struggle reminded me of Shira. She'd barely known how to hold a bow when she'd donned her First Year cloak. If we hadn't become fast friends, she likely would've failed and been sent home within her first few weeks. I smiled, remembering the mornings we woke at unholy hours to drill at the range. She'd barely made it—but she *had* made it. Now, I couldn't imagine my closest friend in anything but green.

I shook my head and tried to think of a way to encourage the boy. "We're not exactly a *thinking* cohort. Our job is to guard the border and keep the wildlife in check, which means shooting things and knocking sense into others at times. I'm not sure knowing the names of dead kings helps fend off a wolf." I watched the color drain from Aaron's face, so I added, "We need scribes, too, and you'll make a fine one, but you have to pass the martial tests first. If you can't pass Archery, where there's no opponent trying to knock you down, how do you expect to pass the others?"

"Stay away from the other man until the round ends?"

I laughed. "Spirits help us if the Kingdom ever invades and you're on the line."

"Why would the Kingdom—"

"It was a just figure of speech, Aaron." I blew out a breath. "Grab your bow. There's enough light for you to empty a quiver. If you can just hit a ring once—any ring—I can pass you. Just once, Aaron."

The boy nodded, then turned, retrieved his bow, and took his place on the line.

"Take your mark," I said.

Aaron shuffled to the line, his bow banging against the ground with each step.

I pinched the bridge of my nose. "Just . . . fire at will."

I'd lost all interest in the formality of the test. Now, I just wanted Aaron to empty his quiver so it could be over.

Chapter Two

Declan

By the time I strode into the dining hall, the sky outside twinkled with stars, and most of the food had been put away. Only a handful of cadets still sat at the tables scattered throughout the dimly lit room. I scanned for other Second Years I might join, but quickly resigned myself to eating alone. To my dismay, I found the redhead and his companion parked in the far corner. Neither seemed to notice me enter.

After a few moments of haggling with an exhausted cook who simply wanted to clean the kitchen and head home for the night, I lowered myself into a chair at a table and began eating my meager supper. The ale was warm, and the food was cold. I sighed and took a sip, washing down congealed gravy and tough meat I couldn't identify. It bordered on disgusting but was filling.

Midway through my meal, I glanced up to find the hall empty and eerily quiet. Most of the candles and lamps had either died or been extinguished, shrouding the chamber in the dim glow from the last remaining hearths still offering warmth. Only two tables remained occupied: one nearby with two officers and one across the hall with Ayden Byrne and his companion.

I focused on my plate, keeping my head down.

" . . . know there's something going on here." One of the officers' voices rose above a whisper and made its way to me. "The Cap doubled the guard at the crossing and has all the patrols on high alert. What in the Spirits happened?"

I snuck a glance without raising my head. The officer who hadn't spoken was looking from me to Ayden's table, probably deciding how freely he could speak in the nearly empty hall.

He turned back toward the other officer. "You know I can't talk about—"

"Come on, Ross. What's going on?" Ross exhaled and stared at his companion, then lowered his voice so I only heard snippets.

" . . . taken from . . . She's Lord . . . daughter. The whole Triad . . . The Guard in Saltstone is . . . minds."

"Spirits," the other officer said.

Ross nodded and sat back, downing the last of his ale. "That's all I can tell you. Not a word—"

"Come on, Ross. It's me."

Ross chuckled and pointed across the table. "Exactly!"

Both men laughed, then stood. As they passed my table, Ross eyed me, but the other man ignored me completely.

A kidnapping? I wondered. Crime in Melucia was fairly common, but it usually involved petty theft or other minor offenses. Serious crimes like murder and kidnapping were extremely rare, even in the larger cities. If a nobleman's daughter had gone missing . . .

Movement nearby made me look up, and brilliant azure eyes locked onto mine. I'd been so lost in thought that I hadn't noticed Ayden and his friend leave their table. The infuriating man had crossed the hall and now stood only a few paces away. A quick scan confirmed that Ayden and I were now alone.

I dropped my head and shoved buttered peas around my plate as though trying to examine their very essence, intent on ignoring the noble arsehole. I managed to scoop a few onto my spoon just as Ayden's voice startled me. I hurled the offending peas across the table.

"Cadet-Sergeant Rea." Ayden's voice seemed to savor the words, and a wry smile teased his lips. "Thank you for allowing us to observe your testing today. It was a pleasure watching you work."

I glanced up. I hadn't noticed how square Ayden's jaw was before, and caught myself staring, before quickly looking back into my plate.

Ayden simply stood, watching.

I couldn't decide which unnerved me more, the little lord's overly polite tone, his compliment about the testing, or the haughty precision with which the prick spoke. Despite being an orphan without two coppers to rub together, I'd grown up with children of the nation's upper crust, and this one reeked of privilege as much as any I'd known.

Slowly, I laid my spoon on my plate, placed my palms on the table, and allowed my head to rise. For the second time in the span of heartbeats, my breath caught. There was no smugness to Ayden's face, no sneer on his lips or glare in his eyes. His friend had borne all of those, but Ayden simply stood with hands clasped before him, his fiery locks stuffed behind his ears.

Those eyes, I thought. *How can eyes be* that *blue?*

I realized he was staring again and gathered myself. "Yes, well, thank you, Lord Byrne. I would appreciate it if, in the future, you and your friend kept your jibes to yourselves."

Ayden's brows rose. "I am not *Lord* Byrne quite yet."

Without another word, Ayden offered a stiff nod and strode away.

"That's all we need, an arrogant little lordling strutting around like some fucking peacock," I muttered, scooping the last of my peas and glaring after the man as he vanished through the door.

The next morning, I rose before the sun, ate a quick breakfast of slightly charred eggs and very charred mushrooms, and headed to the practice yard, where I was surprised to find a lone figure standing near the edge of the sparring ring.

"Aaron, you're early."

The boy shuffled his feet. "I thought, maybe, we could spar and you could count that as my test."

I couldn't hide a grin. Aaron was inventive, no doubt about that.

"It doesn't work that way. You have to face another First Year."

Aaron's shoulders drooped. "There's no way I can win against any of them. They're all bigger and stronger than me."

"But you're smarter than the whole unit combined," I countered, placing a hand on the boy's shoulder and drawing his gaze upward. "And you don't have to win. The rules say you have to finish a round without losing to pass. Next year, you'll have to win to graduate, but we can worry about that later."

"What's the—" His eyes widened. "Oh, really?"

I nodded and pointed to an hourglass sitting on a waist-high stump a few paces from the ring's edge. "The bouts are timed. If you can stay in the ring and not lose any blood—"

"Blood?" Aaron gulped.

"It's a figure of speech, Aaron." I shook my head. "For First Years, just hold on to your sword, the same as every other bout you've fought all year. Leave the ring or drop your sword, and you're out."

"You mean all the other bouts I lost all year?" Aaron muttered a little too loudly.

I balled a fist, then forced myself to breathe. "Do you want to be a Ranger?"

Aaron's head snapped up. "Of course—"

"Then step up and take your place. Stop acting like you can't do things. Just do them."

"Like that's easy. You aren't at risk of getting sent home," Aaron pointed out.

"True." I stepped into the ring, smoothed out some of the sand, then looked back at Aaron. "The others are competing to win, and not just a single bout but the whole competition. The higher they place, the better their standing in Second Year. Find a way to use that."

"How am I supposed to use their desire to crush me so they can advance?"

I shrugged and resumed tending the sand as though the answer should be obvious. To me, it was.

Aaron flopped onto a nearby stone bench and stared into the distance.

A few of the other First Years approached and began stretching. By the time the sun crested the horizon, all ten members of my unit had gathered.

"All right, cadets, it's time for your Test of Swords. No one expects a Blademaster's performance today. Just stay in the ring and don't drop your blade. The goal of this test is to disarm your opponent, not harm them. If you draw blood, you lose, though I doubt that will be a problem with the practice swords." A round of nervous whispers passed through the cadets. They hated using the wooden swords, but none yet held the skill to wield a real weapon without risking everyone within reach. I cleared my throat and continued. "I'll pair you for each round. Winner advances. Losers will have additional pairings to ensure everyone has a chance to pass."

A muscular boy with steely gray eyes spoke, "What if nobody drops or steps out?"

"Good question, Cormac. If time runs out, that would be a draw," I said. "But if I think you're gaming, you'll both lose and have to compete again to survive. Compete with honor or not at all. Understand?"

A chorus of muttered agreement rose from the men and women.

"Anyone else?" I asked. When no one spoke, I called, "Silivan, Wallace, you're first."

Cormac Silivan was the natural leader of the group. A mountain of honed muscle, he was as charismatic as he was strong. His smiles landed as easily as his punches, and the men and women of the unit loved him. As Cormac strode toward the ring, he clapped his opponent on the shoulder.

"Best of luck, Lachlan."

The most reserved man on the team, Lachlan Wallace, stood taller than all the others, but where Cormac's muscles were thick, Lachlan's were lean and wiry. While Cormac smiled, Lachlan stared with an intensity that could frighten a boulder into running. Cormac was powerful, but Lachlan was swift.

This should be good, I thought as I stepped out of the ring and allowed the competitors to enter.

The other cadets gathered a few paces outside the circle, eager to watch and cheer on their companions.

I glanced up as I gripped the hourglass, a flash of *something* catching my eye. I craned my neck, peering past the cadets, and spotted Ayden leaning against a tree a dozen paces back. He wore a different tunic and deep blue leather leggings.

Why is he here? And who has two uniforms? I nearly laughed out loud at the ridiculous question. Why was I thinking about Ayden Byrne at all? I had a test to oversee. I turned back to the men who'd just drawn wooden swords from a rack and entered the ring.

"Ready, fight!"

In the first bout, which stretched nearly until the last grain fell, brawn beat speed. Cormac, realizing time was nearly out, swung wide, forcing Lachlan to parry far from his body, then charged forward, shoving the lithe man so he stumbled and stepped one foot out of the ring.

"Win, Silivan," I announced to a grumbling crowd.

"He just shoved him out," one cadet called.

"Yeah, he didn't use his sword," another echoed.

I shrugged. "Did you hear me say you had to use your sword? I gave you the rules. Silivan followed them and forced his opponent out before time expired."

The whispers of disapproval continued.

I crossed my arms. "Do you think bandits will fight fairly? You lot need to wake up. We aren't preparing you to play games. You're prepping to deal with real-life people and wildlife, often vicious animals who may want to kill you."

"So I can kick them in the balls?" Meave Gallagher, the feistiest of the three female members of the team, said.

I grinned as the assembled men hushed and waited for my reply. "If you can get your boot between their legs, go for it."

The women's grins grew as the men's faces turned ashen. I fought my own crooked grin.

"Don't draw blood. Stay away from eyes or anything that might cause permanent damage. Otherwise, don't droop your bloody sword and stay inside the ring. Got it?"

Uneasy nods were the cadets' only answers.

"Next." I eyed the group. "Gallagher and Campbell."

"No balls to kick there," one of the men quipped as the two women strode forward. Meave turned back and gave all the men a vulgar gesture.

"There's the lady we love," another man called out, earning a chorus of laughter.

"Bring those tasty nuts over here, and I'll show you what kind of lady I am," Meave called over her shoulder, kicking her heel up as she walked.

The men, now more boys than cadets, lost all sense of decorum, hooting and hollering in response.

"Enough!" I barked, quieting everyone, then turned toward the two competitors now inside the ring. "Pick your weapons and take your positions."

I hadn't meant to glance at Ayden, but his brilliant smile shone through the unit and distracted me. The annoying man still leaned against a tree and was clearly enjoying the banter. When he noticed me staring, his smile widened, reaching his eyes.

I looked away quickly and tried to ignore the heat racing up my neck.

"Ready?" I called, focusing on the women glaring at each other from across the ring. Meave twirled her sword and grinned wildly. Her opponent remained calm and still.

"Fight!"

Unlike the previous bout, Meave made quick work of her opponent. Fainting left, darting right, and bringing her full weight down through a sword strike that drove Campbell's weapon to the ground and left her holding her arm.

Two more contests followed before I turned to Aaron.

"Dempsy, Conner," I barked, indicating the weakest of the men would face a woman whose smile rarely faltered, but who all knew was as deadly as an adder, especially when she wielded a blade.

Aoife Conner wrapped an arm around Aaron's shoulders and leaned in. "I'll make this last as long as I can, okay? I want you to look good."

Aaron pulled away, annoyance flooding his face, but looked too terrified to think of a snappy reply.

I had barely yelled, "Fight," before Conner shot forward, whipped her sword in a circle that blurred in the air, and disarmed Aaron. His sword hit the sand before he realized it had even left his hand.

Aaron gaped at his palm as though it had betrayed him, then glanced up at Conner.

She shrugged. "Sorry, I needed a win. Tricks are part of the game."

And just like that, Aaron's hopes of advancing into his second year dimmed.

By the time Aaron lost his fifth bout, I had dismissed all the cadets except Cormac, a skilled swordsman Aaron stood no chance of defeating.

Ayden hadn't moved from his tree, and I caught myself glancing over more than a few times, each gaze earning an annoyingly perfect, toothy grin.

"Aaron, go get some water," I ordered.

"I'm not—"

"Aaron, you *are* thirsty. Get some water."

Confusion remained on the hapless boy's face, but he did as instructed, leaving Cormac and me alone in the ring.

"Cormac, I need you to do something," I began.

Cormac was shaking his head with each word. "I won't throw a round. Honor—"

"I would never threaten your honor." I fought the urge to roll my eyes. Honor wouldn't stop a bandit or a boar from skewering the idiot. "We both know there's no way Aaron can disarm you. A straight-up fight is a waste of your time. I want you to work on your evasion skills in this round. Only defend. Practice your forms, especially dodge and parry. Pretend you're sparring with a king or prince, and you're not allowed to attack, only protect."

"But, Cadet-Sergeant—"

"This is for you, not him." I held up a palm. "Watching you spar against Lachlan made me realize you never have to defend against anyone in the unit. You need that practice."

A moment of silence passed as we stared at one another. Cormac's eyes were defiant, but he nodded once.

"Good. Not a word to Aaron. I don't want him changing his tactics."

"Whatever those might be," Cormac murmured.

"Right." I grunted. "Just work on your own forms, and don't worry about him."

"Yes, sir."

Aaron returned a moment later, looking just as nervous and exhausted as he had before leaving for his drink.

"All right, take your marks," I ordered. "Fight!"

Cormac stared, unmoving.

Aaron waited.

A moment passed, then another.

Still, neither moved.

"You said 'go,' didn't you?" Aaron asked.

I lost my battle with an eye roll. "Yes, Aaron. Time is running. *One of you do something.*"

Aaron lunged forward, sword raised above his head like he was some heroic statue that would never actually have to strike an opponent. When he reached where Cormac stood, the big man simply stepped to the side and let Aaron stumble past. Aaron nearly fell out of the ring without either man touching the other.

Cormac danced to the opposite side and stared as Aaron regained his footing.

I stepped back until I bumped into the bench and sat, wishing I didn't have to watch the mess unfolding before me.

Aaron shot forward, this time more balanced and wary. He swung to the right, and Cormac parried easily. Then he swung left, where Cormac dodged like a dancer changing partners. Aaron dropped nearly to his knees and swung at Cormac's ankles. The big man leaped, nearly hurdling over his scrawny opponent's bent form, then landed lightly on his feet a pace away.

I squinted at the hourglass. There was still three-quarters of the bout to go. I blew out a heavy sigh.

When the sand was nearly out, I stood and shouted, "Aaron, attack! You're almost out of time. Press him!"

Aaron startled, then flew into a gangly blur. His arms flailed, and his sword swung, forcing Cormac to dance faster than he had all bout.

Still, the boy never scored a touch on the mountain.

But that had not been a requirement in the rules.

"Time!" I called. "A draw."

Cormac's face was an unreadable mask as he left the ring. Aaron remained bent, hands on his knees, desperately sucking in air.

The moment Cormac was out of earshot, I stepped forward and rested a hand on the boy's shoulder. "Congratulations, cadet. You passed the second test."

Aaron's head shot up. "What? Really? I . . . wait . . . you're serious?"

A smile filled my face as I nodded. "Yes, Aaron, I'm serious. You needed a draw, and you got one. It would've been nice if you'd touched Cormac, but a win is a win."

Aaron's head bobbed, and his toothy grin made me laugh.

"Aaron, your hair might be beyond cleaning, and the rest of you needs a bath. Get out of here."

"Yes, sir." He stiffened, then bounded out of the ring and raced toward the compound's barracks.

I stared after the boy and shook my head.

"You do him no favors, you know."

I nearly drew my sword as Ayden stepped up behind me. I'd forgotten the man was still watching.

"Why are you here, Byrne? Don't you have somewhere better to be than watching First Years test?"

Ayden inclined his head. "Thank you for allowing me to observe. I have yet to receive my assignment, so I have a bit of free time. Watching your unit yesterday made me curious about how they would perform in the ring. It was . . . entertaining."

I wanted to punch him. "Entertaining? These cadets are working their arses off out here. Show them a little—"

"Easy." Ayden threw up his palms. "I meant no disrespect. You are good with them, and they clearly respect you. This bodes well for after we leave this place and face the real world together."

Ayden's sudden shift from smug derision to complimentary had my head spinning. There was no mocking in his tone or taunting on his lips. Everything about his words and bearing spoke of honest praise.

I stared, trying to decide if I believed the man.

Ayden's deep blue eyes stared back.

"Uh, okay, thanks," I fumbled, finally tearing my gaze away to focus on the practice sword Aaron had left behind. "I'd better put this away." I lifted the sword.

"Right. Very important, that sword. Good thought." A curl twisted the corner of Ayden's mouth. "Nice chatting with you, Declan."

Ayden inclined his head, then strode away toward the headquarters building.

I stared after him, watching curls of sun-kissed hair dangle and wave.

"Arse," I muttered, as I stepped out of the sandy ring and dropped the sword into an empty slot on the rack.

CHAPTER THREE

DECLAN

The next week rushed by. I administered only one more test, the Hand-to-Hand Challenge. As expected, Aaron got his scrawny arse handed to him round after round. I had to use the same sly technique with another of the stronger cadets, coaching them to work on their evasion skills, just to give Aaron a passing draw.

Thankfully, the remaining tests, which involved assignments in the mountain forest, were not mine to oversee. While my underlings battled the elements and struggled to identify edible plants, my classmates and I would undergo tests of our own, the annual Second Year Trial. I'd been so consumed with handling my own unit's examinations that I had given little thought to what we might face.

And that was the *real* challenge of the Trial: it changed every year, so cadets had no way to anticipate or prepare for what might be thrown at them.

One year, the Trial had mirrored tournaments thrown sporadically in the capital, complete with competitions in every aspect of combat and horsemanship. The next year, the Trial was all written exams. More than half failed that year. It was so bad that leadership administered a second, more physical Trial to those who'd failed, so as to not decimate the incoming ranks of new Rangers.

I stood with the nearly two dozen men and women of my cohort outside the main entrance to the building that served as the headquarters for Rangers throughout the country. To call it a building was an offense. It was a compound made of enormous logs designed to house a small city of men and women in green cloaks, containing living quarters, the dining hall, offices, and even a full archery range and two melee rings for wintertime indoor training. At any time, thousands called the place home. Legend credited the Mages, including the Arch Mage himself, in the formation of the structure, as no one believed men alone could've built such a monstrosity. Its size eclipsed every other building in Melucia.

"I heard they're sending us into the mountains to war-game against the border patrols," one nervous cadet said to another behind me.

"They're doing another tournament," another whispered.

"I heard it was a race to the eastern border and back," yet another said in quivering voice.

I bit back a laugh at that last one. It was a ridiculous suggestion that would force us to travel nearly sixteen hundred miles, a journey that would consume a half year or more. I knew leadership already knew their new Rangers' assignments post-graduation, and there was no way they would take them off the field for three or four months just to run a race.

I was about to turn and rib the cadet who'd spoken that insanity, but a familiar figure appearing in the central doorway stilled everyone.

"Cadets," Captain Whitman called, as his senior officers filed out of the building to stand on either side of the low step on which Whitman held court. "My, you're an ugly lot."

A rumbling laughter made its way through the Second Years. Ewan Whitman was well liked, and even more respected. At just under six feet tall, the man had seen nearly fifty winters, and thirty of those were in the Green. His short-cropped hair that now held more salt than pepper belied the corded muscle he maintained beneath his tunic. He was quick to correct, but equally easy with praise, and a joke was never far from his lips. Others called him "a Ranger's Ranger," a nickname that hadn't made sense to me until I'd entered the Academy. It had only taken a few interactions to see why the man was so beloved.

"All right, settle down," Whitman said through a broad smile. "It's time for the Second Year Trial. This is one of many tests you face before receiving your cloak, but I think we all know it's the most important. Fail your Trial, and you will go home. It is simple as that."

A few of the cadets glanced around, checking to see how their peers responded, but most remained fixated on the Captain.

"This year's Trial will test those skills held most dear to every Ranger: wilderness survival, tracking, marksmanship, and stealth. You will need each of these if you hope to pass. Oh, and don't forget speed. This year is a timed challenge. If you're late, you're out."

A groan rippled through the cadets. Most challenges could be solved in dozens of ways, but the clock was unforgiving. No one wanted to face a timed Trial.

"Commander Geros will walk you through your objective and the rules. Pay attention. You break a rule, and you're out. You fail your objective, and you're out. You're late . . ."

The cadets chanted back, "And you're out."

Whitman smiled and nodded. "See, you're not as stupid as you look. Geros, walk them through."

Whitman's second-in-command climbed the step. I tried to watch the man's eyes, but the scar that ran from his granite-like jaw to the edge of his right eye stole my attention. It was both gruesome and fascinating. Geros never spoke of how he'd received it, and curiosity gnawed at me since the moment we met nearly two years earlier.

"All right, lads," Geros said, earning a few glares from the women who represented nearly thirty percent of the class. "Somewhere in the mountains, there are ten deer. Each has been tagged with a bright yellow ribbon. Your mission is to bring us one ribbon. You may capture or kill the deer. However, if you kill the deer, you must dress it and return all usable meat and fur, as well as the ribbon. Before you ask how we'll know if you killed the deer and left it to rot, I will say this. We *will* know. Period."

That sent another wave of glances about the class.

"You will be divided into teams of two. Each pair will work together to achieve the objective. No, you will not pick your pairs. We have done that for you, and you may not switch. Don't ask." Geros unfurled a scroll and stared a moment, then returned his gaze to the cadets. "Red boundary markers establish the perimeter for this challenge. Do not go out of bounds."

A lanky cadet in spectacles tentatively raised his hand. Geros's brows knitted.

"What is it, Sikes?"

"Sir, what if the deer goes out of bounds?"

A few cadets stifled laughs, but others nodded and watched Geros.

"You go out of bounds, you're out. Got it?" Geros repeated the mantra, winning a grin from his Captain.

"A few more rules," Geros continued. "You may not steal another team's ribbon. You may not harm another team. You may not interact with another team in any way, and you most certainly may not collaborate with another team. Your only friend is your partner, and you have no enemies other than the mountains. Understood?"

A chorus of, "Yes, sir," bellowed from the cadets.

"Good. On Captain Whitman's bell, the Trial begins. You have three days. You hear me? Exactly three days. At noon, on this spot, in three days, this Trial ends. Don't be late." He scanned the class, letting his words sink in. "Now, listen up. I'll read the pairings only once."

They stood shoulder to shoulder in a semicircle around the stair, but still, the mass of men and women shuffled forward, as though a few inches would help them hear better.

Geros began rattling off names from his scroll, and each cadet raised his or her hand, spotted their new partner, and stepped aside to begin plotting.

"Shira Fagan," was the third name he called. My gaze shot to her, and my heart raced in anticipation of our pairing. We'd been fast friends from the moment we'd entered the Academy, and there was no one I'd rather be stuck on a mountain with than Shira. She could find a way to make me laugh while mucking out stables. If she hadn't been such a ladies', um, lady, I might've wanted more than friendship. That, and other thoughts, kept us squarely in the best friend bucket, which was a fine place to be with a friend like her.

When Geros called another cadet's name to pair with Shira, she shrugged, and my head drooped.

Great. I'll probably end up with some idiot who doesn't know a tree from a rock.

Midway through the list, the Commander barked, "Declan Rea."

I raised my hand.

"Ayden Byrne," Geros called.

You've got to be—

"Looks like we're partners." Ayden's whisper tickled my ear. Startled, I bumped into the man in front of me.

"Hey!"

"Sorry," I said, dusting off the man's cloak. "Got startled. Sorry."

The cadet nodded and turned back, waiting for his name to be called.

When I turned back, Ayden's stupid grin greeted me. The prick was *enjoying* this.

"Come on, let's get organized," I said, brushing past Ayden and striding beyond the gathered cadets without waiting to see if he followed.

Once free of the crowd, I stopped, ran a hand through my poofy blond hair, and turned to find Ayden staring. "Spirits, you startled me again. Try making some noise when you walk. And why the hell are you even here and not in the fancy Saltstone training house for all the betters? That's where you did First Year, isn't it?"

"Yes, it is," he said without a hint of irritation, despite the acid in my tone. "And the training there was fine, I suppose, but I sought certainty that I received real training, not some pampered lessons for those who would never face danger. My parents forbade it, but I requested the transfer anyway. Command is not swayed by title as much as one might think."

I snorted and shook my head. "Like you'd ever risk your shiny arse for anyone else."

Ayden glared. "What is your issue with me, Declan? I have been nothing but polite, even showing an interest in your cadets and their training. Yet every time we speak, you act as though I am your enemy. Why is that?"

I tried to glare back, but the only thing I saw in Ayden's gaze was curious interest. He wasn't preening or strutting or staring down his nose. He wasn't even angry. He appeared genuinely perplexed at my animosity.

I lowered my head and muttered. "You laughed at my cadets."

Ayden stepped forward. With his head still lowered, all I saw were the tips of his boots entering my field of vision.

"Your entire unit was laughing. That kid—"

"His name is *Aaron*," I snapped, as my head rose and our eyes met again. "He's a good kid, and he happens to be Captain Whitman's nephew."

Ayden's brows rose. "So that's why you've been coddling him."

"Coddling?" I took a step back, planted my fists on my hips, and found the strength to glare. "I haven't coddled him. I've helped him. There's a difference. He's probably smarter than everyone in this yard combined."

"And that helps with archery or hand-to-hand how?"

"Not everyone wearing a cloak is a fighter. He'll make a fine Ranger doing Rangery things . . . *inside* the headquarters . . . with parchment and quill."

Ayden snorted. "Rangery things?"

My eyes flared. "Yeah. We need strategic thinkers helping with battle plans and stuff."

Ayden bit back another laugh.

"What's so funny *now*?" I was getting more pissed, but a laugh kept tickling my throat, which pissed me off more.

"When was the last time the Rangers went into battle? A thousand years ago? The worst thing we strategize against is the annual mating season of boars. Oh, unless you count all that, how did you put it, Rangery things?"

We'd been squared off so long, we'd lost track of the officers and their roll call. Geros had long since stopped reading names, and Whitman had reclaimed the step. When the Captain rang his golden handbell, cadets scattered in every direction.

I remained rooted in place with my eyes boring through Ayden's.

"Do you have a ribbon in your pocket?" Ayden asked after an uncomfortable moment.

My head cocked. "What? What are you talking about now?"

Ayden smiled. "If you do not have a ribbon in your pocket, or in your pack, perhaps, then we'd best get started. Three days will go by quickly."

Three days, I thought. *Three days with the prickiest prick alive. Fuck my life.*

"Lead on, Lord Byrne."

"I'm not—"

I huffed out a sigh. "Just . . . for Spirits' sake, go."

Chapter Four

Ayden

"Where should we start?" I asked.

We stood at the edge of town where the forest consumed the plains and the sun's light was filtered through a million leaves that never stilled. It was at once beautiful and foreboding. The packs strapped to our backs were weighty burdens, constant reminders of the three days we had to spend together.

"You've never been in here, have you?" Declan asked without answering my question.

"No."

He wasn't facing me then, but I could feel him rolling his eyes. What was it with this guy? I had done nothing to earn his derision, yet here he was, refusing to answer my question or even turn and look me in the eye. It hadn't even been a full day and I was already sick of his attitude.

"This is the most dangerous land in Melucia," he said, after taking a few steps into the trees. "It's untamed, like the fires of the Phoenix that formed it."

I didn't mean to snort. It just slipped out.

"What?" He glanced back, his eyes narrowed. "You don't believe the histories?"

"Histories? You mean myths. The whole idea of a legendary bird consumed by magical fire is ridiculous. In the past thousand years, how many times has that bird been spotted?"

"Well, never, but that doesn't mean—"

"A thousand years ago, were people more or less superstitious than they are today? Did they hold on to inane beliefs we now know to be children's tales?"

"Yeah, I guess."

"And do you not think it strange that magic is fading?"

Declan stopped walking, then turned slowly to face me. "What do you mean?"

"Do you see a golden collar anywhere around?" I peered all around the forest, as though searching.

Curiously, Declan's head dropped, and he muttered, "No."

Had something I said struck him deeper than intended? Where had this sullen resignation come from? I decided to shelve those questions and press forward.

"There are more Mutes born every year. Magic is dying out. Even the Mages talk about it."

His head snapped up. "I grew up with the Mages, and I never heard a word of this. Not a single one. Maybe you're just listening to the wrong people."

He turned and began trudging forward again, as though he'd settled the point.

Then his words sank in.

He grew up with the Mages? What did that mean? He hadn't said, "a Mage." He said, "the Mages," as though he grew up with all of them. That didn't make any sense.

"What do you mean you grew up with the Mages?" I asked.

Declan strode forward. "I grew up in the Mages' Guild—well, in their compound, really. I would never be allowed in the guild."

He sounded so bitter, like he was almost spitting out the words.

"My parents died when I was three. The Mages took my brother and me in, raised us. Keelan manifested and is now a famous Constable. I'm here, stuck with you, in these mountains."

Stuck with me? How touching. He really was bitter.

"What about you? Raised by servants? A team of diaper-changers and toe-lickers? Bet they fed you and wiped your arse, just to make you feel important."

His resentment bordered on anger, and I nearly tripped over a fallen limb.

"I am the son of Lord Byrne. Yes, I grew up with servants and loving parents. I never went to bed hungry or wanted for anything. My tutors were the finest in Saltstone, and I was introduced to society before I could walk." My voice rose as I spoke, bounding off the stony mountain. "I know you hate me for it, but I cannot help the circumstance of my birth any more than you can yours."

Declan laughed, but there was no joy in the sound.

"What?"

"You really can't compare being the spoiled brat of a high lord to being an orphan handed off to a bunch of old men because no one else wanted you."

I blanched. Rage stirred in my chest. Everything in me wanted to grab a rock off the ground and hurl it at his back, to lash out and force this man to be kind, or at least to show me the respect I was due.

But I didn't lash out.

My mind and heart struggled with whether to defend my honor in the face of a certain insult or be saddened by this man who believed no one wanted him. I wanted to be enraged, to bite back, to show him who I truly was, but the image of the small boy without parents stilled my tongue.

"Declan, I'm sorry."

"That's for sure," Declan muttered, a little too loudly.

Heat flooded my voice. "What is that supposed to mean? I was being sincere."

"Fine, I'll bite." His steps slowed, but he didn't turn. "What are you sorry about? And why'd you call me Declan just now?"

"It *is* your name, is it not?" I drew in a breath and swallowed my pride. This was supposed to be an apology, not a battle. "I do not know what it was like—what it must have been like—to grow up as you did. I . . . I can't imagine losing my parents. I *am* sorry you had to go through that."

He stopped and turned, examining me through narrowed eyes so long I wondered if he would ever speak.

"Thanks," was all he said before turning back and resuming the climb.

We'd made it another twenty paces before curiosity overtook caution. "What was it like? Growing up with all those Mages, I mean."

Declan stopped again and glanced back. "Can we just not talk for a while? I'd like to focus on tracking deer so we can get this Trial over with."

"Oh. Sure. Okay."

He'd turned away again before I'd started speaking.

An hour passed before he stopped beside a trickling brook and leaned against a large boulder. The shade of the forest canopy kept the worst of the sun's heat away, but it was still a smoldering summer's day. Declan wiped sweat from his brow, then let his pack fall from his shoulders and rolled his neck.

"Drink up. Your body needs it, even if you don't feel thirsty. We can refill our canteens here."

I nodded and dropped my pack on the ground, fishing out my canteen.

"Earlier, you said it was the most dangerous place," I ventured, wondering if we were still not talking. "What did you mean? It does not seem dangerous to me, other than those branches that keep trying to kill me."

He chuckled as I kicked away a branch I stumbled over as we entered the clearing.

"The wildlife does what wildlife does. We're in their home now. If they're bigger than us, we might look like a tasty meal. We might also look like a threat. Either way, bears, boars, and other creatures pose a threat to anyone venturing into their territory."

"Sounds great," I said with no small measure of sarcasm.

He shrugged. "If you understand and respect them, and remain on guard, the forest isn't so bad. If you blunder through without a care, you may not make it out. That's one of the patrols' primary missions, watching out for ignorant people who wander in here and get into trouble."

"The Saltstone Rangers do not speak of this much."

Declan grunted. "There aren't any woods or mountains in the center of the country. The only mission out there is keeping the roads free of bandits. They act more like town Guardsmen than Rangers. This . . ." He waved his arms around at the trees. "This is why the Rangers were formed, to protect the border, the forest, the mountains . . . and the idiots who venture into them."

I stared into the brook while he stood in silence. "You know the mountains well?"

"As well as I can, less than most Rangers." He nodded as he drank. "I came here a year before entering the Academy, spent most of my time roaming these woods, just being alone. A lot of people see this place as scary, but I'm more comfortable here than anywhere in the world."

He rested a palm on the boulder as though greeting an old friend. I suddenly felt as though I intruded on an intimate moment.

Alas, my curiosity knew no bounds.

"Why?"

His head cocked. "Why what?"

"Why did you come a year before—"

"Oh, that." His head lowered again. Another moment passed before he spoke. I expected some story about preparing for the

Academy or learning to hunt, but his answer stunned me. "I was probably running from something more than toward anything. I just . . . I couldn't take being out there anymore."

He looked through the forest, as though Saltstone and the rest of the civilized continent were visible.

I didn't know what to say to that.

Declan Rea confounded me, left me speechless half the time and infuriated the other, and fascinated me all at once. Back in Grove's Pass, with his unit, he was always upbeat, jovial even; but out here, he seemed to lose himself in his thoughts. Maybe it was his past he saw. I couldn't tell, but something about the man drew me to him, made me want to know more, to understand his layers and who he truly was.

"Spirits, it's hot," he said suddenly, then reached down and pulled his sweat-soaked tunic over his head and draped it across the boulder.

I hadn't meant to stare. His body was just so hardened and—

"Need something?" he asked, and I realized what my rebellious eyes were doing. I couldn't pull away fast enough.

"Oh, no, sorry. I, uh, just, you surprised me, with your tunic and all, the whole taking it off thing, I mean."

A grin formed, and, for the first time, Declan Rea looked at me with something other than contempt.

"I never thought I'd see the great lordling fumble his words. This is indeed a beautiful day."

"You really are an ass, you know it?"

"I've been called worse." He laughed, then grabbed his tunic and plunged it into the stream. "You might want to do this with yours. It'll make the rest of our climb a bit cooler."

He wrung out the garment, then lifted it over his head. Once in place, the fabric stuck to every curve of his shoulders and chest. Without thinking, I stared again.

"No? Fine. Be miserable," Declan said. "Let's get moving, then. We have a lot of ground to cover if we want to get to the best hunting grounds."

Either he hadn't noticed me gawking, or he hadn't cared. Either way, I was grateful when he turned away and hefted his pack once more.

He had been right. This really was going to be a long three days.

We spent most of that first day in silence, Declan lost in his thoughts, and me trying desperately not to fall on my face. I wasn't uncoordinated and did not lack strength, but the forest floor was a new experience all its own. Where Declan strode forward with confidence, I tested and prodded each step before taking it. More than a few times, the forest floor rose to greet me. Twice, I'd been gazing at some bird or plant, and a tree limb smacked me in the cheek or head. Thorned brambles snared my legs. I didn't want Declan to think me weak or unfit, so I played each incident off as some intentional act, as though I was testing the snap of a branch, and received a welt for my effort.

He merely grinned, and I was sure he knew better. He didn't rub my foibles in my face, but neither did he miss an opportunity to enjoy them.

He truly was an infuriating man.

As darkness descended over the mountains, we'd still seen no sign of deer, ribbons, or anything useful. We passed the entrance to a small cave, and I suggested it might be a good place to hole up for the night.

Declan snorted. "Do you know whose home that might be?"

"Home? Someone lives out here?"

His grin widened. "Oh, certainly. Many, *many* call this place home. We talked about them already. Bears and boars and whoever else. That cavern likely houses a few critters you wouldn't want curling up next to you in the night. Even if they aren't big enough to spot right now, you wouldn't want to end up with a snake as a bedmate."

My eyes widened as I stared at the opening. "I hadn't thought about that."

Declan shook his head. "Come on, Ranger Byrne, let's find a safer place to camp."

Ranger Byrne? Not little lordling or Lord Byrne? It was a tiny thing. He might not have even realized it had slipped out, but I took it as a step in the right direction.

I thought it odd when he chose an open area where the trees were spread farther apart, but who was I to argue?

We slept on bedrolls under the leaves and stars—on opposite ends of the clearing.

I only glanced over at Declan a few times, maybe ten . . . okay, twenty.

He made a tiny "puh" sound with his lips when he breathed out.

That made me smile.

Still, sleep evaded me most of the night. We were in the middle of the woods on a mountain near the border with another country. One of us probably needed to stay awake and on watch for bears or enemy soldiers. No, Melucia and the Kingdom had not invaded each other or even been hostile in nearly a thousand years, but enemy soldiers could, possibly, by some act of rebellion or whatever, cross the border and attack us while we slept.

In the darkness, with the sounds of the forest hammering my ears, that reasoning seemed perfectly sound.

I was most definitely not staying awake because the thought of Declan Rea sleeping nearby made my skin tingle. I refused to believe something so vile.

Although, the way his hair—

"You're awake?" Declan rubbed bleary eyes.

I looked away, as though those enemy soldiers had snapped a twig and were about to attack.

"Did you get any sleep? What time is it?"

I stood from my bedroll and stepped to the edge of the clearing. Darkness shrouded the trees, though a hint of the morning to come peeked through the uppermost leaves of the canopy. All around, the forest lay quiet and still, as if nature herself refused to wake. I breathed in the crisp air, savoring the scent of pine as it drifted to me. There was peace in these mountains, one I had not known in the capital.

"The sun hasn't risen yet, but she's close," I said as I stretched. The beauty of the forest may have been comforting to my mind, but it lacked anything resembling proper bedding, and my back ached.

"Ugh. I'm going back to sleep. Wake me if somebody attacks."

"Are you trying to make me nervous out here?"

He groaned. "I'm trying to sleep."

Then he rolled over and covered his head with his blanket.

Great. Now what am I supposed to do?

We slept in our clothes, which I assumed was the normal thing to do when on patrol in the mountains. I rolled up my bedroll and attached it to my pack, then stood and stretched. The pressure on my bladder demanded attention, so I stepped out of the clearing. The stream we'd found the day before ran close to our clearing, so I picked my way through the brush, gripping every tree I passed for balance, until I stood before a large pine only a couple of paces from the brook.

"Lose some water, refill the water," I mused aloud as I set my canteen on an outcrop of rocks and turned to face the tree.

I was midway through relieving myself when a twig snapped in the distance.

The forest was still dark, though morning's light was beginning to filter through the leaves. I peered around the tree. There was nothing ahead. A quick glance to my left, then right, also found nothing amiss.

A rustle of leaves sounded some distance behind.

I wheeled around, spraying the ground as I turned. Nothing appeared. The rustle didn't repeat itself, and no animal came charging out of the brush, which was a good thing because, if there had been a bandit or boar, the only weapon I had at hand would have done little good.

Relieved—in more ways than one—I fastened my trousers and took a step back.

That's when sounds exploded around me. I dropped to the forest floor, keeping only my head up to see.

A blur of brown as tall as a man shot by some twenty paces to my left.

Branches rustled, and two more figures raced by on my right.

Then I heard Declan cry out.

Chapter Five

Declan

Ayden finally walked away. Spirits, that man made more noise than any human alive. All I wanted to do was get a little more sleep before we had to trudge through the forest hunting the ever-elusive yellow-tagged deer. He seemed to think that, because he was awake, the rest of the world should rise to greet the morning. How wrong he was.

I covered my head with the blanket and squeezed my eyes shut. There was a rock poking through my bedroll, but I wasn't about to move to get rid of it. The last moments of sleep before rising were the most precious.

Ayden's footfalls faded into the distance, and blessed darkness closed around me.

It didn't last long. I'd barely drifted off when the snapping of branches brought me fully awake.

"Ayden Fucking Byrne. Were you never taught to be quiet when someone is sleeping?" I shouted from beneath my blanket.

Another set of branches rustled.

Two?

My sleepy brain tried to understand.

As clumsy as Ayden was, even he couldn't stumble in two places at once. I yanked the blanket off my head and sat up. The metal tip of an arrow greeted me.

"Do not move," said a voice that sounded more like the grinding of gears than any human.

I blinked away sleep and looked past the arrow. A man wearing a robe the color of bitter coffee held a crossbow awkwardly in one arm. His face was covered with an odd mask formed of a snarling bull with white wings where its ears should've been. Only the man's eyes were visible, and they were stranger than the mask. I stared, searching for some sign of life, but those eyes were more black and hollow than the deepest pit or cavern.

"What do you want? We don't have any money. We're cadets—"

"I want nothing from you. Only silence."

"Ayden!" I cried out, hoping to guide him to help me.

An invisible hand clamped over my mouth, forcing it shut. I reached up, finding nothing with which to fight. I tried to call out, then stand, but my body betrayed me. It felt as though ropes of iron had been wrapped around my arms, clamping them tight against my sides.

I looked down, desperate to see what held me in place, but there was nothing. No ropes, no bands, nothing.

It was magic.

Terror flooded through me.

Eyes wide, I looked up.

The man hadn't moved or reacted. He simply stared.

"You will not speak again," the man rasped. "When my brothers arrive, we will leave you in peace. Follow us, and you will die."

I blinked rapidly, wishing the dream to end, but I was wide awake.

This was no dream.

Where was Ayden?

A second robed man appeared, his mask with the beak of a hawk and tusks of a boar.

"Where are they?" the man holding me captive asked.

"Behind," the second said.

A woman screamed. Her cry died as quickly as it had been raised.

A third man entered the clearing, this one also robed. He struggled under the weight of a woman on his shoulder.

"The bitch wouldn't stop shouting. I made her sleep," the new man rasped.

"You should have done that long ago," the man with the crossbow replied.

The man with the woman inclined his head.

So he's the leader, I thought.

"You two go. I will take care of this one," the leader said.

The others nodded, then sprinted away.

The noise of their passing had barely vanished when a fourth form appeared in the clearing.

Ayden.

In a smooth motion I thought beyond his abilities, Ayden leaped toward the man with the crossbow and twisted his body so his foot flew into the man's back, tumbling him forward and sending the crossbow flying into the woods. Even more remarkable, Ayden landed lightly, immediately ready to strike again.

The pressure around my arms and neck vanished the moment the man was struck.

Recovering quickly, the robed man stood and turned back. Ayden darted forward and slammed a palm into the man's chest, knocking him back into a tree.

The bastard barely flinched, pushing off the tree and lunging forward with one hand outstretched. "You will be silent!" he commanded.

Immediately, Ayden grabbed his throat with both hands and dropped to the ground. His eyes bulged, and he struggled for air.

I scrambled to my feet and charged the man, but his magic proved far faster.

In a heartbeat, I lay on the ground, only paces from Ayden, clutching my own throat and staring, as we each gasped for precious breath. His face was turning a pale blue.

"You will not follow. Do you understand?" the man asked, more a command than a question.

I nodded frantically.

As quickly as he'd arrived, the robed man vanished into the woods, freeing our throats and taking his magic with him.

It took a moment to recover my breath enough to ask, "Are you okay?"

Ayden's head rose. Gone was the cocksure gaze. His eyes brimmed with fear as he rubbed his throat.

"I think so. You?" His voice sounded strained, and he winced as he spoke.

"Yeah."

I tried to stand, but a wave of dizziness kept me firmly on the ground.

"Who was that?" Ayden asked.

"Somebody with a really annoying Gift."

"I bet our throats will be sore for days." Ayden nodded. "Have you ever seen robes like that?"

"No."

"And what was with his eyes? And voice? He sounded more dead than alive."

I shrugged and tried standing again, this time bracing myself with a palm to a tree.

"His eyes were black, like there was nothing there," I muttered.

I released the tree and tried taking a step. The world spun, and I began to fall.

Ayden got to his feet and shot forward faster than I would've imagined. "I've got you. Put your arm around my shoulders."

I wanted to resist, to pull away, but I was either going to hug his shoulders or kiss the ground.

"Thanks," I said. "I'll be all right in a minute. I'm just a little lightheaded."

"Getting the life choked out of you will do that," he said, a gentle smile parting his lips. I'd never noticed how full they were, and, unlike the rest of the forest, they weren't spinning.

"You should sit until your head clears. I doubt we'll see those men again. I am not sure whether they were running toward something or away from someone, but they seemed intent on getting away from here."

"Yeah, good idea." I let him guide me back to my bedroll. "I think one of them carried a woman over his shoulder."

He nodded again. "She was either unconscious or dead. I couldn't tell which."

"Another kidnapping," I muttered.

Ayden's head cocked, and his eyes narrowed. "*Another*? What do you mean?"

I hadn't meant to say that aloud. "Oh, uh, well—"

"Declan, we're on a mountainside in the middle of nowhere. The two of us are all we have right now. Put whatever you think of me aside for a moment and talk to me."

I looked at my hands, then back up. Ayden waited, impatience written on his features.

"Fine," I said, heaving a sigh. "I overheard a pair of officers talking in the mess hall. I couldn't hear most of what they said, but the word 'kidnappings' came up a few times, and they both looked worried. I got the impression they had just received orders related to something big going on."

"Kidnappings? Plural? As in, more than one?"

I nodded. "That's what they said."

"And you think this could be one of those?"

"I don't know. Maybe. That kind of thing doesn't happen a lot. What are the odds this is a coincidence?"

Ayden nodded slowly, his eyes distant as he thought.

"Should we go after them?" I asked.

His focus resolved. "And fight the guy with the Gift to silence anyone who opposes him via strangulation?"

"Fair point. Should we at least go back and report this to someone?"

Ayden thought a moment. "Do you think they would waive the Trial if we did? We would certainly fail the objective."

I shook my head. "No, they would never do that."

He shrugged, as if that decided the question.

"What about the woman? We can't just leave her to them."

He thought a moment, then said, "We do not know she was kidnapped, only that a man carried her over his shoulder. Perhaps they were helping her, taking her somewhere to receive aid."

"Is that what you believe?" I asked, nonplussed.

"No. Of course not." Ayden's eyes lowered. "But how could we help her? By the time we make it back down the mountain, they could be anywhere, even across the border. The patrols have a better chance of helping her than we do."

At any point in time, there were dozens of teams patrolling the mountains, senior Rangers armed to the teeth and ready to defend their homeland.

"You're probably right. They won't make it past the patrols if they're up to something."

We sat in silence a moment, each lost in the implications of our decision.

"We would have to repeat Second Year, too," I said.

"What do you mean?"

"If we abandoned the Trial to report this, we would be forced to repeat Second Year."

"Which would place you in the same class as the cadets you now lead, would it not?" His brows rose. "And I would be the one you would blame, consigning me to an entire year of dealing with a pissed-off Declan Rea, more than he already appears to be, though I have yet to fathom why."

A laugh slipped out, and I grabbed my throat, suddenly aware of how painful laughing would be until the man's magical grip wore off.

"What's so funny?" Ayden asked, lips pursed.

"You talk like a proper lord. I mean, listen to yourself. 'I have yet to fathom why.' Who talks like that?"

"Well . . . I suppose—"

"See! *You suppose*?" I chuckled. "I never would've thought you'd say, 'pissed off' or anything that might offend someone's sensibilities."

He rolled his eyes. "I am trained to swim in deep pools filled with sharks. That does not mean I can't step out of the water and walk about with others."

I fell onto my back, laughter rumbling from deep in my gut.

"What?" Ayden stood a couple paces away, an annoyed wrinkle on his brow. He planted fists to his hips, making me laugh harder.

"Sorry, it's just . . . First, you did the lord talk again with, 'swim in deep pools.' Spirits, Ayden. How far did they shove the polearm up your arse?" I tried to stop laughing, but his expression, somewhere between enraged beast and that of a confused retriever, was more than I could take. "Second, that was a terrible analogy. I mean, it was *truly* awful. What are you supposed to be, some kind of fish with legs and feet? Do you have little webbed toes, too? Maybe a fin on your back I haven't seen yet? That must be why you wouldn't take your shirt off before!"

His eyes widened.

Then his frown twisted into a smile.

"It was bad, was it not?"

"Not bad, awful." I shook my head. "Wait. Let me guess. Your mother is a porpoise, and your father is a salamander? What would that make you? A porpimander? A salipus? That's it! Salipus. That fits you perfectly. I hereby dub you Lord Salipus."

My shoulders heaved as tears pooled. Through watery eyes, I watched as Ayden lost his battle to remain stoic and joined in my merriment.

"You will *not* call me a salipus—or Lord Salipus—in front of others. As you have said, I am a lordling, and I command you to forget that name."

"Or what?" I gasped.

"I will beat you until you stop, and at this point you know I could." His face smoothed as he tried to appear fierce, only driving me into another wave of uncontrolled amusement.

A moment later, after the laughter subsided, I straightened and wiped my cheeks and eyes. He stared, looking wary of what might come next.

"You probably could beat me pretty bad," I reluctantly admitted. "Where did you learn to do that kick thing? That was . . . incredible."

I hadn't meant for wonder to enter my voice, especially related to anything Ayden had done, but his flying, spinning kick was impressive.

He lifted his chin. "One of the advantages to being raised in a noble house is the training."

"Huh. Okay."

He lowered himself to the ground and sat opposite me with his legs crossed.

"I know you think any son of a lord is soft or weak, and that may be true of most, but I am not *that* son of a lord. I received training from the very best tutors . . . from all over the world."

If I hadn't known better, I would've sworn there was resentment mixed with the pride in his voice. He'd been so careful to be polite, even as I shat all over him, that I'd begun to wonder if he had any other emotion inside his chest.

"All over the world? Really?" Judging his words had become such a habit that I couldn't resist the jab.

He simply nodded. "The Triad's historian was my tutor for geography and history. I began studying with him when I was five."

"The Triad's own?" I whistled. As the son of one of the most prominent men in the country, I knew Ayden would receive the best tutoring, but to have the ruling council's own historian as his teacher was beyond any privilege I could've imagined. And to begin at five years old? Such an early start was rare outside of the Academies, and those vaunted institutions took only a handful of students each year.

"I began learning basic forms with the Armsmaster for the Melucian Guard when I was seven. My father hosted a Master in hand-to-hand combat from the isle of Vint—"

"Wait. Seriously? Vint? Nobody but pirates sails near that island. Even the Kingdom avoids it, and it's only a hundred miles to their south."

He nodded. "Yes, *that* Vint. It is a large island with villages the pirates respect. The Masters from that land teach fighting unlike anything we have here on the mainland."

"I saw that," I said, trying to reconstruct his spinning kick in my mind. "What about swordsmanship?"

"My teacher was the Swordmaster of the Melucian Army."

"Spirits, Ayden."

He shrugged. "You said I was privileged. Is this not what you meant?"

"I meant you were rich. This is a whole other level of privilege."

"Perhaps." He grinned. "And now, my privilege is yours."

That furrowed my brow. "How do you figure?"

"We are partners, at least in this Trial. You are a better tracker and mountain man, or whatever you call it. I am smarter and a better fighter."

"Whoa, easy there. Nobody said you were smarter than a stump. You only said you had really smart tutors. There's a difference."

Ayden grinned. "Fine. I will concede that, though I would give any stump you find a run for its money."

"You don't need its money, remember?"

"True." He chuckled. "And yourself?"

"What about me?"

"I have seen you train others but have yet to see you shoot or fight yourself."

"Oh, I'm all right," I said, slowly standing to test my balance. "I had to be when it became clear no Gift would have me."

Ayden stared, and something in his gaze softened as he fingered his barren collar.

"I know something of that."

"I suppose you do."

He stood, mirroring my deliberate movement. Neither of us wobbled badly.

"Why don't we finish clearing the site," I suggested. "We lost a few hours of morning light thanks to our visitors. We need to do some serious tracking today."

He nodded but didn't speak.

I stared a moment longer than I probably should have, but something in his eyes held my gaze. This time, it wasn't simply the depth swirling about that drew me in. It was something else. The square set of his jaw, and how the rusty stubble formed so perfectly around it? His lips, and how they curled just so at the corners, even when he tried to be serious? Perhaps it was the way he looked at me, as though searching inside my soul for something . . .

I jerked away. I was being ridiculous, seeing more than was there. I was probably still a little lightheaded. That had to be it.

I kneeled and rolled my blanket, but the feeling of his eyes followed me, and I knew, without turning, that his examination continued.

Was it odd for such a stare to be both disconcerting and comforting?

Ayden had packed up before trekking off through the woods, so he leaned against a tree and waited. I glanced back a couple of times, catching him watching me. His eyes darted away, which made me smile, as though I'd won a minor victory in chasing him off.

It never occurred to me to wonder why he was staring.

I was so naïve.

"We should go another mile or two north," I said, turning toward him as I slung my pack across my shoulders. "But not too far. We need to stay close enough to make it back before the deadline."

He pushed off the tree, picked up his own pack, and stepped to my side as I picked my way through the foliage. "It's just day two. We have plenty of time."

"Maybe. There are a lot of deer up here, and only ten have the mark we're after. If we can't snag one today, we'll be pressed for time tomorrow. We can't forget to factor in the return trip. It would be a shame to find a ribbon but not make it back by the bell."

He grunted. "That's for sure. We'd be repeating year two without having done something honorable about that woman."

I didn't know how to respond to that. Here I was, thinking about our objective, our future, and Ayden was still struggling with the honorable path to aid someone we'd never even met. I knew he was an arrogant prick, a privileged noble who'd never faced real-world challenges or struggled a single day in his haughty life. And yet, when faced with a real-world dilemma, his first thought, the one that lingered, was consumed by honor and selflessness.

Spirits, I wanted to hate this man, to spit at his feet just to mar his perfectly brushed boots, but the innate goodness I was coming to see in him made that bitter taste turn. It was so much simpler to despise him, so much clearer. The last thing I needed was for the other Rangers to think I actually liked a noble, that we were friends. Surely, they saw the same egotism and feckless arrogance I did. Why would anyone—anyone who wasn't a social climber—befriend someone like Ayden Byrne?

And why was I spending so much time thinking about him?

I shook my head in frustration and focused on the trail ahead. The test required all my focus, especially since I was the only one of us who possessed any tracking skills.

"You alright?"

Ayden's voice startled me, and I nearly stumbled over a fallen log.

"Yeah, just got lost in thought."

"You were shaking your head. Did your thoughts argue back?" There was amusement in his tone. Arsehole.

"I'm fine. Keep your eyes scanning and try not to make noise. We're entering an area where a large number of deer feed. There are salt deposits just past that cluster of trees where they gather." I pointed in the distance.

"What is the plan once we find the deer with the ribbon?"

I patted the bow slung across my back. "Guess you'll finally see what kind of marksman I am."

"You don't want to try to capture it? We might be able to avoid killing—"

I turned. "Ayden, the moment the deer smell us, they'll dart away. We don't have time to set up snares. Besides, deer rarely fall for snares. We have to take it down."

"That means we will have to clean it and haul it back."

I smirked. "Why do you think I brought a sturdy lad with me?"

Ayden cocked his head, something he did a lot. "Of course, I will do my part, but . . ."

"But what?"

"You think I am strong?" He looked down at his arms.

His tunic and cloak hid his muscles, but I could picture them in my mind, corded and lean, pulling taut with each bend and curl. I could see how his chest flexed as he reached forward, how his shoulder tightened.

I shook my head again, something I did often, apparently.

"Yes, you are strong. Strong enough for this, at least. Now keep quiet, or we'll never find the damn ribbon."

I turned and stepped carefully, avoiding twigs and other foliage that might give us away, just as the senior Rangers who'd taken me under their wing had taught me. Ayden tried. I could feel him staring at the ground, weighing where to step, but regardless of his choice, each stride rustled or snapped. His tutors were city men, no doubt experts in their fields, but none had taught him how to move silently through the woods.

We would never find the deer together.

"I have an idea." I stopped and spun to face him. His head was down, staring at the ground ahead of his foot. "Let's find you a place to sit and wait. The deer are more likely to find us than the other way around. If we split up, we can cover more possible ground."

"But . . . if we split up, we might never find each other in time to return."

The hesitation, almost fear, in Ayden's voice made my lips twitch.

"You'll stay in place. I'll be able to find you. Trust me."

He eyed me a moment, then nodded. "Okay, you are the expert in this."

His admission surprised me. I'd pegged him for a man who thought he was the best at everything. Why? I wasn't sure. It just fit with the arsehole noble thing. I didn't like how he kept dispelling my assumptions. The blanket of hatred and resentment I'd wrapped about myself was warm and cozy.

"How good are you with that bow? No modesty now. I need to know the truth."

Ayden's chest rose, and a glimmer entered his eyes. "I would love to compete with you one day. You might have more competition than you imagine."

He knew I was an expert marksman, the best shot in the Academy, and would soon be one of the best among all Rangers. If he really thought he could give me a run . . .

"All right, that's good." My teeth ground against that admission. "Come on, let's find you a spot, then I'll go about a half mile farther, near the salt."

We found a hiding place for him where he could see a wide area littered with deer droppings and tracks. With any luck, they would wander right by, and he would have a clear shot.

As I turned to leave, to find my own place to set up watch, Ayden's hand found my shoulder. It was so unexpected that I didn't turn, I couldn't.

"Be careful, okay," he said. The genuine concern in his voice weighed more than his palm.

"Uh, sure. Okay. You, too, I guess."

I suddenly felt like a child trying to speak to a room full of adults.

Utterly flummoxed, I fled.

Yet, the feeling of his hand on my shoulder remained long after I stepped away.

CHAPTER SIX

AYDEN

Declan certainly knew deer.

In my hours alone on the mountain, I counted more than a hundred passing by. Most were fully grown, some sporting crowns with many points, but I was surprised by how many young deer wobbled past on their spindly legs. At one point, three of the younger fawns pranced and played, chasing each other and eventually knocking one to the ground. I had to stop myself from laughing at their antics.

Each deer was beautiful in its own way. Together, they were majestic. I knew they were a herd of individuals, yet they moved as a mass, as one body, one family. There was a sense of community in their passing, as though each knew and cared for the other. I do not know what I expected, but it was not the remarkable scene that unfolded before me.

A few times, a member of the herd stopped. Its ears perked up, and its head turned from one side to the other, its eyes never settling. It sniffed the air, then scanned the area where I hid. I was sure it spotted me, or at least identified the stranger in their midst. It never started or ran, simply found the odd presence, acknowledged it, then resumed its lazy grazing, satisfied I posed no threat.

The thought of shooting one of those creatures sent a pang through my chest.

There were woods outside of Saltstone. My father often joined others on hunts, though those were more for sport than filling our saltbox. I was an expert marksman, always the youngest among peers to win awards. And yet, I'd not joined the men's parties, not even once. I supposed my studies or other distractions of youth stood in the way. All I recalled was my mother objecting and Father yielding to her desires.

Logically, I knew the meat that landed on our table back home came from such animals. Still, seeing the majesty of the beasts as they passed before me, watching how mothers herded their young and cared for their every stride, made me cringe at the thought of one of them falling to my arrow, dying by my hand.

I chuckled to myself. Declan would likely deride such notions. He strode through the woods like a creature born of bark and bramble. Still, I wondered if his conscience gave him pause as he took aim and a deer stared back at him. Perhaps . . . *likely not.*

Luckily—however odd it might seem to consider such failure lucky, given our mission—I never saw a yellow ribbon. I was never forced to choose between my heart's song and our mission's objective.

As the day's heat ebbed and darkness descended, I began to wonder when Declan might return. Would he break through the trees with a limp body dangling across his shoulders?

I winced at that image.

Success would mean graduation, an attainment of both our dreams; and yet, it also meant the end for one of the herd.

Would I sacrifice my dream for a deer's life?

That sounded so silly in my mind. We ate venison at least once each week, and here I grappled with bringing sustenance back and achieving a lifelong goal?

Maybe that robed man had choked me harder than I remembered.

I was being ridiculous.

Thinking of the robed man brought up the image of Declan, lying on the ground, grasping his throat and gasping for breath. I was doing the same, but my fear, in that moment, was not for myself. I was terrified for him. I could see the life draining from his eyes, and everything inside me wanted to race to his side and give him the last of my breath.

This man I barely knew.

This man who loathed me.

By the Phoenix, I was turning into an idiot. Why was I so obsessed with Declan Rea? He had consumed my thoughts since the first day I watched him with his team.

I knew he despised me. What I did not know was if he even preferred men to women. It was one thing to hope a man might change his mind about one's character, to see past assumptions into the heart of another and find something worthy of love. It was entirely another thing to wish a man to lust after that which he never would.

Melucian society had long since accepted couples of any combination, but within the Rangers and Guard, men still clung to deep-rooted views. If discovered, the Green would not be stripped from my shoulders, but I would be shunned by many of my brothers.

Add to everything else, I was Mute. In every way, lacking a Gift was scorned far more than loving another man. Even simple farmers cherished Gifts that allowed crops to grow larger and deeper into autumn. What use could the world have for ones such as us, ones without even the slightest ability to contribute?

I held less resentment than Declan—he was deeply bitter about his magical lot, that much was obvious—and yet, being spurned by the Phoenix felt a bit like being rejected by one's ancestors, as though the Spirits had pronounced one "outcast" or "beyond repair."

Was finding another to love, another man *and* a Mute, worth that risk?

As if to answer, Declan's image reformed in my mind's eye.

His blond hair was unlike any I'd ever seen, unruly and wild, practically beaming with its own sunlight, a perfect representation of the man I was coming to know. I wanted to plunge my hands into it, tangle my fingers in his curls, lose myself . . .

A twig snapped nearby, and I jolted. As quietly as possible, I reached for my bow. I had leaned it against a nearby tree while watching the deer pass.

Another *snap*.

My heart began to race.

Were the robed men back? Would they . . .

"Told you I'd find you."

Declan's lopsided grin sent my heart pounding even louder. I was sure he could hear it in the night's silence.

"Oh, hi. I heard . . . I mean, I wasn't going to . . . you're back. Good." I forced myself to stop talking.

His grin widened. He loved my discomfort. I should hate him for that, but my chest swelled at his smile, his smile *for me*. I didn't care that it was a smirk of ridicule; it was my smirk, my ridicule, from him.

Spirits, I was drowning and could not see the shore.

"Any luck?" He glanced around, I supposed in search of the mythical deer with the yellow tag I should have slain.

I shook my head. "You were right. I saw many pass here, but none bore the tag."

"Yeah, that's what I saw, too." Declan scanned the area where the deer had passed below, then spoke, his voice distant with memory. "They really were something. There was one buck, he must've had twenty points, maybe more. He was huge, and his muscles were powerful, and his eyes—Ayden, they looked ancient, like he had always been here. I know that sounds crazy, but it's how it felt. I swear he looked right at me and inclined his head. I couldn't move. I could barely breathe. It was the strangest thing."

Listening to his excitement, *I* could barely breathe. It was like watching a child experience something for the first time, at once beautiful and innocent. I wanted to cup his cheek and laugh and ask him to tell me about it again and again.

"That sounds . . . incredible," I ventured.

His smile beamed, lighting the dark forest around us.

"I've never seen anything like it, and I've been in these woods a lot over the past couple of years. You should've seen it, Ayden. It was amazing."

I smiled despite myself.

Leaning my bow back against the tree, I asked, "What do we do now?"

"We won't be able to hunt in the night. Let's get some rest and start early in the morning. If we haven't spotted anything within the first few hours, we'll have to head back and hope we find one on the way."

Declan dropped his pack and unhitched his bedroll. "This is as good a place as any. How are you for water?"

I lifted my canteen and shook it. "Still half full."

"All right, we can work our way back to the stream in the morning. That should take us through another couple of areas where the deer congregate."

My brows rose.

"What?"

"Congregate. Big word, orphan boy," I teased, then realized I might have just hit a very sensitive spot.

He gaped, then scrunched his nose. "Me smart. Me talk good. You no smart *or* pretty."

I burst out laughing. "You are terrible, you know that, right?"

"I've been called worse." He grinned and flicked his hair off his forehead.

As he settled, I couldn't stop words from escaping my lips. "You are not what I . . . what I expected."

He looked up. "And what did you expect?"

"A typical Ranger."

"What does that mean?"

Spirits, he is making me spell this out. Why did I not keep my mouth closed?

"Like Commander Geros," I said. "It is as though someone cut him out of the perfect mold of a Ranger drawn by an ancient hand."

Declan laughed. "You saying I'm not the perfect Ranger?"

"No," I said too quickly. "No, I didn't mean that. I mean . . . you're not . . . perfect . . . I mean . . . shit."

His laugh grew, and my toes began to tingle at the sound.

"Let me try this again." I sucked in a breath and tried to stop the stupid tingling from spreading. "Geros is all the good things we hope for in a Ranger, but he is also proud and strong-headed, sometimes too stubborn. He flaunts his women and wants the men around him to do the same. He is a man's man, and a Ranger's Ranger."

"How do you know how strong-headed he is? We're cadets, and he's one of the senior-most officers."

I fiddled with my fingers, desperate to not make eye contact.

"He and Captain Whitman are seen in Saltstone often. They come to meet with the Triad, but remain to make the rounds in the social circuit. I am sure their goal is to maintain support within the noble houses, but in that pursuit, they expose themselves to people."

Declan snorted. "Are you saying one of them exposed themselves to you?"

"No!" I jerked up, horrified. Seeing the triumphant smirk on his lips, I relaxed. "Of course not. I have simply seen them in social settings, and Geros has a way about him, like a thick-necked ox."

"I have no idea what you're saying, but keep going. This is giving me lots of ammunition for the future." His smile grew with every word. "How am I not—how did you say it—a thick-necked ox?"

I let myself fall back onto my bedroll and stare up through the canopy at the smattering of stars. What was I even doing? Why was I swimming into deeper and deeper waters, where Declan could easily shove my head under and drown me without a second thought?

Maybe he was right. My analogies are terrible.

That made me snicker.

"Private joke?" he asked.

"No, sorry. Anyway. You are just different. I saw it in how you led your team, how you worked with that boy. You care about them, and not just as cadets to shepherd through the process, but as individuals. You see them for who they are and who they want to be. They look at you differently than other cadets see their leaders, differently than they look at Geros or even Whitman. That is special, Declan."

A moment passed, then another.

I began to wonder if Declan had drifted off, then he spoke, his voice halting and barely rising above a whisper.

"Thanks." He paused again. "That may be the nicest thing anyone has said to me in all my time here. Maybe ever. I don't know . . . I don't know if I deserve it, but . . . it means a lot."

He sounded like he was fighting each word, like they sliced into him as he spoke, yet he said them, and I knew he meant each one.

The forest floor grew suddenly warm, and I kicked off my blanket.

"I'm exhausted," he said. "Sleep well, little lordling."

My cheeks hurt from smiling, and I was suddenly glad for the darkness.

We rose with the sun. Declan was intent on using every moment we had in our search, so we packed up quickly and made our way toward the stream.

Everywhere we walked, deer scattered. It was as though the word had spread that we were in the area. The herds were both curious and wary, gathering to see the strangers in their midst, but cautious to sprint away the moment we approached.

We never spotted a single flash of yellow.

The sun was a quarter of the way to her crest when Declan stopped and lowered his head.

"We need to turn toward Grove's Pass. From here, we should have just enough time to make it before the bell."

He sounded resigned, like a small boy who had failed and dreaded the disappointment he knew he would soon find in his father's eyes. My heart ached to touch him, to comfort him, to have him comfort me. I would also face failure, a bitter taste my tongue barely knew yet still dreaded, but I found myself more concerned for him.

"We could find one on the way back," I said, not believing my own words.

He nodded, but didn't look up or speak.

We strode in silence.

Unlike our march up the mountain, Declan took no care for silence, stomping loudly over twigs and brush alike, as though punishing the forest floor for our defeat. I almost spoke, begged him to remain hopeful, but something held my tongue in place.

We followed the stream down. It was the easiest path. When we stood roughly a quarter hour from the forest's edge, Declan stopped and let his pack fall.

"I need more water," he said, kneeling with his canteen in hand. I had never heard a more despondent voice.

"I guess you are stuck with me for another year," I said in a weak attempt to lighten the mood.

His eyes remained fixed on the passing water. "If they keep us."

"What do you mean?"

"I'm sure you're safe, being who you are and all. They might turn me out, though. Failure isn't exactly tolerated in Whitman's army."

"You don't think—?" Movement beyond the brook drew me up short.

"Declan," I hissed.

He didn't answer or move.

"Declan, look up now, slowly."

His head rose, and I could feel the tension as his muscles flexed.

Staring at us through the brush, only his head visible, was a majestic buck whose crown towered above his head and marked him as regal as any king.

"That's him," Declan whispered. "That's the buck I saw. See that chipped antler? It has to be him."

The buck stared directly at Declan as he set his canteen on a rock and rose to his full height. With the stream between us, we posed little threat, and the deer knew it. They stared at each other for what felt like a fortnight, neither moving, no one speaking, even the forest quieting for the moment.

Then something incredible happened.

The deer stepped through the brush and up to the edge of the stream.

He was, as Declan had said, massive. His chest was broad and rippling with muscle, but it was his crown of antlers that stole my breath. I had little experience with creatures of the woods, but even I saw the majesty in this beast.

"Don't move," Declan whispered.

There was no fear in that. I was paralyzed.

Then Declan stepped forward, placing a boot into the trickling brook.

The buck watched.

Another step.

Still, the buck remained a statue.

When Declan stood only a pace away, the buck stepped *forward*.

Declan looked as though he wanted to recoil, to step back, but he held his ground.

The buck sniffed the air only hands from Declan's face, then lowered himself onto his front knees and bowed his head, his antlers mere fingers from Declan's legs.

My breath caught.

My heart stilled.

The buck *kneeled* before him.

Declan dared not move.

When the buck rose, his eyes stilled again on Declan's. He opened his mouth and let out a keening that echoed through the trees. A moment later, a young fawn who could have been no older than a few months strode through the trees and to his side.

A yellow ribbon was tied securely about its neck.

Slowly, Declan reached out his hand, palm down.

The fawn tottered forward and pressed its nose into Declan's skin.

With his other hand, Declan reached out and untied the ribbon, freeing the deer from its bond. The fawn stepped back, lowered its head, then sprung away toward the cover of the forest.

The buck stepped backward until he stood only a pace from the cover from which he had emerged. Declan, seeming to sense some spiritual moment, inclined his head. The buck mirrored his gesture, then turned and bounded away.

PART II

Chapter Seven

Keelan

Anxious whispers rippled through the crowd as Ceryl Burner rose from his seat and approached the podium. Beside the lectern were four leather chairs before a polished table, two of which were already occupied by the Arch Mage and Master of Arms. It was rare for the Triad to gather publicly, but this night held special weight in the hearts of all Melucians.

Merchants' Guildmaster Burner placed one hand on the podium, activating the magic that would cast his voice to the furthest corners of the massive hall. The air shimmered briefly, then settled. With his other hand, he clinked a spoon against a crystal glass to quiet the crowd.

"Meetings of the Triad can become—how shall I say it—a bit lively? It is often said that we could take most any issue requiring a simple vote and wind up arguing over the meaning of 'yay' or 'nay' for hours."

Chuckles rippled through the crowd as Burner paused and smiled broadly.

"And yet, on this occasion, we speak with one voice." The crowd stilled. "As has been our tradition for hundreds of years, we gather tonight to honor one man or woman who has contributed uniquely to our nation, a person who upholds our cherished values of dignity, respect, and duty in both word and deed. Custom dictates the Mages, Armsmen, and Merchants each nominate a candidate for this honor. These nominees are outstanding examples of the Melucian ideal—and we honor each of them—but in the final tally, the Triad's vote was unanimous."

Burner reached beneath the podium and raised a head-sized replica of the Phoenix cast in polished silver. It shimmered with azure light, a touch of the Mages swirling across the surface of their vaunted symbol of magic.

"The recipient of the Triad's Own this year is . . . Guardsman-Lieutenant Keelan Rea."

The crowd shot to their feet and erupted, turning as one toward a table in the room's center where I sat.

I stood and wove through the sea of tables, shaking hands and grasping forearms. Nobles and wealthy businessmen and -women showered me with smiles and praise. I'd been seated near the front; still, it took a few long moments for me to reach the high table.

I'd never wanted to crawl beneath a tablecloth so badly in my life.

Applause lingered long after I accepted the trophy from the Guildmaster.

Burner led me to one of the leather chairs, where I was greeted with yet more smiles and handshakes by Arch Mage Quin, a thin man with a shiny pate, and Master of Arms Vre, whose stout chest and broad shoulders resembled an ox more than a man. Burner motioned for me to sit, then moved toward the last empty chair.

"Let's learn more about Keelan and what led him to receive tonight's honor," Burner said as he took his seat and motioned toward me. "Lieutenant Rea, why don't you tell us a little about how you came to wear that uniform?"

My eyes darted from Burner to the crowd. I swallowed a lump, then spoke in a voice nearly as stiff as my collar. "Well, I lost my parents when I was little. I must have only been five or six at the time. One of the Mages took my brother and me in, so we grew up surrounded by men in robes." A smattering of *awws* rose from the crowd. My jaw flexed as I paused.

Chasing suspects or fighting bandits was one thing. I controlled fear in those situations, commanded it. I was used to hard work and doing what needed to be done out of the public eye, but speaking before the nation's elite terrified me in ways a sword fight never would.

Sweat beaded across my brow.

Burner bit back a gasp as I reached up to wipe it with my sleeve. Apparently, that was poor form.

Brow dry for the moment, I continued, "Sergeant Sted—he was a Guardsman assigned to the Mages' Compound for security—he took me under his wing, taught me how to hold a sword, how to be a man, really. He was one of the best men I've ever known. He made me want to become a Guardsman when I grew up, to be like him."

"You said the Mages took you and your brother in. Where is your brother now?"

I faltered, and my eyes drifted to the table as I spoke. "He's at the Ranger Academy out west, near the border."

"Brothers serving their country. Isn't that wonderful?" Burned ignored my obvious discomfort, glancing toward the crowd, who had already begun applauding. "And you were recently promoted to Lieutenant? I believe the case that won you that chevron is also the one underlying your award tonight. Tell us about it."

"Well, I hope getting promoted was about a lot more than any one case," I said. "But I'll tell you what I can. You're referring to the Potter case?"

Burner nodded. "Yes. Arn Potter was a prominent member of my guild. He likely would've been sitting in this chair next year, had he not been lost. Every Merchant in this city is in your debt for bringing justice to his family."

"Thank you, Guildmaster, but I had a team working with me. It took all of us to solve that one." I fought another wave of heat as my face colored again. "Mr. Potter was found in his bedchamber. There were no signs of forced entry. None of the furniture was disturbed. Even the bedcovers appeared unruffled despite Mr. Potter's position and untimely demise. He'd been stabbed more than twenty times. The murderer had smoothed the comforter and even tucked it neatly beneath Mr. Potter's chin. Without getting into more gruesome details, we determined he'd been murdered while he slept."

Whispers ran through the crowd as I ordered my thoughts.

"We suspected his killer had been in his home many times and knew the layout."

Arch Mage Quin leaned forward. "Mr. Potter hosted a large reception in his home earlier that evening, didn't he?"

I nodded. "There were thirty-two attendees, five of whom were relatives. The rest belonged to the Merchants' Guild. We had to assume any one of those might have been our killer."

"That made for a long suspect list," Burner said.

"Longest I've faced," I agreed. "We spoke with each attendee privately. My Gift offers a significant advantage in interviews."

"Your Gift?" Burner asked innocently.

I glanced at the Arch Mage, who nodded once. "None of us like talking about our Gifts in public, but I'm guessing mine is the worst-kept secret in Saltstone." The crowd chuckled in unison. *The Gazette* had broken with custom and printed controversial stories about my Gift. Outraged citizens had called for the paper to pay restitution all while snatching up the next edition featuring my image as soon as it hit the streets.

"The guys call me the human lie detector. I can sense falsehood. Unfortunately, with a room full of Merchants, it appeared everyone had some private agenda or secret to hide."

"You have no idea how true that statement is," Master Vre said, earning a sharp glance from Burner and a round of laughter from the crowd.

Burner seized control again. "Go on, Keelan. Tell us how your team solved this one."

"Well, as with any case, we narrowed our suspect list to those who had the motive, means, and opportunity to commit the crime. Some had one or the other, but only a handful had all three."

"What ultimately broke the case?" Master Vre asked with his usual impatience.

"Upon thorough examination by a local Healer, it was determined that Mr. Potter wasn't killed with a sword or dagger, but a knife whose blade was smaller and thinner than normal weaponry. There were tears across—"

"I think we can skip the gory bits," Burner interrupted.

I nodded. "Sorry. I guess that isn't exactly fancy dinner conversation."

Another chuckle broke from the attendees.

Burner leaned forward in his chair. "You said you worked with a local Healer?"

"Yes, many here will know her. Her name is Tiana Hurd. She runs the infirmary across from the Guard Compound." I scanned the crowd, then pointed when I found Tiana sitting in the third row of tables. "There she is."

"Tiana, please stand," Burner said, and the crowd applauded appreciatively. A slender woman in her early twenties wearing a gown the color of a cloudless sky rose from her seat. Bright brown eyes scanned the room, as chestnut curls fell past her shoulders. I gave her a warm smile even as pinpricks of nervous energy tickled my skin when our eyes met above the guests' heads.

I cleared my throat and resumed my tale. "At Tiana's suggestion, we searched the kitchen in Mr. Potter's manse and found knives whose serrated edges and slim blades matched the wounds on the victim. That led us to search the staff's chambers and question them again."

"And a kitchen maid confessed?" Burner asked.

"It took some time, but yes. We had previously questioned each member of the staff, but none were on our core suspect list. When we interviewed each of them for a third time, this time with one of the dinner knives sitting out on the table, she finally broke. It was the sight of the murder weapon. She couldn't stand it."

"If you can tell when someone lies, why didn't you just ask each suspect if they killed Mr. Potter?" Quin asked.

"There were five of us on the team. If you add the party attendees with Mr. Potter's family and household staff, that's more than seventy suspects—and that doesn't include individuals who didn't attend the party but had some grudge or complaint against the victim. With a list that long, we were forced to divide up the interviews. I wasn't part of the first two conversations with the kitchen maid."

"Did you find out why she killed him?" Quin inquired.

I nodded. "Murders usually stem from one of three motives: money, love, or revenge."

Quin cocked his head. "Love? Why would someone murder for love?"

"Because they didn't get what they hoped for. In this case, the maid was in love with Mr. Potter and begged him to leave his wife. Notes we found in her chamber evidenced an affair between the two spanning several years. In some of the latter notes, she suggested they leave Saltstone and start a new life together elsewhere."

"That wasn't going to happen," Burner said.

I shook my head. "No, I don't think so either. As you said, Mr. Potter was next in line to join the Triad as Merchants'

Guildmaster. His wife is a prominent Merchant, wealthy in her own right. There was no indication he was willing to part with his well-established life. The maid admitted as much in her questioning."

Arch Mage Quin steepled his fingers, then sat back. "Lieutenant, your work on that case was impressive, and we are all grateful for the justice that was served, but please know that this award represents far more than your solving one crime. As you said, you have provided a critical component frequently, ensuring the safety of our people in ways they may never know. From one of those who understands fully what you have given—and continue to give—thank you."

My head ducked beneath the praise. As applause swelled into a standing ovation, and the leaders of the nation rose around me, I struggled to lift my gaze.

It was all so overwhelming.

Burner stepped to stand behind the lectern again. "Keelan, our city, indeed our nation, owes you a great debt. Your service to the Guard has been exemplary, and we offer our sincerest thanks for your diligence and sacrifice."

The Guildmaster waited for applause to quiet before continuing. "Noble gentlemen and ladies, Merchants and guests, on behalf of the Triad, thank you for attending this year's gala. Please join us in giving all our honorees one last round of applause. Have a wonderful night, everyone."

CHAPTER EIGHT

TIANA

I hummed softly to myself as I tied my powder blue smock about my waist. I loved mornings, the sun streaming through the shutters, the scent of a fresh day wafting through the window. I loved hearing Jewel nicker as she pranced about in back. The horse was no great beauty, a swirl of brown, white, and gray, more mutt than respectable breed, but she'd been my constant companion for as long as I could remember, and I loved her dearly.

I loved being a Healer even more.

Many of my earliest memories were of my father struggling his way up the stairs with an injured man or woman draped across his shoulders. He didn't care what time it was or what their family might've been in the middle of, he never turned away someone in need. The first time I saw him use his Gift, and the brilliant light flared from his palms, knitting a wound back together before my eyes, I knew I had been called to follow in his footsteps.

When he died, Healing saved me.

It gave me purpose and meaning.

It helped *me* heal.

Now, I felt my father's hand in every Healing I performed. A smile born of too many emotions touched my lips as my fingers grazed the bag he'd given me. I packed it with herbs, salves, and tonics to carry nearly everywhere I went. Its straps were frayed, and the fabric along the sides bore patches from where rips had been mended. Locals who'd been the recipient of my Gift's touch had given me replacements made of the finest leather and cloth, but setting aside my tattered bag felt like losing another piece of my father.

I stepped onto the porch and squinted as sunlight flooded my eyes. The summer day was warm, but not uncomfortable, so I decided to walk to my infirmary. Jewel would enjoy the day in the field, not tied to a post, and my legs appreciated the exercise.

I began humming again as I stepped onto the cobbles of Brick Road.

Keelan Rea's stern face and square jaw had consumed my dreams the night before. I'd only met him a few times, each to assist with some investigation he pursued, but seeing him on stage at the award ceremony had stirred something in me I'd not noticed before.

Noticed?

I laughed at the thought. Of course, I'd noticed Keelan. He stood tall enough to duck as he passed through my doorway, and was nearly too broad to enter without turning sideways. His arms, what I could see of them through his navy uniform cloak, were thicker than my legs and far more compact, and his neck was like a tree trunk. I'd never met a living statue until Keelan strode in.

I'd never seen him smile until he sat on stage, fidgeting and stammering before the entire Triad and an audience of adoring nobles. I'd also never seen him rattled or embarrassed. It made me want to laugh and wrap my arms around him and . . .

"Ti, stop that," I chided myself. "He's a Guardsman, and probably has every girl in Saltstone chasing after him."

Then I laughed.

I wanted to chase after him, too. Spirits, I wanted to mount Jewel and race as fast as my mare would take me to catch up to that mountain of a man.

I could've dated.

I was certainly pretty enough.

My wit and widely respected skills made me one of Saltstone's most eligible young ladies; and yet, the men who sought my attention failed to garner it.

Besides, I loved my work, and I was good at it.

People suffering and struggling from all around sought my help, and easing their pain was more fulfilling than anything I could imagine. I had a good life and was happy. I was strong, smart, self-sufficient, and perfectly capable of conquering anything I chose to master. Why did I need a man, especially one of those vacant peacocks who sought to woo me?

Keelan wasn't a peacock.

He certainly wasn't vacant.

He might've been the most intelligent, complex man I'd ever met.

And his chest was even more chiseled than his jaw.

"Now, you're just being silly," I giggled.

Then I giggled because I'd just giggled.

It had been a long time since I'd felt like a teenage girl, but the thought of the beefy Guardsman sent me spiraling toward the innocent joy of youth.

There was only one thing about Keelan that frustrated me: he'd yet to look my way unless some case required it. I'd been around him multiple times, chatted about patients, even collaborated. I'd tried to flirt—well, at least make my interest known. I didn't exactly flirt. The man was too intimidating for that. Still, he'd either been too distracted by his work, utterly disinterested, or ridiculously thick-headed not to notice how I leaned in every time he looked my way. I even allowed our hands to brush and linger once, hoping he might take a hint, but he'd simply glanced down and apologized for "entering my space."

"Entering my space?" I rolled my eyes. "I entered *his* space, and he didn't know how to handle it."

Oh, well, I thought. *There's always next time.*

By the time I made it to the front door of my infirmary, and thoughts of Keelan were replaced by the challenges of the coming day, three patients waited outside. One leaned against the hitching post with a leg raised off the ground, the second held a crimson-soaked bandage over her arm, and the third, a young boy no more than twelve summers with sandy blond hair that hadn't seen soap in far too long, sat cross-legged with his back propped against the rough wooden exterior of the building. The boy's face was a pale shade of green I had seen far too often of late.

"Good morning," I said, looking each one in the eye and smiling. "Come on in and have a seat."

I kneeled a couple of paces from the youngster on the ground. "Do you feel warm?"

The boy nodded. "Like I'm burning inside."

"All right," I said. "Follow me back to the exam room and try not to cough on anyone. I'll get you fixed up."

The boy nodded and struggled to his feet as the others entered.

Sunlight streamed through the openings set a foot from the ceiling, bathing the waiting area in warmth and light. As the two adult patients settled into chairs, the boy and I stepped into the only other proper room in the cabin, the exam room.

"Hop up," I said as I stepped into the store room attached to the exam room. When I returned a moment later, a bottle in each hand, the boy still stood before the table, staring.

"It's a table. It won't bite."

When the boy still didn't budge, I asked, "What's your name?"

"Wil," he croaked, then coughed.

"Wil, I need you to trust me. I'm going to make you feel better, okay?"

He looked from my shoes to my smock, then met my gaze. His bottom lip trembled as he spoke. "I've never been Healed before."

I smiled, finally understanding his hesitation.

"Well, I hate to disappoint, but you aren't getting Healed today, either." I raised the bottles and wiggled them. Amber liquid swished in one, while clear syrup oozed in the other. "What you have can't be treated with my Gift. We'll have to do this the old-fashioned way. These taste terrible, but they'll make you better."

Wil's shoulders relaxed, and his lip stilled. Finally, after staring at the syrup a moment, he climbed onto the table and sat with shoulders slumped.

I felt his forehead, then ran through a few other cursory checks. There really was no need for a full exam. I'd seen this illness spreading throughout the city for weeks.

"We usually don't see this in summer. Guess it's early this year," I mused, making the illness sound routine and boring. Wil relaxed a bit more.

"Is anyone in your family sick? Anyone who lives in your house?"

The boy nodded. "Ma and Pa are both pretty miserable."

"Why didn't they come with you?"

He glanced up, then let his gaze return to his fingers. "We can't afford much. They said I should come get well, and they'd let it run its course."

I stared a moment, then waved a hand. "Nonsense. You tell them I said to come see me when they're sick, and we'll figure things out. All right?"

He nodded but didn't look up.

"I'm going to give you enough of these for all three of you. I'm writing the instructions on this paper. Can you or your parents read?"

His eyes shot up, and a smile nearly touched his lips. "I can. Pa thinks it's a waste of time, but Ma taught me. She's really smart. She can read, too, but nothing fancy."

I resisted the urge to tell the boy what I thought of his father's notions, but bit the inside of my cheek.

"Well, that's good, Wil. You keep studying. I couldn't be a Healer if I didn't know how to read and write." I finished jotting instructions, then held out a spoonful of the syrup. "This will make your throat feel better and help with that cough. Open wide."

Wil stared at the spoon like it might attack, then surrendered and opened his mouth.

I gave him a second spoonful of the other liquid, then had him read the instructions out loud. He stumbled a bit but made it through.

"That was very good, Wil. Go home, and get some rest. Tell your Pa I don't want you working for at least two more days, all right?"

The boy's eyes widened as he nodded. I'd also seen far too many overbearing fathers sending sick boys into the field when they should've been in bed. I hoped Wil's parents would heed my advice.

I sent Wil on his way, then called the next patient, the one with the blood-soaked rag pressed to her arm. This, I could heal with magic.

Such was the life of a Healer.

And I wouldn't have it any other way.

Chapter Nine

Tiana

My fingers trailed across the smooth surface of the exam table, then my eyes roamed the rough-hewn logs of the walls. The military-style building was basically a cabin outfitted for medical use, but it was *my* cabin.

The walls were bare, displaying little more than shaved logs. I'd broken convention by hanging my father's favorite tapestry in the foyer to comfort and distract patients while they waited for care. In the back, I stored bandages, herbs, and a wide variety of potions and creams to treat patients who didn't require a magical cure. If Healing magic didn't sap my energy so quickly, I would prefer to use it on every patient who walked through the door, but I supposed every Healer had to learn when *not* to use their Gift.

The days of my youth, working with my father, were often long and exhausting. Today, I felt like I had worked three of those days in one.

I scrubbed my hands, but my smock was streaked with stains that would take more effort—and a fair amount of lye—to clean. I sucked in a breath, sat for the first time in hours, and rested my head against the wall, visualizing the steam wafting off the hot bath to come.

My eyes had almost closed when a familiar voice called from the front door and shook me from my dream. "Miss Ti, don't pack up yet. One more for you."

I sighed, straightened my smock, and stood to see who had hurt themselves now. Healing was my calling, and I loved it more than life itself, but some days simply wouldn't end when they were supposed to. This was one of them.

Two men in uniform greeted me as I entered the foyer, one holding the other upright. I couldn't help but chuckle when I saw my patient . . . again.

At twenty-two, Constable Ridley Doa stood over six and a half feet tall and had the beginnings of broad shoulders. After three years of Guard training, Ridley's once boyish features now held a hardened edge.

Ridley also normally carried himself with the athletic grace of a sportsman, but today his left leg looked as though it would barely support weight, and he needed help just to get through the infirmary's entrance. He was supported by a man who wore a Lieutenant's chevron on one shoulder and the golden collar of the Gifted around the nape of his uniform. A small sack dangled from a strap stretched tightly across his broad chest and shoulders. Piercing blue eyes offset a rusty scruff-covered jaw.

"What have you dragged in today, Keelan? Our 'Constable in the Making' fall out of his bunk again?"

I gave Ridley a playful mock salute.

"Ti, he hurt himself sparring against a cadet twice his size and ten times his talent. I guess the Guard uniform makes some think they're invincible, even if it doesn't really fit yet."

"Third visit this week, Ridley? One might think you just want me to see your legs again." Ridley blushed as I took his other shoulder and helped Keelan walk him back to the exam room. When they reached the table, Keelan set his sack on the floor and helped the injured Guardsman settle into place.

"Let's see what we've got today." I cut away the lower leg of his uniform trousers and began prodding below his knee. Ridley found his courage, as his eyes sparkled with mischief. "Easy there, Miss Ti. Touch me like that again, and I might question *your* motives."

I dug my thumb into the meat of his leg.

"Hey now." Ridley winced.

"Just making sure the Lieutenant knows you're actually hurt and not just paying me a visit." I batted my lashes, earning a scowl from my patient.

Keelan had to turn away as his shoulders began to shake with poorly disguised laughter.

I held my palms over Ridley's leg and closed my eyes. A familiar warm glow lit my palms.

Ridley stared with wide eyes. Both he and Keelan carried a Gift, but to see a Healer in action inspired awe unlike most other magic. I focused and willed the Light to brighten, causing Ridley's leg to glow faintly. He gritted his teeth as the magic mended muscle, tissue, and bone.

Moments later, my eyes opened, and the glow faded.

I braced myself against the table, fending off the wave of exhaustion that followed every Healing. "That should do it, Ridley. Please try to pick on someone your own size next time."

"Spirits, you're amazing."

"Oh, I'm well aware." I winked.

He stood, carefully placing weight on his leg. Without warning, he shot forward and wrapped me in a tight hug and planted a kiss on my cheek. I started to speak, but Ridley bounded toward the door, then grinned back over his shoulder. "Next time I'll try to get hit a little higher up the leg. You really have quite the touch."

He vanished, leaving me speechless and the usually stoic Keelan laughing through tears.

An awkward silence settled over the room as Keelan's laughter abated.

I eyed him. "Need something else, Lieutenant?"

He ran a hand over his head and glared at his boots. He finally summoned his courage, picked up the sack, and set it on the exam table. "Well, Miss Ti—*Tiana*."

Keelan never called me by my name. The corner of my mouth quirked into a curious grin as the skin of my arms prickled.

"I thought maybe, um, you might like a glass of wine at the end of a long day." He set a bottle, two glasses, and a bowl on the table, then looked up at me with sheepish, nearly terrified eyes.

"Lieutenant, are you asking me on a date? In my infirmary?" My brows rose.

"Well, uh, when you put it like that, I mean . . . the wine was Ridley's idea."

I laughed—not a girlish giggle—a full-throated, from-the-gut bellow. One hand went to my stomach while the other braced against the table.

"I wondered how long it would take you to ask. I mean, this isn't exactly the romantic setting I had pictured in my mind, but it is very Keelan-esque."

The goofy grin that split his face made me laugh again. He fumbled the bottle, nearly dropping it onto the hard floor.

"Please, let a professional," I said, taking the bottle from him.

Once the glasses were filled, I pulled the cloth off the bowl, and my smile turned from teasing to pleasant surprise.

"Hope you like strawberries," Keelan said.

"I love them. Thank you, Keelan." I squeezed my eyes shut as I savored the first bite. Sweet, tart juice flooded my mouth. It tasted like summer.

We spent the next half hour talking of little things. When I turned the conversation toward Keelan's work, his shoulders lifted and his back straightened. Everyone knew that Keelan hated talking about himself. It wasn't a surprise when he dodged my questions.

"Enough about me. I want to know about you. Are you from Saltstone? Did you grow up here? What's it like dealing with sick people all day? Are you always wearing baby blue? I mean, you were even in a blue gown the other night at the ceremony."

I laughed at his litany and was thrilled at his remembering my dress. "So, yes. Yes. And some days I wonder why I chose this path. And no, sometimes I wear a darker shade." I took another bite, and my eyes drifted a moment. "I love being a Healer. It's all I ever wanted growing up, and I can't imagine doing anything else."

"Even with patients like Ridley?"

"Especially with patients like him. After all, without Ridley's unfortunate fall, we wouldn't be having this elegant exam-room soiree." I waved around the room with my wine glass, clearly enjoying teasing him about the setting for our first date.

This is a date, isn't it? Oh, Spirits, I'm on a date with Keelan Rea.

"Promise I'll do better next time."

I might die. He said, "next time."

Resisting an embarrassing death, I reached across the table and placed my hand on his. "You did great."

A blush raced up his neck and filled his cheeks.

He sipped wine, then asked, "When did you start? I mean, you're young to be a full Healer, aren't you?"

I nodded. "It all started with my father."

"I've seen the statue of him over at the Triad's building. It still amazes me you're *that* Healer's daughter."

"That's what everyone says. I guess I'm used to it now." I shrugged. "He was the best. When I was a little girl, I followed him everywhere. I even made my own tiny Healer's smock from one of his old rags, knitting it together with ratty brown yarn. I wouldn't let him take it off me, even to sleep."

"Is he why you became a Healer?"

I nodded, my eyes pooling, "I miss him so much."

Keelan watched as I searched my memories, a swath of emotions crossing my face. He then decided to ask about happier times.

"Do you remember the first time you Healed?"

"Oh, yes. Absolutely." I brightened. "When I was seven or eight, I had this scruffy dog, Ollie. He terrorized our horses, chasing them all over. I think they actually liked it, even though they'd kick and bray."

I grinned and took another sip.

"One afternoon, I heard Ollie wailing from somewhere in the field. He'd gotten his paw caught in the joints of the picket fence. By the time I squatted by his side, the paw was full of splinters, bleeding and raw from where he'd struggled to free himself. He looked up at me with terror in those big eyes, and the sight nearly broke my heart. It took forever, but I managed to free his paw. His howling ceased immediately, but then he started to whimper, and his breathing turned shallow and quick. That's when I knew he'd hurt more than just a paw."

"What did you do? Was your dad able to help?" Keelan asked.

I shook my head. "No . . . I don't remember where he was, but I don't think he was home at the time. As scared as I was, I knew I had to help him myself. I spread him out on the ground, forcing him onto his back to inspect the rest of his body. He squirmed, and the keening that followed was nearly too much. I really didn't know what I was doing.

"His eyes started rolling back, and I could tell he was fading. Keelan, it was terrible. I loved that little dog more than anything. I prayed for help, for anything. When no one answered, I ran a hand across his muzzle, then laid it on his chest to calm him. The glow that flared from my palm startled me so badly I nearly fell over. I'd seen my father use the Light, of course, but now it was flowing out of *me*. Without thinking, I moved my hand over his leg and watched the glow brighten and the wounds mend. Both of us passed out after that. My dad found us sleeping in the field."

"That's incredible," Keelan said.

"Ollie's leg was my first Healing."

Keelan raised his glass. "To the finest paw-Healer in the land."

I giggled and sipped my wine, eyeing him over the rim of my glass. Keelan was getting more handsome with every sip.

"Did you grow up around animals?" he asked.

I nodded. "We had a couple horses, some chickens and pigs, even a few ducks who took over a little pond at the edge of our property. When my dad died, I couldn't take care of them all. My old mare is the only one I have left. In a weird way, she's like having something of him still with me." My eyes drifted, then returned to Keelan. "Enough about me. All I know of you is what's on your uniform and what was said at the banquet. No more squirming out of it. You've got to tell me *something*."

Keelan shrugged. "There's not much to tell. I grew up here, went into the Guard as soon as they'd let me. The rest is in the papers."

I waited for him to continue, but he sat quietly, his gaze stern but not unkind.

"You're going to make me pry you open, aren't you?"

Keelan's cheeks flushed. "Sorry. Guess I'm not used to being on the other end of the questions."

I grinned. "Okay, the hard way, then. You have a brother?"

"Declan. He's a cadet at the Ranger Academy out west."

"Are you two close?"

Keelan's eyes fell again. "We were."

When he didn't explain, I softened my tone and leaned forward. "Tell me about him. Let me know *something* about you. Something the papers don't know."

Keelan eyed me a moment, then blew out a breath as though I'd suggested extracting teeth. "He's my little brother—well, younger. He's as tall as I am now, just not as thick. We lost our parents when we were little. That's when the Mages took us in. I think he'd just turned three."

"The Mages?"

He nodded.

"Is that normal? I mean, for the Mages to take in a pair of children?"

He shrugged. "I really didn't know what normal was back then. Life seemed so upside down."

"Keelan, I'm sorry. That must've been so hard."

"I guess so." He stared into the back of his hand. "Neither of us remember our parents at all. I get flashes now and then, like a dream, of my mother's face, but that's it. In a weird way, that made it easier, I guess.

"I can see it all so clearly, that first day we sat in Atikus's office, when they were figuring out what to do with us. Atikus Danai was the Mage who raised us. He's as close to a father as I've ever known." He sipped his wine and studied the far wall as he spoke, his voice a quiet rumble. "He was so scared—Declan, I mean. I lost track of the nights he cried himself to sleep. I held him until he finally went to sleep and fought to keep my own tears from falling. He needed me to be strong, to protect him."

I reached over and squeezed Keelan's hand, turning his eyes back to mine.

"It didn't take long for the Mages to become our family, adopted brothers, fathers, and uncles. Dec was the puffy-haired demon who made them all laugh. I can still hear his giggle bouncing off the stone hallways."

His lips curled at the memory.

"He always seemed so happy."

I sat back. "Seemed?"

He released another sigh. "We grew up in the heart of the magical world, surrounded by men who lived for the Phoenix and everything she represents. Every child in the school on the grounds was one of Melucia's most Gifted, each from a long line of powerful magic. The Mages said over and over how they were our brightest hope for the future."

When Keelan hesitated, I asked, "What about Declan?"

"Declan never manifested, and every year that passed without a Gift tore at him. He wouldn't talk about it, but I could see it."

"How old is he now?"

"Nineteen."

If it hasn't come to him by now, it likely never will, I thought.

"And still no magic? Keelan, I'm sorry."

"I haven't talked about those years—or Declan—in . . . I don't even know how long." A moment passed in silence, then Keelan said, "Sorry, didn't mean to—"

"Stop that. I like hearing about your family. Thank you for sharing." I gripped his hand again. "All right, Lieutenant, I need to clean this place up and get home. Tomorrow comes way too early."

Keelan brightened and packed up the empty bottle, bowl, and glasses. I followed him to the door, and when he turned to say good night, I reached up and placed a hand on his chest.

"Thank you for a wonderful time. I really do look forward to our next . . . date." I grinned.

I could see the hesitation written out on his face: the crease of his brow, the purse of his lips, the faint flush spreading over his cheeks. When it seemed like nerves might have gotten the best of him, I stood on my tiptoes and gave him a peck on the cheek. "Good night, Lieutenant."

The door closed behind him, and I slumped against it and smiled, thinking of strawberries and wine—and crystal blue eyes. How had he known I loved strawberries? I could still taste their sweet juices clinging to my lips.

Even better, it felt like I'd finally glimpsed the real Keelan for the first time. I was surprised he'd answered my questions. He'd always been straightforward and courteous, an honorable man to his core, but I'd never expected such deep emotion to thread his voice. Keelan was strong and proud, the image of a perfect Guardsman, rarely allowing his stern visage to falter; and yet, when he talked about his brother, the room shrank and everything stilled. There was an intimacy in his opening that door to me. He'd opened up—at least, he'd started to.

I hummed to myself as I wiped down the exam rooms, then put away the small bottles of herbs and balm I had used throughout the day, careful to align them with their neatly printed labels facing outward, my father's habit—now mine.

A wistful smile curled my lips. I missed him every day.

I fastened my overstuffed bag and tossed it over my shoulder.

Keelan's face popped back into my mind, and a girlish grin bloomed.

"C'mon, Ti, knock it off," I chided myself with a chuckle.

The sound of the front door rattling snapped me out of my daydream.

The Creed stated a Healer never turned away those in need, but my back ached, and my stomach was dancing for dinner.

Sometimes, you just have to draw a line.

"I'm sorry. I've closed for the night. Unless it's an emergency, please come back in the morning," I called through the door.

The rattling stopped.

I waited a few moments, hoping the would-be patient had taken the hint. When no one replied, I walked back to the storage room to grab one last bottle for my bag. A loud thud startled me, and the vial in my hand fell, shattering across the floor. Noxious fumes drifted throughout the room.

"Who's there?"

Heavy boots *thudded* slowly against the wooden floor.

I dared a peek around the corner. I had to remember to breathe.

A figure in a silky brown robe stood next to the table, his head swiveling as he inspected the space. When he turned toward me, empty, black eyes glared through a mask depicting the snarling face of a bobcat with tusks that curved upward from its jowls.

Tusks?

I stopped my rational brain from wasting time on the odd combination.

When Bobcat locked eyes with his prey, his raspy voice hissed, "Come, Mistress. It is time to take your place."

Mistress? Spirits, is this man touched?

I instinctively raced through treatments I might apply to a mentally ill patient, professional compulsion overriding a far healthier fight-or-flight response.

At least, they overrode it until the man reached out and grabbed my shoulder.

I screamed and jerked away, grabbing the nearest bottle from the shelf and hurling it at the man. The bottle shattered, and a hazy lilac cloud billowed, causing the man to cough and paw at his eyes.

I darted past, ramming him with my shoulder.

He stumbled backward, then fell against the exam table and crashed to the floor. The front door flew open without protest, its lock dangling from the wooden doorframe.

Two shadowed figures stood only paces from the now open front door blocking my path to the Guard Compound that sat across the main road. Now panicked, I darted behind the infirmary.

The figures launched after me.

I ran past the pond where ducks called.

My heart raced.

A tug at the bag dangling off my shoulder turned my head.

I screamed as one of the figures pulled, nearly jerking me off my feet. The attacker fell backward when the bag came free, scattering its contents across the road.

The second man danced over the spilled bottles and wraps before tumbling to the ground.

The moon was hidden behind a thick haze, shrouding the night in darkness.

I ducked behind a thick hedgerow.

Drawing in deep breaths, I fought to calm my breathing, to remain still and quiet.

A chorus of crickets and the occasional chirp of a night-friendly bird barely obscured my labored huffs.

Then I heard the boots.

Louder.

Closer.

I squeezed my eyes shut, afraid my gaze might draw the eye of the Bobcat or his twisted companions.

And then . . .

They ran past.

I sucked in a breath and held it, ensuring silence before poking my head above the shrubbery and surveying the road and beyond.

Nothing stirred.

I decided to double back, to head for the safety of the Guard Compound. The masked men were running toward my home, and I couldn't think of anywhere safer than the Constables' headquarters—and Keelan.

I only made it a few yards when something snapped sharply behind me.

I jumped.

My head whirled around, but there was nothing there.

I stood in the middle of the road, alone, in the darkness.

Breathe, Ti.

When I turned back to resume my route, I slammed headlong into Bobcat.

His powerful hands gripped my shoulders.

I kicked his shins, earning a loud grunt and doubling him over, then tried to sprint away.

A loose brick gripped the toe of my shoe, and I sprawled onto the cold potter's road.

A sharp elbow pressed into my back.

I flailed and screamed.

"Silence!" Bobcat rasped.

White cloth appeared.

The last thing I remembered before blacking out was the rag pressed into my face and the pungent, strangely sweet smell of the infirmary after a good cleaning.

Chapter Ten

Keelan

At the end of the fourth day following the visit to Tiana's infirmary, Ridley trotted up to me on my walk home. "Lieutenant, have a minute?"

I turned and crossed my arms. "Please tell me you're not hurt again."

"You wish." Ridley laughed. "I saw how you looked at Miss Ti. Doesn't take a world-class investigator to know what's going on there . . . uh . . . sir."

My jaw flexed, and I glared at Ridley, but the color crawling up my neck and into my cheeks spoke of how close my friend had come to the mark.

"Yeah, yeah. What was it you needed, *cadet*?"

"Well, sir, it's actually about Miss Ti. I went by the infirmary a couple days ago to thank her for helping with my leg, but the place was empty. Tried again yesterday and this morning, and it didn't look like anybody had been there since." My attention sharpened. "I don't think Miss Ti's ever taken a day off, much less three in a row."

"No sign on the door? No note about being away?"

Ridley shook his head.

I gazed across the yard. "I haven't seen her since the day she treated your leg."

"You stayed after I left, didn't you?" Ridley asked.

"Yeah. I left about an hour after you did."

Ridley's brows rose.

"Stick to the present, cadet." My half grin belied my stern tone. "Tiana makes rounds in the countryside every four or five weeks, and that's probably where she is, but she's not usually gone very long. Did you talk to people in the area? Has anyone seen her this week?"

"Yes, sir. I checked with every house and business near her building. No one's seen her. I walked around the infirmary and found a couple of packages in the post bin but couldn't tell how long they'd been there."

"I'm sure everything's fine, but I'll sleep better if we take a look. Why don't you get us a couple of horses and meet me at the south gate? I need to run up to my house for a minute. See you in ten."

"You got it, Lieutenant. Two horses coming right up." Ridley offered a quick salute, then turned and jogged toward the stables.

By the time Ridley and I trotted toward the infirmary, the moon had risen and clouds obscured the starry sky. We dismounted and tied our horses to the railing on the side of the infirmary, and I strode to the front door.

"Come, look at this." I bent to inspect the bottom of the entryway.

"Bits of wood?" Ridley asked.

I nodded.

I stood and checked the sides and top. Finding nothing, I turned to get a view of the walkway that led up to the building. There were no marks, no scuffs. Nothing.

Other than the slivers of wood at the foot of the entrance, nothing was out of place. Still, something didn't feel right.

I had learned to trust my gut in my years with the Guard—and it was churning like an angry ocean. I leaned back against the door, my gaze sweeping over the path, when the door swung inward. I tumbled and had to catch myself against the frame to keep from falling. I motioned for Ridley to stay quiet and follow me in, drawing the dagger I carried at my side.

Moonlight streaming through the open door provided the only light in the foyer. I paused and listened, then crept through the foyer into the exam room. After a quick search, I straightened and said, "We're clear. The place is empty. Light some lamps, and let's look around. Check the door again while I search the back."

"You got it, LT."

I froze the moment a lamp flared to life.

Shards of glass lay scattered about the floor. More than one bottle. The closer I stepped toward the storage room door, the more unbearable the odor became.

I rejoined Ridley in the foyer.

"Come look at this," Ridley said, motioning with a hand without taking his eyes off the doorframe.

He held a lamp close and pointed to the inside edge. "See those chip marks around the door lock's latch?"

The latch itself now dangled freely and appeared newly scratched and dented.

"There's more of the same on the strike plate."

I straightened, and my voice lost the last of its humor. "Go back to the compound and let the duty watch know there's been a break-in. Have them send men to Tiana's house to make sure she's okay. And Ridley, tell them I said to keep this quiet."

"On my way, sir. Do you need anything here?"

"No. I'll check out the rest of the building and head back. Until we hear what they find at Tiana's house, there's not much we can do here."

I found a cloth on a side table in the exam room, covered my mouth and nose, and stepped into the storage closet. Earlier in the week, when I had last seen this room, everything had been meticulously organized. I had wondered then at how Tiana kept everything in such perfect order.

Now, the room was in disarray. A couple of shelves were nearly empty, with most of their contents scattered across the floor. A strange odor rose from several of the now broken jars and bottles whose contents had mixed.

I stepped back.

As I turned for the front door, something caught my eye.

Stuck in the corner of the exam table, where the metal joined but didn't meet perfectly, was a small piece of brown cloth. The thumb-sized scrap was silky and held an unusual sheen that reflected the lamp light. I stuffed it in my pocket, gave the other exam room one last scan, then headed back to the Guard Complex.

Chapter Eleven

Keelan

Ridley, the Captain-Commander, and another Guardsman who also wore a Lieutenant's chevron stood outside the headquarters building as I approached. Before I could say anything, a man in blue robes stepped from behind the Commander. In the center of the man's robes was a golden Phoenix, and two lines of gold ringed his collar. It was Arch Mage Velius Quin.

The Captain-Commander spoke before I reached the top step. "Lieutenant Rea, Cadet Doa told us what you found at the infirmary. Arch Mage Quin and I may be able to add to your investigation. Let's step inside where we can have a little more privacy."

I raised one brow at Ridley.

The Arch Mage's presence was unusual, but the need for privacy was even stranger. They stood in the heart of the Guard's complex, one of the most secure locations in the country.

The group wound through the building, passing several administrative areas before approaching the

Captain-Commander's private office. A set of double doors that towered from floor to ceiling bore deep etchings of Melucia's most cherished symbols, the Phoenix, Quill, and Sword.

In direct contrast to the grandeur of the doors, the Captain-Commander's office was simple, bordering on bare. One wall peered onto the training grounds through a glass window that spanned the length of the entire wall. Glass wasn't uncommon, but windows this large were. I smiled to myself as I surveyed the simple furniture, thinking that my plainspoken Commander wouldn't have those windows if he hadn't inherited them from a predecessor who enjoyed finer things.

The only piece of furniture that displayed the prestige of the office was a large desk and chair that sat at the far end of the room. The desk had been used by Captain-Commanders for generations. Melucian lore claimed a distant Arch Mage had crafted the desk to commemorate the only Captain-Commander who had also belonged to both the Guard and the Mages' Guild. The Crest of Melucia, similar to the one on the door, covered the front of the desk but with one significant difference—the Phoenix was inlaid with gold and practically flew off the wood. On the desk's surface, under a cover of clear glass, was a remarkable carved map of the Melucian Empire complete with mountains, streams, and lakes.

Quin smiled faintly as his eyes took in every aspect of the desk, of the wooden piece. I swore there was pride in eyes that rarely betrayed any expression.

"Gentlemen, please take a seat." Commander Albius motioned to chairs around a conference table.

"Lieutenant Rea, let's start with you. Cadet Doa reported the break-in at the infirmary. Did you find anything in your inspection?"

"Sir, we found scratch marks and dents on the lock and strike plate of the front door. Small wooden chips were scattered on the ground beneath. This was clearly a forced entry. The storage room where Tiana—sorry, sir— the Healer kept her equipment had been ransacked. There were broken bottles and jars everywhere. I couldn't tell for certain if anything had been taken, but it didn't appear so. Nothing in the other rooms had been disturbed, including a very expensive tapestry that hung on the wall of the foyer. All of this leads me to believe this wasn't a simple robbery."

I reached into my pocket. "I found this scrap of cloth stuck to the corner of one of the exam tables. Its unusual quality made me take a closer look. I don't recall seeing anyone wearing material like this before." I handed the cloth to Albius, who turned it over, then passed it around the room.

"There was nothing unusual in the perimeter, on the grounds?" Albius asked.

"No, sir. Ridley and I found nothing out of order. There were two packages that had been delivered and were still in the post box behind the building, but nothing appeared tampered with."

The room breathed as silence fell over the group.

"Sir, while I conducted my search, Ridley returned with instructions for Guardsmen to visit the Healer's home. Do you know if they've reported in?"

Before Albius could answer, the large door opened, and his clerk's head appeared.

"Sir, pardon the interruption. Your additional guest just arrived."

"Send him in."

"Yes, sir."

Barely a heartbeat later, the door opened again, and the clerk ushered in a Guardsman whose hair was disheveled and breathed as though he'd just run from across the city.

"Thank you, Del. Close the door behind you." As soon as the door clicked shut, Albius turned to the newcomer. "Guardsman, report."

The man's eyes darted between the Captain-Commander and Arch Mage, and beads of sweat formed on his brow.

"Sir, the Healer's home was empty," he said without further explanation.

"And?"

"It was . . . just *empty*, sir. The door was standing open. There was no furniture, no clothing, nothing on the walls except mounted lamps. The place had been cleaned out. It was too dark to do a more thorough search of the grounds, but the interior was bare."

The group asked a few questions before Albius dismissed the man, then turned to Ridley. "Cadet, this is about to go above your rank. You are excused."

Ridley startled and stood, offering the Commander a sharp nod before leaving.

Albius then turned to Quin. "Arch Mage, a little more privacy?"

"Certainly." Quin removed a silver box no larger than his thumb from the pocket in his robe. Two rubies glittered on the lid, which I saw bore an etching of the Phoenix. Rubies were often used as eyes in statues and carvings of the sacred symbol. And, while most thought it an artistic choice, I knew from my time in the guild they served to amplify powerful magics.

Quin pried the box open and muttered a few guttural words before glancing toward Albius, nodding once.

"Thank you," Albius said, facing the rest of the group around the table. "Gentlemen, the Arch Mage just extended a barrier around this office so we can speak without being overheard. Hold nothing back. What's said in this room stays here, understand?" He punctuated the last word with a stern glare.

The other Lieutenant and I nodded.

"Arch Mage?"

Quin leaned forward and placed his elbows on the table. "The Mages of the various cities often share information that may be useful or have impact across the Empire. Earlier this week, I received word from our Guildmaster in Freeport that a young woman was reported missing in that city. While tragic, this would not usually raise the alarm of Mages across the country. However, this girl is a member of our local guild and the daughter of a prominent Merchant family, so we agreed to assist. The family provided a few personal items from the girl's dressing chamber: her hairbrush, a silver ring she often wore, and a small journal containing poetry that she had written by hand. With more than one item, and the personal nature of each of these, our Mages should have been able to locate her even if she was on a ship in the ocean on the other side of the world, but their scrying failed. That is when they reached out to me."

He cleared his throat and continued. "It is a closely guarded secret that the Saltstone Mages' Compound is built at the base of the Silver Mountains for a very specific reason. There is a vein of natural magic that bubbles like a stream deep beneath its stones. This river of untamed magic gives our buildings more strength and offers our Mages far greater power when they act within our walls. The tower in the back of the compound serves as a focal point, a magical amplifier, if you will.

"I enlisted the aid of our Mage with the greatest scrying ability and led him to the top of the tower. He worked through most of yesterday and into last night with no success, not even a hint of the missing woman's whereabouts. I have never seen him fail."

Quin paused and looked around the room, finding my eyes before continuing. "We had no reason to believe the disappearance of Saltstone's Healer was related to the missing woman in the south, but something tugged at my mind. When Cadet Doa returned, we attempted to scry for your Healer. It was a simple, quick spell that I did not expect to offer anything beyond a general direction and confirmation that she still lived. And yet, for the second time in two days, we failed to sense *anything*, much less discover her location."

Wind whistled against the glass wall as the men stared at one another.

The Captain-Commander broke the silence. "Lieutenant Rea, I know you only took command of the Academy a few months ago, but this situation has implications far beyond our city. I'm putting you in charge of these cases, effective immediately. Lieutenant Eagan, you will take over temporary leadership of the Academy until Rea is finished with these cases."

"Yes, sir," we said in unison.

Albius then turned to me. "Rea, there is no higher priority for the Guard than solving these cases and recovering the women. We've already lost a week on both disappearances."

I nodded and began to speak, but the Arch Mage interrupted, "Keelan, as a member of the Mages' Guild, you already have access to our complex, our Mages, and many of our resources. Due to the sensitivity of this situation, and what we believe may be broader implications, you will also have my personal assistance if you need it. The full power of the Empire's Mages' Guild is at your disposal."

What the hell is going on?

To have the direct assistance of the Arch Mage on a missing person case was nothing short of remarkable. And the Commander's insistence that this case held broader implications, perhaps ones of national import, was even more so. I was clearly missing pieces, but neither the Arch Mage nor Albius appeared willing to supply them.

I gathered my thoughts, then nodded. "Thank you, sirs. Commander, I would like to assemble a small team, including Ridley and a few other Constables."

"*Cadet* Doa?" Albius sat back.

"Yes, sir. I know it sounds odd, having a cadet join an investigation, but Ridley was a solid investigator before entering the Academy, and I've worked with him for years."

Albius considered a moment. "Your team, your men. Just get me results. Anything else?"

"No, sir."

"Good. Keep me posted." Albius stood, a clear dismissal. "Rea, Arch Mage, please stay."

When the heavy door clapped shut again, Albius glanced at the Arch Mage. Quin nodded. "Rea, this stays here. Not a word to your team or anyone else, understand?"

"Yes, sir."

Albius moved to the large glass window, peered out at the night-shrouded practice yard, and lost himself in thought. After several minutes, he spoke into the glass in a low voice that I strained to hear, "Keelan, report your findings *only* to the Arch Mage or myself. The offices of the Triad, the Army command, even the Guard, have been compromised. We've only found one spy so far, but we believe that there are others. Trust no one. Do you understand?"

My head spun. "Sir, what would spies have to do with a kidnapping? What am I missing?"

Albius turned to face me. "We don't know that the two situations are connected, only that more than one fact seems to cross with the others, and I stopped believing in coincidence a long time ago, especially where magic is concerned. I can't read you into the specifics, so you're going to have to trust me. Keep this quiet. Any information you learn stays between the three of us."

"Yes, sir. Understood."

I thought a moment, then turned to the Arch Mage. "Who can I speak with in Freeport? I need to gather information regarding the missing woman and everything surrounding her disappearance. Also, has any of this gone public? If so, we should think through a cover for why investigators from the capital are being called in on a local matter. Our presence will stir the rumor mill."

Quin eyed me. "The second question is easier than the first. Yes, the disappearance in Freeport hit the local papers, and there is talk of little else. Serious crimes, especially kidnappings, are rare. Our greatest advantage is that reporters in Freeport don't know Saltstone may also have a kidnapping. Furthermore, the missing woman from Freeport is prominent in her community. She is the sole heir to a significant family holding, and her father commands political influence throughout Melucia. It would not be unusual for him to call in a favor to get someone from the capital to help find his daughter.

"As to your investigation, we have already assembled some notes, including names of interested parties and reports from the local Constables and their initial investigation." Quin handed me a leather folio.

Albius returned to the table. "Lieutenant, go figure out your teams and how you want to divide up the searches. There's a lot of land between Saltstone and Freeport, and you will need men you can trust to lead the various efforts. The Arch Mage and I will meet you at the Mages' Guild tomorrow at noon to review."

As I took my leave, my mind raced at the enormity of what I'd just learned and the task before me. I'd never seen the Captain-Commander so ashen as when he gave the order to keep information between the Arch Mage and himself, and I shuddered, remembering the sound of the unshakable man's voice. Albius hadn't said that the members of the Triad *themselves* had been compromised—only their offices—but he also hadn't ruled it out, and there was only one member of the ruling council not present.

I understood the sensitivity of a high-profile investigation, especially when a noble's daughter was a victim, but the whole spy thing made my head hurt. Why would a spy care about a few missing women? Who even wanted to spy on Melucia? The Empire barely had a standing army and had never threatened its neighbors. Sure, Melucia was a rich trading nation, perhaps the wealthiest in the world, but who spied on Merchants?

Kee, you're doing it again, I scolded myself. *The Mages always said, "If you focus on the problem, you'll never find the solution."*

I thought through who I wanted on my team and the various assignments involved, then froze and stared at the cloudy night sky above.

This isn't some case involving strangers.

In the excitement and strangeness of the last few hours, I'd nearly forgotten how it all started, with *Tiana* disappearing. The same Tiana I'd just spent an evening with. The same Tiana I hadn't been able to stop thinking about for weeks, despite struggling with the courage to court her.

My old childhood companion, my nagging inner voice, chattered again, asking more painful questions and threatening to overwhelm me:

What happened to her?

Why would someone kidnap a woman who only wanted to help other people?

Is she hurt?

Is she still alive?

If she is, how long does she have?

How long do I have before . . . ?

Chapter Twelve

Keelan

I stepped through the doorway and tossed my boots by the door. Something so simple shouldn't feel that good, but after a day like today, it felt amazing to get out of them. I'd missed yet another dinner in the Officers' Mess and was down to eating tidbits from the pantry, so I grabbed the last slightly-soft apple and the somewhat stale end of a loaf. I really had to get better at keeping the house stocked.

Between bites, I unhooked the leather strap on the folio the Arch Mage had given me and began to read.

Freeport Constable Notes, Addendum to File 4.327-8, Month 10, Day 1, Report Time 23:15

Sergeant Dav Colby, Investigative Lead

Criminal Matter: Missing Person

Victim: Bel Crim

Description of Alleged Crime: *Vic left Mages' Guild at approximately 18:00. Wtns at guild states vic said she was leaving to meet her parents for dinner at Campfire Grille on East Doarn Avenue. Vic last seen exiting and walking east. Vic never arrived at destination. At 22:05, mother and father presented to Constable Beel (4301), who was patrolling area. Vic last seen by Mage-Apprentice Kirin Knight.*

Physical Description of Victim: *Female, twenty-two, average height, slim build, waist-length blond hair/straight, blue eyes. At time of report, vic wore pale yellow ankle-length dress with white lace/Gifted gold trim on collar and cuffs, brown shoes with small silver buckles, small gold signet ring (Crim family seagull flying over ship with sails).*

Additional Information: *Vic's Gift—Mental, Empath, power level strong.*

Freeport Constable Notes, Addendum to File
4.327-8, Month 10, Day 2, Report Time 11:15

Sergeant Dav Colby, Investigative Lead

Criminal Matter: Missing Person

Victim: Bel Crim

Investigation Notes:

1. ***Witness Interview: Mage-Apprentice Kirin
   Knight.*** *Wtns states vic was at guild from apprx 11:00
   to 18:00. Vic was studying with senior Mages. Vic left
   guild at apprx 18:00. Vic told wtns she had dinner plans
   with parents (Lord Jereth Crim, Lady Fely Crim) at
   Campfire Grille on East Doarn Avenue. Vic excited b/c*

*dinner to talk about betrothal. Wtns walked vic to door,
saw her leave and head east. Vic not carrying anything.
Wtns stated vic was upbeat, noted vic was singing as she
left. Known vic for three years.*

2. ***Search of Route to Vic's Stated Destination.***
*Walked route twice. Spoke with multiple Merchants
along route and none reported seeing vic. Found nothing
unusual.*

3. ***Search of Vic's Residence.*** *Vic lives with parents.
Perimeter doors and windows to manor appear
undisturbed. No unusual visitors or trespassers reported
by staff. Interviewed cook, valet—neither reported
anything unusual over past week at manor. Vic acting
normal, seemed happy. Lord/Lady Crim allowed search
of vic's rooms—Lady Crim accompanied to answer
questions. Nothing appeared disturbed or out of place.*

4. ***Public Release.*** *Coordinated with Editor of Freeport
News, included sketch of vic. No tips from public as of
this report.*

I rubbed my temples as a headache threatened. There was so
little to start with, and it was now days after the initial report,
days after the women were taken.

The trail was stone cold.

I dropped into my oversized, overstuffed chair, the one piece
of furniture that wasn't standard issue and held the barest hint
of comfort. I only intended to rest my feet for a few moments.

When the sun broke over the horizon, I struggled to shake the fogginess from my head and the stiffness from my neck. I rose to the edge of the chair and stretched, then stood and hobbled on stiff legs to the hearth. I started a fire and hung an ancient, blackened pot filled with water to boil.

While the water heated, I reviewed the notes. Again finding nothing noteworthy, I turned my attention to assembling my team. I had already put myself in charge of Tiana's investigation. I knew I should avoid any case where personal feelings might be involved, but rationalized that Tiana and I had only spent one short evening together, so there was nothing to compromise.

I added a couple of Guards I trusted to the list, then turned to the Freeport search.

I scribbled Ridley's name, added another, and then wrote *Mage/Telepathy* on a blank line. The idea had come late in the night. I would need to coordinate with the team in Freeport, and having a Mage who could send updates telepathically would be helpful. After some thought, remembering Commander Albius's concern regarding spies who might be embedded in both the Guard and Mages' Guild, I decided against adding any other additions to the teams.

I filled my mug, threw on my uniform, and headed to the Officers' Mess.

Ridley was already halfway through his meal when I flopped down beside him. As I surveyed the mountains of eggs, bacon, and biscuits stacked on plates in the middle of the table, my stomach reminded me I'd been skipping meals.

"Morning, LT," Ridley said, raising his mug of steaming tea in salute.

I grunted acknowledgment through a mouthful of biscuit, melted butter dripping from my fingers. When I got the bite down, I glanced up and whispered, "I want you on the search down south. I know you're still a cadet, but this thing is bigger than we realized, and I need someone I can trust. You'll have one other Guardsman, and I'll get a Mage assigned to your team as well."

"Just three of us? Seems kinda slim for a high-profile case, don't you think?" Ridley asked.

"Lower your voice—and no details here. I'll explain what I can later, but this has to be kept quiet. Bigger teams mean bigger leaks. We'll talk about reporting frequency and timing later, but whatever you report, it stays between the two of us, understand?"

Ridley stared for a moment, his eyes narrowed. "Understood, but what if the search needs more people? Two Constables and a Mage won't cut it if someone grabbed the victim and left town."

"We'll worry about that when we get to it. We might have to get a little creative with cover stories, too, but let's focus on what's in front of us right now. I'm briefing the Captain-Commander and Arch Mage at noon. Meet me at HQ at 14:00. In the meantime, do a little digging into the political situation in Freeport. I haven't heard of anything unusual lately, but the victim is an heiress, and her father is powerful. We might as well learn what we can before splitting up. Your team will need to leave for Freeport tonight."

I stuffed a forkful of eggs into my mouth.

"I'll head over to the Merchants' Guild and see what I can learn. If anybody stays up on the politics of the outer cities, it's the money guys. See you at 14:00." Ridley downed the last of his tea and stood to leave.

"Oh, Ridley, one more thing." I lowered my voice. "Tell me about your Gift. I know it's Physical and endurance related, but we've never really talked about it. Given what we're stepping into, I need to know every arrow we have in the quiver."

Ridley sat again. "It's Physical. Endurance is one way to say it. I rarely need more than an hour or two of sleep. It only takes a few minutes before I've recovered stamina enough for a second round in a fight. If we went on a long run, I guarantee you'd lose that big breakfast before I even breathed heavy."

"Huh," I grunted.

"Came in handy in recruit training. When everybody else was falling out, I didn't even break a sweat."

A few hours later, I signed out a sturdy black gelding and made the short ride to eventually pass beneath the stone archway marking the entrance to the Mages' Guild. The crystalline eyes of the Phoenix engraved in gold at the top of the archway followed me as I passed.

The Guild Hall was a marble building bearing carved glyphs every few paces the full length of its exterior. The ever-present Phoenix was etched across double doors, its eyes of fist-sized rubies flaring brightly every time a Mage entered the hall, as if welcoming that child of magic home.

I grew up within the walls of the Mages' Compound but had never been inside the Guild Hall. I handed the reins to a stable hand, then strode across the courtyard and through the doors into the well-lit foyer. Inside, richly paneled walls lined the corridors. The floors, a black marble swirling with gray tones, created a dizzying sense of perpetual motion. Large basin-like braziers were polished to the point of mirror-like clarity and spaced every few paces. A cerulean flame danced above each bowl, flaring brightly as I strode past.

Before I could wander too far from the entryway, a stubby, rotund man in cobalt robes appeared through a doorway on the far wall. The man's face split into a wide grin when his eyes locked with mine, and he launched himself at a full waddle, nearly knocking me off my feet as he wrapped me in a tight embrace.

"Keelan, they sent *you*! Welcome home, my boy."

I took a step back and said with as much authority and mock offense as possible, "Mage Fergus, as I'm certain you know, it's unlawful to place hands on a member of the Guard. I will have to report this aggression at once."

Fergus straightened as tall as his pudgy frame would allow and scowled up at the giant before him. "Young man, pick on someone in your own weight class. It's taken me two hundred years to get fat enough to squash you, and I'm not afraid to do it."

We laughed, and I embraced the old Mage again. When he stepped back, I had to wipe a hint of moisture from my eyes. For once, the troubled boy deep in my heart smiled, and my inner darkness remained quiet.

"Uncle Ferg, I've really missed you all."

"This place has been quiet without you and your little brother. Oh, we have all those other children trying to show off, but you two breathed new life into these stale buildings—and into the crusty old men who live here." Fergus patted his amble belly as his eyes drifted into the past. "We never knew how badly we needed laughter until Declan the Terrible streaked through these halls, quite literally." He chuckled. "It feels like just yesterday that you landed in our laps. Where is Declan these days? What sort of trouble has he gotten himself into?"

"I think Dec's doing okay. He's struggled to find a path." I sucked in a breath. "We haven't seen each other in the two years since he joined the green squad, and I'm not even sure where they have him stationed these days. He'll graduate next month. Can you believe our Declan will be a Ranger?"

Fergus shook his head. "Spirits help the mountains. They'll never be the same."

I chuckled, then my smile faded.

"Uncle Ferg, he was so alive when he had people to terrorize; now he's surrounded by nothing but animals and trees. It's like he's run away, and I don't know how to get him back." I ran a hand across my stubble. "He's nineteen now and still hasn't manifested a Gift. I know that bothers him more than he's willing to admit, especially since he watched me join the Guard and enjoy some success over the past few years."

Fergus gripped my arm. "Give him time, Keelan. He's still young. It can take time for some to find their way." Fergus patted my arm. "As for his Gift, that is troubling. You say he's nineteen now?"

"That's right." I nodded.

"Well, if it hasn't come by now, I doubt it will. Maybe being out in the middle of nowhere is just what he needs, rather than living in some town surrounded by golden reminders."

A bell tolled, and Fergus's eyes popped wide. "Oh, no. Seeing you again made me forget about who's waiting—you know, the people who run the country. Come on, the others are waiting for you in the Marble Room."

As I followed Fergus down the hallway, the swirling marble and dark paneling seemed to stretch forever. I knew how long the building was from the outside, but it seemed we would never stop walking.

How is this possible?

There were no doors or openings, leaving the impression that we were trapped in a richly appointed mahogany box. The only adornments beyond the braziers were plain, white marble squares set waist-high on each wall. Fergus placed his palm on the square to the left, and a section of wood paneling shimmered out of existence.

My jaw dropped.

Fergus let out a chortle and winked. "Always something new, isn't there?"

An impossibly wide marble table consumed the center of the room we entered. The piece was surrounded by puffy leather chairs that looked like they might devour anyone who sat in them. As we stepped further into the room, I stared at the table and froze. There were no seams, no joints, nothing to reveal how the table fit together. There was only *one* stone.

"How . . . how did this get in here?"

Fergus grinned. "Will you never get used to our magic?"

I shook my head, eyes wide, still searching the table's surface.

Motion near the hearth drew my eye, as a lean man with wispy hair stood. Without turning, the man said, "So, the dashing detective returns home?"

I bounded across the room, weaving in and out of the chairs, to wrap the old Mage in a tight hug, lifting him off his feet.

"Atikus, you're old as dirt!" I beamed, setting my adopted father on the ground and scanning his face.

"I *am* old as dirt!" Atikus quipped, prying himself loose. He gripped both my shoulders. "And from the look of things, you are becoming the best of us. I'm so proud of you, Keelan."

That was all it took. I lost it, devolving into a blubbering child with tears of pure joy.

I grabbed Atikus again and buried my face in his shoulder.

Despite our close proximity, we hadn't seen each other in years, not since I joined the Guard at sixteen. I'd vowed to return often, but the well-intended promises of youth often went unfulfilled when life intervened.

Atikus wrapped one arm around me, giving me a pat between my shoulders. "Calm, Keelan. I may be old as dirt, but you're doing a fine job of displaying your youth."

I stepped back and wiped my face.

As I gathered myself, the wall opposite shimmered, and the Arch Mage entered, followed by the Captain-Commander. Both wore serious expressions but pulled up short when they saw me standing before Atikus.

"Commander, it appears we've stepped into the middle of a family reunion. Lieutenant, are those *tears* staining your Guard blues?" Arch Mage Quin cracked a wry smile.

"Sirs, forgive me. I wasn't expecting to see them." I looked from Fergus to Atikus. "Given the work in front of us, this was a welcome surprise."

Albius gave me a rare smile and surveyed the group. "Mage Fergus, if you would excuse us, we need to get started."

Fergus tossed me a wink, then offered a quick bob to the Arch Mage and vanished through the shimmering wall.

Commander Albius strode to the table and sat, motioning for everyone to do the same. Once we were in place, he turned to me. "Lieutenant, why don't you start with your review of the Freeport notes?"

"Well, sir, there isn't much. It appears the local Constables did a cursory search of the route the victim took and spoke with nearby shopkeepers. No one reported seeing the victim or anything out of the ordinary. My team will head down there today, start with the local Guardsmen, and then conduct a more thorough investigation; but, sir, this is going to be a tough one."

Albius nodded. "That's how I read the notes, too. You mentioned your teams. Who were you thinking of?"

I shuffled through my notes. "For Freeport, I want Ridley Doa. I can trust him. Given the sensitivity of these cases, trust is our top requirement. Arch Mage, I would like a Mage to join Ridley's team, preferably one with Telepathy so we can receive regular reports. If we discover these cases are linked, coordination between the investigative teams will be important. Liv Went is my choice for the third Freeport team member.

"I'll lead the Saltstone investigation, along with Sil Wesser and Wil Buros. Wesser grew up tracking small game between here and Grove's Pass, while Buros has a Gift with arms, specifically archery. He's the best marksman in the Guard. The Freeport team has some traveling ahead of them, but our team will get started on the local investigation when this meeting breaks. If our timeline is accurate, we're already well past the Healer's disappearance."

"Let me fill in one missing link." The Arch Mage leaned forward. "I anticipated your need for a Mage to accompany your investigation, and asked Atikus to step in."

I quirked a brow. "Arch Mage, I appreciate Atikus joining the team, but why choose a Mage with the Memory Gift rather than Telepathy?"

Quin started to answer, but Atikus spoke first, a wry grin twisting his lips. "I know it's hard for you to believe after all this time, but I do have my secrets. Don't you remember all those years ago, when you first came to us, I told you about magic and my Gift? You surprised me by asking about my double gold. We discussed Memory, but you surprised me again by failing to ask about my second Gift.""Telepathy?" I asked.

Atikus nodded.

"All those years . . ." I chuckled and rolled my eyes. "That explains a lot."

Albius cleared his throat. "Now that that's settled, we have one additional piece of information we need to give you before you start, and I'm not even sure what it means. Atikus?"

"We've identified that piece of cloth you found." Atikus tossed the scrap on the table.

I leaned forward. This was our first lead, and it got my blood pumping.

"Are you familiar with the Children?" Atikus asked.

I shook my head.

"They are a tiny, semi-religious cult that dates back to the time of the Kingdom War. It was established after Empress Irina died. Between the Kingdom, Melucia, and our neighbors to the east, the Children are only estimated to have hundreds of members, or perhaps a thousand. They are highly secretive and, until now, were of no concern to anyone."

"Okay." My brow furrowed. "How are they connected?"

"Their members wear full-length brown robes made of the same expensive material you found. I had one of our Mages perform a scrying on the scrap. The image that appeared in the waters of the bowl was of men wearing the masks and robes of the Children."

Chapter Thirteen

Keelan

A couple of hours later, my team and I revisited the infirmary. Finding nothing new, we spent the rest of the afternoon combing Tiana's house and the field behind it. The difference in how the two locations had been treated by the intruders was confounding. In the infirmary, we found nothing missing despite how the storage room had been ransacked, but Tiana's house had been stripped bare. It looked as though she had never lived there.

Sil and I moved slowly around the house to the back of the property. A mottled mare snorted and cantered toward us. Apparently unafraid of the strange people invading its territory, the horse strode directly to me and buried its nose into my chest.

"Friendly gal, aren't ya?" I said, scratching her head between the ears.

Sil walked up and ran her hand along the horse's back. "She's a beauty. Tiana had good taste."

"I bet you know what happened here," I said, holding the horse's head in my hands and staring into her eyes. "Wish you could talk to us."

Sil cleared her throat. "About that, sir . . ."

"You're kidding, right?" My head snapped toward her. "I thought your Gift was all about tracking animals, finding trails and such."

Sil shrugged. "I spent years as a tracker. We talked about that when you picked me for the team, but you never asked about my Gift." The skin around Sil's eyes crinkled at the edges. "I can communicate with most animals."

"Don't think I've ever known anyone with that one." I whistled, then turned back to the horse and rubbed her neck. "Care to make introductions?"

"That's not quite how it works. I don't exactly *talk* with animals. It's more like sharing images, impressions, or emotions. I can visualize things or people and share those images with an animal. Unless the beast is particularly stubborn, they'll return images or emotions in reply."

"Really?"

She nodded.

"Any animal?"

She thought a moment, then nodded again. "Essentially, yes, but the intelligence of the animal determines how clear the images are. A simple bird might only understand basic things, like fear or hunger, while a hawk could share detailed images, perhaps even allow me to see through its eyes."

"That's remarkable," I said.

"I use it for a lot of things you might not think about," she said, pride threading her words. "What if this horse had been spooked by us?"

I stared at the horse. "Could you send soothing feelings? Calm her?"

Sil nodded.

"That really is amazing, Sil." I glanced from the horse to Sil. "Okay. I'm not sure I get all that, but why don't you talk to Bessie here and see what we can learn?"

The horse snorted and nipped at me. Her ears flicked, tail lashing behind her as though swatting a non-existent fly.

"Easy, girl," I soothed.

Sil chuckled. "She didn't like being called Bessie. No idea what her name is, but she didn't like that, sir, not one bit."

I shook my head. "Just talk to her, okay?"

"Testy, testy. You know animals don't like people who aren't patient," said Sil, clicking her tongue. "Horses especially. They take things slowly until *they* decide to take things fast. A different pace from humans, that's for sure."

When I stared instead of responding, Sil got on with it, removing a glove and placing her hand on the horse's neck. She closed her eyes and remained motionless for a long moment. The horse also stood perfectly still, ears pricked forward, warm brown eyes wide and staring both at nothing and everything.

Sil swayed when her eyes fluttered open, and I stepped forward to brace her.

"You all right?" I asked.

"Yeah. Sending an image or two is easy; going deeper makes my head spin. I'll be okay in a minute."

"Here, lean against the fence." I waited a moment, then asked, "What did you see?"

"I started with the Healer, sending images of the woman in her blues. The horse returned feelings of intense warmth at first, then shifted to something akin to longing. She misses Tiana."

"Makes sense."

"I wasn't sure what to try next, so I showed her visions of the empty house, mentally walking through each room. Fear replaced everything as panic welled inside her."

"Did she send back anything? Any images, I mean?"

Sil nodded. "They were hazy, but I saw three men in simple shirts and trousers carrying furniture. Behind the men, there was something odd. I couldn't make it out. Another man just stood there, watching the others work. He wore some sort of mask, like you might see at a masquerade ball, but stranger. That's all I saw before the horse broke our link."

"Did the masked man wear a robe? A brown robe?"

Sil's eyes widened. "Yes, he did. How did you know—"

"Stay focused. What else do you remember?"

Sil turned to the horse and spoke softly. "The man in the mask was odd. I mean, the mask was frightening enough, but it was clear the horse was afraid of him. I didn't get the impression she knew him, but he definitely made her uncomfortable."

"That's all? Was there anything behind the man? Could you see a wagon? Maybe other horses?"

"There might've been a wagon," Sil said. "There was something large, and I think I saw wheels, but it could've been anything. I couldn't make it out very well."

"All right. That's more than we had before. Let's take one last look around and then head back."

A quick search revealed a barrel with feed grain beside the horse's water trough, which Sil used to feed the hungry beast while I finished my inspection.

"Why would they pick this place clean? Nothing about this feels like a robbery," I said aloud, more to myself than to Sil. "We're running out of light. Let's head back to HQ and see if the Freeport team reported anything."

"What should we do with her horse? We can't just leave her here."

I glanced around, then nodded. "Have one of our men bring her with us. We'll stable her until we learn more. Hopefully, we'll be giving her back to Tiana soon."

The next morning, I made my way to the HQ building. I was ushered through the giant doors where Albius sat reading from a stack of parchment. The Commander scribbled something on a page, then set it down and looked up.

"Anything?" he asked without preamble.

I detailed the visit to the infirmary and Tiana's house. The only substantive lead was the "conversation" Sil had with Tiana's horse.

Albius's chair creaked as he sat back.

"I would think this was little more than a robbery if we didn't have the link to the Children popping up everywhere."

"Agreed, sir." I nodded. "I'm not sure where we go from here, though. The road to the Healer's house is so well traveled that Sil doesn't believe we'll find a trail, and she's the best tracker we've got. Atikus should make contact soon regarding the Freeport investigation. I'd like to visit the Arch Mage again and see if he has any other ideas."

"Of course. Report back this afternoon," Albius said, dismissing me.

I crossed the river to the Mages' Compound and filled the Arch Mage in. At the mention of Sil's communication with the horse, Quin perked up. "Now that's interesting."

"Really? How so?"

"Wait here." Quin bolted from his chair and called to his clerk. "Jon, have Daris join us in my office, please."

Moments later, a Mage of indeterminate middle age peeked through the doorway. His thinning hair was losing the battle to mask his balding scalp. "You asked for me, Arch Mage?"

"Daris, don't stand there gawking. Come in." Quin waved his hand in a harried gesture. "Any chance you can scry using a living animal? Say, a horse?"

Daris scratched his head, disturbing the careful swirl and revealing even more skin. "I guess. I've never done it before . . . and I don't know what we'll get. Living emotions and thoughts jumble when mixed with scrying magic . . . and animals don't think or hold memories in chronological order. They live in the moment. The horse may give us something from years ago or an hour past, depending on which is stronger in the animal's mind in that moment. If there's a strong enough emotional tie between a beast and human, we might simply get emotions the animal has for its owner. It could be fun to try, though. Why do you ask?"

"The missing Healer situation. You tried scrying for her a few days ago. Lieutenant Rea found her horse. A Natural linked to it and Communed."

"Really? I didn't know we had any who could Commune in Saltstone." Daris's face lit up. "That's a twist. If the Natural were to join in the scrying, it might get us more information, better images. Think of the Natural as a focus relic, but in human form. They would sharpen whatever we received from the animal." He thought a moment, then added, "We'd also have someone who understands animal communication, like a translator of sorts. That's definitely helpful."

Quin asked, "So it could work?"

"Theoretically, yes." Daris bobbed his head. "It could work."

"Keelan, I think this is worth a shot, but it's not without risks. Scrying magic is unpredictable and often unstable." Quin tilted his head back and narrowed his eyes. "It will be up to you whether that's worth it."

"Risks? What kind of risks?"

"The horse and the Natural would be in the direct flow. Emotions can become intense in any scrying. Headaches are common, sometimes nosebleeds, lingering sleeplessness. Add a horse and another person to the link, and there's no way to guess what could happen. I don't believe there's any danger of lasting damage to either of them, if that helps you make a decision."

It wasn't a call I had been expecting to make. I glanced between Quin and Daris, who still hovered in the doorway. After a few heartbeats, I nodded slowly, "Let's lay it all out for Sil and let her decide. She'll be the one taking the risk. When can you be ready?"

"It shouldn't take long to set things up. By the time you return, we should be ready," Daris said.

A couple of hours passed before Sil, the horse, and I strode into the Arch Mage's office, earning confused looks from passing Mages. We drew even more bemused stares when we ushered the horse through the entrance of the tower and struggled up the winding stairs. The horse's hooves sounded like thunder clapping against the stone, but Sil kept her calmed and peaceful.

The circular scrying room at the tower's peak held a handful of simple chairs set against the walls. In the center stood a pedestal with a shallow silver bowl fixed to its top. On the floor surrounding the pedestal, concentric circles of pearly stone encased a ring of magical symbols inlaid in alternating gold and silver, reminding me of other magical markings throughout the Mages' Compound.

Quin and Daris greeted us as we entered the room. "Please, bring the horse inside the circle."

Once everyone was in position, Quin poured the contents of a pitcher into the bowl. The horse tilted her head to the side and snorted.

Daris addressed Sil. "Place your hand on the horse—it doesn't matter where—and don't remove it until we're finished. The flow of magic may make her jumpy, and we'll need you to keep her calm. I'll hold your other hand to create the link between the three of us. I have no idea what we might see or feel. You may experience strange sensations through your Gift. When I stop chanting, maintain contact, keep your eyes closed, and tell us what you see and feel. I will need to concentrate on the casting, so the Arch Mage will guide you."

Sil did as instructed, and the Mage took her hand. He closed his eyes and began muttering. As he swayed from side to side, the water in the scrying bowl rippled, calmly at first, then violently enough to splash over the rim. The horse danced nervously, ears flicking and eyes going wide. Sil touched her forehead to the horse's neck, and the beast calmed.

Vague images materialized in the bowl's water as the ripples settled into a placid pool. At first, the pictures were so faded that all I could make out were colors and rough shapes that changed every few seconds.

Daris chanted a melodic phrase, and the images sharpened.

I leaned forward, craning my neck to get a better look.

A view of the back of Tiana's house from a distance.

A huge silver stallion.

Tiana's face.

Daris stopped chanting.

"Sil, what do you see?" Quin asked.

She squeezed her eyes shut and shivered. When she spoke, her voice sounded far away, like she was standing at the other end of a long hallway.

"The horse's emotions are so strong. I can feel them racing through my chest."

"What do you feel?" Quin asked.

"Longing and loneliness. Spirits, it's overwhelming. I can see Tiana's face, but the images change too fast . . . it's like trying to grab smoke."

"Take deep breaths. Relax and let it come to you," Quin soothed.

"I'll try to go deeper into her mind." Sil's body suddenly convulsed, and she cried out. "Oh, Spirits. It's so strong. Make it stop! *Please!*"

I wrapped an arm around her waist to keep her upright, but Quin motioned for me to stay silent. Sil was trembling, a leaf caught in a gale.

The images in the scrying bowl shifted so rapidly that it was impossible to process one before the next appeared.

Splashes of color.

Bright, then dark.

The horse.

A man.

A mask.

Tiana.

"Come on, just a little further," Sil muttered as her body shook. She turned her head to the side and pressed a cheek to the horse once more. The scent of alfalfa wafted through the room.

Visions reappeared in the water.

Men stripping Tiana's house bare.

A campfire in a field.

The men again.

The images shifted, and the scrying water splashed as though a stone had fallen in its center, then calmed to stillness.

"I can smell pine. It's everywhere," Sil whispered. I drew her against me as she shivered again. "I see a face. He's looking for something. He . . . he was there. I saw him. His eyes were so—"

Then everything stopped.

The visions vanished.

The water quieted.

Sil's consciousness fled, and her full weight slumped against my arms.

Her body shook violently as she muttered urgently, pleading over and over as tears flooded her face. Her cries swelled into screams. "Save me. Please. Save me. I'm right here in front of you! Don't go! *PLEASE!*"

Chapter Fourteen

— · —

Tiana

The cart hit a bumpy patch and slammed me against its unforgiving side. I was groggy and my head hurt, but I was alive.

I remembered waking a couple of times as the cart stopped. The sudden change jarred my senses. Each time, one of the men would open the heavy cover to the cart's bed and check the ropes binding my wrists and feet, then hand me a vial filled with silver liquid. The acrid taste clung to my tongue, thick and unyielding. If I refused the drink, he would simply stand there until I relented. Something in his bearing told me he didn't care how long he had to stand there, only that I downed the liquid.

The man who tended me was more frightening than the potion he forced me to drink. Like those who'd pursued me before, he wore a carved mask and brown robe. His façade was that of an angry bull with horns on each temple and a long beak that curved downward, ending in a sharp point. Murky, black eyes peered through holes in the mask.

Some hours later, perhaps a day or more, I woke again. It was impossible to keep track of time when nearly every moment was spent drugged and asleep.

The air was cooler, almost crisp, and carried the sticky-sweet smell of pine. The road beneath the cart's wheels had grown rougher, and my muscles ached from all the tossing I'd endured. I could barely see daylight through the tiny cracks between the planks, but sounds of movement from other people and horses came through clearly. My throat was sore, and I felt weak, but adrenaline was a magical force of its own, and the possibility of freedom shocked me into alertness.

The cart came to a crawl, then stopped. It crawled again, then stopped again.

A voice with almost bored authority spoke. "Hold. Where are you headed, and what's your business crossing the border?"

The low rasp that answered sent a chill up my arms. "We are Children returning home."

"Children?"

"Yes. We are *her* Children."

Silence lingered before the first man asked, "What's in the cart?"

I found my voice in that moment and began screaming through the wood. "Help me! I'm in the cart. Please help me!" I yelled again and again, as loudly as my scratchy throat would allow. When no one responded, I tried to kick my rope-bound legs against the sides.

Still nothing.

The cart top popped open.

Fresh air flowed across my face.

The night sky peeked through a canopy of tall, thick trees.

A moment later, a handsome face I'd never seen before appeared overhead. The man's jaw was firm and chiseled, and his light, sand-colored hair curled in every direction; but it was the man's eyes that drew my gaze. They were a brilliant, penetrating green that seemed to bore through me.

"I'm right here. You're looking right at me. HELP ME, PLEASE!" My voice cracked with the force of my scream.

The man scanned the inside of the cart, then rapped the wooden floor next to me with his knuckles. As I continued to scream, he held up a hand as if to signal his companion and his mouth formed a word I couldn't hear over my own voice.

Then he leaned down, as if to listen closer, bracing himself with a hand on the side of the cart. I quieted as my hopes rose, but then he pulled back.

I panicked. "Save me. Please. Save me. I'm right here in front of you! Don't go! *PLEASE!*"

The man didn't seem to hear, as he nodded to someone I couldn't see.

Then I heard, "Going home empty-handed, it seems. That is not always a bad thing. Be careful in the mountains. We have had several traders go up and not return recently. Safe travels."

To my dismay, the cart moved forward. Dejected and confused, I lost track of how much time passed before the cart stilled again and Bull-bird returned. He extended another vial and spoke, "Illusion is my Gift. They see what I want them to see. They hear what I tell them to hear. Scream if you wish, but know you will not be heard."

As the cart lurched forward, starting its ascent through the mountain pass, a trickle of tears fell down my cheeks. As with most storms, the light fall was followed by a torrent that caused my angry stomach to clench. Welcome drowsiness overtook fear and pain, and I fell into a fitful, dreamless sleep.

PART III

Chapter Fifteen

—·—

Alfred

"Crown Princess Jessia Vester, Heir to the Kingdom of Spires, and Second of her Name," the royal doorman announced in a booming voice as the audience hall's massive bronze doors flew open. In perhaps the least dignified entrance in royal history, Jess streaked into the Throne Room at a full sprint. Strips of fabric the color of ripe strawberries flew behind her like a cape made of flowing strands. She darted past the assembled members of the Privy Council, and skidded to a stop at the foot of my throne.

"Father, please don't let her do this," she begged through heaves and tears. Her eyes remained fixed on mine, as to avoid the withering gaze of her mother who sat on the throne next to mine.

Before either of us could respond, Jess hurled a crumpled wad of parchment into my lap and ran out the side door. The note fell to the floor as I stood, staring after my daughter, then shook my head and settled back onto the throne.

"I swear that girl will be the end of me," Isabel hissed through pearly white teeth and brightly painted lips. Even angry, the

Queen was the picture of elegance, though one the Privy Councilors chose to avoid at all cost.

I couldn't hold back a chuckle. Though, I immediately regretted the slip as chilly brown eyes drawn into slits bore into me.

The Queen was not pleased.

My wife and daughter had been at each other's throats for the better part of three years, and no one was brave enough to negotiate a peace, least of all me. Jess might have been the heir, but she was still a teenage girl prone to fits, and no force of nature could tame her. I only hoped age and experience might smooth a few of her rougher edges.

I knew I should reprimand Jess for her behavior, especially in front of the Council, but, more often than not, the proud father in me overcame the frustrated King.

I turned, leaning toward Isabel, and whispered so only she could hear. "My dear, she'll grow out of this. I seem to recall another sixteen-year-old girl with a fiery temper years ago . . . uh . . . a *few* years ago," I corrected quickly.

Isabel's glare narrowed further.

Every Councilor seated at the high table snapped to their feet as the Queen rose. "By your leave, husband, I need some air. The betrothal *will* be complete by the end of this week, no matter what our precious little Princess thinks."

She offered a perfunctory curtsy and glided out the side door opposite the one Jess had fled through.

The Ministers exchanged glances. Some offered a sympathetic grin. They had witnessed similar tantrums several times over the past weeks as planning of the royal betrothal sharpened into focus. The royal family put on a unified public face, but the rift between Queen and Crown Princess was one of the worst-kept secrets in the Kingdom. I did my best to referee larger squabbles but had resigned myself to more of a "duck and cover" approach with smaller tiffs; and, while I cherished my daughter, I was embarrassed my chief advisors had to witness what should have been a private spat.

I turned to my Council with a heavy sigh. "Where were we?"

"The letter from the Triad, Your Majesty." High Chancellor Danai Thorn cleared his throat as the members resumed their seats. Thorn's oily black hair lay slicked back across his head and limp behind his shoulders. "Right." I fumbled through a stack of papers on the table beside my throne before lifting the letter in question. I broke the navy wax seal bearing the crest of the Melucian Empire, then scanned the letter. A page shot forward, took the letter, and delivered it to Thorn.

"It appears the Melucians would like to put a horse in our race. They propose we marry Jess to their Master of Arms, Titus Vre."

Chatter and uneasy laughter flitted about the chamber before I raised a palm, silencing everyone. "Stephan, you have something?"

Stephan Bril, Minister of War, had served for more than twenty years. He was one of my closest friends and most trusted advisors. "Your Majesty, Vre? Are they serious? Isn't he near fifty now? Are they thinking we'll marry her off to any old man just to secure better trade deals?"

"Royal marriage often involves older men or women. This is about strengthening ties." My brows creased as I chuckled. "Besides, he's younger than *you*, Stephan."

"Perhaps . . . but I'm *much* younger than my King, Majesty," Bril said with a tilt of his head and smirk on his lips.

"Your Majesty, forgive me for interrupting such a poignant exchange, but I think we should take this offer seriously. Melucia is our primary trading partner, and securing a stronger alliance could only boost the flow between our nations." Destin Carver was a fairly new member of the Council, appointed to serve as Minister of Trade. His mustache was so thin as to barely be seen, and his cheeks were nearly as round as his enormous belly. An annoyingly dusty wig wiggled as he spoke, spilling powder across his shoulders—and anyone nearby. Still, the man was competent, if a touch full of himself.

Thorn nodded. "Your Majesty, I agree with Minister Carver. Our Gifted ranks are extremely thin. Less than twenty percent of our population now wears the gold, and we believe fewer will in the next generation. Without increased trade and movement between our countries, our Gift may die out when your grandchildren sit the throne."

Thorn served as High Chancellor and leader of the Kingdom's Hall of Mages. His public role focused on magic and its users, but the Council knew that he also served as my Master of Spies, administering the most widely respected network of informants throughout the known world.

Thorn preferred a black robe styled as a military jacket above the waist that flared into a floor-length cloak below. Highly polished golden buttons formed ranks from his shoulders to his belt, and a high collar was adorned with two rows of rich, silky gold. A powerful Mage with hundreds of years of experience, he looked to be in his thirties, though his clothing had fallen out of fashion centuries earlier.

Thorn went on, "I need not remind this Council of the precarious balance of power between our two nations. We are significantly stronger in arms, but the sheer proliferation of the Gift among the Melucian population is a direct threat to our own security. That does not even consider the mundane functions like enhanced farming and fishing, healing—and a hundred other abilities we used to take for granted that are now rare. We need Melucia's bloodline as much as we need their trade if we are to secure our people's future."

I regarded him a moment.

Everyone else seemed transfixed by the shine on the table in front of them. The chamber was silent; the creak of a shifting guard's armor echoed off the walls.

I stood. "Thank you, everyone. I have much to think on. It has been a long day, and I have a family dispute waiting behind those doors. We will resume tomorrow."

The Councilors gathered their notes, bowed respectfully, and filed out, leaving me alone and lost in thought. I'd barely noticed them leave. The Triad's letter stared back at me, daring me to decide.

It pained me to think about betrothing my daughter to anyone, let alone someone who lived across the continent, months of travel from our home. My relationship with the Melucian rulers had always been strong and didn't really need a boost, but I understood the arguments in favor of the match.

No one understood why, but the Kingdom's bloodline *was* losing its magic, and the long-term threat to my nation was plain.

A cynical part of me worried that Jess might actually make matters worse. She had always been spirited, but in her teen years she'd become an unmitigated disaster. A dark cloud of resentment and rebellion followed her into every room. A few weeks with her might turn a solid relationship into a full-blown international crisis. I chuckled to myself at the image of the Triad trying to tame my little girl.

A gong sounded in the distance, marking a turn of the hour.

I had just enough time to make a quick change of clothes before dinner would be served. Most nights, I was surrounded by supplicants, nobles, or hangers-on, but tonight was to be a rare, intimate family meal, something our family desperately needed more of if we were to stand together in the battles to come.

I folded the Triad's letter and placed it in the ornate cabinet that sat by the throne. The box had been a gift from one of the small nations on Melucia's eastern border, at the far end of the continent. Nearly as large as a trunk, the gilded container bore enough rubies and emeralds to purchase a small island. It was easily one of my favorite gifts received during my reign, and held an endless stream of requests and appeals.

But the jewels were not the only things I loved about the piece.

I touched my fore and middle fingers to its lid, activating the locking spell placed on the piece by the last person to live who possessed the Gift of Enchanting. Each time I triggered the spell, I felt a boyish thrill run through me.

Satisfied with the click of the magical lock, I turned to leave, but the crumpled wad of parchment Jess had tossed in my lap crunched under my shoe. I'd forgotten about the note.

I kneeled, retrieved and smoothed the paper, then read:

> *Mother's marrying you to that fat old Duke from Huntcliff. You know, the one with the crossed eyes and squirrel on his head for hair? He's got to be at least forty. I overheard Lord Sneak talking to her last night about it. – J*

I sucked in a deep, calming breath and wiped my brow with a kerchief. Justin was a year younger than Jess, and the siblings were virtually inseparable. Reading the scrawl, my hope for a peaceful evening dimmed.

Chapter Sixteen

—·—

Jess

I stalked back to my room and slammed the door, the explosion of wood against stone ensuring that anyone within earshot knew better than to disturb me. Ever since my sixteenth birthday some months ago, Mother had been determined to marry me off.

The thought made my blood boil.

What was so magical about sixteen?

I wasn't ready to marry, certainly not to some stodgy old man who would parade me around like a perfumed animal.

I was the Crown Princess, after all, and would be Queen one day.

Shouldn't a queen be with whomever she chooses?

Shouldn't she love—or at least not detest—the man she's to

. . .

Oh, Spirits, I would have to make an heir with him, with Huntcliff.

My stomach nearly emptied at the thought.

I rummaged through my wardrobe, searching for something to wear to dinner, when another thought occurred.

Could Father be in on this?

Would he actually agree to something so disgusting?

I had always been his little duckling, his favorite—well, only—daughter. Surely, he wouldn't be in on this plot, too?

That weasel Thorn had to be manipulating him. The Chancellor was always skulking around, whispering in ears. I was sure he was trying to get me out of the way so my brother could take the throne—someone Thorn thought he could better control.

The first thing I'll do when I wear the crown is exile that conniving weasel.

A soft tapping at the door snapped my head up.

"Jess, it's me. Open up," my brother whispered.

I cracked open the door to make sure he was alone, then let him in. He eyed the scattering of dresses on the floor . . . and the writing desk . . . and the dresser, and decided to stay well out of range, landing on the foot of my bed. I returned to my wardrobe and tossed more dresses across the back of a chair.

"Sis, calm down. I don't think they've decided anything yet. You know how things work around here. As long as nothing's been announced publicly, there's time to change their minds." He ducked as my dress tossing escalated to a near-violent level.

Justin Vester was the middle child in the royal family, squeezed between our baby brother, Kendall, and me. At fifteen, Justin was wholly unremarkable with average height, a slim build, and a youthful face that would blend into any crowd; and yet, despite his ordinary appearance, Justin's clear blue eyes and warm nature, combined with his burgeoning Gift of Persuasion, made him hard to refuse and even harder to dislike. The boy didn't even try to use his magic; it just flowed out of him, drawing anyone near to his side.

"You don't get it, Justin. Nobody's trying to marry *you* off. If they pick Lord Parna, Mother could ship me off to his stupid town on the other end of the Kingdom where I'd spend the rest of my life buried under a mountain of snow." I flopped face down on the bed beside my brother.

"Sis, she *can't* send you away. You're the next Queen. Worst case, Parna would have to give up his duchy to become King-Consort and live here with you."

I raised a finger without lifting my head out of the comforter. "*Not* helping."

He chuckled, then shifted so we'd be facing each other when I sat up. "C'mon, Jess. We'll figure this out. Who else is on the list?"

I mumbled something unintelligible into the pillow.

"You can either eat that pillow or sit up and talk. I don't think you can do both."

I flipped over and sat up, glaring at his annoyingly infectious grin. "Well, there's Lord Piggy in Huntcliff. Spirits, I would kill myself."

"Stop that. Who else?"

"Barnabus Dask."

"Father's Crown Treasurer?" Justin thought a moment. "Well, he's not *terrible*. The ladies at court seem to think he's handsome enough . . . and he's rich."

"Justin, he's forty . . . and why would I care if he's rich? I will be Queen. The entire Kingdom will belong to me soon."

"Okay, okay. I get it. Who else?"

"General Marks."

Silence stretched between us as Justin's eyes widened.

"*Uncle* Ethan?"

"Yeah. Uncle Ethan," I said. "You know, the one who held me when Father passed me around after I was born? Guess we can check the box of him seeing me naked, even if I was just a baby."

Justin snorted as I covered my face with my hands.

I peeked through my fingers. "It doesn't matter that he practically raised us; he's a noble and member of the Council, which makes him an acceptable candidate for the royal hand."

"So, you'd be okay if they picked him?"

"Okay? No, but do I have a choice in any of this?" I flopped backward and stared at the ceiling. "It's not like they asked me my opinion. That would be too civilized."

"I'm sorry, sis."

I sighed. "He's actually pretty handsome, if you like that sulky, stone-faced military look combined with the personality of a corpse."

Justin snorted. "Hmm. So, no looking forward to the General's staff in your future?"

Despite my foul mood, I barked a laugh and smacked him with a pillow. "You're such an idiot."

"Yeah, but you love me." His grin widened.

"I'll never know why, but I do, little brother." I sat up and mussed his hair with one hand while putting the other around his shoulder. We sat in silence for a long moment before I asked, "What am I going to do, Justin? This is a disaster, and Mother won't listen to me."

"Have you tried *not* yelling at her? She doesn't respond well to screeching . . . unless it's her own." He scrunched up his face, mocking Mother when she was angry, earning a punch in the arm.

"What happened between you two, anyway?" he asked.

I hugged a pillow to my chest. "I don't know. She used to be so different. I could talk to her . . . about anything, really. Justin, she used to look at me like I was the only thing in the world that mattered. Now, all I get is a nasty stare now and then. It feels like she just wants to get rid of me so her perfect life can go on like it was before."

"I'm sure that's not—"

I quieted his statement with one of Mother's glares.

Justin sucked in a breath and tried another approach. "What about Father? Everybody knows you're his favorite. He'd listen to you."

I flopped backward onto the bed again. "You know how he is when it comes to Mother. He hates telling her no. I just wish they'd ask what *I* want, let me at least be a part of the decision. If I'm supposed to be the future of the Crown, don't you think I should be part of choosing the man I'll rule with?"

"Do you even know what you want? All I've heard you say is what you don't want, not what you *do*."

I stared blankly. I knew exactly what I wanted—and who—but I couldn't trust that secret to anyone, not even Justin.

"Little brother, you can be pretty smart sometimes, but no, I have no idea what I want, just that it's not to be married off to some old man and treated like an ornament. Any girl would deserve better, but especially a future queen."

Justin's eyes dropped to his hands.

"Jess, you've watched Father work more than anyone. Maybe they're right, and your marriage could form an alliance that—"

A firm double rap on the door bolted me upright. The door flew open, and Mother bustled into the room, a tornadic whirl of silks and lace, determined to batter anything—or anyone—in her path. "All right, you two, dinner in twenty minutes. Get dressed. Tonight is just the family, so you don't have to worry about wearing a gown or court business. Your Father had a long day and needs a relaxing, *peaceful* night with his children."

Mother swept out of the room as quickly as she'd entered.

I didn't move, just sat and stared into the empty hearth, wishing it would offer answers.

Dinner was excruciating.

I sulked in my spot between Justin and Kendall. Our parents sat next to each other to keep their flock in view without having to look back and forth. The round wooden table was large enough to fit ten, but our family of five still made it feel crowded.

I couldn't wait to escape.

For over an hour, the King and Queen held court. Thankfully, Justin kept parental eyes occupied, commanding the stage for most of the meal. He rattled on about his training with the Royal Guard, his studies with both the Mages and Scholars, and his tour of the National Treasury with other high-ranking students. As he walked everyone through his day's adventures, I stared in wonder at how passionate he was about even the simplest things and how he held his audience in thrall. His Gift helped, but Justin didn't need magic to enchant a room.

I couldn't imagine a world without my brother in it, but I was also jealous of his easy manner and ability to draw people to him. I would be Queen, but he would always be the leader people admired, the one they turned to.

Kendall blundered into the conversation, asking question after question after question . . . after question. When he ran out of questions, he took a bite and thought of another. As Justin steered the conversation toward his martial practice, Kendall practically leaped out of his chair. The Queen's glare introduced him to the Gift of Gravity, one wielded only by every mother's stern gaze.

As soon as Justin paused to take a bite of pork, Kendall resumed his questioning, drilling his older brother about the Royal Guard. Like most eleven-year-olds, he was fascinated with anyone in uniform, though his passions shifted rapidly. One day, he would want to join the Royal Guard, the next he was planning a pirate raid on one of the islands. No one knew what might catch his fancy, least of all Kendall.

At the moment, copying Justin seemed to be his main agenda.

Dinner ended when servants cleared the table, Justin ran out of stories, and Kendall, somehow, ran out of questions.

"May we be excused?" I gave Father a dovish look.

"I suppose, but Jess, tomorrow we need to have a serious talk, Sovereign to soon-to-be-Sovereign. All right?"

Father's tone sent a chill up my spine. He was rarely formal with me, especially in private.

"I am in His Majesty's service," I said, standing from the table and offering a deep, formal curtsy, never dropping eye contact.

I dashed back to my room and dug beneath the pile of dresses on my chair by the armoire. Once I found my leather riding clothes, I quickly changed and slipped out of my room. I wanted to avoid attention, and this was the most common-looking outfit I owned. Besides, the Royal Guard wouldn't think twice about me going out for an evening ride, even this late. With the war brewing between Mother and me, I fled the Palace most evenings.

Careful to avoid contact with my brothers, I crept down the hallway toward the door at the end. I prayed for silence as I pulled it open, peeking through to ensure no one was in the Throne Room.

Nothing stirred.

I raced toward the opposite wall and sucked in one last breath as I stared at the towering golden doors. Two Royal Guards stood vigil on the other side. They stood between me and freedom.

Tossing back my shoulders, I raised my nose into the air and threw open one door.

I was greeted by crossed pikes blocking my path.

"Princess, forgive us, but where are you going without your guards?" A stern, chiseled man in gleaming armor peered down.

"Where I am going is none of your concern. If I needed guards tonight, I would've asked for them. Clear my path. Now!" The last word cracked like a whip.

I was the spitting image of my mother.

I also knew I was technically too young to give a Protector orders, but I had never been afraid to push boundaries when it suited my mood.

The cocky guard's eyebrows rose, then knitted. He looked to his partner, who shrugged, then snapped his pike upright.

"I'll be late. Don't wait up," I said with a coy smile over my shoulder, then hustled toward the outer door that led to the stables.

It was nearly 2300, and darkness cloaked the night sky. The stable boys would already be settled into their rooms at the end of the stalls, so I expected an easy getaway. Still, I crept as quietly as possible, offering each horse a small piece of apple I had stashed in a pouch on my belt. I rubbed their noses affectionately, and each pressed into my palm. I often struggled to understand people, but my Gift made connecting with wildlife easy. I'd often wished I could talk with them, but was grateful for the empathic connection that allowed me to share emotions.

I made it to the stall that held Dittler, my Cretian stallion. Only five Cretians existed throughout the Kingdom, one owned by each of the principals of the royal family. Dittler's sheer size made the stable masters jealous, and his quicksilver mane shimmered in the light.

He was my baby boy.

I pulled the last of the sliced apples from my pouch. Dittler lapped them up, careful not to nip my skin. It always amazed me that a beast so full of raw power could be gentle, even loving. While Dittler chomped, I gave him a quick brushing and placed my saddle on his back. I laughed to myself as he danced in anticipation of the ride to come.

"No racing tonight, baby boy. We have to be quiet, okay?" I rubbed the inside of Dittler's ear with my thumb.

He cocked his head and huffed in ecstasy.

I scanned the stalls before mounting and trotting out of the stables. Thankfully, the grounds remained quiet and still.

We cleared the perimeter of the highly manicured Palace grounds, entering the large forested area. Dittler slowed and glanced back as if questioning the wisdom of a trek into the woods at night.

"It's okay, Dit. We're going to see Danym. You like him, remember?"

The image of sandy brown hair flopping in front of eyes the color of new grass made my skin tingle.

I passed a series of hunting stands mounted high in trees where Father and my brothers spent hours hoping to spot something to shoot. Moments later, I reached my final destination: a clearing by a stream that trickled down from a neighboring mountain. Danym sat waiting on a boulder, staring into the bubbling water, when we rode up.

As I watched him, a nervous energy rippled through my chest.

Dittler let out a snort.

Danym's head snapped up, and his smile lit up the forest.

A little over six feet tall, Danym's boyish features had yet to yield to his burgeoning adulthood, belying the strength he'd built through hours of practice in the ring. Despite his smooth skin and full lips, the thing that made my heart skip was his smile. Wide and bright, the boy's smile made his eyes sparkle and me lose all sense of time or reason.

Danym stood, brushed his leggings, and sauntered over to give Dittler a gentle stroke on the neck, barely looking my way. At last, his head rose, and he extended a hand. "May a humble subject offer Her Royal Highness assistance?"

Spirits, he has to stop looking at me like that.

Please, don't let him stop looking at me like that.

Those voices had warred in my head since the day we met.

I tried to think up a clever retort, something that flowed easily with my brothers or with Father—and *especially* with Mother—but Danym had cast a spell, and I couldn't speak. I nodded, smiled, and took his hand, allowing him to help me down. I stumbled as I landed, forcing him to wrap me in his arms and pull me close to keep me from falling.

Oh, that worked well. I have to remember that one! I smiled inwardly.

Danym stepped back and gave me a formal bow. "Welcome, my lady. May I tether your magnificent horse?"

I gave Danym my most regal glare. "Oh, my boy, of course, but be careful. He is a keen judge of character, and we're still deciding about yours."

Danym grinned, and my knees nearly gave way.

Once Dittler was cared for, Danym led me around the boulder, revealing glasses, a bottle of wine, and a small wooden plate containing cut meats and cheeses spread across a neatly laid blanket. In the center of the plate was a delicate shell of chocolate.

"You think of everything, don't you?" I reached up and gave him a kiss, dropping all pretense. He cradled my head as our lips pressed together.

We sat and talked, enjoying the cool evening. Danym caught me up on news outside the Palace and the routine of his days, and I carefully avoided venting about Mother. After a brief pause to feed each other a bite of chocolate and pour more wine, Danym reached up and moved a stray lock of hair from my eyes. "I've missed you. I know the Palace can be a crazy place, but I worried when I didn't hear anything for nearly a week."

"I'm sorry. It's been awful. All they talk about is who they're going to marry me off to. Now they're even thinking about that old duke from Huntcliff!"

"Lord Parna?" He nearly spat his wine. "The one who picks his nose and farts at court? They call him 'the ostrich' because he can stick his head up his own—"

"Danym!" I slapped his arm.

He laughed. "Well, that's what they say. Is your father seriously considering him? Isn't he thirty years older than you?"

"Yeah, but he's a Duke. They're worried about securing alliances, and trade, and who knows what else. I get it. I will be Queen, and my hand is a powerful chip, but I hate being treated like some cow at the auction. I should have a say in this. No, I should *decide* who I want to be with—who I want to rule with."

He wrapped his arms around me again, and I could hear his heart quicken. There was no sound in the world that calmed me like Danym's heartbeat. I felt safe with that rhythmic thrumming and his arms around me.

Why couldn't my parents see that Danym was who I was meant to be with?

An eternity passed before he pried me away, holding my shoulders in his hands at arm's length. "I love you, Jess Vester. We'll find a way to be together, but I need to get back before my father realizes I left. It's not easy being the High Sheriff's son. It's like he knows when I'm up to something without even asking."

I nodded. "I need to get back, too. Mother would love an excuse to confine me to the Palace—and she has an entire army to keep me there if she sets her mind to it."

Danym helped me mount again, giving me a kiss on the curve of my neck as he lifted me up. I shivered at his intimate touch.

This boy will be the death of me. Spirits, I love him.

As I prepared to ride back to the Palace, trying to linger as much as possible, Danym packed up the remnants of our picnic. As I finally rode off, he started his trek back to his father's estate. The moon was now high and full in the sky, but despite its best efforts at lighting the forest, neither of us noticed the man standing in the shadows nearby.

He muttered a few words and disappeared, leaving no trace of his presence in the woods.

Chapter Seventeen

Isabel

Thorn held a deep bow, waiting to gauge my reaction before rising. He had spent the better part of twenty minutes recounting the events of the evening, starting with a report from the Throne Room guards of the Princess's departure.

"Your Majesty, the children had clearly met at this location many times. They spoke with familiarity and held each other most of the night, but there was no carnal knowledge. I believe the Princess is still intact."

My eyes brimmed with fire as I listened.

"Are you *sure* the boy was the High Sheriff's son?"

"Yes, Your Majesty. He even spoke of his father as they parted." He straightened but kept his eyes cast toward the floor in front of me.

I reached up and shook my inky hair from its tightly woven chignon, allowing it to fall freely past my shoulders, then rose and strode to stare into the stone fireplace.

It was past time the girl grew up.

This childish crush had to end.

"Danai, I need to speak with the High Sheriff . . . *privately*. It is imperative that no one, not even the King, knows we are meeting. I will personally impress upon our Chief Constable the importance of proper succession and the need for alliances above childish love stories. Sebastiano is a reasonable man, loyal to the Crown; I am certain he will come around and tame that son of his."

Thorn remained silent a heartbeat too long.

I turned with one brow raised.

When he finally spoke, his voice was an indistinct murmur that carried more than a hint of malice. "Your Majesty, we *could* go with a more direct—more *permanent*—solution."

I tilted my head. "That is an option, but let's try diplomacy first. I know your skills and am sure you would make it look like an accident, but we cannot risk angering the High Sheriff at this stage in our plans. He is too influential, both at court and across the country."

"Before the Crown gets involved directly, perhaps *I* should give diplomacy a try?" Thorn inclined his head.

I gave him a sidelong glare. "Go on."

"We should save the royal presence as a trump card in case other efforts fail. Allow me to speak with the High Sheriff. We are both members of the Council, and no one will look twice at a meeting between us. It would be difficult to hide a meeting with the Queen. I think we both know how poorly things might turn if the Crown Princess learned of your . . . involvement . . . in this matter."

I blinked a few times, wrestling with the days of bitter arguments that would result if Jess learned of any of this. "Fine.

You have one opportunity, but I will handle this my way if you fail, no matter how messy things might get for Her Royal Highness." My voice lowered to a near whisper. "Come back tomorrow after the dinner hour and report. I want this tied up quickly. The King intends to put candidates for betrothal before the Princess tomorrow, and we cannot have the Sheriff's boy spoiling our plans."

I turned back toward the fire.

Why does everything have to be so hard with that girl?

Why is it always a battle?

I missed the days when Jess looked at me as if there were nothing and no one else in the world, when I was her entire universe.

Spirits, she was so beautiful and fragile.

I smiled at the memory.

But that sweet little girl had grown into a willful, obnoxious, frustratingly cunning young woman. All I saw in her eyes now was resentment and bitterness. Deep down, I knew this happened between girls and their mothers everywhere, but it was deeply disturbing when it happened with my own precious baby.

Thorn bowed and slipped out the door, leaving me alone with the flames.

The next morning, the Palace staff ensured the boys were shuffled off to their lessons on time, freeing Alfred and me to manage our daughter and the day's agenda. Alfred asked Chancellor Thorn to clear the royal calendar, determined that we would finally settle the question of betrothal.

He took my hand. "Issy, she's only a few minutes late. Take a deep breath."

I nearly crushed his fingers in a vice-like grip. "You have no idea what I've had to do to get all the candidates together on the same day. Duke Parna traveled from the farthest end of the Kingdom. If that ungrateful child so much as whimpers—"

"Deep breath. Please." He pried his fingers from mine, returning them to the safety of his lap. "Jess understands her duty. She will play her part."

We had been watching the side door that led to the residence and were surprised when the golden double doors at the end of the chamber swung open. A page in royal livery appeared and bellowed formally, "Her Royal Highness, Crown Princess Jessia Vester."

When Jess glided through, Alfred stood, his mouth agape.

My eyes narrowed.

What is she up to now?

Jess wore a flowing sky-blue gown trimmed in gold with a silken sash crossing her chest. Her normally ruffled hair was brushed to lustrous perfection and bound behind her neck by a thin silver net that sparkled in the light, and blue and white diamonds glittered from the tiara on her head.

Alfred glanced at me with a boyish grin and practically leaped down the steps.

I followed, gripping his arm. "Not a word out of you until this day is won."

Jess floated down the center of the chamber, head and shoulders high, every inch a future queen surveying her realm. When she reached the bottom step of the dais where the King and I now stood, she gave a deep, formal curtsy and held it a moment longer than custom required, a sign of ultimate subservience in the royal court.

"My Lord King Father and Lady Queen Mother, I am here at your command."

The King peeked at me and raised a brow, one corner of his mouth twisting.

My face was a stone as I stared ice through my suspiciously submissive child.

"Jess, you are absolutely radiant. I have never seen you more—"

I interrupted the King, my voice crisp, "Rise and take your place, daughter. Today we decide the fate of the Kingdom—and our line."

Jess didn't flinch or give me a second look. She simply rose and took her place on the right side of her father's throne, resting one hand on his shoulder. The King smiled and placed his hand over hers.

Believing I couldn't hear, she leaned down and whispered in his ear, "Father, I will make you proud, but please don't give me away to some ugly old man. You want handsome grandchildren, don't you? I love you, Father."

I ignored the exchange and nodded to the High Chancellor, who appeared out of the shadows. While I wasn't happy to hear Jess already grumbling, at least the girl had the intelligence to do it *quietly* this time around.

"Your Majesties, I present you with the list of proposed suitors for the Crown Princess. Members of the Privy Council have reviewed each name, and, after many days of debate, agreed on finalists. We submit them for your review and hope the Princess is well pleased." As he said that last part, he stared at Jess, maintaining eye contact throughout the bow that followed.

Thorn turned to the royal page at the door and nodded. The boy vanished, returned a moment later, and announced, "His Excellency, Kinsley Parna, Duke of Huntcliff, Warden of the East."

A short, balding man whose width nearly outpaced his height waddled into the room. His tiny brown eyes were so close together I thought they might blend into his pinched, upturned nose. The Duke's once black hair swirled on top of his head to form a vortex of failed camouflage for a pale, flaky scalp. Most of it refused to stay in place and flopped down the front of his face as he walked, forcing him to shove it back every few seconds with an irritated scowl.

The Duke shuffled to the foot of the throne and offered the deepest bow his knees and bloated belly allowed, then turned his gaze toward Jess with a predatory grin.

"Duke Parna, welcome. We are pleased to see you again," the King said.

"Thank you, Your Majesty. Huntcliff can be so tedious. One welcomes the change," Parna said in a high-pitched squeal.

A small chortle escaped Jess's lips, one I silenced quickly with a glare.

"How are the borderlands these days?" I asked.

"My Queen," Parna began with a flourish. "One observes trees and mountains. Traders pass through headed to other destinations, rarely stopping in town, and the men and women who live in Huntcliff are as tough as the mountain stones and as friendly as the lions that live in their heights. One does miss the capital."

I pursed my lips. "We understand too well, but how fares the border with Melucia? Relations with their Rangers?"

"One would *never* wish to speak with those barbarians, Your Majesty. Filthy ruffians, they are."

Alfred shifted on his cushion. "Duke Parna, is the border peaceful? Is trade flowing normally through the pass?"

Parna's eyes darted between Alfred and me before answering. "My King, one has not seen a change in trade in years. One's patrols report multiple caravans each week and no disturbance within the pass, aside from the occasional wildlife attack one must expect in the wilderness."

Jess stifled a yawn.

"Duke Parna, you must be exhausted from your travels. The page will show you to your rooms and help with anything you might need. We look forward to spending less formal time together at dinner this evening," Alfred said, motioning for the page to approach.

The Duke bowed toward Alfred, then me, then seemed to remember Jess and gave her a shallow head bob. "One looks forward to it, Your Majesties, Highness."

Once the doors closed, Jess turned to her father and pleaded, "Please no. Marry me to a goat, but not *that* man."

He took her hand. "Baby girl, please just entertain our guests today with an open heart. Regardless of whom you marry, these are the nobles of our Kingdom, and we need their support and goodwill. *You* will need them one day . . . as their Queen."

"Yes, Father," was all she could say.

As she gathered herself again, the page barked out, "Lord Barnabus Dask, His Majesty's Crown Treasurer, and Sir Ethan Marks, Lord General of His Majesty's Armed Forces, Lord Protector of the Realm."

Despite the introduction, the General entered first, striding forward as one marching toward battle. His erect frame was cloaked in a black shoulder wrap made of thick fur, looking more like something one wore on a hunt or trek over snowy mountains than to meet a potential bride.

In contrast, the man who followed behind resembled a hermit or monastic priest. His simple black robe bore no adornment save the golden collar of his Gift.

Jess smoothed her gown and straightened as the men approached the dais and bowed.

"Gentlemen, rise and be at ease. We are pleased to formally introduce a lady you both know well. I present to you my daughter, the Crown Princess Jessia." Alfred beamed as he gestured with an open palm.

Both men offered Jess a bow.

General Marks even attempted a smile, a feat indeed for the most stoic man in the Kingdom.

Jess watched the spectacle unfold. She schooled her features and returned her callers' bows with a graceful curtsy of her own.

"General Marks. Lord Dask." She nodded to each man in turn.

"Gentlemen, we see no need for a lengthy audience. You are well known to us. We look forward to seeing you both at dinner." Recognizing the King's tone of dismissal, the men bowed once more, retreated backward two steps, then turned and exited the chamber.

The doors had barely closed when I shot to my feet and turned to Jess. "Jess, did you see how handsome Ethan is in his furs? And he's so tall."

Jess maintained an air of regal superiority, stepping off the dais and arching a brow toward the King. "Father, I believe Mother would like you to match *her* today. I will gladly give her my betrothal if it pleases the Crown. After all, General Marks is *quite* tall."

I bristled and shook an accusing finger toward my ungrateful daughter, but Alfred cut off whatever incitement I was about to hurl. "Listen, you two. Not today. Jess, you'll learn more about these three at dinner tonight, but we need to discuss one other option that has come to our attention."

"Please tell me it's the Sheriff's son." It looked as if the plea escaped before Jess could think, as both hands flew to cover her mouth and her eyes widened.

The King's brows knitted as he shot a questioning glance my way. "Sebastiano's boy?"

"Your daughter thinks her secret admirer is actually a secret. I imagine she hopes a match with him would appease us since Sheriff Wilfred is so widely respected," I said, settling back onto my throne. "I suppose it might be worth a discussion."

Color flooded Jess's cheeks.

The King laughed, not the good deep belly laugh that meant he loved the idea, more the "you're absolutely out of your mind" laugh that crushed hopes and dreams.

"Ladies, be serious. Wilfred's boy is barely seventeen! There's even a rumor he's a bastard." Jess shot him a mystified look, and he laughed again. "This decision will shape the reign of Queen Jessia Vester and the future of the Spires. It must be treated with the utmost seriousness. Spirits, the fate of the entire world will be affected by this choice. A boy barely old enough to grow whiskers can hardly guide a queen."

The pendulum of Jess's emotions swung from hope to anger, and each pass was visible on her face.

"Guide? You want someone to *guide* me? Did you seriously just say that?"

"Jess, you know that's not what I—"

"I see it now. That is *exactly* what you meant." She paced before the thrones, her anger seeming to boil hotter with each step. "I've been *guided* my entire life. I've been told what to wear, how to hold my head, when to speak—which is basically never. I've been *guided* through every detail of every pointless day. Now you want to arrange a marriage to men more than twice my age because I'm too ignorant or stupid—or *too female*—to rule on my own?"

Her glare shot from me to her father, clearly struggling to decide which parent deserved it more.

"I stood here all morning as you paraded potential buyers for your prize cow. I am *your daughter*, heir to your crown, not some mindless beast to be auctioned off to the highest bidder."

Jess took a breath, but her eyes darkened. "Father, this will be my husband . . . my partner . . . *my Kingdom*. When I am Queen, *I* will do the guiding, and I won't need any man to tell me how to do it."

She curtsied sharply, wheeled about, and stormed out the side door toward her room, her gown rustling nearly as angrily as her voice had.

The King slumped back into his throne.

He removed his crown and held it in his lap, his thumb drifting across the symbol of his office.

I gave him a wry grin. "That went well, dear. For once, it's you and not me receiving our baby girl's ire. I actually pity those poor men coming to dinner tonight."

Chapter Eighteen

Thorn

The office of the High Sherriff sat at the center of Fontaine's trade district in a large stone building with few windows and even fewer doors. The place looked more like a mausoleum than a functional government building. City Guardsmen, Royal Guards, and National Patrol streamed through, reminiscent of an anthill angered by the rain.

The milling crowds of uniformed men and women offered shallow bows and parted as I passed, guided by some involuntary impulse to avoid contact with Mages in general, and me in particular. I strolled the length of the lobby and climbed the stairs to the offices of senior officers and bureaucrats on the third floor. Approaching the familiar desk of the High Sheriff's clerk, I smiled. "Kay, I'd like to see Sebastiano for a moment, please."

A woman in her fifties with spectacles atop gray hair pinned in a tight bun glanced up. "Of course, High Chancellor. Please have a seat."

When Kay reappeared, she was followed by a man wearing a crisp green coat lined with two rows of highly polished buttons.

"Danai? What an odd time for a visit from the King's hand. Is everything all right?" Sebastiano asked with genuine concern.

"All is well. Would you mind if we spoke in your office . . . *privately*?"

Sebastiano paused, then turned and motioned for me to precede him into his office. At the far end of the room, next to one of the building's precious few windows, sat an enormous desk littered with parchment. Either the High Sheriff was in high demand, or he was woefully behind on his paperwork.

We sat at a small table just inside the door. "So, I take it this isn't a courtesy call. What's going on that we needed to talk privately and outside of the Council?"

I leaned forward and lowered my voice. "Are you aware that your son has engaged in private rendezvous—sometimes very late at night—in the woods near the Palace grounds?"

Sebastiano's eyes widened as his head shook. "No. I've been working all hours lately. He's a good boy but has been a little lost since my wife died last year, and with those missing Gifted cases piling up, I haven't been home much. What's he gotten himself mixed up in?"

"Secret, unchaperoned evenings with Princess Jessia."

The Sheriff's eyes threatened to pop out of their sockets as he searched for any sign of humor.

"You're serious?"

"I'm afraid so. In fact, they were seen having a picnic in the woods just last night, complete with wine, chocolates, and a large, comfortable blanket." I peeked at Wilfred's reaction while pretending to leaf through documents.

Sebastiano rose and began pacing, one hand scratching his stubbly head.

"The Queen will have his head for this," he muttered.

"She isn't thrilled with your son complicating her plans. She has her mind set on pairing the Princess with someone from the Council."

"A member of the Council? Which old men are they desperate enough to try now?"

"Dask and Marks."

He barked a laugh. "You're kidding, right? Every rumor I've heard pegs Dask as favoring the Prince, not the Princess. And Marks . . . well . . . he's not as old as the rest of us, but do we really want the leader of our *military* sitting on the throne? What is the Queen thinking?"

"They're better than Parna."

"Now I know you're joking. Parna?" The Sheriff gaped. "One does love talking about oneself, doesn't one?"

I let a rare smile slip.

Sebastiano was one of the few who surrounded the King whose company I genuinely enjoyed. I had been the one to welcome him on the first day he strode through the golden doors. Many on the King's Council were new, with eager eyes and loud voices. Sebastiano held his tongue. He observed. He learned. There was a wisdom in his hazel eyes as he rose to address the Crown his first time. The moment felt only days in the past, though decades had flown by.

We were so young then.

At least, *he* was. I'd lived several centuries by that time, though none in the Palace knew it.

Sebastiano and I were not friends—I could not honestly use that term with anyone—but there was a camaraderie we shared that I assumed to be akin to friendship others enjoyed. I could never lower my guard with Bril or the others on the Council without whispers reaching the King's ears. But, as an enforcer of the King's laws, Sebastiano understood the need for secrecy. He knew when to keep his lips closed and when to speak. He understood the value of information and the need to grasp it tightly in one's fist. In that, we shared a common interest.

"I can't imagine Jess accepting any of them."

I spread my hands in noncommittal agreement.

"So, back to Danym."

Sebastiano held up a palm. "I'll handle him, but I might need your help keeping the Princess away for a while."

There was a pause as the Sheriff leaned against his desk.

I decided to head down a different path. "While I'm here, do you have any update on the missing Gifted cases?"

Sebastiano's head snapped up.

He stepped around his desk and rifled through one of the stacks, holding a page before a flickering lamp. "A fourth was reported missing just yesterday. That's *four* Gifted in the past nine weeks. The only common thread we've found is that all four have a Gift. The latest was taken from Crelt—son of a local Merchant, no one particularly important or famous."

"What was the boy's Gift this time?" I steepled my fingers.

"Looks like . . ." Sebastiano scanned the parchment. "Mental: Clairvoyance."

"So, Strength, Fire, Animal Control, and now Clairvoyance. Doesn't seem to follow any pattern, does it?" I asked.

"I was hoping you or one of your Mages might have more insight. Even the locations where the victims were taken are random, several days' distant."

"Have you discovered a trail to follow in any of the cases? Any sign of where they were taken?"

"No." He dropped into the chair behind his desk and sorted through a different pile. "We did receive some curious, unrelated reports. Our Patrol Captain near Cradle noted a recent increase in activity by the Children. He believes they are migrating further east, possibly over the mountains into Melucia."

"The Children?" My brows furrowed. "I haven't heard anyone mention them in years. They're a cult obsessed with Irina, right?"

Sebastiano nodded. "Every one of them is touched, if you ask me. They run around in robes and the strangest masks you've ever seen. I think they even have their voices altered somehow. Just listening to one of them talk makes my skin crawl."

"Interesting," I said. "Are they still preaching the virtues of the Kingdom War and Queen Irina?"

"Oh, yes." Sebastiano chuckled. "Complete with prophecies of her return and the overthrow of the heretics currently warming the throne."

My eyes widened. "Are you concerned? Should we increase Palace security?"

"No, I don't think so. There aren't enough of them to do much harm."

"All right." I considered a moment. "From what I recall, they've always kept to themselves. Do you suspect their involvement?"

"No, nothing, other than the timing. I have two units in the area, one in Cradle and the other in Huntcliff. If there's anything going on, we'll hear about it."

I stood and nodded. "Thank you, Sebastiano. Please keep me informed. The King is disturbed by these cases and is eager for their resolution."

"We all are, Chancellor. We all are."

Two hours later, I stood in the Queen's study watching her stare into the fireplace. Ancient, leather-bound tomes lined even older shelves, as though the past bore witness to every moment of our present. Aside from the fire crackling in the hearth, the only light in the small chamber came from a lone candle mounted in silver sitting on a table by her leather chair.

"Yes, Your Majesty, the Sheriff understands completely."

She responded in a low, measured tone that was more intimidating than if her voice were raised. "I'd better never see his boy anywhere near the Palace or my daughter again. Do you understand me, Danai? Never. Again."

"I understand perfectly, Your Majesty." I bowed before leaving the Queen to ponder her flames. I couldn't decide which burned brighter in that moment, the ones in the hearth or in her eyes.

CHAPTER NINETEEN

JESS

I had planned to be the perfect daughter, the perfect princess. Today was important to Father, and I desperately wanted to see approval in his eyes. That's all I ever wanted. Father taught me to be brave and independent. He instilled a sense of strength, making me believe that one day I would be a great queen. He painted images of my coronation that captivated my dreams and made me believe that anything was possible.

With one careless comment, he'd shattered his little girl's fantasy.

What if it hadn't been careless?

What if it was what he really thought?

Did he truly believe I needed some *man* to guide me, that I couldn't think for myself?

Did he think the experience of someone older was more important than his daughter's happiness?

The entire conversation made my blood boil.

These couldn't be the words of my father. Perhaps they were those of the King, but not the man who said he believed in me.

Mother is behind this somehow.

The Queen had wanted to be rid of her troublesome daughter for years now.

What have I ever done to deserve to be tossed aside, to be sold off? I can't believe this is happening.

Whatever I did to make her hate me, it's gone on for too long. I can't take it anymore.

I paced my bedchamber, wearing a path of rage into the rug. Then it came.

The knock.

The summons.

The executioner had arrived to escort me to the gallows.

Well, to dinner, but it felt like the gallows.

How am I going to get through this night?

"Stop knocking. I'm coming," I barked.

"The King and Queen request your presence in the formal dining room, Your Highness," the royal porter said.

The man had served the royal family for decades and had seen his share of royal outbursts. He barely flinched as I threw the door open and stormed past. A trail of fury stalked my path as I wound through the hallways of the Palace toward the dining room. With each step, my wrath and pain churned.

When I entered, everyone was already seated and talking quietly. Servants in formal coats lined the walls awaiting the tiniest royal desire. Unlike the intimacy of our private dining chamber, this room was vast and contained a table long enough to seat fifty guests comfortably. Father held court in his usual place at the table's head, while the Queen, who usually occupied the seat opposite the King at the table's foot, was now seated to his right.

Treasurer Dask sat on the side opposite the Queen.

Uncle Ethan—General Marks, I mentally corrected myself—sat across from my chair staring blankly into the opposite wall. He looked almost as uncomfortable as I felt.

The chair to the King's left remained empty, awaiting my royal presence.

Duke Kinsley Parna was seated beside me.

Empty chair beside an empty shirt. So glad they saved me a place of honor.

I froze at the far end of the table. I couldn't move. Anger gnawed at my bones.

"Jess, please come join us. The cook made your favorite tonight, and I'm sure these gentlemen are eager to get to know you," Father said in a tone I thought hinted at contrition.

Good. He should feel guilty.

I forced myself to step around Parna and take my seat. The King handed me a glass of mulled wine and raised his own. "To the future of the realm. To my beautiful daughter, Crown Princess Jessia Vester."

"To the Crown Princess," the men said in broken unison.

And so it began.

Lord Parna spent the night trying to whisper in my ear. He reeked of old musk, and his breath was fouler than that of their twelve-year-old, nearly toothless hound. Every time a servant brought a new dish or a different wine, the Duke spent the following moments droning on about how wines or beef or vegetables—*or anything*—from the East were better, and how, in great detail, the masters of that region made them so. I might've found the lectures educational if the Duke had spoken in anything other than third person.

One can only take so much of one referring to one's own person in the third, I thought, suppressing an eye roll.

And that infernal piece of meat lodged between his two front teeth threatened to fly out every time he lisped an *s* or tutted a *t*. I kept my napkin at the ready in case of an unexpected shot across my brow. As the Duke prattled, I daydreamed about a tiny cannon shooting roast beef out of his mouth. That made me chuckle, drawing a sharp, questioning eye from my suitor.

I didn't bother to explain myself.

Treasurer Dask looked quite handsome and might've been a worthy candidate if he hadn't been so incredibly offensive. He tried a fresh approach at impressing me, the bride-to-be, offering one inappropriate joke after another. As the servants began placing platters of various meats and vegetables on the table, he sprang from his seat, commanding everyone's attention.

The King and Queen shared a startled, uneasy glance as Dask cleared his throat.

"I knew an old Bishop who had lost some of his teeth and complained that others were so loose they might fall out.

'Never fear,' said one friend. 'They won't fall.'

'And why not?' the Bishop asked.

His friend replied, 'Because my testicles have been hanging loose for the last forty years, as if they were going to fall off, and yet, they are still there!'"

The King's uneasy laugh broke the silence that followed.

The Queen glared daggers at Dask.

The Treasurer seemed pleased with his effort and laughed deeply before downing more wine and taking his seat.

I felt hope dim with each passing moment.

General Marks never spoke—not a single word.

He assessed those seated around the table as though they were players on some battlefield board game waiting to be moved or attacked or dismissed. He barely even looked at me. When he did, pity and sadness filled his eyes. In those moments, I thought he might have looked as trapped by circumstance as I felt.

As servants entered the hall carrying trays of decadent desserts, Duke Parna ran his hand up my leg for the third time, adding an extra squeeze of his greasy, sausage-like fingers when he approached the upper part of my thigh.

The indignity of the day finally snapped something inside me.

I couldn't take it anymore.

Not one more moment.

I snatched up a two-pronged fork and stabbed him in the wrist.

Parna yanked his hand back and howled in pain, leaping from the table with a spray of blood splattering in his wake.

"That wicked, awful girl! She stabbed me!" he squealed.

"Jess! What have you done?" Mother rushed to the Duke's side.

"What have *I* done?" I shot to my feet and flung my napkin and bloody fork onto the table. "I did what *you* should have done. I protected myself from this disgusting pig and his wandering hands. Of course, you didn't see or do anything. All you can see is how to get rid of me. Fine. I'll go. You get your wish, YOUR MAJESTY!"

"Jess," gasped the King, his eyes wide as he rose to his feet.

Something more was said but it fell on deaf ears.

I stormed out, purposely knocking a platter of vegetables out of the hands of a servant who was entering the hall.

Once in my chamber, I slammed the door shut, slid the bolt in place, and changed into my riding clothes without so much as a moment's pause. I grabbed a travel bag and stuffed it full of everything within reach. I was almost out the door when I glanced back at my empty desk and released a sigh.

I can't leave without any word to Justin.

I sat and scrawled a quick note, then rose and fled my room for the last time.

Most of the Palace staff had the night off in anticipation of a long dinner and an evening of the royals entertaining their small group of guests. For once, I was thankful for Mother's planning. It only took a few moments to sneak through the corridors to the Throne Room, then perform my well-practiced dance with the guards and exit the Palace. For the second night in a row, I found the stables empty and quickly saddled Dittler.

The reins were a comfort, though my fingers white-knuckled the leather.

Tears streaked down my face, clouding my vision as we entered the forest. The darkness that folded around me was absolute—and comforting. I relished the feeling of finally being alone, of being free.

I was so lost in my own thoughts that I barely noticed where Dittler was taking me until I glanced up and recognized the familiar break in the trees that led to the riverside I loved so much—the clearing where Danym and I would meet. My tears subsided as I thought about Danym holding me, felt his arms warming me, making me feel safe and loved.

I dismounted and led Dittler to the stream, then aimlessly strolled the area, grasping for some sight or scent that would evoke Danym's memory.

How can the thought of him soothe my anger so?

I took my waterskin out of the saddlebag and drank deeply. The adrenaline that fueled my escape was wearing off, as thirst and exhaustion crawled through my veins.

I kneeled to refill the waterskin from the stream.

Dittler snorted nervously and nudged me with his nose.

"What is it, boy? There's nobody out here. Easy."

The moon wasn't as full as it was when I'd met Danym the night before, and I could only see a few paces away. I replaced the stopper on the waterskin and stepped around Dittler, scanning the forest darkness.

Something moved to my left, snapping my head in that direction.

Then the leaves rustled.

"Who's there? Show yourself," I said, trying to sound brave as a bolt of fear shot up my spine.

Dittler's ears flicked and he pranced in place, nostrils flaring.

Another snap from behind made me spin around.

A man in a long robe crept through the trees, headed straight toward me. He was only a few paces away.

Our eyes locked, and the man bolted forward, his arms outstretched, fingers curled like claws reaching for me.

I leaped onto Dittler's back and spurred him forward.

The man dove out of the way with a muffled curse, but reached up and grabbed one of my boots, nearly yanking me out of the saddle.

I pulled free and managed to get my feet into the stirrups.

A second man appeared to my right.

He grabbed at Dittler's reins, but the horse was quicker, bolting deeper into the forest.

"Go, go," I screamed.

I gripped both reins and mane and prayed they would be enough to keep me in the saddle. My knees clamped tight against Dittler's sides.

Another horse whinnied from behind.

I urged Dittler for speed.

Still, the other horse edged closer.

I could hear it, hooves against packed earth, its heaving breath.

My heart felt like it was going to beat out of my chest.

We entered a clearing and wove between fallen trees and resting boulders.

My path was blocked.

Dittler, unable to clear the way, reared high, throwing me to the ground, then bounded off into the darkness.

I lay dazed, surrounded by chunks of stone and towering trees, terrified and alone in the woods.

I'd never been thrown before. The ache was like nothing I'd ever known. The impact drove the air from my lungs. Dirt and leaves caked against my hands when I finally managed to push myself off the ground. The taste of salt from flowing tears tickled my senses. I'd bitten through my lower lip, and copper now clung to it in a crimson flow.

Hooves crushed leaves.

My pursuer neared.

Then a man's voice called out, "I think she went this way. Over here."

I had to move.

Stumbling forward those first few steps, I let adrenaline be my guide.

The forest had never seemed so large; being alone had never felt so terrible.

My head whirled around, searching for anything familiar.

But I was lost.

The trees had long since shed their leaves, coating the forest floor and making stealth impossible. I heard men searching, no longer concerned for secrecy as they crunched through the woods. All I could do was hide and remain as still as possible, hoping the robed men would go away.

I tried to slow my breathing, to be quiet and still. I couldn't stop my hands from trembling.

Spirits, what have I done?

Finally, the sounds of pursuit faded, and I released the tension I'd held, taking deep breaths to calm my racing heart. I lay on a rough bed of twigs. Cold rocks dug into my side. Clouds had obscured the moon, and darkness descended upon the forest, leaving me confused, terrified, and virtually blind. Ever so gently, I pushed myself up into a sitting position, careful to make as little noise as possible.

A twig snapped behind me.

I froze.

My heart stilled.

A hand reached around from behind and covered my mouth, while a powerful arm encircled my waist.

I thrashed and squirmed.

I tried to scream.

The arms were too strong, the grip too tight.

"Jess, stop. It's me," a familiar voice whispered.

"Danym?" I mumbled beneath his hand.

He loosened his grip enough to let my head turn. My eyes widened, and I threw my arms around his neck and buried my face into his shoulder.

"Shhh. Quiet. Those men are still out here looking for you. I found Dittler wandering through the woods and tied him up by my horse. If we can get back to them, we can get out of here."

He wrapped his arms about my waist and held me close.

I nodded into his shoulder, still squeezing him with all of my strength. He had never felt so good.

He saved me.

Danym saved me.

Nothing made sense . . . except Danym.

We couldn't linger, and I was forced to creep through the forest on unsteady legs. It helped that Danym never released me. His arm about my waist gave me strength. His breath against my skin gave me hope.

Nearly an hour passed as we wound our way through the trees to the waiting horses.

Only once did we spot one of the robed men. We ducked behind a large tree and held our breath until he passed.

When we reached the horses, Danym pulled me close and whispered, "Do you want me to take you back to the Palace?"

I stared into his eyes and shook my head. "No. I never want to go back there again. Take me somewhere safe, just you and me."

My heart thrilled as Danym smiled.

—·—

PART IV

Chapter Twenty

Declan

I thought once we came back down the mountain with a yellow ribbon in hand our timed test and perpetual questioning would end, but in the months following our Trial, the instructors who held our fates in their hands became the cruelest of task masters. It felt more like our first few months, when senior Rangers worked to break cadets and send the unworthy home, than any course designed to add finishing touches to successful soon-to-be, newly cloaked Rangers.

Once outside the loving embrace of the Academy, Rangers tended to specialize. One might focus on forestry skills, while another might thrive on guard duty of one sort or another.

But for cadets, each day brought new and different challenges. We were assigned, seemingly at random, to mentors who led us into the mountains on patrols, never fully understanding what we sought until we arrived at our designated patrol zone. We were sent into the countryside to help deal with wildlife outbreaks. On more than one occasion, we were forced to stand guard at the border as traders passed beneath the watchful gaze of our tutors.

There was no guessing what each new day might bring—or how exhausted we would be as we stumbled back into the barracks long after the sun slept.

Through some quirk of fate, or some joke played on me by the Spirits, I rarely enjoyed an assignment without Ayden appearing by my side. I didn't loathe him as I had before the Trial, but something about him still crawled beneath my skin.

I couldn't decide if it was his sun-kissed hair that blazed and billowed in the wind, or his perpetual smile that brightened any room he entered. It certainly couldn't have been the witty banter that flowed from his plump lips, drawing a laugh from anyone nearby.

Spirits, he drove me mad.

And for some reason, I could not stop thinking about him.

Whatever had happened on the mountain with that majestic buck had opened windows in my soul I had never known existed. Ayden had been there with me. He stood by my side. His support never faltered. In fact, in my moments of deepest doubt, it was Ayden who lifted me up, who encouraged me to press forward, to win the day. It was Ayden who offered me his courage when my own faltered.

It was Ayden who'd marveled as the deer bowed his head.

Even that near mystical moment hadn't dimmed his gaze as it cast my way.

Now, I saw him in every cloak that passed—at least, I looked at each cloak in the hope it might be him. His eyes were everywhere, glowing brightly, smiling at the edges at some unspoken quip only he understood. The set of his jaw confounded me, and I woke several times with my hand extended, as my sleeping mind longed to feel his stubble against my skin.

Worse, he haunted my dreams.

In my slumbering rest, he cradled my head against his chest, brushed the hair from my cheek, kissed my forehead until I slept.

I could hear his heartbeat.

I could feel his breath.

I longed to taste his lips.

I had never wanted a man, never seen one in any way beyond that of a brother or friend. And yet, this noble, this arrogant, bright-eyed, beautiful, brilliant, handsome, talented, irritating man . . .

I was consumed by Ayden Byrne.

And I hated myself for it.

I already knew what living outside our society felt like. Magic's abandonment had ensured I would forever be an outcast. If I surrendered my heart, if I gave it to . . . would I worsen my plight, consign myself to a lifetime of jeers and jibes? Would there be anywhere in the world where I might flee and know peace?

Would I lose my Cloak, my Ranger Green . . . before it had ever warmed my shoulders?

These feelings were foreign and frightening . . . and they called to me each time I saw him smile.

They made me want and dream and hope. . . .

"You're quiet today," Shira said, bumping me with her shoulder as she raised her tankard, her third since we'd entered the tavern.

Shira had stood by my side since the day we first darkened the Academy's doors. Daughter of a long line of silk Merchants, she'd struggled with archery and other combat skills. I helped her through. In turn, she ensured I passed every course in history and lore, two subjects about which I had little interest and even less aptitude.

Beyond studies, Shira was funny, bright, and possessed a tongue sharper than any dagger on any belt in the Guard.

"Sorry, guess I've been in my own head lately."

She eyed me over the top of her mug. A group of cadets sang loudly in the corner. Their words were so garbled, I doubted even they knew what they sang.

"This wouldn't have anything to do with a certain flame-headed noble, would it?" A grin crept toward the edges of her eyes.

I furrowed my brow and pretended to not understand. "Who?"

She set her mug down, crossed her arms, and glared. "Declan Rea, don't you dare try toying with me. You may have everyone else fooled into thinking you're married to the Rangers Corps, but I know who makes your heart beat faster."

Dammit, how could I forget about her Gift?

Shira's twin ponytails, wide smile, and innocent eyes made it hard to take her seriously at times. It was easy to forget she was one of the most formidable cadets to enter the Academy in decades.

"You know I can literally hear your heartbeat, right?"

"He just pisses me off, that's all."

"You're a terrible liar." She snorted and grabbed her ale. "Besides, your heart started doing that thing the moment I mentioned Ayden."

"Shh," I said, motioning with one palm and leaning forward. "Fine, you caught me, though I'm not sure what you caught me doing. I haven't figured any of it out yet."

Her nose scrunched like she'd smelled something awful. "What's there to figure out? I mean, besides which of you gets to be the man and—"

"*Shira!*"

She chuckled. "Right. Nobody with hair like yours could ever be the man."

I turned and folded my arms on the bar, then fell over to bury my face in them. I could feel the army of bottles glaring down from their shelves behind the barman, the stares of the others seated at rickety tables packed so tightly shoulders bumped as knives sawed through tough meat. My face was burrowed into my arms, but I was sure the brilliant redness glowing from my ears signaled my utter horror to everyone within sight.

Shira's laughter rose above the raucous singing in the corner.

Then her hand landed on the center of my back and began rubbing circles. "There, there, little one."

I lifted my head enough for her to hear my voice. "I don't know what to do, Shira. He drives me mad, makes my blood boil, pisses me off . . . and I can't stop thinking about him."

"Did anything happen on your Trial?"

"No. Absolutely not." I sat up and faced her, snatching my stein off the bar and downing the last of it in one gulp.

She motioned for the bartender to bring another round, then asked, "Did you want something to happen?"

"No. I mean, I don't think so. I still hated him then. Not that I don't hate him now, although, I don't, not really. I just don't . . . shit. I don't know what to think or how to feel. I sure don't know what to say or how to act. I try to avoid him, but the damn seniors keep putting us in the same classes and pairing us on missions."

"Really?"

I nodded. "We've already been paired for crossing watch. That's another three days straight I have to work next to him."

"Have to? Or get to?" Her smirk said more than her questions.

"Both, maybe. I don't know." The new beers arrived, and I drank half of mine without taking a breath.

"Easy, Ranger," Shira said, one hand on my arm forcing my stein away from my lips. "It's not worth getting so snockered that you can't pull duty tomorrow."

"I guess."

"Have you talked to him? Does he know how you feel? Do you even know how he feels?"

I shrugged. "I haven't said anything, but I'm pretty sure he likes me. He's always smiling and finding some excuse to pat my back and grip my forearm. On the Trial, he got really close once, and I thought . . ."

"Don't stop. You thought what?"

"I thought he was going to . . . you know . . ."

"What? Declan, what?"

"Kiss me."

"That's anticlimactic."

"What the fuck?" I blanched. "A man almost kissed me and you call that anticlimactic."

She shrugged. "Anything short of 'he juggled my nuts' was going to be disappointing."

"Shira!"

"Come on, Declan. You're a big boy—at least, I assume you are. You're tall and—"

"Shira—"

She smirked. "Let's assume you're of juggle-able size. You were alone in the woods on a mountain with no one but squirrels and deer to watch. If you were ever going to figure things out, that was the time. You could've at least let him get a little lip action."

"You're assuming I have myself figured out enough to sort through how I feel about him."

"Oh, really?" For the first time since we'd started dancing on ridiculously thin ice, she looked surprised. "You mean . . . you didn't know? Seriously?"

I opened my mouth, then closed it. Then opened it again, but nothing came out.

"I see," Shira said. "Declan, wow. No wonder you have had a lot on your mind."

My head drooped, and my fingers began fidgeting. I couldn't meet her gaze. I couldn't take any more judgement, least of all from her. I needed her with me, in my corner, no matter what. The thought she might not want me near her because . . .

"Declan, I can see your head spinning. It's going to pop off if you keep that up."

I tried not to smile, but Shira was impossible.

"When did you first think you might, you know . . ." She glanced around to make sure no one was within earshot, then leaned toward me and whispered, "like man arse."

"Shira!" I nearly spit my ale.

"That's what it is, right? I know you like the other bits, but it's mostly about the arse, isn't it?"

"I have no idea. Did you miss the part where this is all new to me?"

"You mean . . . you haven't . . ."

My head shook slowly.

Her eyes widened again.

"Oh, Declan, my little baby bird with his fuzzy feathers and broken wing."

I rolled my eyes. "I'm not *that* bad."

"How old are you?"

"Almost twenty."

"And you've never stuck your sword into a sheath?" She pantomimed exactly that.

"Can you keep your acting to yourself?" I hissed, glancing about for onlookers. Thankfully, no one was paying the least attention to us. "No, I haven't."

"Not even with women?"

I shook my head again.

Her mouth made an O, and her eyes found another level of widening.

I gulped ale, finishing the second tankard in only a handful of minutes.

She eyed me, then sat back, propping one elbow on the bar.

"Wow. A raw recruit, forgive the pun."

I raised a less-than-appropriate finger.

"That certainly explains why nothing happened on the mountain," she mused.

I shrugged. "Are you forgetting the part where I actively loathed Ayden at the time?"

Shira ran fingers across her chin, as if to contemplate the depth of that question. "About that. Why, exactly, did you hate this man? From what I've seen, he's one of the few good ones here. I get to hate him because he plays for your team. You don't have an excuse, unless there's more you're not telling me. Did he shoot you in practice? Abuse a member of your unit? Play with your unit? Never mind, I already know that hasn't happened."

I tried desperately not to laugh knowing that would only encourage her.

"You're a terrible friend. Why do I stay with you?"

"Because you're scared of everyone else who wants to be with you."

"Fuck off."

"You first." She raised her mug, then took a long pull. "Now, answer the question. Why did you hate him?"

"I honestly don't know." I stared into my ale, hoping it would give me answers. "I saw him that first day, like a shiny new copper—or gold, in his case—and it just felt like some rich kid privilege had let him skip First Year and become an instant Ranger, like we were getting stuck with some dandy who'd never be able to have our backs."

Her brows rose. "You really thought about it, didn't you?"

I let out a sigh. "Not really. I did think he looked stuck up, and he did laugh at my cadets, but that was about it. I guess I assumed the rest."

She sipped her beer, a change from the charging guzzle from a moment earlier.

"Do you think you might've actually liked him but were fighting it?"

"No, of course—" Her cocked brow silenced me. I stared into my mug again, then looked up. "Maybe. Shira, what am I supposed to do? You know how the other Rangers look at men who . . . at men who aren't like them. I'm already second class because of my plain collar. If I let this—"

"Declan," she said, her voice suddenly soft. "Look at me."

Reluctantly, my gaze rose to meet hers.

"You are one of the best men I have ever known, and you're a damn fine Ranger . . . or will be soon. The Captain won't drum you out because you fall for another Ranger. He's not like that. You might catch some shit from the guys, but who cares? If it isn't this, it'll be something else. That's just how Rangers are." She leaned forward and gripped my forearm. Her eyes searched mine, and a lump formed in my throat. "I love you so much it hurts, and if you ever repeat that, I *will* kill you."

I chuckled. She glared.

"Life is too short to let arseholes choose your fate. It's definitely too short to let them choose who you love. If you like Ayden, tell him. Let the chips fall. You both deserve the truth, either way."

Shira sat back, and I lost myself in thought again.

"Besides." She seized my attention again. "You getting laid will do more for the morale of the rest of us than anything. You're a whiney prick when your balls are blue."

My mouth opened, but before anything could fall out, she hopped up, grabbed her beer, winked, and strode across the tavern, leaving me alone with my ale and my thoughts . . . and a stupid, boyish grin.

Chapter Twenty-One

Declan

"Why does ale hate me?" I groaned, gripping the sides of my head as I rolled off my pillow. Cadets stirred around me, some already dressed and ready to tackle their day's challenges, while others, like me, groused about the sun's obnoxious early rising.

"Good morning," a familiar voice said with entirely too much enthusiasm.

I squinted up to find Ayden, fully dressed in his cadet leathers, gloves strapped beneath the epaulet on his shoulder, and a wide grin plastered across his annoying morning-person face. Even through crusty, sleep-filled eyes, Ayden looked like a town square's statue with his infuriatingly sharp jaw and brilliant eyes, and the way his tunic struggled to contain his chest and showed off his slim waist. Even the deep greens and browns of his uniform offset the fiery curls that fell across them.

No one should look like that so . . . naturally.

In that moment, I wanted to stare at him and never move.

"I hate you," I mumbled, then covered my head with my pillow.

He chuckled. "Oh, no you don't. You hate yourself for drinking too much with Shira."

"How do you know—"

"Declan, really? You drink with her at least three times each week. You are too conscientious to drink to excess with your First Years, and you dislike most of your classmates. If you're grumbling like this in the morning, it means you were out with Shira."

"Not true," I said, tossing the pillow aside and leaning forward.

"Arsehole," one of the other cadets in a nearby cot called out.

"We hate the fluffy-headed fucker, too," another cried.

"My hair isn't fluffy. It's full!" I immediately regretted engaging with the enemy, as my fingers rose and vanished beneath an ocean of unruly curls standing at attention in all directions.

A chorus of half-hearted laughter and teasing jeers drifted through the now bustling hall. Flimsy straw mats lay empty atop rows of racks lining the walls of the long hall as cadets rose to dress and make ready for the day. For some reason, I'd become the center of attention without even raising my head.

I wanted to crawl back under my green-and-brown patchwork covers and hide.

"Nice chest." Ayden grinned as his eyes roamed my now exposed upper body.

Suddenly even more self-conscious, I yanked the sheet to my neck. I'd lived communally with dozens of men for nearly two years, and somehow this one man made a single comment about my nipples and I blushed all the way to my toes.

Damn you, Ayden Byrne.

"Okay, Prudence. I will let you dress in peace. The Lieutenant is already waiting outside to ferry us to the crossing. I would hurry, if I were you." Ayden turned and took a step, then glanced back. "I am thankfully not you, because you reek of ale."

With another smirk, he strode out of the barracks, leaving me clutching my sheet and nursing throbbing temples.

Ten minutes later, I stepped out of the barracks, shielding my eyes from the obnoxiously bright sun, who seemed determined to make me wither beneath her intense gaze.

"Rea, move. We're already behind schedule because of your drunk arse," our Lieutenant griped. Ayden sat on the back of the cart, one brow raised, a snarky grin on his stupidly perfect lips.

Spirits, I hated his lips.

And I wanted to taste them and lick them and—

"Rea, today!"

I nearly leaped out of my boots. "Yes, sir. Sorry, sir."

I hopped onto the side rail opposite Ayden and clung to the wooden bench as reins snapped and the cart lurched forward. Ayden sat with his back straight and chin high, like some royal about to survey his kingdom. The wind blew his hair just so, brushing it past his scruffy jaw, letting the sun set his crimson stubble ablaze.

"What are you staring at?" Ayden asked, cocking his head.

I startled and looked out at the passing town. "Nothing. Thought you had something on your cheek, that's all."

I could feel him grinning. The arse saw right through me. He had since the first day we'd met.

But rather than rub my discomfort in my face, he asked, "You ready for this?"

"For what?" My mind was clearly not on mission.

"Crossing duty," he answered. "This is our first time."

Each of the two other times we'd been assigned to crossing duty, the full Rangers were out front, handling inspections, making the calls. Today, they would sit back and watch us try our hands, only intervening if they noticed some threat we missed. It was a true test of how ready we were—or were not—to don green cloaks. This wasn't some training exercise. It was proper work performed by real Rangers every day.

I shrugged. "How hard could it be? We check to see if people are hauling what they say they are, then we stand aside. Senior Rangers will be watching. It's not like we'll be out here on our own."

"True." He nodded and stared into the distance. "Still, it is nice to finally be doing something real, something that matters."

I wasn't sure how much crossing patrol mattered, but, then again, it was the primary place citizens of Melucia and the Kingdom entered each other's countries—the honest ones, at least. I supposed those who harbored ill will would try to cross elsewhere along the thousand-mile chain that separated the two nations. How stupid would a bandit need to be to cross where there are the most Rangers possible?

Still, Ayden was right. We were doing something real. There was something exciting and new about that. I felt almost as though we really were Rangers.

As the crossing came into view, the first thing I noticed were the caltrops. Standing taller than my head, the X-shaped wooden braces bore sharpened points facing the Kingdom border. The line of them stretched from one side of the trees to the other, with only a small opening to allow travelers to pass once inspected. On the road that led from the Kingdom, several wooden barriers were placed on either side to force carts to slow to navigate back and forth, preventing anyone from racing forward and punching through our defensive line. I questioned what cobbler or chicken Merchant might try such a feat, but it was standard border protocol.

A team of eight Rangers stood watch at the line. Less than a quarter mile away, another twenty were housed in barracks built specifically for crossing guards. There were more men in green cloaks in this quarter-mile area than anywhere outside of Grove's Pass.

Now there were two Second Year cadets added to their number.

A barrel-chested Ranger whose face looked like it had seen the business end of a caltrop strode up. A forest green cap poorly hid wispy strands of brackish hair. He bore the same Lieutenant's chevron as the man sitting in the front of our cart. "These the rookies of the day?" He glanced back and scowled, though the scars on his face made it hard to tell scowl from smile—or any other expression.

"You know it. That's Rea, and that's Byrne."

The scarred man's brow tried to rise. "Byrne? As in Lord Byrne?"

Ayden's head lowered. This happened more times than I could count, virtually every time we met someone new.

"The same. The little lord is yours to command. Enjoy it." Our Lieutenant glanced back. "Byrne, Rea, get the fuck out of my cart and don't let barbarians invade my country. Got it?"

"Yes, sir." As we made to climb down, I noticed Ayden avoiding eye contact with our officer of the day. He'd lost his usual humor, and a sternness had settled into his eyes. I was fairly certain that had nothing to do with the duty we were about to perform.

The moment our feet hit the ground, the cart jolted forward, then spun about and headed back down the road toward town. Ayden and I turned to face our duty officer.

"Here's how this'll work," he said, his voice somehow rougher than his face. "You two take point. That means you'll inspect every cart, horse, buggy, and fuckin' handbasket. Nothin' gets by without your eyes on it. Understand?"

We nodded.

"Good." He eyed a cart currently being inspected by a team of four Rangers, then turned back to us. "One of you will stay with th' driver, while th' other inspects. *Never* leave a driver alone, and never let their hands touch th' reins."

He paused again.

We nodded again.

"There's an entire team behind you. If ya ain't sure, don't let 'em pass. Get one of us t' help. Don't fuck this up. Got it?"

"Yes, sir," we said in unison.

"Questions?"

Ayden didn't hesitate. "Are we looking for anything specific, sir? I heard rumors of kidnappings."

"Keep your voice down," the Lieutenant snapped, leaning in. "You want to panic folk?"

"Uh, no, sir," Ayden said.

"Ask 'em what they're carryin'. Check for anythin' not disclosed. Anything different. And yeah, look for women with gags stuffed in their mouths and ropes around their wrists. That would be a fuckin' clue. Now get to th' line an' do yer damn job."As he marched away, I heard a muffled, "Fuckin' rookies."

I glanced to Ayden, but he still stared after the Lieutenant, his jaw set with defiance and fire blazing in his eyes.

"Here we go," I said, nudging him forward.

Four hours passed.

Four endless hours.

We stood and waited.

We paced the length of road we'd been assigned, only to have the Lieutenant bark at us to return to the exact spot that marked the crossing, as though walking ten paces to the north might allow someone to race past unchecked and threaten the safety of the Empire.

Ayden fumed, but I was too bored to care.

One cart and one horse passed through the checkpoint. The cart carried potatoes and beets, and the horse bore only its rider, a messenger carrying letters to Huntcliff.

We chatted quietly about what might come through, who might try to trick us, and we played games trying to come up with scenarios of how we might handle a barbarian invasion. There hadn't been barbarians on our continent in four thousand years, but it was a fun game to pass the time. Ayden was confident he could shoot faster than I could strike with my sword. He was probably right.

We stared into the trees.

We watched the road.

We chatted with the Rangers assigned to babysit us.

And we tried to remain upright, though everything in my feet and legs screamed for a chair or bench or boulder, anything that let me toss off my boots and rub my aching toes.

By the time we were allowed to step away from the crossing for a late midday meal, any excitement I had felt over doing "something important" had evaporated into the mountain air.

"Spirits, this is boring," I said, stabbing a piece of stringy meat I assumed was heavily seasoned boar.

Ayden nodded as he washed down a bite with water. "I expected a lot more traffic."

That was an odd answer. How would he know how much traffic there should be crossing to and from our neighbor?

He must've heard me thinking.

"My father is one of the Chief Merchants in the country. Trade flows freely between our house and the Kingdom. House Byrne alone sends dozens of carts per day across the border, yet we have seen three in four hours—and none of them bearing the owl of my house. Something feels off about that."

I chewed my meat, wishing we'd been served anything but shoe leather for lunch.

"You think too much. Maybe it's just a slow day."

He stabbed a potato and pointed it at me. "And you think too little. We are supposed to have our eyes open here, always seeing, always studying. Rangers notice what others miss. It is how Melucia remains safe. I merely point out an anomaly that disturbs my senses."

"It disturbs your senses?" I grunted, somewhere between a laugh and chuckle, the most a full mouth allowed. "My Lord Byrne, how ghastly. One must never disturb his lord's precious senses."

He scowled and glanced away. I'd hit far too close to the mark, it seemed. Shit. I actually hadn't been trying to offend him that time.

"Ayden, I'm sorry—"

He turned back, a dark look in his eyes. "Thank you, but I have had enough of my heritage being mocked for one day. You know I cannot help being born into my station. It is my lot in life, as everyone else is born into theirs. By now, if you do not know I try to be a good man and use my privilege for ... helping others ... perhaps, you do not know me at all." He rose, gathered his plate and tankard, and stepped out of the mess hall, leaving me alone at the table staring into what remained of my boar.

By the time I returned to the line, Ayden already stood watch. The senior Rangers lounged twenty or so paces behind, some sitting in the bed of a cart, while others stood smoking cherry-tobacco in their pipes and chatting quietly. They appeared unfazed by the numbing boredom of their duty or the apparent lack of inspections required that day.

We stood in silence for a half hour.

Ayden never once looked in my direction.

Waves of anger flowed off him, like he was the epicenter of a dying sun.

"Ayden, please. Look at me." I kept my voice low, to not attract the attention of the senior Rangers. They didn't need to know we were squabbling.

"I have to watch the road. It is our job, remember." Ayden didn't so much as glance in my direction.

"Please, stop." I gripped his arm.

He shrugged me off, but finally met my gaze.

The ice in his brilliant blue eyes stabbed through me. Regret crept up my spine.

"Ayden, I really am sorry. I know you aren't your title. I mean, you are, or will be, but that isn't who you are. At least, it's not all you are." I ran a hand through my hair. "Dammit, I'm mucking this all up."

He waited, and I swear his lips twitched, though he was careful to remain perfectly still otherwise.

I looked back into his eyes and made a decision.

It was time to be honest.

He needed to know.

"Ayden, I need to tell you something, and I don't know how to say it or what you'll think or . . . Spirits, I don't even know what I think about it. I'm so confused, and it's eating me up inside, but I can't keep this to myself anymore. You've become . . . I mean, you are . . . Fuck, Ayden, I can't stop thinking about—"

"Cart!"

The crack of the Lieutenant's voice sliced through anything I was about to say, and both our heads snapped up. A lone horse pulled a wooden cart with two men in the front, each wearing mud-colored robes that shimmered faintly when sunlight found its way through the leaves. Each man—I assumed they were men by the width of their shoulders—also wore strange masks. One in the form of a horned bird, the other a heavily tusked cat.

"Fuckin' Children," one of the guards griped loud enough for me to hear.

A known quantity then. That was reassuring.

As the cart drew closer, the occupants became clear, and far more disturbing.

"Are those—?" Ayden asked.

"Yeah," I whispered back as I nodded. "The same as those men in the woods, the ones with the woman."

"And the magic."

I shuddered at the memory of unseen icy fingers gripping my throat, at gasping for air and knowing my end was near. My hand rose to rub beneath my collar.

Ayden rested a hand on my shoulder, as if sensing my disquiet.

"Be alert," he muttered. "The men behind us are standing now, hands on hilts. Even the Lieutenant is on his feet."

I nodded once, keeping my eyes on the cart's driver.

As the cart rolled closer, I could see these weren't the same men as those we'd encountered on the mountain. Their masks were heavily detailed but of a different mix of animal and bird from those we'd seen before, the driver's bearing the likeness of a snorting bull with the wings of some massive bird. But it was the men's eyes that truly caused my heart to seize. Orbs of onyx glared through holes, scanning, never settling. They were the same lifeless eyes we'd seen so many weeks before. When they landed on me, it felt as though invisible hands ran along the length of my body—searching for what, I couldn't guess.

Ayden stepped forward and raised a palm. "This is your inspection. I have the driver."

I nodded and took my position to the side of the cart while Ayden stepped up beside the driver.

"Hold. Where are you headed, and what's your business crossing the border?" Ayden summoned the authority of both his Cloak and House as he spoke.

A low rasp answered. "We are Children returning home."

"Children?"

"Yes. We are *her* Children."

Silence lingered before Ayden asked, "What's in the cart?"

"It is empty," the driver hissed. "We sold our silks and now return for more."

Ayden eyed the man a moment, then nodded toward me. "My partner will need to inspect your cart. Please remain seated with your hands well away from the reins."

The driver nodded and folded his hands in his lap.

I stepped around, scanning the sides of the cart, then the wheels, not entirely sure how wheels could tell me anything useful but knowing it was part of the routine. When I got to the back, I lifted the latch that secured the lid, then raised the lid over my head.

Sunlight brightened the insides of the dark, empty box.

A few wisps of stray straw had gathered in the corner, and a few pieces of lovely white silk cloth lay rumpled to one side. Otherwise, the cart was empty.

I rapped the wooden floor, checking to ensure there were no hidden compartments. It would be our luck that the senior Rangers would send a cart through with all sorts of hidden contraband just to test our thoroughness. I refused to be tricked.

And yet, something about this cart felt . . . odd.

I couldn't hear anything, but I could feel something, as though gentle waves of wind flowed into me, one after the next, and I shivered at the overwhelming sense of being watched.

"Done yet?" Ayden asked.

I held up a hand without looking up. "Almost."

I leaned down, as if to listen closer, bracing myself with a hand on the side. The moment my hand touched wood, my whole arm vibrated. The sensation ebbed as quickly as it began, as though someone had kicked the side of the cart. The waves of air surged, and I pulled back.

I scanned the space again.

There was nothing there.

I was imagining things.

I nodded to Ayden.

He smiled up at the driver, who had remained a statue throughout the inspection. "Going home empty-handed, it seems. That is not always a bad thing. Be careful in the mountains. We have had several traders go up and not return recently. Safe travels."

Chapter Twenty-Two

Ridley

Atikus, Liv, and I rode out of Saltstone's southern gate toward Freeport. Atikus's Gift had already proved useful when he sent word to the Freeport Guild that we were on our way, asking them to make preparations with a few of the local mages. Unfortunately, Telepathy's one-way nature limited the conversation, and the Freeport Mages couldn't respond or even acknowledge the instructions.

The other unfortunate element working against our team and our mission was time.

Even while traveling along Melucia's well-maintained roads and pressing our horses for speed, the trek from Saltstone to Huntcliff would take at least thirty days. By the time we arrived in the southern port town, the trail would be as icy as the border in winter, so said Atikus as he sat astride his horse puffing rings from his pipe.

Nearly a month after we'd set out from the capital, the outskirts of Huntcliff came into view. Summer was yielding to an early fall, and the breeze off the bay carried more than a hint of crispness. Liv and I rode comfortably in our heavy

Guard cloaks, but Atikus had to wrap several blankets about his thin frame to keep from shivering. He claimed his joints had predicted a severe winter, and swore they were never wrong.

We trotted directly through the center of town, slowing as the central home of southern Mages rose before us. In contrast to the marble majesty of the Mages' Compound in the capital, this simple wooden structure appeared as humble as the Merchant quarters in which it nestled. A rudimentary carving of the phoenix adorning the wood above the door was the only indication the place belonged to the men and women of magic.

As we approached, a young boy in a dusty-blue Mage-Apprentice robe took our horses while a snow-topped man stepped out to greet us.

"Mage Atikus Danai, in the flesh!" The man beamed.

"Pel, it has been too long." Atikus returned the warm smile and clasped arms with his brother-Mage, then stepped back.

"Let me introduce our illustrious team: Guardsman Ridley Doa and his associate, Guardsman Liv Went. I know Lord Crim requested the best Saltstone could offer, but we're all you get," Atikus added with a theatrical wink.

Pel nodded to Liv and me. "Thank you for coming. We appreciate your help. Come, let's knock the dust off and put some whiskey in."

Atikus's eyes brightened. "That whiskey sounds wonderful if it might also come with a side of pork. I'm starving, and I'll bet you've never seen anyone eat like young Ridley here. I imagine he's ready to chew on his horse after a month in the saddle. It's a good thing your young groom took the poor animal away before he could do any damage."

Liv shot me a glance, but I simply shook my head and smiled.

As we entered, Pel glanced over his shoulder. "I'm sure you'd like to clean up a bit before supper, maybe even change. That should give the cook time to get something hot on the table. Why don't we meet in the dining hall in, say, thirty minutes?"

I nodded and spoke before Atikus could offer another of his weak jokes. "That sounds great. Thank you, Mage Pel."

We turned down one corridor, then another. Pel never broke stride.

"How big is this place?" Liv whispered.

"It looked tiny from the road," I said.

Atikus glanced back with a grin and a cryptic reply. "You two haven't been around Mages much, have you?"

Pel finally stopped before a simple wooden door. "Who's up first?"

I stepped forward.

"Your room, good sir." Pel bowed, the smile never leaving his cherubic face.

The others continued down the hallway as I stepped inside.

The room was basic, but comfortable, especially after the time spent traveling. Ever the Constable, I took a moment to inspect every corner. Finding nothing unusual, I turned to the washbasin on the table and was surprised to find warm, almost steaming water. I pressed a wash rag to my face and let the water soak away our month-long ride as I rinsed off and changed out of my Guard uniform and into a pair of tan trousers, a simple white shirt, and a blue coat. The team had discussed the need for some discretion while investigating in the port city and decided that both Liv and I should wear civilian clothing.

Answers would be easier to get out of people if they weren't intimidated by a uniform bearing the capital's crest.

A knock on my door startled me out of my thoughts.

"Ridley, you ready? Atikus and I are walking to the dining hall," Liv called.

I opened the door and froze. I'd known Liv for over a year, since joining the Guard, and couldn't remember seeing her wear anything other than leather leggings and a navy cloak. "Liv, wow, you don't look like a Constable anymore."

"Was that a compliment?" She smirked, glancing down at a sage dress that clung to curves I didn't know hid beneath her Constable's garb. "I hate this thing. Makes it hard to ride and even harder to run, but it should help us blend in. We can play the husband-and-wife routine, and Atikus can be our doting grandfather."

"Hey! Let's make that *father*, young lady." Atikus wiggled his bushy brows before turning toward the dining room.

"Sure, Pop. Whatever you say." She poked him with her elbow.

Atikus chuckled as I shook my head, something I'd done a lot over the past month.

The smell of roasted chicken drifted to us as we entered the dining room. A wide variety of vegetables covered the center of a long table that sat alongside two similar tables. Light-colored paneling and candles in silver brackets created a welcoming, almost cozy atmosphere. The flame on each candle flickered with the same magical blue I had seen in the braziers of the guild in Saltstone, though I'd never seen it atop a candle before.

Pel and two other Mages entered through the opposite door and greeted us. The only conversation that survived the start of the meal was that of a fork and knife arguing over a piece of chicken. I was exhausted and starving; still, I couldn't remember roasted chicken ever tasting so good.

Pel must have noticed the rapture on my face. "So, Constable, do you find our cook acceptable?"

It took me a few seconds to chew then wash the bite down with ale. "If I didn't know better, I might think someone used magic. Mage Pel, this is the best meal I've had in a long time."

"Oh, but magic *was* used in your meal." Pel beamed. "Our cook has a unique Gift that none of us quite understand involving enhancement of flavors. He can't alter what something tastes like, but he can accentuate what is already there. That's why we call him Salt."

"Salt? I like that. Funny little guild. I might have to trade in my uniform for a robe if this is what guild life is like." I stabbed another potato.

"We have our moments—and you would be welcome."

We finished the meal with a blueberry pie that made my eyes roll backward. Atikus, perpetually consumed with thoughts of food, never spoke as he focused on crushing his meal as though it were an enemy army. He was licking blueberry juice off his fingers when he noticed the group staring at him.

He turned to Liv. "Dear daughter, I believe you've embarrassed us with your table etiquette."

Without missing a beat, and in a tone nearly as sweet as the pie had been, Liv replied, "Oh, dear *father*, the blueberry clinging desperately to that beard of yours might tell a different tale."

I spit a mouthful of ale, and the rest of the table's occupants devolved into joking and fits of laughter.

When everyone had eaten their fill, Pel's expression sobered as he turned to his old friend. "So, Atikus, I understand you're here asking after Bel. She's a sweet girl. I've worked with her since she was a young thing, helping her learn to navigate her Gift."

"I suppose we should talk business." Atikus leaned forward and pressed his elbows into the table. "Ridley, you're leading this investigation. Why don't you start? We can jump in as we have questions."

This wasn't our rehearsed introduction, but I appreciated the way Atikus deferred to me despite my status as a cadet.

I opened a leather journal and leafed through a few pages. "I've read the reports from the local Constables. They did a decent job with what little they had but didn't find much. Has the guild learned anything new since you were alerted to our visit? It has been more than a month since her disappearance, so anything you might remember will be helpful." I paused, then added, "Oh, one more thing, do any of your Mages have a Gift that might help us locate Bel or recreate her route?"

Pel nodded. "Yes, but the information we gathered was not obtained by any magical means. Unfortunately, it isn't much. A girl on staff who was a close friend of Bel stepped forward. She said she saw Bel leave through the back door of the Hall and walk down the alleyway that runs behind the buildings, parallel to the main road."

"That doesn't make any sense." I sat back.

"How so?" Pel asked, his brow knitted.

"The local Guards have a witness who said she walked Bel out the *front* door and watched her go down the main road. That was around 18:00."

Another Mage chimed in, "The main road is well lit and usually filled with people walking about, especially that time of day. Even with magic, it would've been difficult for someone to take Bel without anyone seeing something."

I made a note, then asked, "What about the back way? The alley?"

"The alley is quiet. Nobody goes back there, really, except for the Merchants who own the buildings nearby, taking out their rubbish, that sort of thing." Pel scratched his chin. "It's mostly unlit and backs up to a large wooded area."

I scribbled again.

Liv and I peppered the Mages regarding the alley, the businesses along the route, and who else in the guild might have seen Bel and lied about it. After an hour, Atikus stretched and yawned, his motions full of purpose and impossible to miss.

I fumbled with my papers, closing the leather journal. "Mage Pel, you've all been most helpful. Thank you. Would you mind if we resumed in the morning? We have had an endless journey, and I'm sure we could all use a good night's rest."

"Of course," said Pel, with a nod of his head. "We'll help in whatever way we can."

I turned to Atikus and Liv. "This has my mind racing, and I won't be able to sleep. I think I'll go walk the alley and see if anything jumps out. Why don't you two get some sleep so we can start early in the morning?"

"At this hour?" Atikus asked. "It's pitch black out there."

I nodded. "I'll have to go back when there's light, but this will at least give me a feel for the place."

Everyone rose and took their leave while Atikus tried to sneak another piece of pie from the table. Liv turned with a grin, speaking loud enough for all to hear. "Pop, Ma would never let you have another piece this late. You know how gassy you get."

Laughter echoed in the dining room as we walked out.

I escorted Atikus and Liv to their rooms, then went outside, where I found a bin with torches. The back of the Guild Hall opened to a tightly packed alleyway. To one side, a densely wooded area ran the length of the alley. Thick pines and gnarled oaks cast shadows onto the dirt path. The back sides of shops lined the side opposite.

The guild sat apart from the row of shops, and I had to walk some fifty yards before reaching the first one. From there, narrow buildings were packed together like children's blocks with only inches of space between them. This was the most upscale Merchant area in Freeport, where the elite came to shop and dine, but the backs of the shops looked the same as those in the poorest neighborhood. Flecked paint, chipped wood, and overflowing bins gave the alley a grunginess that wrinkled my nose almost as much as the smell of rotten food in some of the bins.

The alley appeared to be infrequently traveled. With each step, I watched the path grip my print and hold it. Tracks would remain if undisturbed. The ground was hard-packed and dry. I didn't think there had been any rain in the last couple of days.

I walked past a door marked *Cobbler*, then *Moira's Naughties*, then *Men's Grooming House*, before reaching a door that read, "*Gil's Royal Tailoring*," in faded black script. This was the last place Bel had been seen.

I searched the outer wall of the building, then held my torch up to the space between the building and its neighbors on either side. There wasn't enough room for a person to squeeze through, and nothing looked like it had moved in years.

A rat scurried into the shadows.

I turned toward the woods.

There was nothing remarkable, and the trees were just as still as when I first strode by. I stepped to the edge of the path and moved slowly, carefully examining the ground before taking each step. A few yards further down from the shop's door, deep grooves in the dirt headed off the trail. The tracks didn't continue onto the forest floor, but broken branches and disturbed leaves led in that direction. I kneeled to get a closer look, and something glinted in the torchlight. I brushed loose leaves away, revealing a ring. Curious, I picked it up and turned it over in the torchlight. It was a golden signet. I couldn't be sure without checking the crest with the Mages, but my gut screamed that it belonged to this missing victim. She must have dropped it for someone to find, leaving behind the only clue she could.

Good girl, Bel, I thought as I stuffed the ring into my pocket.

There was nothing else of note in the brush, or at least nothing else that could be found in the dark, so I decided to return in the morning with the team. My mind raced. The leads weren't much, but they were more than we had a few hours ago.

The next morning, Atikus, Liv, and I were greeted in the dining room by spicy smoked bacon and biscuits, platters of eggs, and an assortment of fruit and nuts. Pel was already seated, attacking an overfilled plate that struggled to contain a sampling of everything. Atikus snatched a plate from the stack and began forming his own mountains.

As the group ate, I filled them in on what I had found during my walkabout, then turned to Pel. "Would you ask the local Guard to return to the rear of the tailor's shop with an experienced tracker and see if they can follow the wheel marks I found? That may give us an idea of the direction the kidnappers went."

"Shouldn't they have found them in the first place?"

I wanted to laugh. Of course, that was the case. The locals had done a shoddy job from start to finish, but I couldn't afford to say so and maintain any hope of receiving their support and aid. I kept my expression smooth and said, "Possibly, but that doesn't matter. The only thing we should focus on right now is finding Bel and bringing her home."

"Of course, you're right." Pel wiped his mouth with a napkin as he stood and motioned to a serving boy. "Let me send someone to do that right now, before any rains come in and ruin tracks." When the boy left the room, he turned back to me. "Let's talk about that ring you found. I know the Saltstone Mages failed to learn anything with their scrying, but I'd like to try again using that ring. We don't have a focus tower like they do, but I believe an item that was so highly personal to Bel might yield more information."

"Anything you find will be more than we have right now. Atikus?" I raised a questioning glance at the old Mage.

"It's worth a try. When our Mages used the scrying bowl in the tower, we didn't even get a ripple, much less a picture. They believed Bel was alive at the time based on the energy given off by the items, but something was blocking their Sight, and they couldn't break through. Even if we can't pinpoint a location, the ring may at least confirm if Bel is still alive." He thought a moment. "Pel, I would like to help with the scrying by linking with the Mage performing the spell. With my Telepathy and strength, we may be able to break through whatever is shielding us."

"That's an excellent idea." Pel nodded. "We'll need to make some preparations. Meet me in the lab in an hour. You remember where it is?"

"The one thing I can't remember is the last time someone asked me, 'Do you remember?'" Atikus snorted as his eyes glittered with amusement. "You forget that I can't forget, even the things you've forgotten."

Mage humor. Hilarious, I thought as I rolled my eyes.

The group disbanded, and Atikus explained that the scrying would take about an hour to prepare and then another two to complete, so Liv and I decided to pursue other lines of inquiry in the meantime. We began with interviews of both the serving girl who had revealed Bel's backdoor departure and the young apprentice who'd lied about showing Bel to the front door. The latter was in tears, horrified that her deception might've brought harm to her friend. She explained that Bel was meeting her parents for dinner, so she'd sneaked out the side door to visit the tailor's shop. She'd wanted a new gown for the occasion, hoping to surprise her parents. She had asked the apprentice to cover for her.

Through her tears, she managed to say, "I wanted to be a good friend. What if she's dead now? What if I killed her?"

Neither Liv nor I had answers. Even when the girl finished crying and composed herself, she had little else of use to add.

Both interviews were dead ends.

We retraced the back-alley route, searching for clues I might have missed under torchlight. When we reached the tailor's shop, Liv walked over to the ruts in the dirt and began following them into the woods. In daylight, we could see that the trees were old and towered over the town. They were also spaced several paces apart, allowing their roots to spread and intertwine. The floor of the forest was mostly leaves, dirt, and the occasional shrub, leaving a visible path of wheel marks.

After a few minutes, Liv returned. "The locals should be able to follow those tracks. That should give us some idea of which direction they headed. I doubt we'll get much more than that."

"That might be useful if this case is actually linked to the missing Healer in Saltstone."

"I can't see how it is," Liv said.

"Honestly, neither can I, but we don't have enough to rule anything in or out at this point," I said. "All right, let's go talk to the tailor, see what they remember."

We made our way to the front of the building and entered a door that led into a small brightly lit shop filled with the scent of leather and incense. A stout, graying woman with thick spectacles shoved atop her head and a tangle of measuring tape around her neck greeted us. "Please come in and make yourselves comfortable. I'm in the middle of a measurement, so look around a bit. I'll be back in a few moments." Then she vanished into the back.

With little to do but wait, we strolled around the tiny shop. The walls were lined with dresses and coats, displaying what might be possible for Freeport's wealthiest customers. Nearly a half hour after we entered, the woman who'd greeted us returned and curtsied. "Please forgive the wait. It's the busy season for us, and so many young ladies are getting married. Now, young miss, is that what's brought you my way?"

I chuckled a little too loudly at the brightness of Liv's blush, earning a raised brow.

"On, no, ma'am," Liv said quickly. "We are here on official business. Guard business."

"Oh, my goodness! I just assumed, with your fine dress and handsome escort, that you were a couple. I hope I haven't stepped in something." She smoothed her dress and began fidgeting with a thimble that materialized from her pocket.

"No, ma'am." Liv smiled and softened her voice. "Not at all."

"Oh, good." The woman's eyes darted from Liv to me. "So, what's this all about? What would the Guard want with my shop?"

"Do you recall making a dress for Bel Crim recently? She's the daughter of—"

"Lord and Lady Crim. Oh yes, I do. Of course I do!" She nodded, nearly losing her glasses in the process. "I remember just about every dress I make. And Lord Crim, well, that family has been a customer for years. They're very good customers. Horrible business, Bel going missing and all. Just terrible."

Liv sat and motioned for the woman to do the same. "Tell me about Bel, about the dress you made for her recently."

"We spent hours together, just the other day, even brought in a hairdresser. She was so excited. Couldn't stop babbling about some dinner she had that evening. I wasn't paying much attention. She's such a sweet girl, but you must understand, Bel Crim could talk your ears off. You don't think her going missing had anything to do with my shop, surely?"

"No," Liv reassured her. "We don't think so, but we're talking to everyone who saw her the day she went missing. Would you mind telling us about her visit that day? We never know what little detail might fit with other things we've learned."

It took the dressmaker a moment to gather herself and recount the events of that day. I was impressed with the level of detail she recalled, down to the stitch patterns Bel preferred, but there was nothing surprising—or particularly useful—in her recitation, other than that Bel asked to leave through the back door rather than the front. She said she wanted to avoid running into her parents and ruining what she called, "her grand entrance."

Liv stayed with the dressmaker as I spoke with her assistant in the back of the shop. She confirmed the same series of events and became emotional talking about Bel's disappearance.

"Any read on either of those two?" I asked as we strode back to the Guild Hall.

"I think the shop's a dead end, other than the tracks and the ring."

I couldn't argue, which meant we had nothing new to go on—unless the Mages had managed to find something.

It was lunchtime when we stepped through the humble door of the Guild Hall, so we headed straight for the dining room, confident our older partner would be holding court before any plate within range of his lanky arms. As expected, Atikus, Pel, and two other Mages were already devouring mounds of food. Atikus used his fork, still saddled with a roasted turnip, to motion for us to sit.

"Father, we met the most skilled seamstress today. Perhaps, after all these wonderful meals, she might let a little room out of those robes of yours. I believe the twins are kicking down there." Liv poked Atikus in the ribs as she sat next to him.

Pel was so caught by the comment that a piece of turkey shot out of his mouth and smacked Atikus square in the forehead. The room erupted. The next half hour was spent eating and laughing, the group having bonded over what Pel dubbed, "the great flying turkey incident."

As the plates were cleared, Atikus turned to me. "I'm afraid we were successful in our efforts with the ring."

"Afraid? That's great. Why don't you sound happy about it?" I asked.

Pel stepped in. "We were successful in creating a scrying link using the ring. We could sense Bel's presence and even ascertain a general direction and distance of her whereabouts. As hope rose of learning her exact location, the link snapped. Worse, the ring's aura faded and winked out."

"I'm sorry, Pel. My Gift has nothing to do with scrying. I haven't done it before and haven't spoken to many who have. Can you explain what that means?" Liv asked.

He nodded. "When an item is personal to someone, it often takes on some of that person's aura. The longer it's worn or used, the stronger the pairing of the auras becomes. In simple terms, the ring's natural aura, which is very weak to begin with, is replaced by a linked version of Bel's aura. Think of it as a mirror of her own."

Pel cleared his throat. "She had worn the ring only a few days earlier. It was a family heirloom with deep significance to both Bel and her family. Their auras weren't simply connected; they were intertwined. What we witnessed in the scrying was Bel's life force fading. Her location and distance were still hazy, but we know one thing for certain: Bel is dead."

Liv and I sat back in our chairs. Our shoulders slumped.

Our mission was to locate and *save* the young woman, yet here we were on day two of our search, and she was dead. It was hard not to let frustration and disappointment overtake us.

Pel spent the next hour explaining the process of scrying and the information they had gathered. I listened numbly; it was hard not to take each explanation as an accounting of our failure. Bel had been taken from Freeport and traveled west to somewhere beyond the mountains at the border, where we assumed she was killed.

Pel and his Mages excused themselves, allowing Atikus, Liv, and me to discuss our next steps alone. It took me a few long moments to set aside remorse and focus on the future. We'd known our mission bordered on impossible, especially starting a month following the kidnapping, but still . . .

"Atikus, would you mind sending word directly to the Arch Mage and Keelan? They'll want this information right away," I said.

Atikus placed a fatherly hand on my shoulder as he rose and excused himself to send the message, preferring the quiet of his room for such a task.

We decided to let the local Constables inform Bel's parents, concluding there wasn't any point in remaining in Freeport. It was just a couple of hours past noon, and we wanted to start home before the sun set.

An hour later, we had gathered our packs and thanked our hosts. Pel presented each of us with a small bag of provisions that Mage Salt had prepared for our ride home. Atikus grinned like a schoolboy as he stuffed his bag of goodies into his saddlebags. By 16:00, we were on the road headed north, each dreading conversations that waited at the end of our journey.

Chapter Twenty-Three

Tiana

I woke from a fitful sleep surprised to find I was no longer in a cramped prison but laid out on a bed of pine needles and leaves beside a small campfire. Both my wrists and ankles were secured by ropes that scored angry lines across my skin.

The crisp air was thick with the scent of mountain pine.

As my mind cleared, I glanced around to find the cart just off the dirt road, tethered to a tree by a heavy rope. The horses and masked men were nowhere to be seen. In fact, I couldn't hear anything other than the sounds of a forest at night and the soft crackling of the burning wood.

I tested the ropes on my wrists and sighed as they refused to budge, then turned my focus to the rope around my ankles. I wiggled my foot and bent it as straight as I could. After a few moments of uncomfortable squirming, my left foot popped free, followed by my right. I stared at the rope as it slipped to the ground.

My heart stilled, then began to pound.

My eyes darted about the clearing, sure blackened eyes watched my every move.

But none did.

I was alone.

Blinking at my now unbound feet, barely believing my good fortune, I tried to stand. The world wobbled. A thousand needles pricked my skin and nearly sent me toppling to the ground. I braced myself against a tree and waited for warmth to return to my legs before attempting to move again. It felt like an eternity before the itching faded and I could move freely. Even then, my ankles throbbed and my shoulders ached.

Wasting as little time as possible, I stumbled into the forest.

My mind raced with images of everything I was running from: the robed men, the rolling coffin, the endless possibilities of how the journey might end if I couldn't free myself.

What do those men want with me?

Where were they taking me?

Tears streaked my cheeks.

The glassy eyes of the masked men seemed to stare from behind every tree.

My skin pimpled against the chilly breeze.

Twigs lashed my arms and face.

I felt none of it.

I was *free*.

It was dark and tough to navigate, but slivers of moonlight peeking through the ever-shifting forest canopy guided my way.

I'd made it a half league from the campfire when I heard someone clomping through the forest. I scurried toward a few large boulders and threw myself behind the largest stone, tucking into a ball as the rustling grew closer.

My breath caught as torchlight illuminated the clearing, and I thought my heart might leap out of my chest.

I was hungry, weak, and cold.

After an eternity in a box, then racing through the woods, my breathing labored. I tried, but it wouldn't settle.

"Whoever's there, come out now and you won't be harmed," a stern voice ordered.

I tried to hold my breath and remain still. I would *not* go back in that box; they'd have to kill me first.

After a moment, the man's voice darkened. "Don't make me come back there. Rangers don't like surprises in our mountains, especially after dark."

I sat up and peered over the top of the boulder, finding a man wearing the deep green cloak of a Ranger standing before me; but as I gained my footing, two of the robed men blundered through the foliage, panting heavily from their chase.

Terror stabbed at my chest.

I ducked back down and pressed my body against the cold stone.

The Ranger's bow drew back, its distinctive cry I knew well from my youth. Then he spoke, "Stay where you are. What are you doing in the woods after dark—and why are you wearing those masks?"

"We lost one of our own," one rasped. "A young woman. She wandered from our campsite some time ago, and we are . . . worried for her safety in these dark woods."

I found some sliver of courage and peeked over the boulder. Only the top of my head and eyes were visible. I hoped the shadows kept me hidden. If they were coming for me, though, I had to know.

My breathing had steadied somewhat, but I struggled to control my shivering.

The second my head appeared above the boulder, the Ranger sensed movement. His eyes darted toward me, locking with mine. Unsure, I ducked back down.

The Ranger hesitated only a second. "I've been patrolling these woods all night and haven't seen anyone, but it's a wide range. She could be anywhere. I can help you look for her, but it will be morning before I can get more of the Rangers to join us. From the looks of your robes and shoes, you're not dressed for a mountain search anyway."

"We cannot return without her," the robed man insisted.

"She'll be cold by now—and lost. I'll go back to the station and get my pack, along with some medical supplies and a blanket. I know this mountain well and can cover it quickly. You two will slow me down more than help. Go back to your camp and wait. I'll let you know when I find her."

After an eternity of silence, I heard the robed men's footfalls as they returned the way they'd come.

I stirred, but the Ranger whispered, "Stay where you are. They stopped nearby and are watching to see what I do next. I don't think they saw you."

I froze.

Drained by exhaustion and fear, I pressed my forehead against the stone and closed my eyes, hoping the masked men would leave quickly. The idea of either of them spotting me, of the chance they might recapture me, was almost more than I could take.

The Ranger continued his faux search of the area, kneeling as if asking the forest floor for answers.

The rustle of pine needles.

The crack of twigs.

The soft thudding of his steps.

Then nothing.

The men did not come back and demand I be handed over.

They didn't return at all.

Another twenty minutes crawled by before the Ranger's soothing voice drifted over the boulder. "They've gone. You can come out now."

I untangled my tight, sore legs and stood, peering over the boulder to find the Ranger watching, his bright eyes assessing. A deep green cloak drooped off his lanky frame, and unkempt hair the color of spilled ink sprouted from under a murky brown cap. A quiver of arrows rose over one shoulder, and a long knife in a weathered scabbard dangled from his belt. A bow lay propped against a tree nearby.

"It's okay, miss. Come on out. I'm Ranger Wilk. Donovan Wilk."

The cautious, protective voice inside my head vanished as I hurtled from behind the boulder and blundered into Wilk, knocking him back a step. He had to wrap his arms around me just to stay upright.

I pressed myself close and began sobbing uncontrollably as the last of my control slipped away.

"Miss, you're safe now. Easy," a startled Wilk whispered. "Tell me what's going on. I need to know what we're dealing with before it tries to deal with *us*."

I startled as the Ranger pulled his dagger from its sheath and reached for me.

His brows rose, then he motioned toward the ropes binding my wrists.

I closed my eyes and breathed out, willing calm I didn't feel to enter my body and mind, then held out my arms so he could cut me free.

"Thank you. Spirits, that hurt," a distant, unfamiliar voice escaped my lips as I tried to rub life back into my hands. I was startled that I didn't even sound like myself. My throat was raw from crying, and my tongue was so dry it rasped like sandpaper against my teeth. The sleeping draught they'd given me hadn't likely helped.

"Please take me somewhere safe. There are three of those men. They kidnapped me as I was walking home. I've lost track of how many days have passed because they kept me drugged in the bed of a cart." I shuddered at the first memory of waking and realizing where I was. "It feels like we've been riding forever. I woke up about an hour ago by a campfire, and the cart was there, but the men weren't. I tried to get away from them, but I don't know how far I can go on my own. Please, *please*. You have to help me."

He eyed me a moment, testing the truth of my words, then nodded once. "All right. My station's not too far from here, up this mountain. It's not the easiest climb, but I'll help you up. I want to hear everything, but not until we're back at the station. Last question for now. What's your name?"

"I'm Tiana."

"Tiana, everybody calls me Donny. Well, that's what I think the animals call me. They're about all I see these days." He chuckled with an awkward, oddly comforting smile. "Let's stay quiet until we get to the station, okay? I'll snuff the torch to make it harder to spot us. My Gift is Night Vision, so we'll be fine without it. Just stay close and follow my steps."

As Donny led me on a winding trek through the forest, my mind raced. I thought I saw robed men everywhere, stumbling twice when I heard some animal fleeing our approach.

Donny reached out and took my hand after the second stumble, guiding me forward. He was clearly at home in these mountains; still, it took a little more than an hour to make it to a tiny cabin on stilts Donny called Station Twelve. Safely inside, I fell into a chair and my sobs returned, a storm of emotions overpowering me.

Once the clouds opened, the true storm raged.

Donny grabbed a blanket and gently wrapped it around my shoulders, then placed his calloused hand on my arm while using his other to lift my chin.

I didn't mean to flinch at his touch.

"Tiana, you're safe now. I promise. Just try to breathe while I start a fire and make us something hot to drink. Don't make yourself sick with crying."

I wanted to be angry.

How condescending was it for him to tell me not to cry? After all I'd been through, a good cry was exactly what I needed;

but I couldn't find the will to be angry with the boy in the man's uniform, with his kind eyes and lopsided grin. He meant well. I knew that. Neither of us knew how to act following a rescue from cultist kidnappers.

I placed my hand over his and whispered through tears, "Thank you, Donny. Thank you."

Donny had saved my life; I was sure of it. I was grateful in a way words could never fully convey.

By the time he'd hung a pot of water over the flames, I felt some of my old heart return. Strength had also returned to my voice. It no longer rasped or quavered, at least, not as it had when he'd first found me.

"I'm a Healer in Saltstone. They took me while I was on my way home from the infirmary a few nights ago."

"Saltstone?" He whistled. "The capital's a month's hard ride from here, a week more with a cart."

I replayed what I could remember of my journey through the drug-induced haze I'd endured. There were holes in my memory, but I pieced together what I could.

Donny listened without interrupting.

"After so many days in a traveling box, most would have given up," he said.

"I just wanted to be free of them." I yawned. "They never said why they wanted me or where we were headed . . . and they kept calling me Mistress."

"Mistress? That's strange."

I nodded and yawned again.

"Tiana, forgive me. You must be exhausted." He scrambled to his feet. "Why don't you take the bed. I'll keep watch while you sleep. In the morning, we can finish sorting this mess out."

I wanted to thank him again, but words failed as I crawled onto the bed and sank into the comfort of warm, heavy blankets. For the first time since being captured, I slept peacefully and dreamed of a quiet house with a picket fence and an old dappled mare.

Chapter Twenty-Four

Isabel

Anger burned through me as I nearly shook with rage.

Jess's performance had been outrageous, beyond any act of childish defiance to date. Her insolence threatened the very future of the monarchy, and fury resonated through my chest.

In contrast, the King stared into the rich wood of the table before him. He hadn't spoken or moved since the room had cleared. He hadn't even looked up.

My mouth twisted at his weakness.

Our guests had been dismissed to relax, be it in their quarters or with a stroll of the gardens, while servants cleared the table and retreated beyond the ire of their monarchs.

"I am going to wring her spoiled little neck," I fumed. "How could she show us up like that in front of two members of the Council and the Warden of the East? Does she have no clue what it means to rule, to be subject to the needs and whims of the nobles? Tongues will wag across the Kingdom before this week is done, mark my words. This will reflect on you, Alfred, on *us*."

Alfred's eyes closed as his weathered fingers pinched the bridge of his nose. "Issy, she was out of line stabbing the Duke like that, but did you see what he was doing all night? At one point, he practically *licked* her ear."

I shoved my chair back and stood, then paced a warlike path in the marble floor. "Alfred, don't you dare go there. Do you think *I* have never had to put up with a noble whose hands decided to explore into territory well beyond his reach? Or had to face the humiliation of a man looking down his nose at my judgement because I am *only* a woman?"

The King straightened and stared, his eyes wide.

"Are all men so naïve? Sweet Irina!" I threw my hands in the air. "Of course, I have. *Every* woman has. It makes me so angry I want to burn everything down, but it is the way of many men. Women understand it, and we learn to deal with it in our own way, in a way that maintains peace and order in the household."

My voice lowered from a near shout to a menacing growl. "What we *never* do is embarrass our King and Queen in front of the most important men in the Kingdom. Just one night we needed that little brat to see the bigger picture, and she couldn't do it. Just. One. Night." My voice rose, punctuating each word.

Alfred sucked in a breath and rose to stand before me, halting my pacing. He took my hand in his own and waited for my gaze to meet his. Then he spoke in a measured tone, as one hand reached up to brush my cheek. I wanted to recoil at his touch, but leaned into it instead. "My Queen . . . my love . . . if *any* man ever touches you the way the Duke touched our daughter, promise me you won't 'deal with it in your own way.' Promise you'll tell me so I can see him locked in the tower while his offending hand is fed to our hounds.

"I am not naïve enough to think that men always behave well, but I will never allow *anyone* to dishonor you or our daughter—ever. Am I clear?"

My mouth opened, then closed.

I grasped at anger, but it slipped away as though I tried to hold smoke between my fingers. My husband's eyes held such passion and a simmering, protective rage, something I had thought long lost to years of marriage. A tear rolled down my cheek for the first time in years.

Alfred wiped the tear away, then pulled the hand he held to his lips and kissed it.

"None of these men are right for our little girl. The Crown can wait until we find the right match—a match who will offer her the respect and love she deserves. Besides, none of these men truly offer the Kingdom any new strategic alliance or advantage. Men of the Council? The Duke of Huntcliff? There is no risk of that weasel rebelling, save to fight against something squirming on his fork." He shook his head with a wan smile. "What were we thinking, Issy?"

I blinked away another tear. "My King is far wiser than his Queen."

"Nonsense." He smiled, and his eyes glittered in the lamp light. "My Queen gives me strength, unburdens my heart, makes me wise."

He kissed my forehead and drew me into his arms, then sighed. "We have had enough for one night. Let's get some rest and start fresh in the morning. We are young still, and Jess will not inherit the throne for many years. I do not know why we were in such a rush that we would ever consider Lord Piggy."

I snorted into his chest and slapped his arm. "Now who's besmirching honor, Your Majesty?"

"My dear, being a sovereign has its privileges. If I say he's Lord Piggy, then that is who he is," he said with a wide grin. "Sometimes it truly is good to be the King."

The next morning, as the King and I ate breakfast, a page scurried into the room and whispered into Alfred's ear.

His face darkened.

"Show them in at once," he said.

I set my fork down and gave my husband a sharp, questioning gaze, but before he could respond, Chancellor Thorn, Minister of War Bril, and Sheriff Wilfred marched into the room.

"Your Majesties," Thorn began through a hasty bow. "Forgive the interruption, but this couldn't wait for Council this afternoon."

"It's all right, Danai. What is it?"

Thorn nodded to Wilfred and Bril.

The Sheriff fixed his eyes on the King and spoke, "Your Majesty, we know some things with certainty, and we suspect others. I'll start with what we know."

Alfred crossed his arms. "Get on with it."

Wilfred's head bobbed as he cleared his throat. "As you are aware, four Gifted have been kidnapped from various locations throughout the Kingdom. Chancellor Thorn and his Mages worked closely with my team to ascertain some pattern for the kidnappings but came up empty. Both men and women were taken, their Gifts varied widely, and each individual was stolen from their home city or town, which are hundreds of miles apart. We traced the victims' families, some of which were prominent, others not, some wealthy, others poor.

"We found only three common threads. First, each victim was Gifted. Second, every trail we could follow led east. Finally, brown-robed members of the Children were seen by witnesses in two of the four cases." He paused, but Alfred remained silent.

"Based on these facts, and some witness statements, Chancellor Thorn and I believe the victims are being taken through the mountain pass into Melucia."

"What?" Alfred nearly shot out of his chair as I leaned forward. "Melucia? Surely you do not think the Melucians—?"

"We don't know enough to be sure, but that is exactly what we fear," Thorn said. "Whether it is some group within their country or the government itself—"

"The Triad? You think the Triad is kidnapping our Gifted?" Alfred's gaze darted from one Councilor to the next.

Bril cleared his throat, drawing the monarch's eye. "Sire, our border forces posted at Huntcliff have reported an unusual level of activity by Melucian Rangers in the mountains. Some time ago, they began a new practice of stopping all caravans passing through the mountains for inspection. Two Merchants interviewed said they had never been stopped and inspected before, and that the Rangers appeared to be anxious and looking for something specific."

"Do you think our caravans are at risk? Were they threatened?" Alfred asked.

Bril shook his head. "There were no explicit threats, but in each case, Rangers handled the inspections. Heavily armed men stand guard while others conduct their search. We've never seen such measures by the Melucians and have no idea what sparked this escalation. On the advice of the Merchants' Guild, we have ceased all outbound trade through the pass until we can better understand the situation."

"Halted all trading?" Alfred muttered.

Thorn barreled forward, "Your Majesty, it is reasonable to assume the two situations may be connected, that the Melucian Rangers had knowledge of the kidnappings and were searching for our missing Gifted."

My chair creaked as I leaned back, one brow raised. "That is quite a leap, Danai. For all we know, there was theft and they are simply being cautious. Our patrols would do similar, would they not?"

"Of course, Majesty, we certainly would." Wilfred beat Thorn to respond. "I would agree with Her Majesty if we had not also received reports of unusual movement of the Children along the pass. Nearly a dozen robed men were seen going to and from Melucia during the same time period. In my years as High Sheriff, I have never seen a single report of that faction traveling abroad. They are rarely seen traveling beyond their compound in Irina's Seat."

Alfred steepled his fingers and mused, "After a thousand years of peace . . ."

I frowned.

After another moment of silence, Alfred asked, "Recommendations?"

Our Minister of War was normally reserved and rarely spoke at Council but didn't hesitate on this occasion. "Yes, Your Majesty. We recommend full closure and reinforcement of our eastern border. The Third Infantry and Sixth Archery divisions are posted nearby and could be repositioned within the week. There's already a complement of scouts stationed near Huntcliff. We should increase patrols in the mountains and gather intelligence on Melucian numbers and movements, focusing on their Rangers. Additionally, we recommend a team of engineers be dispatched to assess the structural defenses along the border. Both Huntcliff's walls and those of our defensive forts require attention."

"There has been no need for defense for centuries," Alfred said.

"Are you sure we shouldn't just invade?" I broke in, unable to hold my tongue.

Thorn took a step forward. "Your Majesties, these are our *scaled down* recommendations. Many of our Council preferred a more . . . how should I say this . . . robust approach."

"Has anyone simply *asked* the Rangers what they are looking for?" I asked.

"Of course," Thorn snapped, quickly adding, "Your Majesty." He eyed the King before continuing. "They have yet to reply to our messages."

"What is it, Danai? I can see you still hold something back," I pressed.

"Our spies in Grove's Pass have missed two reporting intervals. One miss is uncommon, but happens on rare occasion. Two? That has never occurred. *Never.*" His head lowered. "We fear they are lost."

The room held its breath as the King pondered.

Finally, he nodded once to Bril. "Fine. Do it—the reinforcements, defensive fortifications, and increased patrols. But, gentlemen, keep these suppositions quiet. If questioned, this is a training exercise and nothing more. I do not want the country rallying to war before we even know what is truly happening."

"Yes, Your Majesty," Bril said, his head bobbing crisply.

The three men exited, leaving Alfred and me staring at each other in disbelief. A moment passed before I reached for my tea and took a sip. The delicate porcelain of the cup and saucer rattled in my quivering hands.

"I just hope one of those scouts doesn't get nervous and take a shot at a Ranger. One frightened soldier could bring a thousand years of peace to an end—and there would be nothing we could do about it," Alfred grumbled.

He was worried, I thought, and for good reason.

Chapter Twenty-Five

Jess

Danym led us to his home on the eastern end of the city. Despite his position in the King's Council, his father was a humble man, preferring to let his performance as High Sheriff impress rather than the size of his manor. Danym guided us around to the back of the house, revealing a barn at the far end of a large grassy field. Once inside, we removed our saddles and brushed the horses out. The ride from the forest had been uneventful, but we were exhausted, both physically and emotionally. I helped feed and water the horses before Danym and I headed to the house.

"My father won't be back until late. There's something going on that he won't talk about, but it's big enough to make him work long hours, sometimes overnight. We can get a good night's rest and leave before sunrise," he said.

My mind still reeled from our escape in the woods.

I reached over and took Danym's hand as we walked. The tangle of our fingers was a comfort. When we entered the house, I was surprised to find the outside was matched by an equally modest interior. We passed through a sizeable sitting room with comfortable chairs. On the wall above the hearth was the head of a deer crowned by a giant rack of antlers. The deer's eyes stared accusingly, and I looked away to escape its scrutiny.

We entered a bedroom, and Danym bowed. "The royal suite, Your Majesty."

I chuckled, letting the beautiful boy's antics calm my nerves. "None of that. Remember, we're trying to *not* be recognized. We have to forget titles, maybe even come up with different names until we're safe somewhere."

"You're probably right, but you will always be *my* princess." He gave me a peck on the cheek before backing out of the room and closing the door.

I sat on the neatly made bed and scanned the room. I couldn't stop replaying everything in my mind: the smugness in Mother's eyes as her peacocks paraded through the Throne Room, the smell of the Duke's breath as he whispered against my ear, the feeling of his oily hand on my skin, insinuating his intentions should we ever be alone.

I shivered despite the warmth of the room.

Then my mind turned to the robed men in the woods and the frantic flight that led me into Danym's arms.

Who were those men, and what were they doing in the woods?

Had they been waiting for me?

I hadn't even known I would be out there. How could they?

It might have been chance. Perhaps those men were up to their own sour deeds and spotted me by chance, recognizing me as a princess whose ransom would be worth a lifetime of petty crimes.

That might've been a logical explanation, but it didn't feel right.

They wore those strange masks.

I understood the need to hide one's identity better than most, but to pick something so hideous seemed insane. The thought made the men's eyes flash before me—dull, lifeless eyes that stared at everything and nothing, like the deer mount in the sitting room.

Perhaps they *were* insane.

I suppressed another shiver.

Trying to calm myself, I focused on simpler things: getting ready for bed, brushing my hair, the simplicity and comfort of routine. I pulled back the covers and climbed into bed, reveling in the fluffy warmth of its multi-colored quilt. As I drifted off to sleep, the tenderness of Danym's smile overtook my dreams.

Hours later, I woke to a gentle tapping at the door. I rubbed my eyes and stretched, finally surrendering the warmth of the comforter to answer the incessant knocks. Danym had one finger over his lips when I cracked the door and peered through.

"My father came home a couple of hours ago. He should be asleep, but we need to be quiet," he whispered.

I nodded and closed the door. After changing into riding clothes, I made the bed and checked the room, erasing any sign I had slept there. The last thing we needed was for the Chief Constable of the country to spot something amiss and spoil our escape.

Once satisfied, I grabbed my bag and padded into the hallway where Danym waited. We hurried out of the house and raced across the field, the grass crunchy and wet with morning dew.

When we reached the barn, Dittler danced but overcame his excitement at the sight of an apple in Danym's hand.

"I know," I told the horse, remembering how he'd tossed me to the ground and fled into the woods. "You were scared. I'm not mad. You didn't mean to hurt me."

Dittler calmed at my words and snorted. His eyes were wells of brown, deep and mournful, and it felt like he was trying to apologize. I gave him a kiss on his velveteen nose before moving on.

As we saddled the horses and strapped bags into place, Danym turned. "Are you *sure* you want to do this? To leave? You're going to be the next Queen. Running away may make your father think twice about your place in the succession."

It took a moment to gather my strength and meet his eyes.

"I can't go back, Danym," I said, my voice as small as I felt. "I need to be free to make my own future, my own choices. Nobody outside our family sees the invisible chains attached to the Crown. When I was little, I wanted to be Queen more than anything, to rule over a glorious nation, but I've seen what ruling does to my father—what it's doing to my whole family. I can't wear those chains. I just can't."

I tried not to think of my brothers.

I was sure they would be fine, even Justin—*especially* Justin. He was made to wear the crown. He would do better than I ever could.

Danym took me in his arms and held me close, kissing the top of my head. "You don't have to go back. I'll help you be free. I'll keep you safe."

We stood there for a long moment enjoying the simple peace and comfort of an embrace. Finally, he stepped back. "So, where would Your Majesty like to go?"

I smirked at his continued use of my title. "Let's think this through. We could follow the coast through Clude and Oliver, maybe to Cooper on the Hook. I love the tiny villages with their dirty beaches and brilliant sunsets, but Cooper is the only town of any real size west of the Spires. I'd probably be recognized the moment we passed through."

"We can't give anyone a trail to follow. Let's rule that out for now," he said.

I nodded. "That leaves the King's Road through the Spires toward Spoke, or east to Featherstone on the northern coast."

"Please, not Featherstone. My father talks about pirate raids from Riz and how his teams struggle to keep the peace along the coast. The thought of having to fight our way to freedom is almost as scary as staying here," he said.

"Agreed." I stroked Dittler's neck. "So that leaves the King's Road. It's pretty heavily traveled, but that might actually be good. There'll be more people to blend in with, and it should be well patrolled. We'll be okay as long as we can get some distance between us and the capital before anyone realizes I'm gone."

"The King's Road winds through the Spires, and those are some cold mountains. Taller than any others in the land, too. We'll need better gear and warmer clothing if we're making that trip. Why don't you keep Dittler company while I go back into the house for a few minutes?" He turned to walk out of the barn.

"Danym," I said, causing him to turn back as he stood halfway through the open door. "I just want to say thank you. You saved me from more than you'll ever know."

"No, Jess. You saved me, and you don't even know it." He smiled and closed the door behind him.

Dittler snorted, and I let out a sigh, resting my head against his strong back. "I know, Dit. He really is amazing."

Barely a heartbeat passed before Danym burst back through the barn door, struggling to catch his breath. "We have to go. Now! There are two of those robed men poking around the front of the house. We can cut through the neighbor's field and worry about the mountains when we get to them."

He helped me mount Dittler, then walked to the back of the barn and opened a sliding door.

When we got to the neighbor's rickety fence, Danym dismounted and took a hunk of meat out of his saddlebag. My questioning gaze was quickly satisfied as a giant mastiff thundered toward us with globs of saliva flinging from the hound's flopping jowls.

"Let's hope he doesn't bark. He can make the mountains shake with his howl." Danym half whispered, half shouted, "Timber, come here, boy! Treat!"

At the mention of the T word, Timber bolted forward. I released a breath as he accepted the bribe and a scratch behind his ears as he chomped. When a silent peace had been established, Danym dug into his saddlebag, retrieved a large meaty bone, and dropped it before Timber to keep him occupied.

"Let's go," Danym said, climbing back atop his horse.

We'd nearly made it through the neighbor's field when a man called out, "Over here! I've got fresh tracks."

Danym spurred his horse into a gallop, and we raced through the neighbor's gate and onto the main road, urging speed from our mounts the moment their hooves struck firmer ground.

The sun had yet to make an appearance, and the quarter-moon offered only milky light.

When we finally reached the Cathedral of the One, the last major landmark before crossing beyond the borders of Fontaine, I slowed Dittler to a halt.

"We shouldn't stay here long. The sun's coming up, and people will start showing up for morning prayers," Danym said.

"I know," I said. "But Dittler needs a rest. He's blowing hard, and your horse looks even worse. We should find water for them, too."

We walked the horses in a wide arc around the Cathedral, pleased to find a wooded area that shielded us from view. I fed the horses while Danym retrieved a bucket of water we'd spotted near the Cathedral's hitching post.

"They really love you." Danym's voice held wonder as he watched both horses eating out of my hand and nuzzling my shoulder.

I smiled and rubbed Dittler's ear. "I adore them, and they feel it through my Gift."

"Really?"

I nodded. "Unlike with people, they can't hide their emotions from me, and I can't shield mine from them. There's a purity in that openness. I know that sounds silly, but that's how it feels. It's honest in a way people never are."

"People . . . other than *us*, right?"

I turned back to find his brow raised. "Yes, other than us."

The King's Road crossed from one end of the Kingdom to the other and was wide and well maintained once travelers made it past the Spires, but within the shadow of the mountains, the road was narrow, winding, and often covered in ice. From our vantage behind the Cathedral, we could see the western leg of the mountains, and I already felt a chill in the air that heralded the onset of the infamous northern winter.

Danym noticed me staring at the frosty peaks. "That's what we have to pass through. Are you sure you still want to go through with this? Last chance to change your mind."

"No turning back." I packed as much confidence into my words as I could. "They're beautiful."

"Tell me that after a few days of riding through them." He smirked. "All right, here we go. It should take about an hour to get to the base of the mountains, then another seven or eight days to Spoke."

"That long? I've never made the trip, but it doesn't look that far on my father's maps."

"It's not that far, but the road winds up and down, around and through. You'll see. It's a challenging trip, and we risk laming the horses if we push too hard, especially in places where rocks or limbs have fallen onto the road. In another month, snow and ice will cover everything, and it'll be impassable."

"Well, good thing we're leaving now. Lead on, my dear boy." I waved in a commanding gesture.

Danym gave a half bow from his saddle. "Yes, Your—my lady."

Chapter Twenty-Six

Alfred

What should have been a peaceful morning chaperoning Jess and her suitors devolved into a circus of activity. I had spent much of my time in my sprawling study, staring at detailed maps spread across a large table, as an endless flow of Generals and advisors streamed through to offer updates or advice. Minister Bril, General Marks, and Chancellor Thorn buzzed around me like angry hornets waiting to sting anything that met with their displeasure.

Zumi Bacras, Minister of Foreign Affairs, joined the discussions around midday and objected to every word uttered by the military leaders. "Your Majesty, none of my envoys have reported anything beyond peaceful trade and negotiations. There has been no talk—not even a rumor—of hostilities by anyone. Please, let me go to Saltstone and speak with the Triad, see what I can learn before we shatter over a thousand years of peace."

"If war is coming, we can't give up the initiative. The Minister could tip our hand and give away a significant advantage," Bril said.

"I agree with Minister Bril." Marks nodded. "If it comes to a fight, I'd rather hit an enemy who is ill prepared. Anything we do beyond readying our troops will give them time to dig in and fortify, possibly even rally the eastern border nations to their side."

Bacras snorted. "The eastern nations barely maintain Constables. They spend their days squabbling over fishing rights and whose Gifted farmers raise the largest cows. They wouldn't know what to do with a sword if you handed it to them."

Thorn wormed his way into the debate. "Their magic makes them powerful. We have no idea what Talents they may have developed. Our Mages in Saltstone have monitored the research of their guild, which has been conducted in concert with their military command. It is troubling, Majesty. We have nothing to match what they can do with magic."

"Gentlemen, that's enough." I had listened to this argument for hours. My head was throbbing. "No one is going to war. We're repositioning a few units to conduct military *training exercises*. These are war games, nothing more, and the fields near the mountains are the perfect location for those exercises. There is no need to engage in any peace talks because we're not doing anything unpeaceful."

Bacras pressed, "But we are, Your Majesty. In your twenty-three years on the throne, we have *never* conducted war games. At least let me notify the Triad of these exercises and their peaceful intent, allay any fears sparked by our troop movements along their border."

I looked to Bril.

After a moment's thought, the Minister nodded. "That might actually work to our advantage, Your Majesty. If they think the games are peaceful, they won't try to respond or prepare when they see the buildup."

"Minister Bril, these are peaceful *defensive* maneuvers. Period. No more talk of war. Is that clear?" I snapped, then turned back to Bacras. "Send word to our Ambassador in Saltstone of the exercises but say nothing of the increased patrols in the mountains. Our scouts need to see what's going on, and I don't want the Rangers masking their movements because we've tipped them off."

"Yes, Your Majesty." He bowed low and backed out of the room.

As the door closed behind Bacras, Justin appeared in the doorway.

Isabel, who had been watching quietly from a chair at the opposite end of the conference table, rose to intercept our son.

"Justin, not now. We're very busy." She reached to stop him.

"Mother, it's important, and I don't think it can wait," he said, standing his ground before the most powerful men in the Kingdom—and the most feared woman.

I noticed the exchange and held up a hand, silencing the room. "Justin, come here."

Isabel scowled but stepped aside to allow the Prince to approach. "What is it, son? I don't think you've ever interrupted the Council, and you look terrified. Take a breath and tell me what's going on."

Justin's eyes darted up, then fell to the floor. "Father . . . Jess is gone."

My head cocked. "Gone? What do you mean, son?"

"I think she ran away."

I glanced at Isabel. Her scowl had darkened as her eyes flared.

"Run away? Why do you think that?" Even as I asked, my heart sank. Justin would know Jess's movements as well as anyone in the Palace. He was her closest confidant.

Justin handed me a folded note. "I found this on her pillow. None of the staff have seen her today, and the guards are acting weird."

My forehead creased as I read the note, then slid it down the table to Isabel.

As she read, I barked at a page. "Bring the Throne Room guards immediately . . . and call the Captain of the Guard."

The page gave a quick head bob and scurried out of the room.

All eyes turned toward Isabel as she read aloud.

Justin,

I'm sorry to leave without saying goodbye, but I can't do this anymore, and I didn't want you to have to cover for me. Mother will never let me be happy, and I won't marry Huntcliff, no matter what they say.

Father may take the crown away from me for this, which means you will have to do more than you

*ever wanted. I'm sorry for that, too, but you will
make a great king, one people will look up to and
love.*

I hope we can see each other soon.

Please know how much I love you, little brother.

Jess

The Queen hurled the note across the map-strewn table. "I really am going to wring her little neck."

"Can we make sure she's *safe* before we start plotting her death?" My icy glare silenced her.

None of the Generals or Councilors dared speak.

The page returned with a Palace Guard sporting golden epaulets.

"Captain, I presume you know the Princess is missing. What have you learned?" I asked.

The man offered a crisp bob. "Your Majesty, the two men who were on duty last night are not in the Palace. I've sent for them and expect their arrival shortly; but sire, I doubt my men will be much help. We are charged with keeping people *out* of the Palace, not keeping them in. Your daughter is . . . forgive me .

. . rather forthright. She rarely offers much explanation. She has not been seen since leaving the grounds late last night."

"Very well, Captain," I said, turning back to the page. "Send for the High Sheriff, and tell him it's urgent."

Isabel's eyes snapped to mine. "What do you want with *him*?"

"The Sheriff controls more watchful eyes than anyone outside of the military. Even if the local Constables maintain their distance, we can offer Jess *some* protection as she roams the countryside. The thought of her out there alone . . . It makes me sick."

"Uh, Father? She might not be alone."

I had nearly forgotten Justin was still in the room and turned toward him. "Who do you think she has with her?"

Justin stared at his shoes.

"She's . . . umm . . . well . . ."

"Out with it, Justin. We don't have time for this. Say what you know." Justin startled at the familiar sound of the Queen's whip-crack.

"I think she's with Danym, the High Sheriff's son. They've been seeing each other in secret almost every night for . . . a while." Justin spoke fast, as though that might lessen the blow of the words.

"You knew?" Isabel leaned across the table as though she might lunge at her son. "All this time, you knew?"

A battle raged in my chest as my heart warred with anger, fear, and pain. Anger at our son who'd held a secret that might risk our daughter's safety. Fear at the thought of Jess on the open road. And pain, so deep and twisting, at the knowledge of how far our family had fallen into disrepair.

We were royals. No, we were *the* royals, the ones all others looked to, aspired to be. We were the ideal. And yet, regardless of how hard we tried, we were so far from ideal.

My heart ached in that moment.

Justin stepped back, bumbling into Minister Bril.

"Right now, we need to focus on *finding* her." My gaze darted from Justin to Isabel. "There will be plenty of time to deal with who knew what later."

I took a deep breath, then began issuing orders. "General Marks, this isn't just some wayward girl; she is the heir to the throne. I want flyers with her picture distributed to every man in uniform. With the movements to come, their eyes may be as useful as any."

"Yes, Your Majesty."

"Chancellor Thorn, have your best scrying Mages search for her. Justin, take the Chancellor to Jess's bedroom and find something personal of hers, whatever he needs." I thought a moment, then continued. "Minister Bril, send word to the officers on the border to be on the lookout. Everywhere else, our men should observe at a distance; but if Jess makes it to Huntcliff, I want them detained. Under no circumstance are they to be allowed across the border."

Everyone stared.

No one moved.

"*Now!*" I snapped.

The room burst into a flurry of activity.

Justin took advantage of the chaos to leave before his mother could vent her anger in his direction again. Smart boy.

I took a seat at the table and slumped back with a heavy sigh.

"I pushed her away," I muttered to myself.

"What are you talking about?" Isabel asked as she sat.

My eyes didn't leave the tabletop as I spoke. "I've always been closer to Jess than anyone else. Our bond is special. She's my heir, after all. She's the only person in the world who will truly understand the weight of the Crown."

Isabel bristled, but I was too lost in thought to care.

"To rule means committing to a lifetime of service to everyone else, giving up your own hopes and dreams for those of your people. The burden is . . . it can be almost unbearable. Anyone might crack." I wrung my hands, then met Isabel's gaze. "What baffles me is that Jess actually likes Council meetings, regardless of how long or tedious they are. Some days, she stays with me in the Throne Room and talks for hours, walking through what she's seen and how I handle situations. Spirits, she asks so many questions, especially when the Ministers go at each other. She calls that 'the old men's blood sport.'"

I shook my head, and a tight smile curled my lips.

"Issy, I know she's headstrong and volatile, but she's more mature and thoughtful than the boys, far more than *we* were at her age. I thought she was starting to understand—"

Isabel rose and placed her hands on my shoulders. "What are we going to do with her? Jess knows her responsibility, *her duty*. If she would run now, what would stop her from trying to escape the Crown in the future?" She spoke in a soft, almost pleading voice. "Maybe . . . one of the boys would be better suited—"

I stilled her words with a pointed glare. Debating how to parent was one thing. Tinkering with the line of succession was an entirely different matter, one I had no intention of entertaining. "She is still young. Unless you have some other plans, the Crown will remain ours for many more years. There is time to help her grow into the role. Spirits, I've felt like running away a time or two myself."

Isabel set her jaw. "But you didn't. You honored your duty to the Kingdom above your own desires, hopes, or fears. I am starting to think she may never put anything above her own desires."

Before I could respond, another page entered with High Sheriff Wilfred following close behind.

The Queen made to speak, but I patted her hand and stood, our private signal that I wanted to lead the conversation. I locked eyes with the Sheriff and held his gaze. When I spoke, my words were slow and measured. "Sebastiano, we have another situation. Jess is missing. We believe she ran away . . . and that Danym is with her."

The Sheriff staggered back, bracing himself on a chair. "Your Majesty, I just heard about the Princess but had no idea *Danym* . . . When I got home last night, he was asleep in his room. I checked before I turned in. Nothing seemed out of place."

I lifted the note from the table and handed it to Sebastiano. "This was found in Jess's room. It doesn't reference Danym, but Justin seemed to know quite a lot about the pair and their little rendezvous, far more than *we* knew. He believes they've become serious, and their relationship drove her to rebel against our betrothal efforts."

"I . . . I don't know what to say, Your Majesty. I would *never* encourage or condone—"

"We know, Sebastiano. We have no doubts about that. Our concern right now is locating Jess and Danym. We will figure out how to deal with the pair once we know they are safe," I tried to reassure the Sheriff. "General Marks and Minister Bril have the military angle covered and will be on alert at the border in case they get that far. How would you suggest we best use your Constables?"

"I'll send word to the Chief Constable in every town right away. Our resident Mage is a Telepath and can get the word out quickly. Every office already has likenesses of the royal family, but we'll work up a new flyer and get it distributed. We'll also increase our patrols on the major arteries," Wilfred said.

"Good. If Thorn's scrying turns up anything, we will make sure you are informed. Report to me immediately if you learn anything—and Sheriff, start with a thorough search of your house. We believe they left early this morning. If Danym slept in his own bed, as you say, Jess might have been somewhere nearby. That would at least give us a place to start."

"Of course, Your Majesty. With your permission, I'll get started now." The Sheriff barely finished before I nodded his dismissal.

Finally alone, I took Isabel's hand and pulled her into my chest, wrapping my arms around her and holding her close.

Please, I thought, *let her come home to me safe.*

Chapter Twenty-Seven

Declan

I stared as the cart rolled away and vanished around a turn.

"Declan? What is it?" Ayden asked.

I remained still, my gaze fixed on the last place where I could see the vehicle.

"That was well done." I heard the Lieutenant's gruff voice behind us.

"What is bothering you?" Ayden asked, not even acknowledging the Lieutenant's praise.

"I can see it all over your face."

I ran a hand through my hair and looked past Ayden into the woods. "I don't know."

The Lieutenant stepped between us then, facing me. "Did you see something?"

I shook my head. "No, sir. There was nothing in the cart. I checked several times, even tested for a false floor."

"What's the problem, then?"

I hesitated. "It just . . . didn't feel right. Something felt strange."

The Lieutenant's eyes began to roll.

"Sir, I know it sounds insane, but I swear—"

"Cadet, out here, you learn to trust your gut. It can save your life; but, if there was nothing in the cart, there was nothing in the cart. It's simple as that."

"Yes, sir," I said through gritted teeth.

The Lieutenant eyed me a moment longer, shook his head, then said, "You two, take a break. Be back in half an hour."

"Yes, sir," I said as the man strode away without waiting for a reply.

"Come on, I could use a drink," Ayden said. He gestured for me to follow him.

As we passed the group of soldiers who stood back up by the crossing, we could hear them laughing as the Lieutenant joked about the "jumpy" cadets and their imagined dangers. My head lowered.

"Great. The men already look at me sideways for the damn collar, now they'll wonder if I have something loose between my ears." I could feel embarrassed heat crawling over my cheeks.

"We already know that is the case. You *are* bat-shit crazy, Declan Rea," Ayden teased.

I barely glanced up.

"Come on, Declan. You know I jest."

"Yeah." I didn't have the heart to laugh.

We reached the wagon's flatbed. Nestled among the other crates of supplies was a massive metal pot filled with water. Ayden grabbed a ladle and filled two mugs, handing one to me.

"Thanks," I mumbled, raising the mug to my lips.

Ayden looked about and, finding no one within earshot, asked, "What was it about that cart that bothered you?"

I stared at my boots. "It's stupid. The Lieutenant is right."

"Stop that." Ayden reached up, gripped my shoulder, and turned me so we faced each other. "Talk to me, Declan. Tell me what you saw."

My eyes squeezed shut as frustration flowed through me. I felt stupid and embarrassed—and *sure* something was amiss—though I couldn't see through my own doubts how to resolve any of it.

"I didn't *see* anything. It's what I couldn't see that bothered me." I felt silly, but the sincerity in Ayden's eyes urged me on. "I don't know, Ayden. It felt like there was something there, just out of reach. As though . . . if I could just look closer or reach out, it would be there. At one point, I put my hand on the side to lean over, and I swear it vibrated."

"Vibrated?"

"Yeah." I nodded. "Like someone kicked the side. It was sudden and violent. I could feel it thrumming through the wood. I nearly jumped back, but I knew the guys were watching and didn't want to look foolish."

"Could you hear anything?"

I shook my head again. "No. Nothing but the forest."

Ayden thought a moment. "The men were pretty strange, too. Did you see those masks?"

I nodded but was lost in thought and didn't respond.

"I remember something about a group called the Children from my studies a few years ago, but I have never seen one . . . at least, not before today."

"You think that's who that was? The Children?"

Ayden nodded. "The man even said something like, 'We are Children headed home.' While you were searching the back, I was scouring my mind for anything I could remember from those lessons. All I could recall was that they wanted to bring Irina back."

"Irina? Queen Irina? The one who died, what, a thousand years ago?"

Ayden nodded.

"Why would they want to do that?"

"Who knows? Why do fanatics do anything? Blind allegiance to their faith? Following their leader? There could be a thousand reasons, none making any sense to the rest of us."

"Right." I was still a moment, then glanced up. "You believe me?"

"Of course I do." Ayden's lips curled upward, and he placed a hand on my arm.

My eyes fell to his hand.

My heart danced.

Heat flooded through my chest and up my neck.

My mouth went dry.

"Yes, I believe you. If you say you felt something odd, then there was something odd. You have good instincts and are an honest man." Ayden stared into the forest, not catching all the signs of my discomfort. "Although I am still unsure what you experienced. What you describe sounds like magic, but we would need a Mage to truly help us understand."

"Magic," I snorted, my voice dripping with derision. "No fear of that being involved, at least, not with me around."

"Declan—"

"Fucking Gift. Even out here, in the middle of nowhere, the damn collars find a way to shove themselves in my face. I hate magic, hate it with everything I have."

"I get it," he said quietly. "Even with my father's name, the Gifted nobles see me differently. It feels like . . . like they're watching a cripple struggle by. I guess I've learned to live with it, but still . . ."

"Exactly." I nodded, looking up to find pain in Ayden's eyes, a pain I hadn't noticed until that moment, a pain I knew too well. "I wish the stupid Phoenix would just fly away or die or whatever . . . just never come back."

A heartbeat passed, then Ayden's head shook as a smirk teased his lips.

"What's so funny? Don't tell me you're laughing at me, too?"

"I am not laughing at you. Neither of us has a Gift. Why would I laugh?"

"You've got that shit-eating grin on your face, the one you always have right before you make some snide joke."

Ayden's smile grew, finally reaching his eyes. "You know my expressions?"

I rolled my eyes. "You aren't exactly subtle, little lordling. So, out with it. What witty bit of wisdom do you have about the Phoenix for the poor little Mute?"

"Poor little Mutes? I like that." Ayden chuckled, flicking his own barren collar. "And the Phoenix couldn't truly die. She would simply be reborn from her ashes in a new form. You know that's how Phoenixes work, right?"

I crossed my arms like an angry three-year-old. "That's not funny, and it doesn't help."

"I thought it was funny, especially with you plotting her death."

"I wasn't plotting. I was *wishing*. There's a difference."

"Oh?" Ayden's brows raised.

"If I plotted, she might have a reason to eat me . . . or whatever she does when she's pissed."

Ayden laughed. "Eat you? The Phoenix. That's great."

"Oh, fuck off."

"I doubt she would do that either, no matter how handsome you are."

An uncomfortable silence stretched between us, as the possible implications of that comment sank in.

"Anyway," Ayden returned to the topic at hand. "We would need a Mage to help us truly understand what you experienced, assuming magic was involved."

I chuckled. "If we were in Saltstone, I know a few hundred men in blue who'd love to help."

Ayden stared, waiting, but I didn't say more.

His hand had remained on my arm throughout, forgotten . . . almost. I could feel the reassuring heat of his palm.

"So," Ayden said, his voice low, unsure. "You started to say something before."

"What?" I woke from my daydream of Mages back home. "Before that cart rolled up, you were going to say something. It sounded important."

"Oh." My cheeks flushed. When Ayden's hand fell away, my arm suddenly felt empty, like something was missing. "It was . . . um . . . nothing. I was just thinking, you know, about graduation, our postings . . . and stuff."

Ayden eyed me.

I dug both hands into my mop of hair and tugged. I wanted to be honest with Ayden now, to tell him everything I thought and felt, but my nerves were raw and my courage was well and truly gone.

"We should get back," I said. "Thanks for, you know, believing me and all."

I didn't wait for Ayden.

I nearly ran to the crossing.

Two hours after the sun fell behind the mountains and the autumn chill consumed the air, Ayden and I were allowed to return to Grove's Pass.

"Spirits, that was a long day," Ayden said, rubbing his neck as the cart rolled to a stop in the center of town.

"I don't think I can feel my feet anymore," I agreed. "And I think I could eat a whole cow. I've never been so hungry."

Ayden laughed. "Should I warn the mess hall? They might never recover. I have seen you eat."

I brandished a petulant finger, earning another laugh.

"I think the mess is safe. It's too late for them. By the time we get to the HQ, they'll be put away."

"The tavern, then? My treat?" Ayden asked.

My brow lifted. "Dipping into the royal purse? How could one refuse?"

Ayden punched my shoulder. "We have no royals in Melucia, but if you wish to address me as Your Grace, you may do so."

I snorted. "I've seen you fight. There's *nothing* graceful about you."

"Hey!"

I winked and darted across the road toward the tavern.

Raucous laughter and music greeted us the moment the doors opened. First Years mingled in small groups near the bar, while Second Years packed around tables at the center of the sprawling common room. Some laughed and ate, while others gambled with dice or cards. Green-cloaked Rangers huddled in twos and threes, mostly in darkened corners where the younger men and women were less likely to disturb them.

"Ayden!" one Second Year called the moment he'd entered. "Bring that fat purse over here. We need a sucker to donate to our very worthy charity."

The men around the one who'd yelled laughed and raised tankards in salute, shouting for Ayden—and his purse—to join them.

"Somebody's popular," I mused.

Ayden shook his head. "My coins are popular. Me, not so much."

He'd meant the comment in jest, I was sure, but there was something behind his words that pricked at my senses, something deeper.

"You want to join them?" I asked.

"No, I'm hungry, too. Maybe after we eat."

I nodded. "All right."

The only unoccupied table was wedged in no-man's land between the First and Second Years. Ayden begged off gambling and led us on a circuitous route to our table. A young girl flew by, leaving two tankards of ale in her wake and calling back, "My brother will bring your dinner in a moment."

I raised my ale. "To a hard day's work."

Ayden returned the toast, "To the Cloak."

Men around us overheard and mirrored Ayden's words. "To the Cloak," echoed off the walls. Even the full Rangers hiding in the corners lifted mugs at the centuries-old salute.

Those around us quickly returned to their games and drinking, leaving Ayden and me hungrily waiting for our promised meal. Thankfully, we didn't have to wait long. A rotund boy with sandy hair and pockmarked cheeks shoved through the crowd.

"Roasted chicken, potatoes, and green . . . something," the boy said, as he laid plates before us. "There's stew if you want some, but I don't know what's in it. Smells a little funny, if you ask me."

Ayden's nose wrinkled. "I will stick with the chicken, thank you."

I raised my fork. "Bring it on. I'm starving."

The boy nodded, then melted back into the crowd.

"After what he just said? You're really—"

I pooched out my belly, rubbing in circles. "Man hungry. Man need food."

Ayden shook his head and stabbed at the unidentified greens.

When we finished eating, Ayden was pulled into a game of dice. I stood behind him, my empty pockets unnoticed by the gamblers.

The rules were simple. Three dice were rolled. Any combination without a three turning up was a win for the roller. Any three displayed meant victory for those gambling against him. If more than one three showed up, the damages doubled or tripled. The entire game was a tip-of-the-hat to the Triad who ruled in Saltstone, and had been played for centuries by Guardsmen and Rangers alike.

A half dozen rolls in, Ayden had yet to stand a turn without hitting at least one three, doubling twice.

"You really suck at this," I said, laughing behind him.

"That's our little lord!" one man called as Ayden doubled again.

"Purse! Purse! Purse!" rang across the bar.

Ayden stepped back and raised both palms. "I am out."

A chorus of *boos* and *awws* followed his retreat.

Ayden threw his hands wide. "A Ranger must know when to withdraw."

Grime-covered cloth napkins pelted him from every direction.

"We'd better get out of here before your subjects rebel, Your Grace," I teased, my breath thick with ale.

Ayden allowed himself to be ushered through the pack of cadets and out to the road. A cool, brisk wind whipped our tunics, as a misting rain pelted our skin.

"When did this mess start?" I called over the wind, my stagger increasing to a trot. "Come on. Let's get back to the barracks before this opens up."

We ran across town, weaving behind buildings and down moonlit alleyways, nearly making it halfway before Ayden stumbled, his footing still unsure from his five tankards of ale. I grabbed for him, but he fell onto the dirt-packed cobbles and lay unmoving.

My heart thudded at the sight.

"Ayden." I leaned down and gripped his shoulders, turning him over. Mud smeared his forehead, but I couldn't find any cuts or blood. "Are you all right? Look at me. Ayden!"

Ayden's eyes opened and found mine.

The world froze.

My breath caught.

Ayden's hand rose, and his fingers trailed the stubble of my jaw, so gentle, yet firm.

I shivered.

I couldn't move.

I could barely think.

Without a thought, I leaned down, so close I could taste Ayden's breath, now rich with the ale and cherry from cobbler. Sweet upon sweet. I longed to taste everything, to feel him, to know—

"Declan," Ayden whispered, his voice hoarse and raw.

His hand sank deep into my curls, gripping my hair, claiming me.

My whole body tensed.

My heart raced.

Our lips were so close.

Lightning flashed in the distance, framing Ayden's face.

Copper curls fell limp about his shoulders, an aura of gold and flame.

His eyes sliced through the gloom, pearls of endless blue that pierced my soul.

Spirits, he's beautiful.

I gulped back fear, swallowed years of terror and longing, bit back every doubt I'd ever known.

Thunder clapped.

Ayden's fingers dug into my scalp.

I leaned closer, our lips and tongues now only a breath apart.

And the storm raged in earnest, dousing the alley and us with it.

I pulled back, gripped Ayden's shoulders, and lifted.

"Come on. Let's get to the barracks before we drown."

Chapter Twenty-Eight

Jess

Throughout our first days crossing the Spires, Danym and I barely saw any wildlife, much less other travelers. The road's elevation soared, and the air turned cool, then frigid. The leaves had fallen from the trees, masking the edges of the road and forcing our pace to slow further. Despite it all, my worries over Mother's reaction and our robed pursuers began to fade.

For the first time in my life, I tasted freedom.

Danym remained quiet.

At first, I thought he was simply being cautious, not wanting to be heard by anyone who might be on the road, but as distance between us and the capital grew, I suspected his silence was more thought than caution. He was always thinking, working through every possibility, planning for each unforeseen obstacle. His constant planning made me feel safe, cared for.

Our ninth day was brutal, as the road steepened and the air became thin. Danym struggled with the altitude more than me, and we had to stop often to rest. As the sun reached her peak, we pulled off into a small clearing that butted against a rocky cliff. Lunch consisted of flavorless dried meat, nuts, and the last of our bread, which had grown stale in the cool air. As we gnawed through our tough meal, my stomach grumbled at daydreams of steaming, freshly made bread from the Palace kitchens. While life in that place might've felt like a prison at times, the food was amazing.

The view beyond the cliff was breathtaking, with brushstrokes of azure clouds and snowy peaks in every direction. Standing on what felt like the edge of the world, I suddenly understood why the ancients had named their land the Kingdom of Spires. I couldn't imagine anything more beautiful and majestic than these mountains. Danym appeared and wrapped his arms about my waist, nuzzling my neck with his nose and playfully nipping my ear. I closed my eyes and painted a mental portrait of that moment—that *perfect* moment I never wanted to end.

When Danym released me suddenly, I opened my eyes, surprised by his absence and the way he squinted off into the distance. I followed his gaze down the slope of the cliff and spotted movement.

Two figures in brown wound their way up the road on horseback.

"I guess thinking we'd lost them was too much to hope for." Danym sighed. "Let's get back on the road before they get any closer."

"They're close," I said, my voice near breaking.

"Maybe a day back, I'd guess."

I couldn't think.

Terror I'd thought shed back in Fontaine strummed through me, a symphony of fear echoing through every corner of my mind.

Mother's face flashed in my mental vision, her mouth twisted in a sneer, her eyes burning with brilliant accusation. Then I saw the inky eyes of the robed men, lifeless and unseeing, yet missing nothing.

I couldn't decide which fate scared me more.

In one hand, I was a slave to the whims of the Throne, a tool to be used and sold when it suited some royal needs. In the other lay an unknown future, one where men with dead eyes and long-buried goals sought . . . what?

Would they also use me?

Was I a tool to them as well? A means to wealth or power?

Or did they seek something darker, some unspoken purpose that might cost more than . . .

I refused to accept that fate. I couldn't. My life was meant to be shared with Danym. I was meant to be happy, to be free, to grow old in his arms, safe and loved.

Numb, I turned to mount Dittler.

"We're about to start down the other side, and it'll be steep for a bit before leveling out, so we can't let them scare us into moving faster than the horses can handle. They might catch up a bit, but they'll have to slow when they get to this point, too." Danym patted his horse's neck as we resumed our trek.

The afternoon sped by, then the night.

The next day, finally headed down the other side of the mountain pass, we stopped to rest. Danym's lungs burned, and the horses struggled. I searched for another hiding place off the road but returned with a shake of my head. "There's nothing on either side but steep declines."

"It'll be okay. Just give me a few minutes to catch my breath." Danym lowered himself to rest against a tall pine. His cheeks and the tip of his nose were red from the wind.

I took the break to give each of the horses an apple, then poured water from one of our skins into a bowl and held it up to let them drink. They lapped greedily and nudged my shoulder in hopes of more.

"We'll find a stream, and you can drink as much as you want. Just hang in there a little longer," I said, stroking Danym's horse's neck.

Dittler huffed, his ears flicking with impatience.

The wind picked up, whistling an eerie tune through the trees. The air had grown even colder, and I shivered, wishing we'd had time to retrieve heavy furs before making our escape.

We mounted and continued downward for another hour before the sun began its rapid descent. We had to slow to round a sharp turn when something whizzed by. A loud *thunk* sounded, and Danym's head snapped up as an arrow lodged into a tree a few paces away.

"Jess, go!" he yelled, dropping any pretense of secrecy.

We spurred our horses, but the steep descent denied a quick escape. The sounds of hooves on gravel and men shouting grew louder as another arrow flew past. We were too far ahead for our pursuers' aim to strike true, but the whiz of arrows unsettled Danym's horse. His tail lashed angrily behind him, and he snorted and stamped, prancing and trying to rush forward.

Danym had to pull at the reins to keep him from taking off at a gallop.

The trees fell away, revealing sheer cliffs on either side.

I urged Dittler for speed, but our beasts were exhausted.

As we reached the end of the road, the forest faded and the town of Spoke appeared across a distant field. I spurred Dittler, begging him for one last push.

We were going to make it.

Three hundred paces to town, to the safety of high walls.

Danym cried out, "Jess, faster. They're right behind us!"

Fear gripped me.

Dittler shared my terror. I felt it through my Gift.

He whinnied loudly and pushed past his pain.

I glanced back as smears of brown crested the hill and began to grow larger.

Two hundred paces.

An arrow flew past, then another, then a third.

One fell harmlessly to the brush-covered dirt, but the second struck true.

Danym cried out, swaying wildly, fighting desperately to stay upright.

"Danym!" I screamed, unable to turn, to see if he remained in his saddle.

One hundred paces.

A voice ahead boomed, "Halt!"

Uniformed men gathered just beyond the edge of town, each with nocked arrows in longbows aimed directly at us.

"Help!" I screamed. "Help us!"

One of the men shouted a command, and the others fired high over our heads.

Horses screamed behind us.

After a second volley nearly hit one of the pursuers, our hunters turned and melted back into the forest.

I tried to slow, but Dittler was spooked and charged through the line of men. When he finally came to a halt, I looked back and realized Danym was nowhere behind, though his horse raced alongside Dittler.

There was blood in the saddle.

Panic seized me, and I yanked Dittler's reins, racing back to where the Constables stood over a prone body.

Danym lay face down with an arrow poking through his shoulder.

His tunic was soaked with blood.

He wasn't moving.

Two of the men kneeled as the third man turned toward me. "What's this all about?"

I ignored him, leaped off Dittler, and threw myself by Danym's side.

I couldn't lose him.

He'd left everything to be with me, to keep me safe. This was *my* escape, and now he might die for taking part in it. I convulsed with tears as I gripped his hand and pulled it to my chest.

"Danym, look at me. Please—"

"Miss, let us help him. The Sergeant's a Healer. Your friend should be okay if we can let our man work." He then turned to a third man. "Go get two more units. We need to chase those bandits down before they cause any more trouble."

The man gave a crisp nod and raced away.

I watched as the Sergeant took a thick-handled knife from a scabbard on his belt. One edge of the knife looked razor sharp while the other had a jagged edge. He pressed the serrated edge against the shaft of the arrow and sawed through it, taking care to not disturb Danym any more than necessary. "Sir, come help me turn him over. I need to get this arrow out before doing any Healing."

As the leader kneeled, the Healer handed him a palm-size cloth that had been folded several times and drenched in a sharp-scented liquid. "When I pull the arrow out, press this against the wound on his back. Hold it there until I'm done, and you"—he looked at me—"hold him down. This is going to hurt."

I kneeled and pressed my hands against Danym's good shoulder.

The Healer prodded the flesh around the shaft with the tips of his fingers, then gripped it.

"On the count of three. One . . . two . . ." He surprised me and yanked on two.

Danym shuddered, but the shaft slid free. The Healer tossed the arrow aside, then placed his palm above the wound. A dim glow traveled through his hand into the whole of Danym's shoulder.

Danym moaned and tried to roll over, but I held his weakened frame in place.

Midway through the Healing, six new men in uniform arrived. The leader dispatched three of them to hunt for the robed men and instructed the others to remain with the group.

The Healer finally rose, the glow fading from his palm, and a look of fatigue creasing his eyes.

"Thank you," I said, glancing up, my voice sounding as unsteady as I felt.

The Healer patted my back, obviously unsure how to respond. The leader chuckled.

While the Healer packed up, and the other men prepared to carry Danym into town, the leader pulled me aside. "We'll take you and your friend to the local inn and get you settled, but I need to know what's going on. Who were those men chasing you?"

My mind spun.

I hadn't thought about needing a cover story this early into our trip. Of course, we would be stopped by Constables or asked basic questions by innkeepers. How stupid could we have been? The Guardsman in front of me wasn't asking anything unusual, especially of someone he'd just rescued from bandits.

"I . . . I don't know. We saw them about halfway from Fontaine, up in the Spires. They tried to steal one of our horses. Danym wrestled the reins away and knocked the man down, but they didn't give up and chased us all the way here."

The man nodded but didn't say anything. He simply stood there staring, waiting for the rest of the tale. I had no idea what to say and decided to try something Mother once did to get out of a long, boring day at Court. I put the back of my hand to my forehead and feigned a dizzy spell, then toppled to the ground.

The Healer was by my side in a flash, waving a small bag of something vile under my nose. I sneezed and gagged. As I sat up on my elbows, the Healer checked my pulse and watched my breathing.

"She's exhausted but otherwise fine. Nothing a good dinner and night's rest won't fix." The Healer stood and brushed off his trousers.

"All right, let's get them into town. Miss, we'll want to hear more about your trip, but for now, we'll settle for your names," the leader said.

I paused a beat too long. "I'm . . . I'm Petti, and he's my brother, Gil."

The Healer and the leader exchanged a glance and a raised brow, then looked back at me. "All right, Petti, let's get you somewhere safe. My men will bring Gil on a stretcher."

Though reluctant to leave Danym, the thought of dinner and a bed was tempting. As I turned to mount Dittler, the Healer extended a hand to steady my climb, then let out a low whistle as he took in Dittler. "Only Cretian stallion I ever saw was carrying King Alfred through the countryside at the head of a column. Where'd you come by this handsome fella?"

Spirits, this is going to be a lot harder than I thought.

"He was . . . a gift," was all I said as I mounted.

"That's a *regal* gift!" he said in amazement, hitting far closer to the mark than I would've liked.

The leader signaled to two of his men to form up as an escort, and a moment later, we trotted through the heart of Spoke, the town often referred to as the Gateway to the Spires. It was almost dark, and lamps hanging from tall wooden poles were already lit, casting a dim glow across the dusty road. Most of the buildings and houses were made of rough logs with sharply sloped roofs designed to allow seasonal snows to slide off to the back. The people milling about were even less colorful than the rough-hewn wood of their homes, wrapped in simple hides and heavy furs.

I was shocked when we stopped at a three-story stone building, the largest I had seen since leaving Fontaine. A sign bolted into the wood above the double doors depicted a large black bird with its wings outstretched, and read, "The Crow's Nest."

A boy rushed out from around the side of the building and reached for Dittler's reins. When I resisted, the Healer stepped forward. "This is my nephew, Ben. He'll take good care of your horse."

"I will," echoed Ben, with a bob of his head so fierce it sent his shaggy hair fluttering. "Promise you that, miss."

Dittler eyed the boy and snorted.

I patted his neck, then reluctantly passed Dittler into the care of the youngster.

The Healer led me into a wide, open room typical of any inn across the Kingdom. Rough tables and chairs lay scattered about, and a grand bar sprawled across the opposite wall. Rows of colorful bottles lined shelves in front of a mirror mounted to the wall.

The leader stepped to the bar and greeted a short, round woman with enormous ears that reminded me of a comical mouse whose illustration I'd once seen in a book. The innkeeper gave him a warm smile and giggled. Then, without warning, she reached chubby arms across the bar, took his face in both hands, and pulled him into a long slobbery kiss. The man wiped his lips with his sleeve and gave the woman a wink and a smile. The woman peered over his shoulder at me a couple of times with one brow raised.

When the leader turned back toward where I sat, the innkeeper disappeared through a half door behind the bar and returned through a side door at the edge of the room with a different young boy in tow. "Miss, follow this lad to your room. There'll be a hot bath shortly. Come back down in an hour for supper. Your brother should be here soon. I'll make sure he's brought up to ya."

I gave the woman a weak smile. "Thank you. A warm bath sounds wonderful."

Moments later, I was submerged in steaming water. The heat penetrating my skin and sore muscles was so soothing I'd barely noticed how brown the water had turned. I was about to close my eyes for a long soak when someone banged on the door. "Miss, we have your brother."

"I'll be right there," I called, hopping out of the bath and wrapping a large fluffy towel around my body.

Bath, you stay warm. I'll be right back.

The guards stared at my towel a bit too long as they carried Danym in on a stretcher, then placed him carefully on the bed. "Healer says he'll be out another few hours, then he'll be hungry as a bear."

I gripped the towel's edge and held it tight through crossed arms as one of the men snuck another peek.

"That is *quite* enough," I snapped, my regal bearing nearly knocking the man down. "Thank you for bringing my brother. You may withdraw. Take your wandering eyes with you."

Men!

I bolted the door behind them, returned to the tub, and sank beneath the soothing water.

CHAPTER TWENTY-NINE

JESS

I dressed and sat on the edge of the bed, watching the rise and fall of Danym's chest as he slept. My hair was still wet from the bath, but I was restless and uncertain of what to do with myself. Eventually, curiosity won out. I pried Danym's shirt open and marveled that the hole left by the arrow had vanished, leaving only fresh pink skin in its wake. There wasn't even a scar.

Relieved Danym was truly safe, hunger rumbled through me. I exited our room, descended the narrow stairs, and stepped into the common room through which I'd entered when we'd first arrived. Mouthwatering scents of savory meats drifted from the kitchen, and my stomach clenched at the prospect of its first hot meal in days.

When we'd first arrived at The Crow's Nest, the common room had been empty and quiet, a stark contrast to the crowded affair unfolding before me. Most of the tables were filled, and the room roared with laughter, music, and the clanking of utensils. A jubilant fire crackled in the massive stone hearth, somehow making the enormous room feel warm and cozy. At the opposite end, a handsome young man dressed in chestnut leggings and a festive patchwork vest played catchy, upbeat tunes on a mandolin. A group of teenage girls clustered around his stage and squealed with delight as the music rose and fell.

I had attended countless balls at the Palace, replete with the finest musicians and entertainers in the land. I'd tasted food crafted by renowned chefs who traveled from all corners of the known world to serve their masterpieces to the monarchs of the Spires. I'd even traveled from one end of the country to the other with my parents, touring towns and villages, sampling whatever made them proud.

And yet, this humble tavern was unlike anywhere I had ever been, unlike anything I'd ever seen. None of the people appeared wealthy or particularly refined. Their clothing was simple, and the lack of teeth in many mouths spoke of even simpler lives. Still, they appeared so happy, so content. I marveled at the comfort I felt in the place, at how it suddenly felt like home.

I chuckled at how ridiculous that sounded. I was a princess. This place could never be home. Still . . .

The innkeeper paused from flitting about the room and made straight for me.

"Young miss!" She grabbed my arm and pulled me through the crowd toward an empty table near the fire. "Sit, sit. Looks like you cleaned up real nice. Real nice indeed! Now, let's get ya something to eat. Sorry to run, but we're very busy."

The woman scurried away before I could speak, leaving me alone at a table for four.

I leaned back and enjoyed the warmth of the fire.

As I scanned the room, I realized there was more than a random scattering of patrons laid before me. Near the stage were teenage girls who appeared to already know each other.

At the far end, several tables were pressed together, barely containing twelve massive men in worn, rough-spun shirts and thick leather trousers. Most had sleeves rolled up, revealing faded tattoos and crisscross patterns of scars, both new and old, a sure sign of lumberjacks who spent much of their time wrestling limbs and trunks. The conjoined table was a blur of pitchers and mugs as the serving girl tried to keep up with the thirsty men.

In the opposite corner, three Constables in their olive cloaks spoke quietly. They leaned forward, their eyes never focused on one place, always roaming about the room. They reminded me of how the men of the Privy Council would huddle and scheme in the Throne Room.

Thank the Spirits I'm out of that awful place!

In the room's center, a few tables were occupied by several families. The adults laughed and ate at one table while a pack of rowdy youngsters entertained themselves at the two adjacent. One of the children appeared to be my age, but the rest couldn't have been more than ten. Every few minutes, one of the adults would turn and half-heartedly address the chaos stirring within their brood. The children promptly ignored the admonishment.

Those seated at tables near the fire were older, reminding me of my Nan before she died. An ancient man, bent from seven or eight hard decades, sat peacefully holding the hand of his silver-haired wife. Her face was leathery and creased but held a beauty that warmed my heart.

The old couple ate quietly and chatted even more so.

I watched, transfixed, as the man's face brightened each time he looked up and caught his wife's eye.

"They're here almost every night." I startled, turning to find the innkeeper standing beside me, staring in the same direction. "Been coming here longer than I've owned the place—and that's a good thirty years. Makes your heart full just watching them, doesn't it?" She sighed loudly. "Anyway, here ya go, miss. Beef stew, cornbread, some roots and greens. Oh . . . and a mug of ale to wash it down. Let me know if ya need anything else. My boy'll bring ya more ale as ya empty that one."

My eyes widened at the mounds of food laid across the table. The innkeeper barked a deep laugh. "If that Healer knows anything, your brother should be down before long and will want to eat it all himself. You'd better get started before he shows up."

I smiled at the mention of Danym and thanked the innkeeper as she flitted away.

The stew was flavorful and hot, perfect on a cool night. I didn't recognize what root I was eating but savored the earthy beginning followed by a hint of spice. I took a sip, expecting the infamous watery taste that seemed to plague the reputation of innkeepers throughout the Kingdom but was pleasantly surprised by the richness and depth of the fall brew.

The musician's tunes took a romantic turn, transforming his loyal following's squeals into dreamy stares and swaying shoulders.

I sat back again, pleasantly stuffed and enjoying the contentment that comes with a full belly, when Danym appeared in the doorway near the stage. He scanned the room before settling on me and winding his way through the crowd. A pair of the teenage girls noticed him, giggled, and stalked him with their eyes. An unfamiliar wave of heat blazed through me, and I nearly leaped out of my chair before recognizing my own foolishness.

"Don't hate me for my fans. Fame is such a burden." Danym flopped into the chair beside me with a self-satisfied grin. He winked and flicked his hair dramatically.

I punched his arm before leaning across to give him a peck on the cheek. "Somebody sounds a lot better."

"Feels like I slept for a week, but yeah, I do feel a lot better. I'm starving, though." He grabbed a bowl and filled it with the now lukewarm stew, then loaded a plate with the last of the vegetables and cornbread.

We chatted about simple things, weary of weightier topics haunted by robed men and monarchs, both aware those were tales that would come soon enough. At one point, between bites of stew, Danym grinned up.

"Uh-oh. I know that look. What?" I asked.

"Me? I'm pure and innocent." His mouth twisted into a lopsided grin as I snorted and rolled my eyes. "I've been meaning to ask about your horse."

I cocked my head. "You want to ask about Dittler?"

"More about his name. It seems kind of . . . different. How'd you come up with it?"

"It is different—and very special." I donned a serious, almost somber face. "It's actually a sad story. He's named for a pet I had as a little girl."

Danym's face sobered. "Go on."

"My room's always been in the back of the Palace, close to a door that leads to the stables. We have a large barn and fenced field out back, too. Growing up in . . . that place . . . could be really lonely. Until Justin was old enough to carry an actual conversation, the animals kept me company and became my best friends. I had my own private door to their magical world." My eyes drifted and filled with memories. "If I opened a window, I could hear barks and snorts all day and night. There were horses, cows, sheep, pigs, chickens, ducks, and I think we even had some geese in the garden pond. Oh, and there were always dogs and cats chasing each other. I had more fun behind our, um, *house*, than I ever did in it. I loved that place."

I sighed.

"My father spoiled us with new pets, especially for our name day. It became something of a family tradition. One year, when I was four or five, he gave me the cutest baby chick. He was so tiny, and his feathers were silky soft. He had a streak of brown on his tiny forehead between his eyes that Father called his crown. He teased that he would be my heir one day, so I'd better take good care of him. Justin was still a toddler back then. Every time the chick peeped, Justin would point and squeal, 'Dit, dit, dit.' So, I named him Dittler."

I took a long sip of ale.

"Okay," Danym said as I drank. "That's kind of cute, I guess. Where does this turn sad?"

"I was getting to that part." I set my mug down and cocked a brow. "It was a few days after I got the chick, early in the morning, just as the sun was rising. I was half-awake, and all I wanted to do was sleep, but Dittler peeped and peeped. I reached down from my bed to get him out of his box. All I wanted to do was hold him, put him in my bed so he'd be quiet. When I reached for him, his leg got stuck between my ring and finger. He squawked and squealed—jolted me right out of the bed, scared me to death. Without thinking, I yanked my hand away, pulling his leg with me, snapping it right in half. It was terrible. The more he squealed, the more I waved my hand in the air. The poor little guy was flopping all around, leg juice staining everything he touched."

Danym's eyes twinkled as I finished my tale.

"Stop that! It was traumatic!" I feigned offense. "I couldn't be around chickens for weeks!"

Danym lost all composure and a good mouthful of ale as he doubled over. Tears burst from his eyes. I fought back my own laugh, but other diners around us had overheard and were chuckling.

That's when my own tears began to flow.

"Leg juice? Really? Is that a thing?" Danym spat as he gasped for breath.

I tried to gather myself. "If you make me piddle in the middle of this room, I'll knock *your* Dittler off!"

Everyone sitting near the fire burst into laughter, and I heard the echoes of "leg juice" several tables away. A few heartbeats later, the musician caught the fever and struck up "The Chicken Dance" on his mandolin. Utter chaos ensued as the crowd leaped to their feet with their voices raised and arms flailing to the rhythm of the music. Danym and I laughed until our sides hurt.

That night might have been the most fun I ever had.

It took a while for the common room to settle following all the wing flapping. By then, I felt sleep tugging at my lids. Out of the corner of my eye, I noticed the older couple from earlier, still holding hands, turn and stare with knowing smiles.

"Danym, look at them. They make me believe happiness really is possible." My eyes fogged.

"Is that what you see for us? Sitting across a table, holding hands, wrinkles deepening with each passing minute? I could do with fewer wrinkles, if we're being honest."

"I'm serious." I snorted, turning my gaze back to the couple. "Other little girls dream of being a princess, wearing fancy dresses, and living in a palace. I've done those things, lived them my whole life, and I'd trade them all for a lifetime like those two."

Danym reached across the table, took my hand, and drew my gaze to his. "You already did, and here we are."

A knock startled me awake.

"Sorry to wake you, miss, but the Constables are back and asking for ya both." The innkeeper knocked two more times for good measure.

"We'll be right down. Give us a minute," I called out.

The night had been awkward at first, each of us dancing around who would sleep where and in what clothing. Eventually, we decided to sleep in the bed together, but remain clothed in deference to propriety.

It was the first time I ever slept in Danym's arms.

I felt his breath on my neck, the beat of his heart against my back, the warmth of his arms wrapped around me.

As tired as I was, I lay awake for the longest time, breathing in his scent and reveling in his touch. I hoped that night was the beginning of a lifetime of peaceful slumber wrapped in his embrace.

Danym whispered as we rose. "We never talked about who we're supposed to be. What have you told them so far?"

"I told the leader of that city guard unit that you're my brother."

Danym laughed. "Well, we blew that last night. Our only hope is that he didn't talk to the innkeeper or the Constables in the corner—or any of the other hundred people in the common room."

"So, what now? What do we tell them?" Panic churned in my gut.

"My dad always says the toughest guys to crack are the ones who tell mostly truth but weave a lie inside it. Let's just tell them we ran away together, that your parents wanted to marry you off, and we couldn't live without each other. That's the truth, isn't it?"

Danym finished lacing his boots and stood. He seemed confident in his tale.

"I guess. What are our names? I told them I was Petti and you were . . . oh, hells, what name did I give them? Danym, I don't remember." I began to pace. "What if they ask who our parents are? Or where we live? Or—"

"Jess, breathe. We'll figure it out. If you act nervous, they'll know we're not telling them the truth." He took my hand, gave it a squeeze.

"Nervous? Why would I be nervous? My parents are the King and Queen. We just ran away from the Palace. The entire Army and national Constable force are probably looking for us, and we're being pursued by men in strange masks and robes who shot you. Oh, and we're about to be questioned. I can't imagine what there is to be nervous about."

He dropped my hand and gripped my shoulders, then reached up and tucked a stray lock of hair behind my ear. "If you feel like the room is spinning, just let me talk. We'll be fine."

With that, we headed downstairs.

The common room was once again empty and quiet, except for the ever-present innkeeper, who was buzzing about as though the place was still packed with restless diners. Two uniformed men were seated at a table in the middle of the room facing the door we entered through. I recognized the leader of the team who'd rescued us immediately.

"Good to see you again." He looked Danym up and down. "And nice to see you on your feet. You had us scared for a minute."

"I was too out of it to be scared, but thank you. I hear we owe you our lives." Danym had an easy smile about him.

I felt like I might throw up.

"Just doing our job. Please, take a seat. We just have a few questions." He smiled warmly as we approached the table.

"Why don't we start with an introduction? I'm First Sergeant Betz and this is my partner, Constable Wilover. You are?"

I watched as Danym never broke eye contact with Betz. "Beryl. And this is my fiancée, Sylvia."

Pause.

"So . . . you're not brother and sister?"

I shifted in my seat and stared at the table. "No, sir. I'm sorry about that. It's just . . . everything moved so fast . . . and Da—Beryl was shot. I couldn't think."

Betz's gaze bore into Danym. "Beryl, where are you two headed?"

"Probably east toward Huntcliff. We haven't thought that through all the way, but we had to get out of Fontaine." Danym reached down and grabbed my hand beneath the table.

"Were those men chasing you in Fontaine? Is that why you're going east?"

Danym laughed. "Oh, no. We just wanted to get away from her parents."

"Is that right, Sylvia?"

It took me a second to realize that Betz was addressing me. I nodded nervously. "Yes, sir."

Betz leaned forward. "Sylvia, did your parents hurt you?"

"Oh, no! Never. Nothing like that." Genuine shock flooded my face. I couldn't imagine such rumors about my parents. Mother might want to send me away, but she had never laid a hand on me in anger, and Father would execute anyone bold enough to do so.

Pause.

They were waiting for something.

I couldn't figure out what I was supposed to say, so I opted to remain silent.

Betz leaned back. "So, what can you tell us about those men who were chasing you?"

Danym squeezed my hand. "The first time we saw them, we were at the eastern edge of Fontaine, near the Cathedral. We'd made it a few days, almost a week, into the Spires before we saw them again. That's when they started shooting, and we realized we'd better run. You know the rest."

Wilover scribbled notes. Betz glared.

And stared.

I noticed a bead of sweat forming on Danym's temple.

Abruptly, Wilover closed his journal, and Betz stood.

I nearly jumped out of my chair.

"Well, I think that's all we need for now. Our Healer thinks you'll need a few days to fully recover, so I suggest you stay put for now," Betz said.

"I'm not sure we can afford to stay too many nights in this place. We really should get going," Danym said.

"Oh, don't worry about the cost. *The Crown* has you covered." Betz smirked on his way out the door, leaving Danym and me frozen in our seats.

CHAPTER THIRTY

KEELAN

I sat on the floor holding Sil. The minutes that followed felt like hours as her body calmed and she finally stilled.

"That was unlike any scrying I've ever witnessed. What happened?" Arch Mage Quin asked Daris.

The Mage ran his hand over his balding pate, straightening hair that hadn't been there in years. "Honestly, I'm not sure. I felt Sil connect to the Healer through her link with the horse. I've never heard of such a thing, but there was a close bond between the animal and its owner. Add my scrying magic focused on the Healer, and I suppose it makes sense."

"I think it's safe to assume that Tiana is alive and being held captive. Daris, did you get any sense of her location, even a direction?" I asked.

"No. Nothing from the scrying. When Sil wakes, she may be able to fill in some gaps. She saw and experienced things we couldn't see in the water."

"Keelan, I suggest we adjourn to my office where Sil can rest more comfortably," Quin said. "We can figure out what to do next while we wait for her to wake."

I rose and lifted Sil, bracing myself for the downward spiral of tower stairs. We opted to leave the horse in the event a second scrying was required. Either way, Quin suggested the grooms might be better at handling the beast on the stairs than any of us.

Upon entering Quin's sprawling office, I laid Sil on a couch and dropped into a nearby chair. The Arch Mage settled into a large leather seat behind his desk.

"Should I send for the Captain-Commander?" I asked. "He will want a full report."

Quin responded, "No. We can fill him in once we've spoken." He looked over at Sil and was quiet for a moment. "Keelan, I hate to wake her, but we need to know what she saw before deciding our next steps."

I nodded and kneeled, then placed a hand on her shoulder. When she didn't wake, I shook a little harder. "C'mon, Sil, we need to talk."

Quin stepped around his desk, leaned down, and pressed his index finger to the middle of her forehead. A quick pulse of light traveled from his fingertip into her skin, and her eyes popped wide.

"Keelan, Arch Mage? What happened?" She tried to sit up, but I gently pressed her back down.

"Easy," I said. "You passed out while we were scrying with Tiana's horse. You looked terrified and kept saying, 'Save me,' over and over."

Sil tried sitting up again, but then closed her eyes and fell back as if dizzy.

"You'll be disoriented for some time and need to rest. We just need to know what you saw during the scrying, then you can rest," Quin said.

"It was so much more than just images. I've never felt anything like it. Emotions flooded through me with each new scene. Warmth and love at Tiana's face. Sadness at images of her house. I think those were the horse's memories and feelings.

"Then everything became so vivid . . . so intense. I don't know . . . it was overwhelming. It wasn't just the horse's emotions anymore. It was as though I was inside Tiana herself, seeing through her eyes, feeling what she felt." Sil clutched herself as she spoke. "There was so much fear . . . and pain. A feeling of loss and loneliness. When that man appeared overhead, I felt a spike of hope and excitement, then confusion and panic. Then it all went dark."

The office was still, save the crackle of the fire.

Sil remained slumped on the couch.

I stood and walked aimlessly across the office. My mind was a jumble. It felt like the puzzle pieces were there, but someone kept shuffling them before I could snap the full picture into place. "What do we know so far?"

"What do you mean?" Quin asked.

"Let's go over everything again. What do we know?" I scratched my chin.

Sil finally managed to lean up, pressing her back to the high arm of the couch. "The southern investigation ended abruptly after their scrying revealed the victim had died."

"Right." I nodded. "Before she died, the victim was taken and moved west, likely beyond the mountains into the Kingdom."

"That sums up the report we received from Atikus," Quin said.

"I wish Atikus were here." I smiled at the thought of my adopted father. "He would help us sort through all of this."

Quin grunted agreement. "His team is still twenty days away. If only we had a Mage who could teleport. It's been nearly a hundred years since one of our people possessed that Gift."

"Right," I said, my mind already moving on. "Okay, let's turn to Saltstone. Tiana was taken at some point over the last seven to ten days. Her infirmary was ransacked and her house emptied, down to the pictures on the walls. She ended up in the mountains, surrounded by the smell of pine, and was transported in a wooden container. What else?"

Sil cleared her throat. "Don't forget the man with the green eyes. I don't think he was one of her kidnappers. A strong feeling of hope came over me when I saw his face, like he was a Constable or something."

"Can you describe him again?" I asked.

"He was leaning over, looking down as if Tiana was lying on her back looking up at him. He searched around but didn't appear to see her, then turned away," Sil said. "From that angle, it was hard to tell, but he looked tall and had a strong jawline. His hair was wavy, almost curly. It was really blond, almost yellow in the sunlight. His cloak was light green of a uniform, like a Ranger's but not that dark. The one thing I saw more clearly than anything was his eyes. They were the brightest emeralds I've ever seen. There was a sadness to them . . . I don't know . . . maybe I was just feeling Tiana's sadness."

"Did he have any weapons? What else did you see?"

"I think . . . yes. There was a bow and maybe a quiver over one shoulder. I'm sure I saw arrows."

"What color was their fletching?" I pressed.

Sil screwed up her face as she thought. "Green, I think? Maybe? They were dark, I know that."

I glanced up at Quin. "The border?"

Quin nodded.

"You saw his bow and uniform? Blond hair and green eyes? Big hair?" I tried to cover my surprise.

"I'm sure of it," said Sil.

Dec? What have you gotten involved in, little brother?

"Is there anything else we can do using magic? We've narrowed our search to west of the mountains, which leaves us a land mass the size of Melucia and all our neighbors combined."

Quin shook his head. "I don't think so. The horse will only give us more jumbled memories, and I don't like the idea of subjecting Sil to another scrying so soon after the last one."

"I'm all right—" Sill protested.

"No. The Arch Mage is right. No more scrying," I said. "We need to follow the trail west. It's really all we have now."

"I agree. If the Healer's captors are moving slowly with a cart in tow, you may be able to make up ground on them."

"Seven to ten days' worth of ground?"

Quin shrugged. "If they stop to rest, sleep overnight in Huntcliff? You never know what might happen with a cart traveling over the mountains."

"True," I sighed. "Could you get word to Atikus? Redirect him to meet me in Grove's Pass? If we left in the morning and he cut west when his team reached Crees, we would get there at roughly the same time, give or take a few hours."

Quin tapped a finger against his cheek. "We can't send word telepathically, but the old-fashioned way will work. A raven should make it to Crees well before the team. I can have one of our Mages relay word once they arrive."

"That would work. Add Ridley to that order. I'd like him with us, too.""What about the rest of the team?" Quin asked.

"Have them return for reassignment." I scratched my scalp, then turned to Sil. "I wish we could leave you here to rest, but we may need your Gift before this is over. You've made more contact with Tiana than anyone else. I'll send Buros and Went back for reassignment, as well."

"Arch Mage, is there anything you can give Sil to help her? I need her on horseback first thing tomorrow morning."

"I'm sure we can come up with something," Quin said.

I walked out as the glow of Quin's magic flowed into Sil.

We set out early the next morning, making good time on our way out of the capital. Quin assured us that his raven was on the way, and that Atikus and Ridley would meet us as planned.

The trip from Saltstone would take more than three weeks if we pushed our mounts to their limits. Despite Quin's best efforts, Sil's condition post-scrying was still shaky, something I knew would force additional delays.

I tried not to let frustration get the best of me as I thought about Tiana folded up in a cramped wagon. I didn't want to imagine her terror in the hands of those men and the pain each bump in the road must inflict as her body slammed against hardened wood.

I didn't want to think about those things or see them in my mind's eye, but my thoughts rebelled. Within hours of leaving home, I'd already begun spiraling toward that dark place.

Chapter Thirty-One

Ayden

"It has been three days since the storm, and Declan had not spoken a word about those moments on the cobbles, those moments when we'd been so close to . . . so close to becoming more than fellow cadets and friends." I drained the last of my tea and stared at the flakes that remained in the bottom of my mug. "Shira, I saw it in his eyes. I felt it in my heart. Hell, he was lying on top of me with his lips a hair's width from mine."

I knew I shouldn't be talking with Declan's best friend about my feelings.

I knew it was a mistake to tell her about that night and what I thought it meant, what I *hoped* it might mean.

I knew better.

And yet, as popular as a lord's purse might be, I felt alone within the walls of the Rangers' Compound. I had plenty of companions willing to gamble with my fortune, but no true friends who might listen and understand.

As much as I admired Declan for his social skills, his ability to make people laugh and endear them to him, I also envied those skills. It wasn't that I lacked the good graces to win friends. I didn't mistreat others or talk down; at least, I didn't mean to. I couldn't help it if my highly educated use of the language came across as better-than to folks raised in more rural parts of the Empire.

Still, I longed for simple friendships like the one Declan had with Shira. And since this was about Declan . . .

She rested a palm on my forearm, drawing my eyes to hers.

"Ayden, you need to tell him how you feel."

I nearly tumbled off the bench. "And risk him laughing at me—or worse? I don't even know for sure he's interested in, well, boys."

She snickered.

"What? Don't you laugh at me—"

She held up a hand. "I'm laughing because, first of all, you were practically swapping spit with him in the alleyway. That might be considered *a clue* as to his intentions. Second, and possibly even funnier from my perspective, we're sitting in the middle of the Rangers' headquarters, the center of masculinity and strength in the known world, and you talk like you two are seven-year-old boys debating if girls eat boogers or have some mystery pox."

I threw my head into my folded arms. "I don't know what to call any of this."

"Head up. I don't speak garble."

I lifted my head. "Sorry. I'm just new to all this."

Shira's brow shot up.

"Okay, I'm not new to *all* of this. I bedded my share back home. Okay, not my share, but some. A few." Her gaze was unflinching. "Fine, more than a few." I glared at her annoying smirk. "There were always nobles or other students or even the occasional stable hand who wanted to lend a hand, if you know what I mean. Come to think of it, I *tried* to bed every boy I could find, but I never had feelings for any of them. I never thought about any of them when they weren't around or dreamed about holding them all night or, fuck, just being near them. I can't get Declan out of my head. He's everywhere—at least, I look for him everywhere. That's the same thing, isn't it? Why do feelings make all this so much more—"

"Complicated?"

"Yes. That's exactly it. Complicated. Why can't this just be simple? Pinning a stable boy with thick arms and an even thicker cock against the wall of a barn is simple. There's no messiness involved. I mean, there is, but that's different."

Shira scrunched her nose. "Too much, Ayden. Way too much."

I grinned. "Really, it wasn't too much. If you could've seen him. He had an ass that—"

She squeezed her eyes shut and raised a palm.

"Fine. No more about stable sex." I chuckled. "What am I going to do, Shira? Why can't this be simple?"

She shrugged. "It can . . . if you just *talk* to him."

"What if—"

"I am not your priest. You asked my opinion. I gave it. Now, do whatever you will, but get on with it. Graduation is in two days, and I don't want either of you moping around like lost puppies when they drape the Green over our shoulders. Got it?"

I ducked my head beneath her withering gaze. "Yeah, I get it."

She pushed back from the table. "I have crossing duty today. Shoot me now. You two have fun up there in the mountains, all alone, with no one but the trees to see or hear anything if you get—"

"I get it," I nearly shouted, turning heads at nearby tables. I lowered my voice. "Thanks, Shira. Sorry to put you in the middle."

She laughed. "I'm *definitely* not getting in the middle of you two. Neither of you have the tits for what I like, no offense."

I cupped my chest with both hands, lifting. "You don't think these are pretty enough for you?"

She snorted, "They're pretty all right. They're just not big enough. I like 'em milk-ready, if you get my meaning."

I groaned. "I'm going back to moping. Please, Spirits, take that mental image out of my head."

Shira chuckled all the way out the dining hall door.

Declan and I met at the quartermaster's station, a log cabin twice the size of most homes in Grove's Pass, situated roughly a hundred paces from the main headquarters building. Supply carts came and went so frequently that a Captain some hundred years ago had removed the quartermaster's section from the main building to keep the traffic clear. It was one of only a handful of functions not housed in the main compound.

Declan was already sifting through his pack when I arrived.

"Did somebody sleep in this morning?" Declan teased in greeting.

I shook my head, failing to return Declan's easy smile. "Ran into Shira at breakfast."

Declan's brows rose. "Oh?"

I shrugged. "She's funny. Told me—well, us—to have a good patrol."

Declan stared a moment, then went back to checking his pack. "I checked out your gear already. You'll still want to go through it. Last week they left a canteen and flint out of one guy's bag. Screwed up his whole patrol." He pointed a few paces away. "It's over there."

I followed Declan's finger, finding a backpack with a bedroll neatly tied to the bottom leaning against the side of the building. I stepped around Declan, unstrapped the bag, and began reviewing its contents, peeking up every so often.

Declan caught me looking a couple of times but didn't say anything.

"Overnight?" I gulped.

Declan nodded. "Yeah, unless we find something worth reporting. Orders are to return tomorrow at noon. Another team will head up then."

"They're keeping a lot of patrols up there these days. Is that normal?"

Declan shrugged. "Don't think so, especially with winter coming. The snow usually handles most of our winter patrols for us."

I slung the pack over my shoulder and wriggled the straps into place. "What do you think's going on? Have you heard anything?"

"Not a word." Declan rose and hefted his pack. I hurried behind him and held it so he could slide his arms through the straps. "Thanks."

We made our way to the edge of town, and Declan checked his map and compass. "Looks like about a two-hour hike to our route. Not too bad."

I peered over his shoulder, close enough to nibble his ear if . . .

"Isn't that near where that buck was?"

Declan nodded. "Same general area, yeah. Would be amazing to see him again. He was a beauty."

I held my tongue, thinking more about the whole bowing down before Declan thing than any aesthetic nature the beast might possess. If Declan wanted to focus on the deer's rack and ignore the odd deference the buck paid him, who was I to argue?

The climb was steeper than I remembered.

The trees were now barren, and leaves littering the forest floor made the trek treacherous. Hidden logs and fallen limbs lay everywhere, waiting to twist an ankle or send a Ranger tumbling back down the mountainside. Declan led us, prodding the ground ahead of each step with a long walking stick, a process that kept us both focused and quiet, nearly doubling the time it took to reach our destination.

"Are you ready for graduation?" I asked as Declan dropped his pack in the clearing we'd chosen for our campsite. The spot sat at roughly the center of our patrol zone, making it easy to work rounds without facing an eternal return trek for rest.

"As ready as anyone is to wear the Green for the first time." Declan glanced up. "You?"

"They will wrap us in that cloak in two days. Two. Can you believe it? After all this time, we are so close." I leaned against a tree. "I think I am ready. It's funny, though."

"What?"

"To hear the cadets talk, so many of the other Second Years are beating their chests, like they have already won some prize."

"Haven't they? How many usually make it? Half?"

"That may be, but still . . ." I brushed hair from my forehead. "As much as we have trained, I cannot help feeling we have so much more to learn. Think about it. When we were working the border crossing, those Rangers looked at us like we were clueless."

Declan snorted. "*You* were clueless. I was masterful."

"Right. Mister 'I feel something' despite the empty cart."

Declan winced.

"Forgive me, Dec," I said. "That was unfair."

Declan looked up, something foreign in his eyes.

"What is it? I did not mean anything—"

"You called me Dec."

I nodded. "It just slipped out. If you dislike it—"

"No, it's fine," Declan said. "It's just . . . that's what Keelan always called me, ever since we were little. He's the only person in the world who calls me that."

"Your brother?"

"Yeah."

"I will refrain—"

"No." Declan stood and took several steps toward me, and I felt my stomach twist. "Please. I think . . . I think I like you calling me that."

My mouth opened, but I couldn't find words. Declan was almost within reach, almost close enough to touch, and there was such sincerity in his eyes. Sunlight filtering through the trees fell across his shoulders and lit his hair.

"Declan . . . Dec, I need to tell you something."

He nodded slowly, his eyes drinking me in, consuming me. My throat went dry.

"Me too, but you go first," he said.

I blinked. "I have tried to say this for some time now but could not find the words. I mean, every time we were alone and I tried, something happened or someone interrupted us."

"Just say it," Declan urged. "You can tell me anything. I hope you know that by now."

My heart raced. "I do."

Spirits, give me courage. I have to get this right. I want him to be—

A twig snapped beyond the clearing.

Both our heads turned.

Declan raised a fist, holding us in place as we listened.

Another snap.

Declan motioned for me to move to the south of the clearing as he worked north as quietly as the forest floor allowed.

I removed the bow still strapped to my back and nocked an arrow.

Declan motioned for us to move forward into the trees. His head swiveled, scanning the area before him.

I mirrored him.

Leaves crunched and twigs snapped as something—or someone—suddenly raced away.

Declan bolted forward.

I followed, maintaining my position well south of Declan's line.

After a dozen tense moments of searching, we returned to our campsite.

"Did you see them?" Declan asked.

I shook my head.

"Let's see if we can find where they were hiding." Declan stepped through the brush in the direction the sounds had come from, careful to watch for tracks or other signs. A moment later, he kneeled by a depression in the leaves.

"This looks like where they were lying."

I nodded and kneeled, scanning the forest floor. I brushed back leaves at the base of a fern and pointed. "What's that?"

Declan stepped carefully around the impression, then lifted a flask. The dull tin barely glinted as Declan held it beneath rays of sunlight.

"Check out that symbol." He held the flask up for me to see.

"Mountains on a shield. That is Kingdom Army issue."

Declan nodded. "What's a Kingdom scout doing up here? We're nowhere near the border."

"Good question," I said before letting out a frustrated sigh. "So much for a peaceful night on the mountain. We need to head back. Command will want to know about this right away."

"Guess we just found out why there are so many patrols these days." Declan rose and brushed off his pants. "Let's grab our gear."

Chapter Thirty-Two

Keelan

The Rangers had served Melucia as the nation's first line of defense for over a thousand years, claiming dominion over woods and mountains alike. Their headquarters were based in a towering building made of immense wooden logs, reminding me of Tiana's infirmary on a palatial scale.

"When you said we were coming to see the Rangers, I had a tiny shack in the woods pictured in my mind. This place is enormous!" Sil stared up with wide eyes.

I laughed. "Most people have that reaction, I think."

"Do you think Atikus and Ridley beat us here?"

I shrugged. "Possibly, but I doubt it. Their route is about the same distance as ours, but we traveled along a larger roadway. Plus, by our third day into the trip, you were nearly at full strength. Atikus talks a big game, but he's still an old man. I doubt they were able to match our speed."

"Fair point. I hadn't thought about Atikus slowing them down."

Green-cloaked Rangers streamed in and out of the building, barely glancing up at the strangers stepping up to their doors. As we entered, hoping to get settled for the night and have a quick supper, an excited voice shouted out from across the foyer.

"KEELAN!"

Sil had to hop out of the way as a tall, green-clad man bounded across the room and slammed into me, knocking me to the ground. Before Sil could blink, we were wrestling and laughing like children.

Atikus strode through the door and took in the scene. His face lit up with a bright, wide smile, and the old man dropped his pack and shouted with mock indignation. "Declan Rea, what do you think you're doing down there on the ground? Did no one teach you manners, young man?"

My assailant and I froze.

The green-cloaked man squinted up to find Atikus towering over us with fists planted on his hips. Tears of joy threatened to overwhelm both of us as Declan leaped to his feet and wrapped the old Mage in a tight embrace.

"I can't believe it. I can't believe you're really here." Declan's voice was muffled by the fabric of Atikus's robes.

When he finally released Atikus, the Mage stepped back. "My boy, it's only been three years, and I think you've grown into a tree."

Declan tried to wipe the boyish grin from his face. I still towered over the others but was now only a few inches taller than my brother. "I had to match my surroundings somehow."

"Wait, I just realized you're here," I said to Atikus. "How? There's no way you kept pace with us."

Atikus grinned. "The Mages in Crees offered fresh horses. They even added a little magic to spur them on. If my beard wasn't snowier than the peaks, we would've beat you here."

"Huh." I shook my head at the old Mage.

Sil cleared her throat.

I startled, then turned Declan around to face Sil. Ridley had walked in while we were chatting and now stood behind her. "I'm sorry, guys, this is my little brother, Declan. Dec, meet Guardsmen Ridley Doa and Sil Wesser."

Ridley stepped forward and clasped forearms, but Sil stood transfixed, her eyes wide. Declan gave her a head bob and a bright smile. "Nice to meet you, ma'am."

All color had drained from her face, and she wobbled.

I reached out to brace her. "You all right, Sil?"

"It's *him*. He's the man . . . the one in the vision."

Ridley wrapped his arm around her shoulders and led her to a nearby chair.

"What's she talking about? What vision?" Declan asked.

Atikus cleared his throat to get their attention. "Could we get settled, maybe have some supper first? Then we could talk somewhere more private."

Declan eyed Atikus a second, then nodded. "Of course." He called out to a Ranger who sat behind a desk at the far end of the entryway. A moment later, a young cadet in a light green cloak appeared and led the group through a series of hallways to a room with a simple wooden table and padded chairs.

As everyone sat, the cadet looked up at Declan. "Sir, the mess hall was already shutting down for the night. It'll take 'em a good half hour or more to scrape up supper."

"That's fine. Tell them we'll be there in an hour."

"Yes, sir." The cadet wheeled about and closed the door behind him.

"I want to catch up with you two more than anything, but let's talk through things while we wait. My Ranger sense is going nuts, and it never lies. We can have our family reunion over dinner. What's this all about?"

Atikus and I locked eyes.

I know your orders, but you should tell him. He needs to know if he's going to help us. He's your brother and is now a full Ranger. You can trust him, Atikus's voice brushed against my mind.

I stared at the Mage a moment, then nodded.

"Strange things have happened since you left Saltstone. Most recently, two Gifted were kidnapped."

Declan winced at the word Gifted but remained silent.

"One team pursued the case down south but ended their search when the victim died. Our team, Sil's and mine, has been searching for the missing Healer, Tiana Hurd. Sil, why don't you fill in the gaps and tell the group about the scrying? I doubt the Arch Mage was able to give Atikus and Ridley much detail in his missive."

Atikus leaned in. "That's right. Most of this is new to us."

Sil gathered her thoughts, then walked the group through their investigation, from the search of Tiana's home to the scrying. When she reached the part where she'd seen Declan in her vision, she could barely keep her eyes from his, and her voice broke.

"I still don't get why you think the man in your vision was me. I haven't seen anyone who matches your missing Healer's description, and I would've heard about it if another Ranger had run into her," Declan said.

"I believe you looked right at her but didn't see her. It would've been weeks ago, perhaps a month. You would've still been wearing a light green cloak like that boy who was just here."

"Before graduation," Declan thought aloud.

"What about men in brown robes? Have you seen anything like that?" Sil asked.

He nodded slowly. "Yeah, I remember a pair of men in robes. They wore strange, twisted masks, like a masquerade gone wrong. Gave me the creeps. Their eyes were all black."

"When? Where were you?" My heart pounded.

"Ayden and I were on crossing duty. It was a month before graduation, I think." He stared into the far wall, searching his memory. "The men were taking a cart through the mountains. Looked like a Merchant's return trip after selling whatever they'd brought into the country. I searched their cart, but didn't find anything. Still, I remember the whole thing feeling *off* somehow. There wasn't any reason to detain them, and they continued through the mountains."

"The Mages haven't figured out how, but we think a kidnapper used magic to disguise the Healer's presence," I said.

"Huh," Declan grunted.

I leaned forward. "Dec, when was this? It's important."

"We've only been on crossing duty once this fall. I can check the logs, but I'm pretty sure it was only a few weeks ago, maybe five."

"How long would it take them to make it through with a cart this time of year?" I asked.

"I didn't see anything wrong with the cart that might slow it down. It was empty; that would help with speed. The pass crosses five different mountains. I'd say an experienced team could make it in ten days, no less. If they didn't have the cart and pushed, they could do it in less, but they didn't appear to be in a hurry." Declan paused, narrowing his eyes.

"Kee, I know what you're thinking. You can't go after them. The road through the mountains is tough enough in the daylight, but it's deadly at night, especially up top where snow's already piling up. We find dozens of travelers each year who try it, lose their footing, and die at the bottom."

Atikus leaned in and placed a hand on my arm. "Keelan, listen to your brother. No one knows these mountains like a Ranger. We need a good meal, Sil needs rest, and I want to hear who this Ayden fellow is your brother keeps mentioning."

Declan's face flushed.

My brow furrowed. I hadn't even taken notice of the name.

"Let's get you settled into rooms." Declan stood quickly and turned toward the door. "We can meet back in the dining hall. You've got to be hungry."

There was a pause, then he met my gaze. "We can talk more over food. You and me?"

There was a hopeful lilt to his voice.

I nodded.

Declan stepped out, returning a few minutes later with a different cadet, this time a lanky youngster with a crooked nose and worse teeth. "Your packs are already waiting for you, so there's no need to go back up front. Evan will show you to your rooms."

A short time later, the group was huddled around a large wooden table piled high with slices of roasted boar, stewed greens, crusty potatoes, and several platters of berries and fruit. Pitchers of ale and water were scattered throughout, reminding me of the raucous inns I'd visited throughout my time with the Guard. The dining hall was empty, save for our group and a serving boy who scurried to and from the kitchen as we ate.

Atikus usually lost himself in his plate, but he couldn't stop smiling and laughing as he listened to us bantering like teens, reliving our years growing up in the guild. Declan would start telling a story but could barely finish a sentence before I would take over. It was like another wrestling match as we twisted and tossed our way through each tale. Atikus couldn't resist adding his own embellishments in places, a few times adding details both of us denied were true.

The old Mage's habit of making grand gestures as he spoke became a hazard when he forgot he was holding a full mug of ale and threw half of its contents all over Declan. I sat back in my chair and watched the spectacle with tears streaming down my face. I hadn't experienced such simple pleasure since our investigation began.

A pang of guilt pricked at me as I wiped my eyes.

Here I was, laughing and reminiscing with my family, while Tiana was alone and afraid. *I'm being insensitive,* I thought; but then Atikus started in on another tale from our childhood, and I couldn't fight the joy in my heart.

When the conversation slowed, I glanced over my mug and asked, "You mentioned someone before. Ayden?"

Declan blanched, and color rose to the tips of his ears.

"He's a Ranger. We get paired up a lot, have since he showed up over the summer."

I waited.

Atikus leaned in.

Declan's eyes avoided us both.

He's not ready to tell us whatever this is. Let's not press, Atikus whispered in my mind.

I opened my mouth to object, but Atikus added, *In good time. Be patient.*

"So," I struggled for a new line of questioning. "How do you like that fancy new cloak?"

Smooth, Keelan. Real smooth. Atikus smothered a grin.

Before Declan could answer, Sil and Ridley stood. "Lieutenant, would you like to meet here in the morning?"

"Guys, I'm sorry. You must be exhausted." I stood. "Yes, that's fine. We'll eat a bite and make our plan for the day. Declan, can you join us tomorrow? It would be helpful to have a guide who knows the mountains."

"I already cleared it with the Captain. He had a few ideas on where to start. I can go over it with the group tomorrow."

As Sil and Ridley offered their goodnights, Declan suggested we move our discussion to a more comfortable setting and guided us to a small reading room next to the library. We talked late into the night, recounting childhood adventures, most involving Declan terrorizing some Mage or staff member. Declan peppered me with questions about my Guard training and subsequent cases. Atikus grinned as he watched the two of us buzz back and forth.

The name Ayden came up more often than it didn't, but Declan avoided questions about this mysterious Ranger.

"Kee, I still can't believe you're this bigwig Guard in the capital," Declan said, swirling his tumbler of whiskey. "I mean, I *can* believe it. You were always gonna be in the Guard, and they all loved you for it. Everybody knew you were the rising star."

The sharp edge that crept into Declan's voice caught me off guard.

Atikus leaned in and gave Declan a pat on the knee. "That cloak seems to fit you pretty well, too, son. I'm proud you've found your way."

"Found my way?" Declan stared into the fire. "I guess I have . . . I like being a Ranger, but I spend a lot of time wandering the mountains, trying to figure out what I'm doing up here. It's almost as lonely as it was in the halls of the Mages' Guild."

"What are you talking about? You were the most popular kid in the guild. They fell all over themselves for adorable little Declan," I said, now surprised by the bitterness seeping into my own voice.

"Yeah, right. I was right up there with the kitchen staff. The cute little Mute with the big hair that nobody thought would ever amount to anything." Declan snorted.

"Declan, that's not true," Atikus said. "I've always believed in you, even if you never gave yourself much of a chance."

"How was I supposed to give myself a chance when magic decided I wasn't good enough?"

A fog of silence enveloped the room.

Declan finally rose and refilled his glass.

"Why did you come out here? Join the Rangers?" I broke the silence.

Declan flopped back into the chair, set his glass down, and leaned forward with his elbows on his legs. When he spoke again, his voice was a whisper. "I don't know, Kee. I had to do *something*. You were the one that was good at everything. All I ever did was make people smile a little, make 'em laugh at me." He stared into the fire again. "Maybe I was just trying to fit into a world that didn't make any sense. Maybe I was running away. Or running toward . . . I don't know . . . to a place without all those damn collars. Somewhere I could figure things out."

"Collars? You mean the *Gifted* collars?" Atikus asked, bewildered.

"Yeah." Declan sucked in a deep breath. "You won't get it. Nobody can. Well, Ayden does, but none of *you* can."

"Perhaps it's time you told us who this Ayden is." Atikus leaned forward and put a hand on his shoulder. "Go on, son. I *want* to understand."

Declan took in another breath, then sipped his drink, eyeing the ice cubes as if they would hop out and run away.

"Magic is *everything*, especially in a place like Saltstone where your collar doesn't just represent your ability but your social status, too. Keelan never even had to think about it. You handed him a gold collar the day you found us, but no matter how much I wanted it, how much I tried or begged or prayed, magic never came. Yes, I made people love me by acting out and being a character, but that's not the same.

"Growing up, it wasn't that big of a deal because there was always hope: hope magic would come, hope I'd one day make you proud when you put the collar around my neck, too. That day never came."

Declan met my eyes. "People treat Mutes differently. Either they look down their noses and say we're stupid or give us a look of pity, like we're crippled or somehow broken. Like *I'm* broken."

My throat was tight.

I wanted to try to argue with my brother but found the words wouldn't come.

"To answer your question, Ayden is a Ranger, and was a cadet in my class. He's the only other Mute in Grove's Pass, and far as I know might be the only other one in the whole damn corps. He gets it." Moisture reflected in Declan's eyes against the firelight. "When I was sixteen, maybe seventeen—you'd left for the Guard by then—people started looking at me differently. They were afraid for me, for what I couldn't do, for the life I wouldn't have. I could see it in their eyes. Spirits, Kee, I could see it in *your* eyes when I was a lot younger than that." He snatched his glass off the table and downed the last of his drink in one large swallow.

The fire crackled for a long moment before Declan spoke again. "I had to get away from it all. I couldn't take it anymore. Out here, at least there's one other person like me, somebody who gets me and doesn't look at me like . . . like that."

I leaned back and ran a hand over my head, not believing what I was hearing. Declan had always been a little lost, never knowing what he wanted to be, but what kid didn't feel that? What child didn't wonder if the world was too big, of if his dreams were too small?

He'd been a cheerful boy.

Always happy.

The Mages had thrown every subject they could think of at him to spark his interest, but studying just wasn't for Declan. He was a free spirit who thrived on making everyone around him smile and laugh. I couldn't remember a time when Declan was ever down or sad. To hear what he'd carried inside for so long, what he *still* carried . . .

"We need to get some rest before tomorrow. It'll be a long day." Declan set his glass down and, without another word, turned and walked out of the room, leaving Atikus and me staring at each other.

"It's funny," I finally said after a long moment and a few sips of whiskey. "I was always jealous of Declan. Everybody loved him. No, they *worshipped* him. We would walk into a room together, and it was like I wasn't even there. He's several years younger, a lifetime apart when you're a kid, and I looked up to *him*. I wanted to be that crazy and funny and . . . I don't know . . . free. Declan doesn't get how tight these collars fit."

"Keelan, give your brother a little time. He started talking tonight. Maybe this trip will do you two some good, get things out in the open so you can help each other." Atikus offered a fatherly smile. "You know, when I look at you two together, I can't help but see those two scared little boys who walked into my office just yesterday. Well, maybe a few yesterdays ago."

Chapter Thirty-Three

Isabel

I kneeled and cupped a delicate flower. The heart-shaped petals with their bright purple line were among my favorites.

I sat on the ground and crossed my legs.

The bloom's sweet fragrance hung in the air and heightened my awareness as I closed my eyes to meditate. The garden was the one place in the world where I, Queen of the largest nation in the world, could be alone. There were no courtiers, no ladies, no peasants begging for this or that—and no children.

Sweet Irina, no children!

What a wonderful thought.

I cleared my mind, erasing the images of the garden, turning toward blessed emptiness. In that place of nothing, that darkness, I was most aware and could See beyond.

My mind's eye opened, and darkness was replaced by a wide road, the King's Road. Thousands of archers marched in orderly columns.

I shifted my Sight to the head of the columns to find the tail of another line of mounted knights. Dark tunics lay beneath cloaks of emerald and ash. Each man wore sharply pointed helms that glinted like the peaks of the Spires themselves. Verdant banners framed in gold fringe, embroidered with the white outline of the Spires, snapped in the breeze.

Ahead of the horsemen, the eastern mountains towered.

My Sight shifted again, and a town came into view, little more than a village really. I focused intently on memories of my daughter and was rewarded with a vision of Jess and Danym sitting at a table by a roaring fire.

"Issy, the Council is assembling." Alfred's voice startled me, and the vision winked out. He knew I meditated, but I'd never told my husband about my Sight. Some Gifts were better not shared.

I blinked a few times and rubbed my eyes. "I'll be right there. Give me a minute or two."

Alfred patted my shoulder and left me alone in the garden.

I sighed.

For one blissful moment, I'd had the world to myself. As always, it didn't last.

I unfolded my legs and stood in the fluid motion of an acrobat, never touching the ground with my hands. It was a point of pride that, at forty-one winters, I was still athletic and limber. I reached down toward my toes, stretching tight legs and a stiff back, and spotted the gold-and-purple bloom inches from my face. A smile parted my lips as I cradled it between my fingers.

My second Gift stirred, and the bloom burst into flame.

When I entered the Throne Room, the Council was already assembled. Alfred was seated on his throne watching a heated discussion. I ascended the dais, surveying the body language of the Councilors before us.

All eyes were on Trade Minister Carver, whose cheeks were flushed and breathing was labored. Chancellor Thorn sat at the foot of the table, back straight, chin high, a stone unmoved by the storm. General Marks and Minister Bril whispered at the table's other end while the remaining Ministers filled seats in between.

Carver waved his arms wildly as he spoke, lace ruffles flapping and snapping with each gesture. "Your Majesty, this is madness. Melucia is our largest trading partner, and, if the Chancellor's information is correct, they have four or five times our number of Gifted. Why would they need to *steal* what few we have? Why would they risk so much to gain so little?"

I had never seen the pompous man so flushed. His powdered wig was disheveled and cocked to the side while his exquisite coat lay rumpled on the back of his chair.

Thorn barely let the room breathe. "Because they know our military might would crush them without magic. They want to take the last of our Gifted to ensure we can never attempt to master them again."

"Master them? Who wants to master anyone?" Carver spit back.

While the Councilors argued, I leaned toward Alfred and whispered, "What did I miss? You have them worked up this morning."

The King didn't return my smile. "We have new reports from Sebastiano's network tying the missing Gifted to Melucia."

"Melucia?" My eyes widened.

Alfred rose, silencing his advisors. "Sebastiano, walk us through your reports again. The Queen hasn't heard this information, and I need a moment to think."

"Of course, Your Majesty." The High Sheriff stood and gathered notes scattered across the table. "The first reported kidnapping occurred in Marlon, a small fishing village that only has two Constables. Only one item was found where we believe the kidnapping occurred: a button embossed with the symbol of an owl, wings outstretched, which matches those worn by Melucian Rangers.

"We disregarded the button as coincidence until our team in Cooper reported finding a few Melucian coins on the floor of the home where that kidnapping occurred. Cooper is the furthest town from Melucia, and it's unusual to see foreign gold turn up so far west.

"In Ario, where the Natural was taken, we found no relevant evidence. However, in Crelt, where the most recent kidnapping occurred, an old man selling clams at the docks witnessed two men in brown robes helping what he assumed was a drunk friend onto a small boat. One of the men stepped off the boat, removed his cloak, and bent to tie his boot laces. The old man served in the Royal Guard for twenty years, was stationed in Huntcliff for most of that time. He said he would recognize

Rangers' boots anywhere because of the embossed owl on the ankle. He described the symbol perfectly."

The King remained silent as he paced before the throne, hands clasped behind his back.

The Sheriff spoke again, "Your Majesties, this is all still coincidental. As Minister Carver said, Melucia is our greatest trading partner, and the items found are common. No one has seen the missing Gifted cross the border, and there has been no aggression or incursion into our territory by the Rangers, or any other Melucians, for that matter."

"Perhaps no aggression, but they have increased patrols and their presence in the mountains." General Marks joined the fray. "Your Majesty, we must prepare for every possibility. The two units currently headed to the border will not be enough if the enemy attacks. We need enough to counter . . . or preempt—"

I stood and joined Alfred. "Preempt?"

"Yes, Your Majesty. If we wait to defend, we allow Melucia's generals to choose the time and manner of the battle. With their advantage in magic, our border would be nearly impossible to defend; but, if we attacked first, caught them unaware, we set the terms for the engagement. With our advantage in numbers, that is a battle I'm confident we can win."

The Councilors around the table erupted, each shouting to make his point above the others.

Alfred whispered to me, "What do you think?"

"We both want to reign in peace, but I fear others may have already chosen the path of war."

Alfred's head drooped as he rubbed his temples. When he spoke, his voice was low and quiet but somehow stilled the chaos of the Council. "General Marks, how long would it take to get the Army into position?"

"Winter is nearly here, Your Majesty. No one, not even the Melucians with their magic, could move an army over the mountains once the snows begin. That gives us four or five months to prepare."

The King turned away and stared at the back of his throne for a long moment.

He spoke in a near-whisper, his gaze never leaving the ornate crown carved into the top of his seat of power. "Get the Army ready, General. No one crosses the border without my order, but I want the men in place before the spring thaw."

My mind raced as I hurried through the halls of the Palace toward my study. The pieces were falling into place. The clues left at the kidnapping sites had worked perfectly, especially the Rangers' boots. Those little droppings had been Thorn's idea. His network of spies was buried so deep inside the High Sheriff's organization that he knew about the kidnappings before even Sebastiano. Adding a little seasoning to the crime scenes had been a simple task.

My well-rehearsed performance, challenging preemptive action, forced Councilors to actively defend their suppositions and press for action. For thirty years, Alfred droned incessantly about preserving the peace he was gifted by a thousand years of kings before him. Yet today, we had won even the King to the side of battle.

The Council ultimately supported action—everyone except that horse's ass Carver—and the entire Army would move toward the border soon.

The Kingdom was preparing for war.

Now all I needed was to get Jess back under control.

The thought of my spoiled, willful daughter made my neck flare with heat. That girl had been given everything. Years had been wasted coddling Jess, giving her a soft youth in exchange for the future to come.

Then, at the first hint of a required sacrifice, Jess had rebelled.

How dare she defy her mother when the family needed unity now more than ever? If her little adventure became widely known, it would shake confidence in the throne. Jess had to realize that some things were more important than her pitiful little heart.

I had come to that conclusion long ago.

Thanks to my Sight, I knew exactly where Jess was hiding. The girl wasn't even doing *that* very well, sitting in the middle of a public tavern like some peasant.

How should I bring her home?

I could simply have her taken by force and returned, but that would only heighten tensions between us.

No, it needed to be Jess's idea to return.

Thorn was waiting when I entered my study.

"You did well this morning, Danai. I expected more of a fight, especially from Alfred."

"Thank you, Your Majesty, but I believe your deftness added the final blow."

I glided to a tea cart and poured a cup. "So, where are we?"

"Things are moving along nicely. Council broke three hours ago, and Minister Bril has already ordered units into action. He only held back four, one for protection of the capital and three to guard the port towns of Cooper, Kitchton, and Brighton. He also ordered our fleet to begin patrols of the Fersh Bay and the waters off Freeport. They'll be in position to form a blockade when ordered. Bril even increased training quotas at the Academy and other military recruitment offices. I think he's actually excited to see some action.

"As for our little escapee, my agents note their every move. They stand ready for whatever you command."

"Good. Have them remain out of sight. I am still debating how to handle her." I took a sip. "What about on the Melucian side? You still haven't told me your plan there."

Something shifted on Thorn's face.

"The Melucians discovered one of my agents who was embedded in the Guard. I ordered all other agents into silence until further notice. We are blind for the moment."

"They were bound to find one at some point. You have, what, ten, twelve embedded throughout Saltstone?"

Thorn shifted in his seat, avoiding my eyes. "Roughly, Your Majesty."

I shook my head. "After all this time, you guard your secrets, even from me."

"Forgive me, Your Majesty. It's an old habit and for your own protection. You know that one effect of my Telepathic Gift is protection from mental intrusion. Without that Gift, your mind is vulnerable to those who might use theirs to sift through your memories. I merely act to protect our plans."

This was a painfully familiar conversation. I remained dubious. I'd never heard that magical theory from any other Mage. Then again, there were no other Telepaths in the Kingdom's Guild. Maybe he was being honest, but something made me pause every time he repeated this lesson.

"Fine. How long will you keep the network quiet?"

"That depends on the Melucians. They are searching for more agents—quite aggressively. We dare not move too quickly, or we risk the entire network."

Something didn't feel right. I needed to think. "What about the Conclave? The King will need to present the case for war to the nobles. They feed and supply our armies."

Thorn spun the ruby ring he wore. "Yes, he will need to be impressive on that day, but nothing decided today would force the Conclave, so we have some time to build the public case for war. If the people support the King, the nobles will have no choice."

"You're probably right, but the entire plan hinges on their support."

I stood and moved to a bookshelf, not really seeing any of the books. "I need to think, Danai. Leave me."

The door's latch clicked, and I smiled at the silence that filled the room. I scanned the ancient leather-bound volumes. Running a finger across faded leather, I realized I'd never even looked at many of the books that filled the shelves. Histories of every nation, stories of distinguished men—*Why always men?*—even fictions of magical lands, creatures, and people.

I noticed a few my mother read to me when I was a child and smiled fondly at the memory.

As I turned, a dusty tome on the top shelf caught my eye. Its leather had been dyed an odd crimson that time had worn to near black. Cracked gold script on the spine formed words I couldn't comprehend, but curiosity overcame me. I slid the rolling ladder into place and climbed a few rungs. I squinted to make out a date on the spine—nearly *twelve hundred* years ago. My heartbeat quickened as I reached for the book, gently running my finger across its spine.

With a reverence few things warranted from a queen, I pried the book from its neighbors. Standing on the ladder, I opened the cover. Pages crinkled as I flipped them. Still, I smiled at how well preserved they were. I couldn't puzzle out any of the strange symbols scrawled across the parchment but discovered a map on the last page. It was stunning, both in its detail and artistry. I traced a finger over the familiar shape of the continent, surrounded by a smattering of islands. Gold filigree surrounded bright greens and blues, giving the map a richness rarely seen even in modern works of art.

Then two things seized my eye: on a large island to the southeast of the Melucian end of the continent was a concentration of the shimmering gold, as if the artist had accidentally dripped a large amount of the precious ink onto the page.

That was curious, given how meticulous I'd found the rest of the book.

I grinned at the second revelation.

There were *no borders* inked on the continent. The massive land was wreathed in gold but not separated by it. I scanned the page again and realized there was only one name large enough to represent a nation, and that's when it hit me—there was only one nation, one Kingdom.

This had to be *Irina's* map, crafted when every lord bent the knee to her power and majesty.

The histories all agreed that the Melucians ultimately rebelled against her rule, but Irina's banner still extended from sea to sea throughout much of her reign. This book was a priceless relic of a time long past, a time when all people were unified under the rule of one woman.

This was the sign, the sign I'd sought.

The Spirits, or whatever was looming over humanity's shoulder, had led me to this moment, to a new age.

This would be *my* time.

Chapter Thirty-Four

Jess

"What do you think he meant by that?" I stared at Danym across the table.

"Well, I'm guessing your mother and father know where we are. That would explain why we haven't seen those robed men anywhere. Constables are probably posted all around the inn to keep you safe."

"That makes sense." I leaned forward on my elbows, then put my face in my hands, mumbling, "Danym, she's going to make me go back."

Before he could respond, the innkeeper appeared at my side and placed a hand on my back. "Is everything all right, dear?"

I began sobbing. Before I knew what had happened, I found myself wrapped in the innkeeper's arms, my head buried in her shoulder. "Please help me. I can't go back."

The innkeeper stroked my head. "Of course, I'll help ya, Your Highness."

I jerked back. "What did you call me?"

"It's all right, Highness. I've known since ya walked in." The woman's warm, toothy smile nearly eased my shock. "I've dreamed of a life in the Palace since I was a little girl. Following the lives of the royal family has been something of a pastime for my sisters and me. I'd know you anywhere . . . Highness."

I gave Danym a questioning look.

"Why don't we go back into the kitchen to talk in case someone else walks in?" The innkeeper motioned toward the door behind the bar, then released me and turned.

On the far wall of the spacious kitchen were two enormous fireplaces whose suspended pots were already boiling with the day's lunch. The innkeeper sat on a stool and motioned for us to do the same.

"Highness, why don't you tell me what's going on? Maybe I can help."

I hesitated, but Danym reached over and gripped my hand. "I think it's all right. She already knows who we are."

"We just want to be together. My parents want me to marry someone else, someone truly horrible. He's forty years my senior and ugly as a pig, with hands that wander. They wouldn't listen to me, so running away was our only option. Now it looks like they know where we are, and it's only a matter of time before they make us go home."

"If we could just get to Huntcliff, I think we could be free," Danym said. "That's where we were headed before we were attacked on the mountain pass."

The innkeeper kneeled in front of me and took both of my hands. "Constables are watching the inn. There were a few inside and more surrounded the building last night, but our stables are across the street, and I doubt they're watching them since you're trapped in here. If I can get you into the stables, ya should be able to take your horses out the back."

I asked, "You would help us? Why?"

"Love does tricky things to a person," said the innkeeper with an almost tremble to the words.

Danym stood. "How do we get into the stables?"

"The inn shares a storage basement with the building next door. We keep meats and barrels of ale down there. It opens into the neighboring building but also into the stables."

"Do you really think this could work?" I worried.

"I don't know," Danym answered. "The worst thing they can do is send us back, and they'll do that anyway if we just sit here. It's worth a try."

I sat immobile for a moment before nodding once.

Danym rested a hand on my shoulder. "We need to pretend we never heard what the Constable said today. We show up for lunch and dinner and act like we don't know anything. If they get a hint we're up to something, they'll drag us back."

I wiped a tear. "All right."

I raised the innkeeper's hands to my lips and kissed them. "I don't know how we can ever thank you for your kindness."

The woman beamed. "Your Highness, you're letting me play royal for a day. What more could a poor girl like me want? Now, ya two go back up to your room before one of those men comes looking for ya."

Danym and I held hands as we strode upstairs. Once the door was locked, I pulled the curtain back and peeked out. The innkeeper was right. Now that I was looking for them, I spotted four Constables across the road, opposite the main door to the inn.

I felt sick.

I had spent my entire life being watched, and I hated that it was happening again.

Luckily, the rest of the day passed without incident. Lunch in the common room was a simple meal of pork stew, greens, and cornbread—remarkably similar to dinner the previous night. Afterward, we retreated to our room and decided not to go back down to the common room unless we *truly* needed to.

Night fell soon enough. Danym and I sat on the bed, bags packed, when a knock sounded. The innkeeper might've offered a limited menu, but she was pleasantly prompt. She bustled us downstairs and into the kitchen before speaking.

"There's no one stirring right now, but that could change any moment. We'd best get ya on your way."

I nodded. "Thank you."

The woman smiled. "No thanks. Just move quickly now."

As we crept through the kitchen to the wall beyond the second hearth, I noticed a large metal ring on a door I hadn't seen earlier in the day. The innkeeper grabbed a candle and lit it, then pried the door open and led us down a short stair. The air was musty, and the floors were packed dirt with a few wooden platforms built to hold casks, clay jars of honey, and a variety of pickled, salted, and dried foodstuffs. We walked twenty paces before coming to a wall with a ladder bolted into its boards.

The innkeeper stepped aside and motioned up the rungs. "That's your exit, Highness. It'll open into the middle of the stables. I gave the stableboy the night off, so there shouldn't be anyone up there. The hinges on the stalls squeal something awful, so be careful. The Constables are probably standing just outside on the street."

I stepped forward and surprised the innkeeper with a tight hug. "Thank you so much. One day I will find a way to repay you."

"Dear child, just be happy." She cupped my cheek and smiled. "That would be repayment enough."

"Oh, I almost forgot." The innkeeper reached behind a cask and handed Danym a sack. His grip sagged under its weight before he righted himself. "You're a week and a half to the next town. I can't let ya starve on your way to freedom."

I gave the woman one last hug, then followed Danym up the stairs and began saddling our horses. Dittler nuzzled me as soon as I opened his stall.

Once the packs and saddles were in place, Danym gave my arm a quick squeeze. "We'll walk them out to the street and make sure nobody's there, go three or four blocks to be safe, then we can mount up and get out of this town."

I nodded. "I'll follow your lead."

He opened the back door, and we led the horses onto gravel. The skies were clear, and the night was dark and cool. There was no one in sight. As we passed the third block without alarm, Danym motioned to mount and we trotted away.

It took another hour before the last of Spoke's houses faded from view, and I released a breath I didn't know I'd been holding. "We actually did it."

Danym smiled. "I told you, Jess. We'll be all right. I'll make sure of it."

Chapter Thirty-Five

Isabel

I let my Sight fade as my mind raced to process what I'd just seen. Jess was truly convinced she would be able to escape her duty; but there were larger plans in play, plans Jess knew nothing about and would never understand, plans to give the Kingdom more power and wealth than we had ever enjoyed.

I had spent decades preparing for the coming spring, and *nothing* would stand in my way, not even my bullheaded, selfish little daughter. The answer to the question that had been weighing on me suddenly became painfully obvious.

I made up my mind.

I would do what needed to be done.

I would pay the required cost to set *my* kingdom on the most righteous of paths.

"Your Majesty." Thorn bowed as he entered the study. "Were you able to See anything useful?"

"My Sight is *always* useful, Danai. Never forget that," I snapped, unwilling to suffer foolishness this day. "They left Spoke by the King's Road, headed east."

"So, my innkeeper played her part well?"

"It appears. See that she's well rewarded. We may need her services again one day." I reached for my wine.

"Yes, Your Majesty. What about the loving couple?"

"It is past time we end this. Before they go beyond the limits of my Sight, send *your* men to follow them. There's nothing but farmland and wilderness between Spoke and Cradle. Bring her in when they're halfway between the two towns—but Danai, whatever you do, there can be no witnesses."

"Yes, Your Majesty." Thorn bowed, then backed out of the room.

I savored a sip as I stared into the fire.

The wine was sweet, tart, and black as blood.

CHAPTER THIRTY-SIX

JESS

We rode until the sun crested the mountains, offering a hint of light to come. We found a small wooded area a few hundred paces off the road where we could get some rest. Danym was adamant we only travel at night. It would add days to our trip, but he argued safety was more important than speed.

It felt strange to stop during the day.

I found that even though I was tired, the sun kept me awake. I drifted over to Danym's horse. It was a rather portly chestnut who looked as though she would rather be grazing in a pasture than serving as their get-away mount.

"Can you talk to her?" Danym asked.

"That's not really how it goes," I said, stroking my hand over the bridge of the mare's face. "I think she likes you."

"I don't think she has a name," he said.

"I don't think so either."

I was tempted to question our stop but reminded myself that Danym had yet to be wrong about such things, and I knew very little about the King's Road past the Spires.

We would wait during the day, whether I could sleep or not.

Throughout the nights that followed, something unexpected and beautiful unfurled before me: I began to realize how vast and empty much of the Kingdom was. I lost track of how many miles we'd traveled without seeing a single building or house.

My tutors had drilled me in the history and geography of the land, but the Kingdom was quite different when seen from horseback. I peered up at the unending ocean of stars and laughed softly to myself. Only a short time before, I'd seen the Palace as huge, a world unto itself.

Now, everything seemed so small.

My focus shifted to a forest above the ridge ahead. A family of deer was grazing and darted away at our approach. Places on the map seemed so distant and irrelevant when they only existed as part of a lecture or exam. I stared in wonder at the majesty of the land I felt I was meeting for the first time.

Then my mind wandered back to the innkeeper who'd risked so much for us, all in the name of love. She was kind and caring, ultimately aiding us in our flight for freedom. We hadn't even thought to ask the woman her name.

It felt strange that an old woman would be so enamored with the royal family. Then again, I supposed that was the point of having royals, to give commoners something to look up to, an ideal to which they could aspire. But as much as I enjoyed our time in the inn, I couldn't imagine spending thirty minutes *working* in one—certainly not thirty years. Still, the woman had treated me more as a daughter than one of her betters.

Father would tell me to look for the lesson, to find the kernel in every experience that might reveal how to understand our people, to see their needs and hear their desires, to be a better ruler.

Spirits, I heard that a thousand times.

So, what was the kernel with the innkeeper?

Or with the Constables who saved us and healed Danym?

I hadn't really thought about them, and they hadn't even known who I was when they'd risked their lives on my behalf.

Would I have been kind in the innkeeper's place, sheltering strangers running from powerful parents?

Would I risk myself to save another?

The answer that stirred deep within sent a chill of shame down my spine.

I'd spent the last ten years fighting my parents every time they tried to teach me; and now, when I'd finally won my freedom, I couldn't stop trying to find the lesson.

Danym's horse snorted, and I watched as he bent to stroke its neck and mutter calming words.

I smiled, and my mind wandered back to the day we first met. I'd been riding Dittler through the capital after heavy rains. Murky water filled pockets in the city's crumbling streets, making the jaunt both hazardous and filthy. As I rounded a turn, Dittler stomped squarely into a puddle, splashing muck all around, coating the young man walking toward me. I remembered every clump of mud and how it had clung to his hair. Even more, I remembered the indignant bird-like squawk that escaped Danym's lips and the way he flapped his arms in disgust.

A laugh slipped out, causing Danym to turn. "Did I miss something funny?"

"Oh, no. Just remembering . . . something." Despite my exhaustion, I was finally happy.

Danym turned back to peer at the road ahead.

He sat so tall and proud, yet he was so warm and gentle—and beautiful. I couldn't miss that. His youthful face caused music to play in my heart, and its beat quickened at the thought of his caress on my cheek, his eyes meeting mine.

He'd also shown himself capable of making shrewd decisions in the face of challenging situations.

I definitely made the right decision leaving for a new life with him.

Leaving.

That word tasted bitter on my tongue.

Something inside tugged, some annoying prickle in my chest that nearly made me squirm in my saddle.

My entire life had revolved around duty, serving the needs and whims of others. It was all I'd ever known, all I ever expected to do.

And yet, here I was, *leaving* all of that behind.

Leaving my duty.

Leaving my people.

Nausea threatened as I pondered my choices and the ripples they had created.

A high-pitched shriek brought me back to the present. Danym's head whirled around, and he traced an arrow as it crossed the full moon.

"That's a patrol signal. They've spotted us." He urged his mare onward. "Come on, we can lose them if we move fast enough."

The King's Road was long and straight once travelers made it past a major bend that occurred roughly halfway through the journey toward Cradle. As we raced for our freedom for the third time in less than a month, that bend loomed in the distance.

The sound of hooves thundered behind.

A plume of dust billowed in the distance.

So many.

Danym turned and yelled, "They're gaining on us!"

"Come on, Dit. Give me more, please."

Danym's head whipped about, then fixed on a break in the trees off the road.

He yelled back over his shoulder, pointing. "We're not going to lose them, not like this. Keep going straight, Jess. I'll break off and lead them away. Meet me in Cradle!"

"Danym, *no*! Don't leave me alone!" I screamed as he turned and headed off the road.

The rump of his mare vanished into the darkness.

I was alone.

As badly as I wanted to follow, I focused on the road ahead and begged Dittler for speed. He relished the chance to run after so many days of trotting and soared in a blur of fur and mane and hooves. If I hadn't been so terrified by the thought of being captured, I would've loved the wind in my face and the thrill of flying through the countryside.

But there were men chasing me, men who would take me back.

As Dittler flew, the gap widened, and I lost sight of my pursuers as the bend came into view.

We finally reached the crest of the hill as the road began its turn, forcing Dittler to slow.

As we rounded the bend, my heart stilled.

I was too stunned to scream.

Eight men in dark robes waited, four on horseback and two standing on either side of the road. The mounted men held bows, nocked and ready. Those standing lifted small tubes to their lips.

"*Danym!*" I screamed, finally finding my voice.

He was nowhere to be seen.

One of the men raised a palm and called out in a metallic voice muffled by his mask, "STOP!"

I spurred Dittler, but he was spooked and spent.

He reared.

I barely held on.

"Come with us, Your Highness," the man said, his voice a whisper brushing against my ears that somehow rose above the clamor of hooves.

Tears streaked down my face.

My mind raced.

How could this be happening? Where were those damn Constables?

I looked closer at one of the men, at his terrifying mask.

This isn't happening! my mind screamed. *I have to turn back. The Constables will help.*

I gave Dittler a sharp kick in his flanks, and he whinnied, but before he could wheel about, two darts struck, one in his shoulder and the other his neck. He reared once more, then staggered as two of the robed men raced to our side.

A sharp pain pierced my shoulder, and I stared down in horror to find a dart poking through my tunic.

The world spun and blurred.

The two men, one wearing the face of a lion, the other an angry raccoon, pulled at my numbing limbs and lowered me to the ground.

I stared up at the night sky.

Terror faded to emptiness, and the face of a raccoon appeared overhead.

I gazed at the mask, trying to make sense of its snarling features. It reminded me of something that I couldn't quite grasp—someone I knew.

Then I saw its eyes.

They weren't black.

I *knew* those eyes.

His eyes.

I'd know them anywhere.

They were so deep and green.

"Danym? No . . ."

Chapter Thirty-Seven

Declan

The next morning, the group met in the dining hall for a quick breakfast of fresh biscuits, eggs, and bacon. I hoped that if I was my friendly, gregarious self again, they would act as though the conversation from the prior night had never taken place. I was at home with Sil and Ridley, entertaining them with Ranger jokes and mountain tales, and had them laughing through most of the meal.

I noticed Atikus and Keelan exchange the same questioning gaze before giving up and focusing on the meal.

As Atikus reached across the table to fill his third plate, Keelan cleared his throat to get everyone's attention. "Declan, before we make a plan for the day, something's been bothering me since we walked through our cases last night."

I glared, trying to decide which conversation was bothering my brother and whether I should be angry about it being raised in front of the others.

"Has there been anything else strange going on up here? When we talked last night, you sounded guarded with how you described things at the border."

I hadn't expected that question. I stared at the table for a moment to gather my thoughts before speaking. "That's a question for my Captain. I'm sorry, but I really can't say any more."

Keelan's mouth dropped, and Atikus nearly choked on a biscuit.

"Declan, really?" Atikus said.

"I'm sorry. It's just—"

Keelan rescued me. "Would I be able to speak with your Captain today?"

"Of course. We don't get visitors from the capital often, especially famous Guardsmen, so I'm sure he'll want to meet you anyway." I hadn't meant for the edge to return to my voice. "Why don't the rest of you get ready to leave while I take Keelan to see Captain Whitman."

Keelan took the hint and downed the last of his tea, offering Atikus a shrug. I turned and led him two tables down from where we'd been sitting. A pair of men were finishing their own breakfast when I interrupted. "Sir, sorry for the interruption, but I'd like to introduce you to my brother, Guardsman-Lieutenant Keelan Rea."

Captain Whitman rose slowly from his chair and wiped a bit of egg from his chin. He eyed Keelan, then extended a hand.

"I've heard a lot about you, Lieutenant. Good stuff, except what Declan here tells me, of course." He chuckled.

Keelan grasped his forearm while keeping his eyes locked on the Captain's. "It's a pleasure, sir. Thank you for putting us up for a couple of days. Most of us have never seen Ranger HQ before. It's an impressive place." He released his grip as the

Captain sat. "Would you mind if I stole a couple of minutes before we head out?"

"Glad to have the company. Please, take a seat." Captain Whitman sipped his coffee. "What's on your mind, Lieutenant?"

"It's about something rather sensitive, sir." Keelan glanced across the table at the Ranger who was eating with the Captain and gave Whitman a meaningful brow raise.

The Captain's own brow lifted. "Please meet my second, Commander Geros. You can speak freely at this table. Just keep it low."

"Thank you, sir," Keelan said. "We're here investigating the disappearance of one woman and the murder of another, two cases we now have reason to believe are linked. We are confident the kidnappers recently brought their victim through the pass to cross the border. Declan stopped a cart recently driven by two men in brown robes that matched the description of our suspects. The cart was empty, but we believe magic was used to conceal the woman from his inspection."

Captain Whitman nodded, his gaze steady, then took another sip of his coffee.

"Sir, we're headed into the mountains today, following the trail we think they took. Before we do, I need to know if we're walking into more than just a kidnapping. Has there been anything else strange reported recently?"

Captain Whitman's face was granite. "What did Declan tell you? I assume you asked him before coming to me."

"Yes, sir. He said it was a question better left to his Captain, sir."

Whitman nodded and glanced up at me. "Geros, give us the table."

Once Geros had left and we sat across from the Captain, his eyes found Keelan's again. "I understand your orders are from the Captain-Commander and Arch Mage directly."

Keelan's spine stiffened as his eyes widened. "Yes, sir."

"Take a breath, Lieutenant. Your Commander sent word that you were on your way and asked that I give you whatever help you might need. He was vague on the details, but I'm used to that these days, especially when a courier is involved." He leaned forward. "Most people don't remember that the Rangers were originally founded to protect Melucia's borders. The war had just ended, and tensions with the Kingdom were still high. It took more than a hundred years for things to settle down enough for our mission to expand to forest patrols and wildlife conservation. Despite all that, our primary mission remains border security and ensuring the free flow of trade between the nations."

The Captain finished his coffee. "Six months ago, a trader and his family left Grove's Pass and headed over the mountains bound for Irina's Seat, a town on a large lake close to Huntcliff. The whole trip should've taken them three weeks, maybe a little more with the children in tow. Two months after they left Grove's Pass, we received word they never arrived. In fact, the Constables in Huntcliff report they never saw them come through. Not long after, another trader went missing, then a caravan of three. During that time, we haven't seen a single trader from the Kingdom headed *into* Melucia. We would normally see one or two pass through every day. It's getting cold, and traders are usually racing to get into or out of the mountains before the snows. In six months, we haven't seen one—*not one*—inbound from the Kingdom."

He waved a serving girl over and asked for more coffee.

"I sent a couple Rangers to the border to check things out. We've always been on cordial terms with our counterparts, even have friendly competitions now and then, but not recently. The pair I sent reported that the Kingdom's border had been closed. Large wooden barriers were erected to prevent passage. Their border hasn't been closed in ten centuries, and I can't get any of our men through to see what's going on. The Commander of their forces in Huntcliff hasn't responded to my messages in months, and our birds don't return.

"Honestly, I have no idea what to think, but I'm worried. Your team will need to be careful as you get close to the dividing line. If you learn anything, I want to hear it immediately."

Keelan ran a hand over his head, scratching as if to spark some thought that eluded him. "Sir, I barely know what to say. We need to head into the mountains to follow our missing girl's trail. Beyond that, we'll keep our eyes open and let you know what else we find. I assume this needs to stay between us?"

"Atikus is cleared for this information. The Arch Mage was specific on that point. No one else needs to know unless things change dramatically. Use your best judgement, but understand something: I've been doing this a long time and have never seen anything like this. Something serious is starting that we aren't prepared to face. Hell, Melucia as a whole isn't prepared for this. If you trust the wrong person, people will die. That is a fact, one you need to be aware of. Be sure before you share any of this."

"Yes, sir. Understood," Keelan said. "Thank you, sir. If there's nothing else, I want to get started before we lose too much light. It gets dark fast up here."

"You just said more than you know, son," Captain Whitman muttered to himself just loudly enough that Keelan and I heard it as we walked back to our table.

An hour later, we stood in the middle of the road on the edge of Grove's Pass.

I couldn't help eyeing Keelan as I made an overdue introduction. "This is Ranger Ayden Byrne. He worked crossing duty with me the day the cart passed. While I inspected the back, he held the driver in check. He and I have also been on patrol in the mountains several times, and I thought he might be helpful as we move beyond this checkpoint, especially if we need to split into two search teams."

Ayden nodded to the group. "Good to mee you all."

Keelan remained fixed on me. "Sil, why don't you check this area before we move into the mountains? I doubt there's much here, but it's worth a try."

"You got it, LT."

Sil spent a long time crouched over dirt and twigs. Unfortunately, even she failed sometimes. There'd been enough traffic this close to town to muddle any tracks that might've helped in their search, and I reminded them that I never saw the cart veer off the road, so looking for tracks on either side was pointless.

Keelan finally called the group back together. "There's nothing here. Where would you suggest we go?"

I turned to Ayden and whispered, "What do you think?"

"This is a waste of time. The road is too packed for tracks, and we both saw the cart. There is nothing to follow." He glanced down at the road a moment. "We could travel the road, but in hopes of what? Catching up? They are too far ahead for that."

"What about the stations?"

"If they left the road, one our men might have seen something." His gaze narrowed. "Short of crossing the border, we have no other real options."

I nodded, turning his words over in my mind, then looked back toward Keelan. "We could just follow the road to the border and hope we see something, but that's more of a wish than a plan. There's a station about halfway to the top of that mountain." I pointed at a spot in the distance cloaked by trees. "The Ranger on duty up there might've seen or heard something. We don't rotate the men in stations like we do patrols, so he would know this area better than anyone."

"Anyone else? Other ideas?" When no one said anything, Keelan nodded. "Lead the way. Sounds like the best we've got right now."

It took the better part of the afternoon and half of the next day to reach the station. By the time the stilted shack came into view, the sun was setting over mountains that were already well shaded, and we could barely make it out when I held up a fist.

I motioned to Ayden, who circled wide to the opposite side of the building. I waited another moment before whispering to Keelan, "Something's not right. There should be a fire going, and those look like arrows in the ground over there."

I pointed to the ground twenty yards from the base of the station.

"Keep everyone here until I come back," I whispered before creeping forward.

I edged toward the base of the station and climbed the ladder. Ayden took up a position at the ladder's base, an arrow nocked and ready.

The angry buzz of flies greeted me as I stepped inside. The scent of rotten meat nearly made me gag. I wrapped my cloak about my mouth and nose before stepping fully into the room.

It was empty and eerily quiet.

The hearth was dark and cold.

Nothing stirred.

I crept toward the center of the room.

A Ranger lay sprawled face down on the floor in a pool of dried blood. One arrow had pierced his neck, its head sticking completely out the other side. Another was lodged in his upper chest near his shoulder. The glass of the one window was shattered, and shards were scattered everywhere. The Ranger's bow had fallen by the window and was now lodged behind a rickety desk. Furniture was overturned, and the two lamps used to light the cabin had been smashed.

I stepped out and said, "Broken arrow," the code phrase for a fallen Ranger.

Ayden's eyes widened, then closed. I knew he spoke silent words of peace for the fallen man's passing; still, his thoughtful moment of reflection in the midst of such a scene surprised me.

I motioned for the others to join us.

Despite their experience, Keelan, Sil, and Ridley flinched at the scene. Atikus remained by the door.

"No sign of Tiana?" Keelan asked as he surveyed the scene with his inspector's eye.

"No. Looks like somebody put up a pretty good struggle, though," I said.

"His name"—Ayden nodded at the fallen Ranger—"was Donny."

"I'm sorry." Keelan winced. "I didn't mean—"

"Right." I started toward the door. "Keelan, investigations are your thing. Why don't I go look for some firewood while you inspect, see if you can figure anything out? Atikus, would you send word to HQ that we lost Donovan Wilk and ask for a team to come recover his body? He has friends down there. They'll want him burned or buried. Ayden, would you come with me, please?"

Ayden and I made our way down the ladder, then began walking deliberate circles around the station, looking for anything that might aid our search. A quarter hour later, Ayden froze near the edge of the clearing and motioned for me to join him. With one glance, I turned and sprinted back to the ladder.

"Keelan, bring your tracker. We found their trail," I said through labored breaths. "Let's go, now!"

Keelan made for the door, calling over his shoulder, "Ridley, pick up where Sil left off. Sil, you're with us. Atikus, with your memory, can you take a snapshot of the room, all the details?"

"Of course. My Gift will pick up everything in sight. Anything under an item or covered up won't get captured, though," Atikus said.

"Do it, then join us outside."

Keelan and Sil descended the ladder and strode across the clearing to where I kneeled about ten paces from the northeastern side of the station, staring at something on the ground.

"Sil, come look at this." I pointed. "Looks like they were in a hurry—or struggling with your Healer."

Sil studied the area, looking from different angles. Saying nothing, she walked into the woods, focusing intently on debris before taking each next step.

"Behind you," Ayden said, following her with his bow nocked.

After twenty minutes, they returned to the group. Sil reported, "Their trail is pretty obvious. They were hurrying through the woods without any care of hiding it. There are three sets of footprints in places, sometimes only two with long stretches of bent and broken twigs, indicating they were dragging the third. About thirty paces in, the group stopped and rested. There are a few flattened places in the foliage where they made their camp. From that point, there are only two sets of prints and no more drag marks. They probably carried her the rest of the way."

She looked to Keelan. "Sir, they're headed for the border, I'd guess to Huntcliff. The main road is just over that rise in front of us. It's weird, though. They'll have to take a kidnapped girl through a border checkpoint without raising suspicion."

"Actually, it makes sense," I said. "Their magic masked the Healer's presence from me when I stopped them. I couldn't see or hear her at all, and you claim she was right in front of me. That same magic might be what they're counting on to get them into the Kingdom without trouble. Any search will turn up empty, confirming whatever the Kingdom soldiers are led to believe.

"Our biggest problem is beyond the border. Once they get through Huntcliff, they could go anywhere. The Kingdom is huge; we'll likely lose them for good."

"We have to try. Dec, can I speak with you a moment?" Keelan placed a hand on my shoulder and steered me some distance from the others. "Is there a way into the Kingdom other than through the pass at Huntcliff?"

"There are several, but getting to those entry points will be a problem. Other than the road on the pass, the mountains are pretty steep. Getting over them and through to the other side is dangerous, even for the best climbers. Ayden nearly broke a leg on Black Bluff last summer. If the Kingdom really is up to something, I bet they'll have patrols all over the base of the mountains. All of our reports from their side went dark months ago, and we have no actual intelligence to help with a plan."

Keelan's eyes narrowed, as if he spotted movement in the distant forest, past the road. After a heartbeat, he whispered urgently, "Everyone down."

We all dropped, except Atikus, who cocked his head at Keelan, not comprehending the sudden change.

"Atikus, get down. *Now!*" Keelan whispered. "Man in a Kingdom military uniform moving through the woods. He's scanning back and forth, bow in hand, nocked."

I signaled for the group to lie flat and not move as I edged carefully to the top of the rise. What I saw made my heart catch. I crawled back, again sending Ayden in a different direction, then signaled for the others to follow in silence.

When we were back in the clearing beneath the Rangers' Station, I whispered, "Keelan, the scout you saw in the woods was one of several I could see from the ridge, all walking in a line about a hundred paces apart from each other heading southwest toward Grove's Pass. I couldn't see anyone on the road, but the Kingdom isn't scouting the area for the fun of it. We need to warn the Captain."

"What are they up to?" Keelan asked no one in particular.

"We've had troubling intelligence of movement on their side of the border. Traders, back when they could actually get through, described formations of tents popping up in the fields around Huntcliff. We initially thought they were just reinforcing their border or running some sort of exercise, but those scout movements look offensive. I'd wager they're testing our defenses, at least trying to identify what we have out here."

"Atikus, can you send word to the Captain-Commander, Arch Mage, and Declan's Captain right now?" Keelan asked. "Whatever's going on, they need to know."

"Of course. It shouldn't take more than ten minutes." Atikus disappeared into the station.

I turned to the others. "We need to learn if this really is the start of a military operation. After so many years of peace, we barely have a standing army."

Sil spoke up for the first time since they spotted the incoming army. "Lieutenant, if we can get anywhere near a bird or some other animal, I may be able to help without putting any of us in direct danger."

"Your mountain, your call," Keelan said to me.

I nodded. "It's a good idea, but I suggest we abandon this station as quickly as possible. The scouts will find it before too long, and I wouldn't bet on a friendly meeting. Our best advantage right now is that they don't know we're here.

"Kee, we need to climb. They won't be looking on the mountaintops once they've cleared the lower areas around the road, and the height would help with finding the birds Sil needs. We'll still need to be careful to stay out of sight. They may not be looking up, but movement is easy to spot up there where the trees thin out."

As Atikus emerged from the station, Ayden returned. His breathing was heavy as he spoke. "More scouts walking in pairs, bows at the ready. They're searching or testing. I am not sure which, likely both."

"We need to move, now," I said. "We need speed and silence, two things the mountains rarely offer, especially this time of year. If we get split up, stick with either Ayden or me. We'll be able to find the others. Do *not* go on your own."

The initial hour of the trek passed easily but grew intense as we started our steep ascent to the top. Atikus's breathing became labored, forcing us to stop and rest frequently.

Four hours later, we stood about two hundred paces from the peak of the neighboring mountain. We hadn't seen another patrol for some time, allowing everyone to relax a bit. The mountain on which we stood was one of the shortest in the range, but the view was still breathtaking. As far as we could see, emerald mingled with flashes of gold and orange. Peaks of the taller surrounding mountains sported snowy caps and were shrouded in a mist that shimmered with shades of dusky purple and gray.

Keelan smiled as he sucked in the crisp air. A white plume billowed from his lips as he exhaled.

I chuckled, and everyone turned. "I remember my first time up here. It took me a few minutes to stop staring, too. Now it feels almost like they're family, those peaks—living, breathing family. I know, I know, they're just mountains. It's hard to explain." A hint of pride crept into my voice. "But that's how most of us Rangers feel."

Ayden nodded with a knowing twist forming at the corner of his lips.

Atikus stopped rubbing warmth into his arms long enough to rest a hand on my shoulder. "Son, I believe you're growing into that cloak of yours after all."

As the group snapped out of the peaks' trance, Sil stepped away and sat cross-legged on the ground. A short time later, two massive birds landed in front of her and cocked their heads, glancing between Sil and the rest of the group. She reached out and gently stroked one of the birds. It cooed and stretched out its neck to help her get a better angle. After a moment, the birds took flight, and Sil stood and walked back to the group.

"You're not going to like this," she said. "All I get when I commune are images. The smarter the animal, the better the image. Blackbirds aren't on the higher-intelligence end of the scale, so what I saw was quick and fuzzy."

"Whatever you saw is more than what we have now. Go on," Ayden encouraged.

"First, they showed me a glimpse of their nest. I think it overlooks the fields to the west of Huntcliff. I could see the town to the northeast and got my bearings from there. The next few flashes were in flight looking down at the ground, probably of those same fields around Huntcliff, but it's hard to be sure. There wasn't any point of reference to help fix a location other than the mountain range to the right, and the view was dizzying."

She rubbed her temples as she spoke. "Lieutenant, the birds were pretty high up, but there was no mistaking the orderly rows of tents covering the landscape. The image came and went too quickly to count, but I would estimate tens of thousands of soldiers camped there. The birds grew bored and severed the connection before I could see anything else."

Everyone gaped in silence, trying to absorb what Sil had seen.

For over a thousand years, the Kingdom and Melucia had lived in peace. The two nations were never overly friendly thanks to the historical resentment that followed the Kingdom War—a war that no one living had experienced; but they were cordial and generally good neighbors. I couldn't fathom what could provoke the Kingdom to invade Melucia and disrupt everything we'd worked so hard to build together, but I knew we needed to find out if there was any hope of avoiding another disastrous war.

"Can we start by getting a little farther down this mountain? We can't help anybody if we freeze to death," Atikus grumbled while rubbing his hands together.

I led the group down the northern face of the mountain, the Kingdom side, but under cover of the thick forest that surrounded us. The descent wasn't nearly as arduous as the climb, but the threat of Kingdom patrols and the frigid temperatures of the higher elevation slowed our pace. After an hour of cautious progress, we stopped to rest and refill skins with water from a stream that wound its way down the mountain.

I spoke as we sat on a pair of fallen trees near the water's edge. "We don't have time to go back to our side of the border for orders. We need to gather as much information as possible on the Kingdom's forces and get it back to command. Now's the time for ideas, no matter how crazy. Talk to me."

For the next few minutes, the group debated our options.

Sil suggested focusing on using more animals to view things from a distance. Ridley wanted to take out a scout or two and find a way into Huntcliff wearing their uniforms. He reasoned that counting troops was helpful, but they wouldn't be able to learn *why* the Kingdom was acting without hearing people on the streets and in the pubs, where alcohol would loosen lips.

"We need to get word back to the Captain. If those scouts really are testing our defenses, he needs to raise the alarm and alert Saltstone," I said.

"You're not suggesting—?"

"Besides you, I am the only one who knows these woods, the only one who could make it through their lines. I'll go."

"No!" I hadn't meant to snap, but unfamiliar terror spiked into my chest. The thought of Ayden facing however many enemy scouts, the thought of him getting shot, was too much. "No, that's too risky. We'll find another way to get word back." I glanced toward Atikus to find him and Keelan watching our exchange, his eyes narrowed and never settling on either of us nor betraying his thoughts.

I gathered myself, then spoke in favor of finding an alternate route through the mountains a little farther south to avoid conflict as much as possible. I was concerned that any information we gathered would be wasted if we were caught by enemy scouts.

Atikus remained uncharacteristically quiet throughout the discussion.

As the conversation slowed and everyone gazed at the ground, struggling to come to consensus on the best path forward, a snapping sound turned all our heads.

I bolted upright, thrusting a fist into the air.

Ayden shot to his feet and nocked an arrow.

Several snaps followed the first.

Someone *was* out there, and they weren't worried about staying quiet.

I motioned for everyone to remain still while I vanished into the trees. Ayden remained and stood guard.

I returned a moment later, my own bow nocked and ready. "There's a team of four scouts headed this way. I spotted another team about a half mile down the other side, also headed toward us. We have to move. Now."

We scrambled as quietly as possible, but Ayden and I were the only ones trained to move quietly in the woods. A shout from behind spurred us forward, trading silence for speed.

Sil and I led the way down while Keelan and Ridley helped Atikus. The old Mage's knees struggled in the cool mountain air and rocky terrain. Ayden took up the rear position, guarding our flank.

"Dec, we're never going to make it. I can hear their voices now," Keelan whispered when I raced back to help.

"He's right, son. I can't keep up," Atikus said.

I didn't hesitate. "Listen to me, both of you. We're *all* getting off this mountain. Keelan, Ridley, get Sil and Ayden and meet me down the southern side of this mountain, about a hundred paces. We'll hide Atikus and deal with the scouts. Tell Sil to have her bow drawn and ready in case they spot you before we're back together."

I tucked my shoulder under Atikus's arm and practically lifted the Mage off the ground. "This may hurt a little, but we'll be fine. Just stay quiet, all right?"

Atikus grunted but didn't protest.

A moment later, I stopped and pointed to a crack in the mountainside. "You'll have to squat to get in, but it'll keep you hidden. Don't come out until you hear my voice."

As Atikus bent to wedge himself into the crevice, the others trotted up.

I motioned for everyone to gather around me. "There's four of them, all armed with bows. We need to lead them west to a clearing where two mountains meet. Ayden, go get in position on the south side. Sil, you and I will set up on opposite sides. That'll give us the high ground. Keelan, you and Ridley stay here with Atikus, keep him safe. You're our last defense if one of them bolts. We can't let any of them escape, or we might be dealing with the whole Kingdom Army up here."

The sounds of pursuit grew closer as we sped down the mountainside. One of the Kingdom scouts called out, "I see them. Down here!"

We barely made it to the clearing in time to hide.

All thoughts of finding the Healer had vanished.

Even my concern for Ayden was a distant hum in the back of my head.

The enemy scouts formed a diamond, the first three men looking in different directions while the trailing man scanned behind. Sil's arrow struck the lead man through the neck, dropping him before he could cry out. My bolt hit the center of the chest of another. The other two men stepped back into the trees, stunned by their fallen comrades.

I could still see their bows, arrows scanning back and forth for a target.

I nocked another arrow and slowed my breathing.

The scouts split up, one circling the clearing toward me, the other toward Sil's position.

Ayden dropped the man headed toward Sil.

One left.

The final scout heard his fellow cry out and turned to run. It was his last mistake.

I took two paces, aimed, and dropped him with a shot between the shoulder blades.

A few tense moments later, the team stood together in front of Atikus's cave.

Again, I rattled off orders. "Keelan, Sil, you need to lead the way north, be our forward eyes. I'll help Atikus. Ridley, you and Ayden, watch our rear. Try not to get more than a couple hundred paces ahead. It's too easy to lose each other in these woods, and we obviously can't go calling out anymore."

Keelan and Sil nodded and headed north. As I braced Atikus again, the Mage whispered, "Declan, wait."

The almost desperate tone in Atikus's voice made me freeze. "Are you all right? What's wrong?"

Atikus's voice was quiet and carried a strange tremor. "Son, I'm sorry for what I'm about to ask of you. This was supposed to be my mission, but with the scouts in the mountains, I won't make it—and *everything* hangs in the balance."

"Atikus? What are you talking about?"

"You know our border security better than most. It's thin. The state of Melucia's army is closely held, but even a slight challenge would pose a grave threat, and our neighbors to the east are so weak and fractured to be worthless in a fight. Without serious help, Melucia won't last more than a few months."

"What are you saying—?"

"War is coming. The guild is preparing, but we're not enough. We need help."

I leaned against a tree for support and stared into the forest. Atikus remained silent, allowing his words to sink in. When I finally spoke again, my voice carried the steel of command.

"I don't have any experience with the eastern border, but Rangers I know who served on that side of the country talk about the border states like they're backward, stubborn children, always squabbling. You're right about them being useless in a fight. Who else is there? The islands barely have roads, much less standing armies."

"The islands may not hold great cities or armies, but they contain something far more powerful." Atikus glanced away. "The help only *magic* can give."

My head snapped up.

My brow creased.

Simmering rage bubbled deep within.

Spirits, I don't even have a Gift.

Why wasn't the old Mage talking to Keelan about this . . . or Sil . . . or Ridley . . . or *anyone* else who wore that stupid collar?

The more I thought about it, the angrier I became.

It was like Atikus was dangling the one thing I'd wanted my whole life, and I knew it would get yanked away before I could grasp it.

Atikus seemed to read my mind and snapped with the tone of a disappointed father, "Declan, look at me. This is too important to let your personal grievance cloud your judgement."

I turned and faced the only father I'd ever known, matching his scowl. "Nothing is clouding my judgement."

Atikus ignored my protest. "What I'm about to tell you has been passed from Arch Mage to Arch Mage for thousands of years. I may be the only person in our lifetime to know this secret beyond our own Arch Mage, which is why he ordered me to join this party. You must guard this with your life and reveal it to no one, not even your brother. Do you understand?"

I nodded cautiously. "Go on."

"Rea Utu, southeast of the coast of Drea, is more than the capital of a small island nation; it is the very heart of magic itself—some say the birthplace of magic. Deep in one of the mountains that shelters the village lies a wellspring the Arch Mage believes is the source of magic and the heart of the natural world.

"There are legends about the place. Most are ridiculous and designed to scare children into their beds, but one kernel of truth weaves its way through all these stories: living in the mountain, as the protector of magic, is a person known only as the Keeper. They are said to be the wisest among us, possessing an understanding of magic like no other."

I huffed in annoyance. "There's a thousand miles of land and over fifty miles of ocean between us and Rea Utu. The Kingdom Army is at our backs. How can any of this help?"

"I'm getting there," Atikus snapped. "The Keeper doesn't simply have a Gift; they actually commune with magic at its source. The way it was explained to me, the Keeper doesn't actually wield magic so much as they speak to it, and it flows through them. I'm sorry. What we know was passed down through the centuries. It's vague and confusing."

My head swiveled, listening for approaching enemies, my patience wearing thin with this ridiculous tale.

"Declan, the point is this. Appealing to the Keeper for aid is our ultimate safeguard when all else has failed. We are out of cards to play, and we need help if Melucia is going to survive."

"Again, I don't see what this has to do with me." Acid dripped from my every word.

"Declan, for once in your life, stop being angry and listen." Atikus let out an exasperated sigh. "Trust the Arch Mage if you can't trust me. Keelan and his team have a different mission. We don't understand what's going on with these missing women, but we believe it has something to do with the Kingdom's recent military buildup and potential aggression. There are too many coincidences tying things together, and Keelan is the best investigator we've got. You know I won't make it on my own, and I think Keelan may need my Telepathy before his search is over. You're all we have left. We need you to do this in my place, to appeal to the Keeper."

"Atikus, we don't even know for sure that war is coming—or if your Keeper is even real," I argued stubbornly.

"Yes, we do. In your heart, you know it, even if you don't want to admit it. *Spirits*, none of us wants to admit it, but war is still coming." He closed his eyes and tilted his head back so it pressed to the wood of the tree.

Atikus looked like he aged a thousand years in that moment.

"Declan, I've known you since you were barely old enough to walk. I know you're still searching for where you belong and what you should be—who you should be—but right now, I also know that this is *your* journey. It's time for you to believe that you are here for something larger than yourself and accept the calling before you."

I stared at him with caution and disbelief—and more than a little curiosity. A moment later, I nodded. "Fine, I'll go, but only if Ayden comes with me."

"No," Atikus said with finality. A distance entered his gaze, then he refocused on me. "This must be you alone. This was a secret never meant to be shared. We cannot risk another owning this knowledge . . . not even one as close to you as Ayden."

His words fell about my shoulders like links of iron, though I couldn't decide in that moment whether it was his implication or his refusal that nettled me more.

I blanched. "What do you mean no? You need me—"

"Declan, we don't have time for this. You *must* go, or Melucia will die. *Everyone* you love will die. Keelan and I . . . we will die. You must go, and only you. Please, if you have ever trusted me, trust me on this."

I gaped, searching the old man's eyes for any sign of deceit or exaggeration, but finding only desperation and hope.

"Okay," I said, my voice barely audible above the breeze. "Fine."

Atikus peered up, gripping his arms in both hands.

I reached out to brace him again, to take him to Keelan and Sil, but the Mage stopped me with yet another raised palm.

"There's more," Atikus said.

I cocked a brow. "Really? More than you sending me across the world to chase down magic's last hope?"

"I am not too old to bend you over my knee, Declan Rea." In any other situation, I would've doubled over laughing, but the steel in Atikus's eyes froze me in place. "What I'm about to tell you has security implications you'll appreciate more than any of us."

Atikus waited for me to hold eye contact before continuing.

"There's a cave in these mountains that contains an ancient gate. It is one of a pair, the only pair known to still exist. When a person passes through this gate, they are transported directly to its twin in the mountains of Rea Utu."

Atikus removed a folded parchment from inside his coat and handed it to me. I opened it and stared in disbelief.

"You mapped the mountains, both here and on the island, *from memory*?"

"Oh, son, you forget my Gift. I could draw every hair on your younger two-year-old head even today." Atikus smiled wistfully before continuing.

I studied the sketch as Atikus spoke. "The gate is not on the same mountain as the Keeper. You'll likely need to go into the village for supplies, maybe even rest for the night, then head to the Keeper's domain. No one knows what the Keeper looks like, and some fables spin the tale they appear to each person differently, in a way that he or she will best receive their teaching. You'll have to use your best judgement.

"Inhabitants of the island differ greatly from our people. For a tall, pasty mountain man like you, blending in will be impossible. You should expect to be watched by skeptical eyes the moment you set foot on the island."

"Sounds familiar," I grumbled.

"Oh, remember this, don't tell any of the locals where you're headed. The Keeper is sacred on the island. You're likely to earn more enemies than friends if they find out you're looking for them."

"All right. Is there anything else I should know? Secret mission, magical gate, island, hostile villagers, mysterious

Keeper person. Nothing else?" I hadn't meant to sound sarcastic, but the moment was so ridiculously surreal that it flowed freely.

Atikus again ignored my snark. "Only to be careful and try to *learn* something while you're there. Visiting Rea Utu has been a dream of mine from the day I first heard of the place." He was quiet for a moment, and a deep sadness entered his eyes. "And son, just know that . . . that I'm sorry. Please don't ask why. Just forgive me when you have the chance."

I stared in confusion, expecting more.

No more came.

A half hour later, we rejoined the others. Atikus took the initiative, speaking before anyone else could start. "Declan has new orders."

Ayden stepped forward, eyes fixed on me. I tried not to wither beneath his gaze.

"His Captain gave them to me before we left, and I was instructed to give them to him as we neared the border. The scouts changed the timing, but not the orders. They were sealed, and Declan was told to keep their contents to himself. What I can say is that his mission is extremely sensitive, and he won't be continuing with us from this point. He needs to leave immediately, so say your goodbyes now."

Atikus patted me on the shoulder, but his eyes tracked Ayden, whose stare bore a hole in my chest.

Sil and Ridley offered me a respectful nod and offered their thanks for Ayden's guidance in the mountains.

Keelan strode over and grabbed me in a tight, awkward hug. "Be careful, little brother. You're all the family I've got."

As we pulled apart, I was surprised to find a tear forming in Keelan's eye. Something lodged in my throat.

"Kee, walk with me?"

Keelan cocked his head, then nodded.

I led us a few dozen paces away from the group and struggled to meet Keelan's eyes.

"Dec, what's going on? What is it?"

"Keelan, I'm sorry." I tried to order my thoughts, but I hadn't rehearsed any of this, and words tumbled out. "I'm sorry about the other night, for ever thinking you were anything but my big brother who wanted to protect me. I'm sorry I was so angry and bitter for all those years, and that I never talked to you about how hard I fought, how much I struggled. I'm . . . I'm just so sorry."

Those last words squeaked out in barely a whisper.

Both of us had tears trickling down our cheeks as we embraced. I tucked my face into Keelan's shoulder as he pulled me into him and muttered into my puffy hair. "I love you, little brother. I always will. You don't need to apologize to me, not ever. You hear me."

My shoulders shook as waves of emotion dammed for years released, waves I had never known lay just beneath the surface. Keelan's hand pressed my head tight against his chest, and he kissed my brow.

When we pulled apart, Keelan draped an arm around my shoulder and turned toward where the group waited.

"Keelan, wait." My voice was that of a small, dandelion-headed boy from so many years ago.

Keelan waited.

I lifted my head and wrestled with my own courage. "I . . . I don't know how to say this. Spirits, I'm still figuring everything out. I feel so stupid."

"Declan, spit it out. There are armed men out here."

"Right." I sucked in a breath. "It's Ayden."

Keelan's brow rose, but he remained quiet.

My hands found my hair and tugged.

I turned away, then back to face him.

Spirits, why is this so hard?

"Ayden is more than just another Ranger, I think. I'm not sure. I mean, I am sure, but he doesn't know . . . though, I think he does."

"What is he, then?"

Fuck, he's making me say it.

"I think . . . I mean, I know, but I'm not sure, but I think. Shit. Keelan . . ."

He crossed his arms.

"I'm crazy about him, Kee. He makes me feel stupid and silly and warm . . . and I can't get him out of my head."

Keelan stared.

I tried to stare back but couldn't.

When an eternity passed, and I couldn't take it anymore, I blurted, "Say something, please. I'm dying here."

"Fuck me, Declan. We all already knew. We knew the first time you said his name; we've just been waiting for you to tell us." Keelan shook his head, a bemused smirk forming. "Just talk to the man. Have you seen how he looks at you? And you . . . for fuck's sake, Dec . . . you're like a lovestruck teen sneaking peeks at him when you think nobody's watching. It took everything I had to keep Atikus from cracking jokes."

I couldn't believe what I was hearing.

They figured it all out?

Hell, I hadn't even figured it out.

And he wasn't angry.

He wasn't ashamed.

He wouldn't run or turn his back or . . .

"So . . . you're okay if . . . I mean . . . if I'm—"

"You're a fucking idiot. They need a new rank just for you, Ranger, Idiot Grade." Keelan grabbed me and jerked me against his chest. "You're my brother, and that's that. As long as you steer clear of sheep . . . livestock might be a deal killer."

I snorted.

"I told you I would love you no matter what, and that's what I meant. Don't argue with me about it again."

Just as I thought he would push me back, he squeezed the air out of my lungs and added, "Oh, and he'd better treat you right or I'll crush him, and you know I can. I'm bigger than both of you."

Despite the mountains and forest and scouts and war, despite kidnappings and killings and *everything*, I laughed.

It had never felt so good to laugh.

"Come on, the others are probably getting worried, and you have a secret mission to go on, fancy man."

I snorted again, blowing snot across Keelan's tunic.

"Okay, gross. You are officially disgusting." Keelan shoved me away then led us back. Once in view of the others, he announced to the group, "All right. Ranger Boy is on his own. Let's get moving toward the border while there's some light left. If we're going to cross near the coast southeast of Huntcliff, we have a long hike ahead."

Everyone hefted their packs.

Keelan hefted Atikus.

And the group said their last goodbyes.

With the skies painted brilliant hues, and the forest rustling in a near-winter's breeze, Ayden stood by my side as I watched my brother vanish, wrapped in the dark cloak of the forest.

Chapter Thirty-Eight

Ayden

I stared at Declan as he watched his brother walk away.

I wasn't sure whether to be happy for him or let my heart break as they separated again. He had said little about their time together, but the tension between them was palpable.

It wasn't much better between us, though our training had kicked in, and we had worked well when faced with dangers on the mountain. Whatever we were—or were not—the brotherhood we shared as Rangers remained strong.

That was reassuring.

He stared into the trees long after the others were gone, an odd mix of sadness and something peaceful I couldn't identify written in his features. I wanted to ask, but the moment felt too personal to disrupt.

"Well, I guess this is it," he said without turning toward me.

He hadn't spoken about his secret mission in front of the group, and I wondered if I was to play a role in whatever scheme he was now steeped in.

"I have to go," he said.

"Where?"

"I can't tell you."

Rangers hadn't been truly militarized in centuries, so I supposed it was a bit odd. Still, I waited for him to say more.

Declan turned.

His eyes were so deep. The forest somehow drew the verdant brightness out of them, breathing life into them and granting them more power over me than the man already possessed. I could barely move beneath his gaze.

"I need to tell you some things." His voice was halting now, as though he wanted to speak, but struggled to find the words—or courage—I wasn't sure which.

My heart began to race. I didn't know why.

But I hoped I did.

"Okay."

He started to speak, then looked around, then back to me. Sweat beaded on his brow. "Shit, I can't do this standing up. Can we sit down?"

I glanced around and smirked. His discomfort was adorable, and begged to be prodded. "I am fresh out of comfortable chairs. May I offer you a log?"

He groaned and shook his head, a smile playing at the corners of his mouth.

"There. Let's sit on that." He pointed to a log near the stream.

His fidgeting had found its way into me, and ants began crawling beneath my skin.

We sat a few paces apart.

The brook's bubbling should've been a comfort but only stirred the nerves already swirling inside my chest.

There was weight to this moment; I could feel it, like the mountain itself rested atop whatever Declan was about to say. It would either raise me up or crush me beneath its mass.

Declan eyed the distance between us, the space on the log that could've fit Atikus and Keelan both, probably Sil, too. He stood and sat so close our knees touched.

I thought my skin might crawl off and run away into the woods.

His eyes rose, and I wondered if I would ever be able to move or look away again.

"I really suck at figuring things out." He ran a hand through his hair, a nervous tick that made me swoon the first time I saw him do it.

My chuckle quivered. "I could have told you that."

He held a finger to my lips.

His touch stilled my soul.

"Let me get this out while I still have the courage to say it."

I nodded like a terrified boy awaiting a strapping.

"Ayden, I hated you. I mean, I *really* hated you." He smiled, that lopsided grin that made my knees weak, the one I hoped was only for me. "Spirits, I thought you were such an arrogant prick."

He looked up at the canopy above, then laughed. "You know that day, that first day, when you showed up to my testing? I saw you standing off to the side, just the pair of you, like you were better than the rest of us, and we should be grateful for your presence."

"I never—"

"Then Aaron fired into the trees, and you started laughing. I didn't care that my cadet had just failed miserably, or that the rest of our team made fun of him. I mean, I did care, but they're teammates. Making fun of each other is what they do." He reached up and wiped sweat off his brow. "All I knew was that *you* were laughing at my team. An outsider, standing next to my cadets, was laughing at one of our own. I wanted to snatch that bow out of Aaron's hand and plant an arrow between your cocky little eyes."

My cocky little eyes widened.

"From that day, every time I saw you, my blood boiled. Hell, it was a low simmer already. You just cranked up the heat. I spent the next however long dreaming up all the reasons you shouldn't be here, shouldn't even be a cadet. I assumed your father bought your entrance. Spirits, it made me crazy that you were allowed to do your First Year in Saltstone then transfer to the Academy. How unfair was that? To all the men and women who worked their arses off to be here, to even *try* for the Green . . . I'm still not convinced that wasn't the case."

My mouth opened, but his finger pressed against my lips again.

I had to resist the urge to kiss it.

"Ayden, you *are* an arrogant little lordling. There's no doubt about that. You talk like you were trained in the Kingdom's court. Hell, have you ever even used a contraction? Who talks like that? And . . . you walk like there's a stick up your arse. And most of the time your nose is stuck so high in the air you might drown if it started to rain."

Wow, this is brutal. He really did hate me. Did? Does?

My brows rose, but his finger didn't . . . this time.

His smirk grew.

"But . . ."

Oh, fuck, there's a "but."

"I really hope I'm not about to make a total fool of myself . . . I mean, more than I already have, because I'm pretty sure I've done that already. Shit, I said already again." He ran both hands through his hair. When they stayed beneath his curls and he yanked, I knew this was getting serious. "Spirits, I'm such an idiot."

His eyes drifted into the forest beyond, and words lodged in his throat.

"Dec, just say whatever it is."

Without thinking, I rested a hand on his leg.

I only meant to encourage, to comfort, but somehow my hold became like an adder's fangs sinking deep into his flesh.

He tensed but didn't pull away.

His eye flew to my hand.

I yanked it back.

He looked up.

A heartbeat passed.

Then another.

I thought I might die from the damn waiting.

Then something resolved in his gaze, his hands reached up and gripped my head, and he leaned forward and pressed his lips to mine.

I couldn't think.

I couldn't breathe.

I knew I should kiss him back or pull away or run into the forest . . . or something . . . but my body wasn't listening. It was frozen.

The forest vanished.

The world disappeared.

There was only Declan Rea . . . and his kiss.

I sucked in a breath.

He pressed firmer, gripped tighter. His tongue teased against my teeth, then the tip of my own.

Sparks of light and fire and sunlight and . . . every other sensation and emotion I'd dared dream of throughout my nineteen winters raged through me. My chest swelled as I breathed him in, drew his breath into me, tasted him deep within my body and mind and soul.

Slowly, my hand rose, as if by its own power. Frightened fingers trailed down his stubble cheek, tracing the line of his jaw as I had done a hundred times in my dreams.

It felt better than any dream, rough and smooth and perfect.

With his lips still searching mine, his head tilted, melting into my touch.

He moaned.

Too soon, he pulled back.

Far too soon.

"I have to go."

The heart he'd just filled now wept. Panic welled in my chest.

"Will you be all right?" was all I could think to ask.

"I think so. This shouldn't be dangerous—at least, I don't think it will be." Declan brushed hair back from my forehead. I wanted to curl into his touch and never move again. "I bet you'll have more fun getting home than I will."

I tried to look down, to pull away, but his grip was absolute, his gaze infinite.

"I'm sorry, Ayden. I'm so sorry I wasted all this time fighting with myself . . . with you." He blinked a few times, as if tears might erupt. "I'm so crazy about you it hurts. You're all I think about, every day, all day. You're in my dreams. I've never . . . . Nobody . . . fuck. I've never kissed a man before now. I've certainly never fallen in love with one."

I don't know what I was about to say, but all thought flew far from that mountain, abandoning me to stare helplessly into his emerald gaze.

"I am in love with you, Ayden, and it's killing me to walk away right now. All I want to do is talk to you, know you, feel you. Hell, just be with you." He swallowed hard and waited for me to speak.

When I didn't, he pleaded, "Say something. Spirits, you're killing me. If this isn't what you want, if I've—"

"Fuck, Declan, really?" That wasn't the romantic thing I'd hoped to voice, but it's what tumbled out. His mouth split wider than I'd ever seen. "I have been in love with you since that first day on the range, you idiot. Did you not see me staring every chance I got, making up excuses to be near you, arranging for us to be paired on every damn patrol?"

Shock flooded his eyes. "You did that?"

I nodded.

He laughed, and it was the most beautiful sound I'd ever heard.

"Spirits, I thought they were playing with me. All the seniors knew how much I despised you."

My head lowered, but my smile remained. "No, that was me."

"You little sneak." He shook his head.

I shrugged as pride welled in my chest, yet another emotion to add to the list of the day.

Then his eyes drifted . . . and hardened. The distance he'd closed by sitting next to me somehow grew wider than before, though we hadn't moved. When he looked up again, sadness had returned.

"This mission, this thing I have to do, it's important. It's bigger than both of us."

"I know—"

"No." He shook his head firmly. "You don't. Ayden, if Atikus and the Arch Mage are right, the whole war, if that's what we're about to have, may rest on what I'm about to do. I'm not sure what I'll find or how dangerous it will be . . . or if I'll make it back home."

"You fucking better."

He stared a moment, then grinned. "I like it when you curse, little lordling."

"Fuck you."

His grin widened, then fell away.

"I need to go, and you need to get back and report to the Captain."

He stood, his hands drifting to my arms to lift me to my feet.

I fell forward into him, and his arms wrapped around me.

"I just found you, Declan. Spirits, don't you die on me now," I whispered into his shoulder.

He kissed my forehead, then lifted my chin.

"Ayden Byrne, by the Phoenix, I will come home to you."

"You fucking better."

His smile returned as his lips met mine one last time.

Without another word, he smoothed my hair, rebellious as a wildfire, then retrieved his pack and stepped toward the edge of the clearing.

My heart froze as he glanced back, and the hint of a smile curled his lips.

Then he turned and vanished into the shadows beneath the trees.

Did you know that reader reviews are important to the success of an indie author? Not only do they validate our work, but they are also used by retailer algorithms when deciding which books to share with new readers. If you enjoyed An Archer's Awakening, please take a moment to leave a review filled with stars. Ayden and Declan thank you!

Don't forget your free gift . . . click here to tell me where to send your free copy of *My Accidental First Date*, a fun, cheeky contemporary romance novella.

Of Crowns & Quills continues in the next book in this series, *An Archer's Destiny*.

ALSO BY CASEY

Romantic Fantasy
Of Crowns & Quills

An Archer's Destiny
COMING SOON

An Archer's Reconing
COMING SOON

An Archer's Reconing
COMING SOON

Romantic Spy Thriller
Of Shadows & Secrets

Casey's Tawdry Tease

Contemporary Romance
Heartstrings of Honor

Untitled: The EMT
COMING SOON

Untitled: The Policeman
COMING SOON

Untitled: The Coastie
COMING SOON

Contemporary Romance
Nashville Spicy

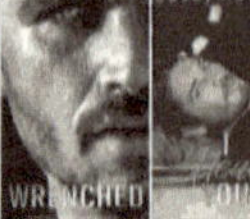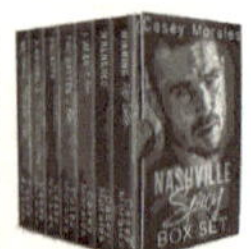

Contemporary Romance
Raised by Wolves

ABOUT YOUR AUTHOR

Casey Morales is an LGBT storyteller and the author of multiple bestselling & award-winning MM romance novels. Born in the Southern United States, Casey is an avid tennis player, aspiring chef, dog lover, and ravenous consumer of gummy bears. Learn more at AuthorCaseyMorales.com.